"DO NOT BE AFRAID . . .

. . . I'm not going to let him hurt you. I promise."

"How can you make such a promise?" Rose shuddered, blue eyes haunted. "The man will be my husband in two days' time. No one could protect me from Bertram, and no one can protect me now."

Rand clutched her head between his hands and forced her to gaze into his eyes. His eyes blazed with conviction. "Listen to me. I know I failed you before, but I am going to make it right. I swear to you, Sir Golan will never have the opportunity to hurt you again."

"Why should I believe your promises after you lied to me?"

"Because despite what you think, I care about you. I do not wish to see you forced to marry a man I now know is a danger to you."

"What are you saying, Rand? Edward insists I marry; there is naught you or anyone can do to sway the king when he has decided upon a course."

Rand took a deep breath. "I shall marry you instead."

BOOK YOUR PLACE ON OUR WEBSITE AND MAKE THE READING CONNECTION!

We've created a customized website just for our very special readers, where you can get the inside scoop on everything that's going on with Zebra, Pinnacle and Kensington books.

When you come online, you'll have the exciting opportunity to:

- View covers of upcoming books

- Read sample chapters

- Learn about our future publishing schedule (listed by publication month *and author*)

- Find out when your favorite authors will be visiting a city near you

- Search for and order backlist books from our online catalog

- Check out author bios and background information

- Send e-mail to your favorite authors

- Meet the Kensington staff online

- Join us in weekly chats with authors, readers and other guests

- Get writing guidelines

- AND MUCH MORE!

**Visit our website at
http://www.kensingtonbooks.com**

Vow of
Deception

ANGELA JOHNSON

ZEBRA BOOKS
KENSINGTON PUBLISHING CORP.
http://www.kensingtonbooks.com

ZEBRA BOOKS are published by

Kensington Publishing Corp.
119 West 40th Street
New York, NY 10018

All Kensington titles, imprints, and distributed lines are available at special quantity discounts for bulk purchases for sales promotion, premiums, fund-raising, educational, or institutional use.

Special book excerpts or customized printings can also be created to fit specific needs. For details, write or phone the office of the Kensington Special Sales Manager: Attn.: Special Sales Department. Kensington Publishing Corp., 119 West 40th Street, New York, NY 10018. Phone: 1-800-221-2647.

Zebra Books and the Z logo Reg. U.S. Pat. & TM Off.

ISBN-13: 978-1-4201-0858-3
ISBN-10: 1-4201-0858-1

First Printing: November 2010
10 9 8 7 6 5 4 3 2 1

Printed in the United States of America

Chapter One

Westminster Palace
In the year of our Lord 1276
Fifth year in the reign of King Edward I

"The lady who shall be my next wife shall have no reason to find fault with my lineage." Sir Golan de Coucy chuckled. "Indeed, 'tis no boast when I say that the de Coucy's are endowed with certain attributes women greatly esteem in a spouse."

Sir Rand Montague, escorted into King Edward's chamber by a dark-robed clerk, glanced at the knight speaking amongst a group of lords.

Hazy light filtered into the long, narrow room through three glazed windows on the longer east wall. Opposite this, a table was pushed up below a map of the world painted on the plaster wall. Rand approached Lords Warwick and Pembroke, and de Coucy standing before the table.

Sir Golan was tall, of broad muscular frame, with dark brown wavy hair that swept back from his smooth forehead. At court, rumors abounded about the comely, well-sought-after knight who was searching for a new bride. The gossip mainly revolved around the knight's prowess with the opposite sex and the tragic story of how his first wife died giving birth to their stillborn son.

But another dark rumor claimed Golan had had a hand in his wife's demise.

Rand truly despised the courts' ruthless preoccupation with other people's personal affairs. He knew firsthand the destructive force of speculation and innuendo. His cousin Kat was nearly destroyed by scurrilous lies spread by vicious nobles who reveled in court intrigue.

Rand greeted each man with forceful slaps on the back all around. On the long board were what appeared to be a large rolled-up map, and a lighted branch of candles, a flagon of wine, and several jewel-encrusted drinking vessels.

Golan passed Rand a chalice of claret, or rosé. "I believe I have boasted enough for the nonce," he said, grinning broadly. "Rand, tell us about your mission to Gascony."

The Earl of Warwick added, "Aye. I had not heard you'd returned to England. Was your journey successful?"

Rand patiently answered all their questions, savoring his claret. He recognized the excellent vintage from his family's Bordeaux vineyards that he imported in his cargo ship.

"My lords, well come we meet," King Edward intoned behind them.

In unison with the other lords, Rand spun round and bowed low before his sovereign liege lord. Edward waved a negligent hand for them to rise, then moved to the table. They gathered round the king, who unrolled the map, which was a very detailed representation of Wales and the western border of England. Without preamble, the king began discussing war plans.

"Here and here," Edward said, pointing to the Welsh Marches along the English border, "if it comes to war, as I expect it will, is where I plan to cross into Wales. These troops will advance into the south and central regions of Wales, but I'll send the bulk of the troops into Llewelyn ap Gruffydd's territory in Snowdonia in the north, harrying him and any resistance we meet." A red flush crept up Edward's face as he continued, "If the man does not come to pay homage to me as his overlord, I intend to crush and subdue him." He rapped his knuckles on the table, punctuating his statement. "No man, prince or otherwise, shall defy me without retribution."

Rand listened with half an ear as Edward discussed his plans. With war appearing imminent, he could not help but worry about Rosalyn Harcourt, Lady Ayleston, and her young son, Jason.

Staring at the map, his eyes strayed to the cartographer's mark that indicated the town and port of Chester near the Welsh border. The manor of Ayleston lay in the Marches five miles southwest of Chester, making it vulnerable to Welsh raids once hostilities broke out. It was too dangerous for Rose to remain at Ayleston without proper protection. But Rand did not think she would listen to him if he tried to reason with her. She ought to move to one of her dower manors farther inland for the duration of the war.

"Well, cousin. I have lost you, haven't I?"

Startled, Rand glanced up at the king.

Several inches taller than him, Edward had long golden hair and a drooping left eyelid. The king slapped him on the back good-humoredly. "Come. Tell me what troubles you."

Rand glanced around, realizing he and the king were alone. Consternation filled him at his breach of etiquette, but Edward, seemingly unperturbed, moved to the table to pour more claret into his chalice. Rand followed suit, taking a big swill of his wine.

"Now. I would hear what had you so distracted earlier that war plans could not hold your interest. Most unusual for you, cousin."

Rand *had* been feeling rather out of sorts of late. The pride and satisfaction he usually took in being a trusted and highly valuable knight in the king's household no longer fulfilled him as it once had. Something was lacking in him, but for the life of him he could not deduce what.

"'Tis Lady Ayleston, Sir Alex's sister."

Edward chuckled. "Ah, of course. I should have guessed. After warring, you are renowned for your amorous conquests."

Rand chuckled. "Nay, Sire. My interest in Lady Ayleston is not of a prurient nature. Verily. My concern is her proximity within the border of Wales, war with Llewelyn appearing inevitable. As Alex is my friend, I cannot help but feel it is my duty to keep her safe from harm."

Rand shrugged, grinning as though his apprehension was naught but a trifle.

"Ah, Rand, you are a good and dutiful friend. But let me set your mind at ease on that score. The good Sir Golan has offered to marry the lady, and offered a hefty sum to acquire the wardship of the lands of Lord Ayleston's heir. He shall make a worthy protector of Lady Ayleston."

Rand's stomach felt as though it had dropped to his knees. He knew it was inevitable she would marry again. But thinking of Golan caressing the delicate perfection of Rose's body—kissing her soft, luscious lips—was too awful to bear.

Rand took several deep draughts of wine. It burned a path down his throat, clearing the images from his mind. "Has the lady given her consent to the marriage?"

"Nay. I have not informed her yet, but Lady Ayleston will do as she is told. As you have noted, the seat of the Ayleston barony is in a strategic location near the border between our two countries. It also has a total of thirty-two knight's fees, and fifty men-at-arms and archers. Ayleston will need a strong leader to rally her fighting men under one banner."

Perhaps just as importantly, Rand thought, silver from Sir Golan's purchase of the wardship would flow into Edward's coffers and help pay for the war.

Edward quirked his blond head at him and a twinkle of humor flashed briefly in his eyes. "Have you given some thought to seeking a bride yourself? 'Tis time you married and saw to the begetting of heirs."

"I have not thought about it, Sire. I have plenty of time yet before I need concern myself with siring heirs. Besides, I doubt any lady with good sense would have me," Rand said good-naturedly.

"Nonsense. Any lady would be proud to have a knight of your renown to claim as a husband."

Nay, there would be no wife for him. Rand turned to stare blindly at the portrait of Queen Eleanor above a cold fireplace. What he did not tell the king was that he would never marry—for everyone he ever loved died. The waking dreams of his sweet, vivacious little sister were a constant reminder.

A pain throbbed at the base of his skull as the memory returned.

The river's current tugged Rand under, and he sputtered, choking up water even as he gripped Juliana tighter. "Rand!" she cried out in desperation moments before they were dragged under again. The water's embrace drew them deeper and deeper into the dark depths of the river. Holding his breath, lungs bursting, he couldn't breathe. A bright light burst inside his head.

Oh, God. Rand released Juliana. Her narrow arms slipped from his neck and she floated down.

Suddenly he kicked his legs and shot straight up. He burst free to the surface, gasping for breath. His mouth opened wide; a long, agonized wail of grief ripped from his throat until his voice was sore and raw.

". . . you are to escort Lady Ayleston to court without delay." King Edward's commanding voice pierced his waking vision. "Certes, keep your counsel regarding her marriage to Sir Golan. I shall inform the lady of her duty when she arrives at court."

"Sir Rand." The same dark-robed clerk as before appeared

at his side, his arm extended toward the door by which Rand had entered.

Reeling, Rand bowed and then exited the chamber. His agitated footsteps echoed down the torch-lit corridor, while it felt as though a vulture pecked at his exposed innards. Not only would he have to watch Rose marry another man, but now the king had tasked him with delivering her into that man's hands.

When he finished his distasteful task, it was time to consider his position in the king's household. He'd risen to knight banneret, yet still he was not content. Perhaps he was destined for dissatisfaction—guilt was his burden and his curse.

Juliana's death was not all he had to atone for. His mother's violent, painful death was on his conscience, as well. Rose, he had wronged her, too . . . But she made him swear never to speak of it and he honored her request.

Ayleston Castle
Chester County
Welsh Marches

Rising at daybreak, Rose exited the Keep down a set of steep stairs, and went round back to the kitchen garden. She dug her fingers into the moist earth, weeding the medicinal herbs she grew for treating the various wounds, ailments, and diseases of the dependents of Ayleston Castle. It was a responsibility she learned at her mother's side, and one in which she took immeasurable comfort in, easing the ills of her people.

Entering the kitchen by the back entrance, she met with Cook to plan the meals for the following week. Then after instructing Lady Alison on the supervision of the servants in clearing and replacing the rushes in the Great Hall, she went to her steward's office.

A corridor off of the Great Hall's entrance led to a chamber. When she stepped inside the small room, David ap Qwilim rose from the stool behind the table and bowed. "Good morrow, my lady." He smiled in greeting. A hank of his thick, dark auburn hair flopped on his broad forehead.

"Good morrow, David. Has a message from the Bishop of Coventry and Lichfield arrived for me yet?"

In addition to the table, a number of open cupboards on one wall were stacked with parchment rolls full of estate records.

"Aye, milady. Bishop Meyland's messenger arrived early this morrow." David searched the rolled parchments on the table until he found the bishop's sealed missive. He came around the table and handed it to her. "I insisted the man wait while I informed you of his arrival, but he refused and departed hastily."

Rose broke the wax seal, unrolled the parchment, and read the untidy Latin scribble. A quiver shot to her stomach, but she did not reveal her distress. She had learned well at Lord Ayleston's hands how to suppress her emotions.

"The bishop informs me that his annual progress has been delayed, yet again, and he will not be able to travel to Ayleston for some while." She looked up from reading the message and met the steward's concerned black gaze. "Well, David, if Bishop Meyland cannot come to me, I shall go to him. Ready an escort for me for the journey to his residence in Lichfield. We depart on the morrow, at dawn."

Rose left the chamber, her steps calm and measured, a counter to the pressure building in her chest. Anxiety spread its wings inside her, a feeling of imminent doom growing that no amount of mental reasoning could calm. She exited the castle in search of Edith and Jason, the heat of the sun already foretelling another sweltering day.

She found Edith on a bench overlooking the orchard, keeping a watchful eye on Jason. Crouched on his haunches,

Jason, large for a boy nearly three summers old, dug for worms with a stick beneath the sheltering branches of an apple tree.

Rose raised the missive in her hand and waved it at Edith. "The bishop has cancelled his trip to Ayleston, again. I wonder what can be keeping him?"

Edith set one of Jason's hose she was mending down on the bench beside her. She rested her right arm, bent at an awkward angle, in her lap. "Milady, calm yourself. I am sure there is a perfectly reasonable explanation for his delay."

Rose smiled at her former maidservant's observation. Rose could not be any calmer outwardly, but Edith knew her very well and understood her agitation.

"I cannot help feeling something is amiss. Not till the bishop takes my vow of chastity will I feel safe. I shall *never* marry again," she swore, a dark thread of conviction drawing her voice taut.

Rose plopped down on the bench beside Edith. Jason tugged a worm from the earth and squealed in delight, his cheeks dimpling. Rose's gaze softened as she watched him.

"Are you sure you wish to take such a drastic measure? A vow of chastity is irrevocable. Perhaps you will want to marry again one day."

Rose jerked her head to Edith. Jason's nurse gazed at her, eyes shadowed, her left hand rubbing her crippled arm.

Guilt reared. Rose reached over and began massaging the shrunken muscles and tendons of Edith's forearm. "Oh, forgive me, Edith. Here I am rambling on about my troubles when you are in pain."

A significant pause, then Edith whispered, "'Twas not your fault, milady."

"If only I had been obedient and dutiful, Bertram would not have broken your arm and forbidden me to set it properly for you."

Rose gazed off in the distance, her thoughts returning to

the past. Rose had been spoiled and indulged as a child, and her father, Lord Briand, had taken an unusual step in allowing her to choose her own husband, provided the man was of equal or greater rank than she. But Rose had chosen unwisely, to her everlasting shame and regret. When she threatened Bertram that she would return to her father and tell him of Bertram's perverse sexual proclivities, her husband struck out at Edith instead.

From that moment on, she learned never to defy him. No one was safe from his violent tendencies, not even Jason, his own son.

"Once I take my vow of chastity, I shall never be compelled to marry and be at the mercy of a man again."

Marriage required enduring the humiliating debasement of conjugal duties. She had barely survived her first.

"Wurm, Mama. I found a wurm." Her son's excited voice drew Rose from her devastating memories. She looked down at Jason standing before her. The worm lay in his dirty palm as he raised it up for her inspection. She relaxed her tight grip on the crumpled missive.

Her eyes grew big as she stared at the worm he dangled before her. "Oh my, you did find a worm. A big, fat, wiggly one." She growled beneath her breath, then reached out and tickled his tummy.

He burst out giggling, his little body wriggling as he tried to escape her marauding fingers. "I can't breathe, Mama," he gasped between giggles.

Rose relented, bent forward, and kissed his sweaty brow. "Jason. How would you like to help me collect some herbs in the woods? You are always such a great help to Mama."

"I'm a good helper, Mama." He jumped up and down, a huge grin on his face, his gold curls bouncing in his exuberance. Her heart twisted at the resemblance to his father, but she pushed the guilt away.

Regrets could not alter the past. She lived in the present,

her sole purpose to rear and educate her son to prepare him for responsibilities he would assume upon his majority. Her son was her life. Indeed, she would protect him to her last breath from anyone who would harm him. She would teach Jason to revere and respect women, like his uncle and grandfather. They were the rare exception of what was good and honorable and chivalrous in a man.

"Good. Why don't you go put the worm in your pail?"

Jason skipped away.

"Milady. What do you intend to do?" Edith looked up at her, her hand shielding her eyes from the glare of the sun.

"We leave for Lichfield at dawn. I dare not delay one day longer."

"I shall go and have Lady Alison pack for you and Jason then." Edith rose and hurried toward the Keep.

Rose's gaze returned to Jason, drawing in the dirt with his stick. Her only regret about her decision to formalize her vow of chastity was that she would not have any more children. But it was a sacrifice she was willing to make for her independence. Not to mention her emotional and mental welfare.

Rand swiped his moist brow upon entering the shadows of the squat stone building shrouded in thick, twisting green vines. Unusually warm for early autumn, it was darker and moderately cooler in the still room. Rand sighed in relief, even as he braced himself for the duty he was about to perform.

"Papa. Papa." Rand heard the childish chant moments before a small whirlwind crashed into his knees. Startled, Rand nearly buckled his legs. Rand stared down at a towheaded boy about three summers old. The lad wrapped his chubby arms around Rand's knees and clung to him as tenaciously as the crusty buildup on the bottom of Rand's ship's hold.

It was Jason, Rose's son. He looked just like his mother, except for his blond hair and blue-green eyes. Rand's heart twisted in yearning, and then he knelt and greeted the little Lord Ayleston.

A soft, deferential voice spoke behind him. "Make your bow, Jason. This is Sir Rand Montague."

On his knee, Rand twisted to look over his shoulder at the lady of Ayleston. Rose stood framed in the doorway, backlit by the sun. Her short, slender form was hidden beneath a sleeveless surcoate of drab gray wool worn over a tunic of white linen. Her beautiful hair and swanlike neck were completely covered by a wimple and veil, the headdress customarily reserved for nuns and older widows.

If he closed his eyes, he could still imagine her dressed in gaily colored silks, with her straight copper hair hanging loose to her waist, and her eyes flashing with life and innocent joy. But when Rand returned from the Eighth Crusade, he'd found Rose's appearance and personality drastically altered. He'd recognized the signs of abuse—docile obedience, avoidance of eye contact, dispirited disposition—because he'd seen the same characteristics in his own mother.

Taking Jason into his arms, Rand climbed to his feet. Rose stepped into the room. Rand's gut clenched at the sight of her. Despite her drab garb, she was the most beautiful creature he'd ever seen. With bright blue eyes that pierced a man's soul, when they were not darting away from direct contact.

Rose's cheeks appeared slightly flushed as she stared at Jason, in his arms. "Good day, Rand. What brings you to Ayleston Castle?"

"Must I have a reason to visit you, Rosie?" He grinned.

She winced, but otherwise ignored the hated nickname. "Nay, of course not. 'Tis just now is a busy time for me." She held up the basket of flowers in her arms. "I am drying flowers and herbs for my scented bath oils and soaps. Half the fields have yet to be cleared of the harvest. I'm planning to leave on the morrow for Lichfield to visit Bishop Meyland of Coventry and Lichfield. Now, you have arrived—"

She stopped in midsentence and cocked her head. "Why have you come, Rand? Has King Edward sent you on a matter to do with his wardship of Ayleston?"

Rand knew how clever Rose was and was not surprised she grasped the significance of his arrival so quickly.

Rose strode around a large cauldron in the middle of the room and laid her basket down on the worktable along the north wall. On shelves above the table were various vials and jars and bottles, their mysterious contents used for numerous treatments and cures for the habitants of the castle and village. A number of plants and herbs, including marigold and thyme, hung from the low ceiling in various stages of drying.

Her arms outstretched, Rose came forward to take Jason from him.

The boy leaned his head on Rand's shoulder and clung tighter. "I want to stay with Papa."

Amused, Rand watched Rose redden in embarrassment.

"Come, Jason," she said sternly. "Edith is here to take you to bed." Then her voice softened. "If you behave, Cook shall give you a treat when you wake from your nap."

With only a little fuss, Jason went to his mama, who kissed him and ruffled his hair before handing him over to the plump nurse who had appeared silently at the door.

Rose turned around and wiped her dirt-grimed skirts in a nervous gesture. "I pray you forgive Jason. Ever since I told him he had blond hair like his father, Jason calls every blond-haired man he meets Papa."

"You need not apologize, Rose," he said softly. "I was not offended—quite the opposite actually. He seems like a fine boy. I would be proud to claim him as my son. Indeed, you are to be commended."

Her eyes shuttered, but he saw the comment pleased her. "Thank you. Would you care to go to the Great Hall? We have some excellent mead and you can explain your visit while you refresh yourself."

"Aye. I would appreciate rinsing the dust of the road from my parched throat."

Rand followed Rose outside, past the flourishing kitchen garden, and around to the inner courtyard. "You have made some improvements since I last visited."

Her eyes jerked to his, almost fearful as though she expected censure. She relaxed when she read the admiration in his eyes. "I do not like speaking ill of my husband, but Bertram neglected the estate when he was alive. So I have expanded the gardens and repaired the dilapidated outbuildings. I've increased the arable and grazing lands, also. But there is much more I wish to do. When Jason reaches his majority, I want him to have a prosperous, well-run barony to inherit."

Rand felt a sudden stab of guilt as Rose spoke proudly of the improvements she was making to Ayleston. She had no idea that soon all control of the estate was to be given into the hands of Sir Golan, along with her person. But the king had vowed him to silence, and Rand could not think of breaking his sworn oath to his king. Rand's father had berated him, calling him a disloyal, disobedient son. But Rand had proven him wrong. Honor and duty were his personal code, his only pursuit that of faithful and dutiful service to his king.

So he shook the guilt away. Rose certainly knew as an heiress she would have to remarry eventually. Except for older widows, it was rare for a woman to be allowed to run vast estates without the protection of a husband.

But Rand just smiled and said, "A worthy goal, indeed."

The double doors of the Great Hall were open. He took her arm to escort her up the steps. She flinched, subtly leaning her body away so only their arms touched. Though Rand kept his expression bland, her reaction saddened him. There was a time she did not despise his touch. Once, she even . . .

When he reached the dais, he pulled out the chair at the

head of the table for her. She looked up, her big blue eyes startled, then dropped her gaze and sat down.

Did her husband never do her this courtesy? But it was the least of the man's transgressions. Not for the first time Rand hoped Bertram was burning in Hell for his foul treatment of Rose.

Rand took the only other chair beside her at the trestle table, and a pretty dark-haired servant promptly appeared. Her name was Lisbeth if he remembered aright. Leaning past his shoulder, the maidservant plopped down a tankard of mead on the board. Slow to withdraw, her bodice gaped, the smooth upper slopes of her breasts inches from his face. He flashed an appreciative glance at her offering, then winked at the bold wench. She sauntered away with a saucy, inviting smile on her lips.

"Why are you here, Rand?" Rose's voice snapped like a whip.

She sat stiff and straight with her hands clasped demurely in her lap. His knights and squires, already partaking of the mead and ale, were laughing and conversing boisterously at the lower table.

Smiling at his men, he drank deeply. Wishing to delay the interview, he changed the subject. "You left court rather abruptly after Kat and Alex reconciled."

"It was time. Though I enjoyed serving the queen, I was gone from Jason too long. And Kat no longer needed me. By the by, have you news of my brother and Kat?"

Rand could not keep the huge grin off his face. "News, indeed. Kat is with child and Alex is elated. I daresay you will not recognize Alex next you see him. He is already making a toy bow and arrows for the child, which he insists will be a girl." Rand envied them their familial bliss, though he hid it behind a cheery facade.

"What marvelous tidings. I know Kat always wanted children. They both deserve to be happy after what they have endured."

"Aye. Lady Lydia caused them a lot of grief. It is still hard to believe a woman was behind the attacks on Kat and Alex. You can never know where evil exists when it hides behind such beauty."

A shudder raced down Rose's spine. She wholeheartedly agreed with Rand as she stared down at her hands in her lap. Bertram had been such an evil man, hidden behind the face of a Roman god. She was glad he was dead, though her soul was damned for her thought.

Rose took another drink of mead. "I heard the king confined Lydia to a nunnery for the rest of her life."

"Aye, he was reluctant to execute her, but I believe a nunnery a rather fitting punishment. She will no longer be able to seduce men into doing her evil deeds. Edward even ordered her beautiful hair shorn."

Rose agreed the punishment was rather diabolical and just. Bertram's mistress had been a curse on many people and there was no way to know how many lives she had destroyed. Her evil machinations had even reached into Rose's own marriage. "What became of Sir Luc? I heard he recovered from his wound."

"Though Sir Luc conspired with Lydia, he had no knowledge of her murder plot or the attack on Alex in Outremer. So Edward banished him from court forever, a stiff punishment for a courtier. Last I heard, Sir Luc returned home to reconcile with his estranged brother."

Rose was surprised she had not heard this news. Sir Luc's family seat was in the neighboring shire of Derby. As long as the man caused her family no grief, he was not her concern. But Rand's untimely arrival was troubling.

Surely it had naught to do with the bishop's repeated excuses to delay taking her vow of chastity?

Rose looked up into Rand's eyes. They were greenish gray or grayish green. His thick blond hair was similar to

Bertram's, though that was the only similarity. "Tell me. What brings you to Ayleston?"

He shifted in his seat, a nervous gesture that surprised Rose and put her on guard.

"King Edward requests your presence at court. In that vein, he ordered me to escort you safely to Westminster. You have today to pack. We leave on the morrow."

Her heart sped up. She waited several beats and forced her voice to remain steady and calm. "I'm sorry, but I must decline." She licked her suddenly dry lips. "As I said, I'm traveling to Lichfield for an audience with Bishop Meyland. 'Tis imperative I meet with him. I can delay no longer. Prithee, give the king my regrets."

Rand stared at her lips. Rose reddened. Her hand fluttered over her lips and then dropped limply into her lap.

Rand looked up and cleared his throat. "Edward's invitation is not a request, Rose. 'Tis an order. You shall have to postpone your visit with the bishop."

"Do you know what Edward wants of me?"

"Alas, I cannot say."

Rose frowned and studied her friend's open countenance. Whatever the king wanted, it could not be to her benefit. Since Edward had become king, Llewelyn ap Gruffydd, the prince of Wales, had refused to pay homage to Edward as his overlord. The king was losing patience, and it appeared England was on the verge of war with Llewelyn.

Because Ayleston Castle was in the Marcher lands of Wales near England's border, it would be vulnerable to attacks and raids by Welsh rebels. With Bertram dead, and Jason in his minority, Edward held wardship of Ayleston and could do aught he wanted with the barony.

Now more than ever it was imperative she take her vow of chastity.

"Very well. I've already made arrangements to travel to

Lichfield. Once I meet with the bishop there, we can continue on to Westminster."

"'Tis out of the question." His voice was adamant. "The king has ordered me to escort you directly and forthwith to Westminster. You shall have to delay your audience with the bishop for another time."

A throbbing pulse jumped at her throat. Oh, this was not good.

Rose raised her chin, bravely holding his intense stare. "My audience cannot be delayed. Bishop Meyland has agreed to take my vow of chastity. I wish to see it done immediately."

A flash of surprise brightened Rand's eyes. "A vow of chastity? When did you decide to take such a monumental step?"

She dropped her gaze and rubbed her fingers in her lap. "I have been considering it for some time. I have no wish to be compelled to marry, or be dominated by a man who shall have complete control over my body and my estates. I imagine some ambitious lord may try to claim my wealth for his advancement. I shall never be at the mercy of a man like Bertram again."

His voice a soft caress, Rand offered, "Not all men are like Bertram, Rose."

She shook her head. "I cannot take that chance. The king can force me to marry any lord of his choosing. The character of the man shall not matter to him, only what advantage he may gain from the transaction. King Edward will not coerce me to marry once I profess to God my vow of chastity before the bishop. Unless he wishes to risk excommunication."

"I am afraid you have no choice in the matter. Your vow shall have to be postponed. The king sails for Gascony in a fortnight." He shoved up from his chair. "Our journey cannot be delayed for any reason. You may bring one servant and one chest of clothing for each of you."

She scrambled to her feet. "What of Jason?"

His brow puckered. "We shall be traveling swiftly, with brief stops and mostly sleeping in tents out of doors. It would not be conducive to a child. Jason will have to remain at Ayleston."

He waited patiently for her acquiescence. What choice did she have in the matter? she thought bitterly. She'd never defy King Edward and put her son's welfare in jeopardy.

"Very well. I have already begun packing. My attendant, Lady Alison, and I shall be ready to depart for Westminster, as you command," she said, her voice monotone.

Rand nodded and left the dais to join his men. Will, Rand's brown-haired squire, said something to him. Rand threw back his golden head and laughed. Dimples creased his cheeks, softening the sharp angles of his face.

She dropped her eyes, her stomach agitated. Deep in thought, she stared down at the pale rose liquid she swirled in her chalice.

Chapter Two

Ayleston Castle, Chester County
In the year of our Lord 1274, January 3
Second year in the reign of King Edward I

Rosalyn, the lady of Ayleston, froze in stunned horror at the landing of the Keep's stairs. Right before her eyes, Lord Ayleston whirled his arms like a windmill, teetering backward, one foot on the top stair. Her husband's handsome features—honed as if by the hand of God Himself—suddenly contorted in stark fear.

Rose clutched her infant son to her chest protectively, though he was asleep and cradled securely in the makeshift sling around her neck. Feeling sluggish as though swimming in deep waters, Rose at last reached out her free hand to Bertram. His fingers brushed her sleeve before he hurtled backward down the steps, an open O of terror on his lips. *Thump, thump, thump,* the sickening sound of his body hitting the rough stone stairs drummed inside her ears.

Legs moving without volition, Rose raced down the wide spiral stairs after him. When his golden head hit the last step, a loud crack echoed up the stairwell. Bertram landed in a crumpled heap at the bottom.

Rose stared wide-eyed at her husband, her temples pounding in rhythm with her agitated heart. Her cheek burned from Bertram's recent violent slap, while a scream of horror reverberated inside her head. It echoed like a pack of hellhounds in Purgatory.

Light from a single torch illuminated Lord Ayleston. His body was facedown, but with his neck twisted at an awkward angle; his vacant eyes stared up at the heavens. With gory fascination, Rose watched a dark red pool of blood begin to form on the step beneath his head. It slowly spread, until a drop of blood dripped over the edge and plopped on the stone floor of the Great Hall.

A noise in the hall shattered her stunned observations. Beads of sweat popped out at her temples and her heart thundered as though it were going to explode. If she was found with Bertram's body, she might be blamed for his death, whether she was responsible or not. A hue and cry would be raised, and if accused of having killed her husband, she would be taken to gaol, away from her young son, a prospect she could not bear. Even more frightening, if she was indicted and convicted of killing her husband, hence her lord, her punishment would be harsh: burning at the stake.

Rose clutched her tunics in one hand, spun around, and made quickly for her chamber at the end of the corridor. After easing the door closed behind her, she rushed into her son's adjoining chamber. Jason's usually vigilant nurse remained sound asleep on a pallet beside the boy's cradle. Rose had slipped a sleeping draught into her drink earlier. When Rose's disappearance was discovered in the morning, she wanted Edith to be able to truthfully say she knew naught of Rose's intentions.

But everything had gone awry when Bertram had stumbled out of his chamber just as she had reached the stair landing.

Now, she slipped the cloth sling over her head, laid Jason in his cradle, and removed the swath of wool from beneath his warm body. The boy made not a sound as she pulled the colorful quilt up to his chin. Ever since his birth, Jason had been a quiet, happy baby. And Rose was thankful for it in this moment as she listened for any signs of a commotion below stairs.

She thought she had measured with exacting care the belladonna she put in Bertram's favorite evening wine, in order that she did not overdose him. But apparently she had been too careful. Rose tiptoed back to her bedchamber, hung up her garments on the pegs beside the door, and slid into her bed to wait for the raising of the hue and cry.

Her heart continued to pump sporadically. She stared wide-eyed up at the canopy, her lips moving in silent prayer. Not for her deceased husband, may God forgive her, but that no one would ever discover her involvement in this night's deeds. It was a confession she would take to her grave; she lived for her son alone now.

Rose jerked awake. Panic beat like the wings of a bird inside her chest. Her mouth was open, a scream deep in the back of her throat. But no sound escaped. It wasn't that she could not scream, but she knew better than to voice her discontent.

Rose blinked, but the solid blanket of darkness surrounding her did not lessen. She crawled across the soft mattress, gripped the velvet bed curtain, and yanked it aside. A glimmer of moonlight from her open shutters illuminated the disheveled sheets and coverlet of her canopy bed. Her medical books were on her table too.

A sigh of relief escaped her.

It was only a nightmare. She was safe in her own bed. Alone. Taking deep breaths, she willed her fear to recede. With her husband dead nigh onto three years, her degradation and humiliation at his hands was a thing of the past. But deep inside, she knew she would never be the innocent, naïve, happy young woman she was when she married Bertram. Her heart was a hard, cold lump—she was a frigid woman who despised a man's touch.

She reached for her Trotula medical book—a gift from her mother—and caressed its beloved well-worn Cordoba leather covering. When Bertram was alive she'd hidden her books because he forbade her to practice her healing arts. She put the text back and chose another book. It was a special collection of healing recipes, prayers, and charms collected and passed down through the generations by the women in her family. Upon Rose's marriage, her mother had gathered them together, then commissioned a local monk to transcribe and bind them into a beautifully illuminated manuscript. Flipping open the leather cover, she allowed the vellum pages to unfold, and closing her eyes, she stuck her finger on a random spot in the book. It was a ritual she performed as a way to ease her dark mood. Many times offering her insight and guidance and wisdom.

She opened her eyes and read the Latin script. She stopped midentry; scoffing, she snapped the book shut. She'd touched on a charm for making a man fall in love with a woman. *What superstitious nonsense.* Her mother had taught her to use her intellect and observation to deduce whether a cure was effective or not. No spell or charm could make a man love a woman. She knew. Had she not tried a similar love spell when she'd discovered Bertram had a mistress—on the night they wed?

Rose plunked the book back on the table and determinedly locked the memories away. She'd dwelled much too often of late upon the misbegotten cur.

Rose slid off the tall bed, and her nightshift dropped down to cover her bare feet. The cooler air of the room dried the film of perspiration that covered her completely. Her linen shift clinging to her skin in damp patches, she shivered. A chill seeped into the soles of her feet as she padded across the floor to her washstand, which stood against the west wall opposite a cushioned window seat. Double arched windows above the seat looked down on the ornamental garden next to the Great Hall.

Grabbing the open neck of her shift, she tugged it over her head and tossed it onto the bed. She plucked her chamber robe off the peg beside the washstand and slid into its enveloping warmth. Then Rose poured water from the chipped painted pitcher into the basin, splashed cool water over her face and chest, and finished her bath by drying off with a linen towel.

An instinctual sensation tugged at her soul, drawing her into the adjoining chamber. A small bed, a chest, and a stool were the only furniture in the room. No one could enter her son's chamber unless first coming through her bedchamber. Next to the small bed in the corner, Jason's nurse and fierce protector lay curled up on a pallet snoring loudly. Rose quietly approached the foot of the bed and stared down at her sweet, innocent son. He lay on his side facing her, with his thumb stuck in his pursed lips and his other dimpled hand clutching a curly lock of light blond hair.

Her heart seized with love, and she could not keep a huge smile from forming on her lips. It was a side of herself she revealed to only a few people. Though she adored her son, she took care never to indulge in sentimental excess. She controlled her inappropriate passions behind a stoic manner befitting a widow.

Jason's cherub lips drew down, and he kicked off his quilt. Rose pulled it back up under his chin, kissed his warm temple. She trembled with a sudden urge to grab her son and escape into the night. But her maternal instinct was stronger. Jason would be the one to suffer—loss of his inheritance, his title, and all the privileges that accompanied it.

Did she have the right to steal it from him because of her fears, her insecurities, her cowardice?

Rose started at a loud bang that echoed from her chamber. She left Jason and went in the other room. The door rattled on its hinges. The sound of a deep voice, a soft giggle drew her curiosity. Rose opened the chamber door and peeked out.

Near a lit torch, Rand trapped Lisbeth up against the wall, his face pillowed between her indecently exposed plump breasts. The maid's hose-clad thigh curled around Rand's hip like a coiled serpent, pulling him flush against her, seeking to devour him inside her.

Rose inhaled sharply in surprise. A quiver of repulsion raced through her. The man was an incorrigible lecher. As far as she knew, Lady Elena was his current mistress, or had been when Rose was at court a couple of months ago. Apparently not content with Elena, Rand had to debauch Rose's castle servants too.

Rand glanced up just then, and stared, gaze glittering. He winked at her, a wolfish grin on his face. Flashing him a look of contempt, Rose pulled back and slammed the door shut.

Her gaze blurred as she stared at the oaken door. She regretted ever . . . Rose shook her head. The past was unalterable; she could only learn from her mistakes and never repeat them. Not that she had any desire to repeat them. Rubbing her arms, she turned and stared at her rumpled bed.

She should get some more rest before the long trip on the morrow. But she could not bear the separation from Jason, so she went to his chamber, crawled into bed beside him, and wrapped her arms around his sweet-smelling form.

When the oaken door to Rose's chamber slammed shut, Rand jerked. His vision blurred with too much drink, yet the fog of desire dissipated with the rapidity born of . . . what? Shame? Embarrassment? Certainly not, Rand assured himself. A man had a right to indulge his baser instincts when a comely maid showed an interest in his manly attributes.

Yet, his rock-hard shaft shriveled beneath his braies.

Lisbeth reached out and palmed him with her hand, with dismal results. Rand drew back and patted her derriere, winking. "Too much drink, sweet."

Lisbeth huffed and, tugging up her bodice, she flounced away and down the stairwell.

He refused to acknowledge the real culprit of his shrunken cock: guilt. It niggled at the edges of his drink-induced haze as he recalled the fiery determination that sparked in Rose's gaze when she'd declared her aversion to marrying again. It'd been nigh on four years since he'd beheld such passion blazing in her eyes, albeit for a different purpose altogether.

It was a clear indication of the fear she bore, and he was leading her down the path of her affliction without any warning. But there was naught he could do to change the outcome. Rand groaned and leaned his forehead against his forearm, which he braced against the rough wall. He was torn between the duty he owed his king, and the loyalty he owed Rose for their past friendship and what they'd once meant to each other.

He could offer for her instead—the thought slipped unbidden from the recesses of his sluggish mind. Rand jerked back and stared at the flickering torch. *Jesu.* He must have drunk more than he thought. Rose would abhor marrying him as much as anyone else. Probably even more so considering the heated parting they'd had several years ago, which she pretended never occurred.

Even if Rose would agree to marry Rand, he'd never inflict himself upon the lady he admired above all others. She deserved a man who was not haunted by the demons of his past failures.

As he stared at the torch flame, images flashed before his eyes. His body jolted as he felt the burning beam fall on his back, felt the searing pain scorch his skin. Trapped, he stared wide-eyed in horror as his mother ran, flames engulfing her.

The stench of burning flesh filled his nostrils, while his mother's agonized screams echoed in his ears, damning him.

God, would the nightmare never cease. He jammed the heels of his hands painfully into his eyes to dispel the grotesque image of his mother's charred body. But he could never escape the guilt he lived with every day, for it was his fault that she had died in the stable fire.

His sister was dead, too, because he'd let her drown to save himself.

Rand had even failed to protect Alex from being abducted in the Holy Land after they'd sworn an oath to protect each other as comrades in arms.

Anyone he loved was cursed to suffer abominably. For that reason, he could never marry Rose and risk growing emotionally attached to her.

Golan was not an ogre. Rand was sure once Rose married Golan she would come to see there were good men who would not wield their superior strength as a weapon over their wives.

Rand stumbled to his bedchamber door, shoved it open, and collapsed onto the bed fully dressed. Unable to sleep, he stared unseeing up at the canopy.

Rose knelt before Jason inside the large open door of the Keep. She clasped him by the shoulders and gazed into his tear-filled eyes.

"Mama, don't leave me. I want to come with you." He knuckled away the moisture in his eyes.

She swallowed back tears. "Oh, darling, I do not wish to leave you. But the king has commanded my presence at court and the journey would be too taxing for you. I will not be gone long, though. I promise."

"The king is a mean man," he spouted, his bottom lip puffed out and his arms crossed.

Rose could hardly agree, but she did not have the heart to reprimand him. She hugged him hard. "I shall miss you terribly, sweetling. Promise me you will study hard with Brother Michael and obey Edith in all things. Will you do that?"

Jason pulled back. "Don't be sad, Mama."

He reached under the neck of his tunic gown and removed the smooth, shiny brown rock attached to a leather cord. "Take it. When you miss me, rub it. It helped me 'member you when you left last time." His lip trembled.

"Darling, are you sure? I gifted the stone to you."

It was a rock Rose had discovered in a creek years ago in her happy youth.

He nodded emphatically. "Now I'll always be with you."

Rose smiled tremulously, clutching the necklace, and smoothed his hair back off his forehead. "I shall treasure it, Jason."

A giggle from the courtyard drew Rose's attention. Her lips clamped tightly at Lisbeth's coquettish smile. The servant curled her finger at Rand, who was sitting on his horse with a mounted party of armored men and Lady Alison. When he bent down, Lisbeth wrapped a hand round his neck and gave him a long, deep kiss.

Whistles and shouts of encouragement filled the courtyard. Rose pinched her lips tighter in disgust at the public display. At that moment, Rand glanced up and stared directly into her eyes. His own darkened with an emotion she could not glean, and sent her heart racing. She jerked her head away and said her farewells to Jason and Edith.

When she approached her mount, Rand's squire, Will, assisted her onto her palfrey.

Rand sidled his horse up next to her. "Are you ready, Rosie?"

"I shall thank you to refrain from calling me by that absurd name."

Rand could not resist needling her. "You do not like it when I call you Rosie?"

"Nay. It reminds me of childish things. I am no longer a child."

He searched her gaze, and then his eyes dropped to her lips. They were bowed in a softly sensual shape that begged a man to kiss her. Begged him to kiss her. The pull was strong as her lavender and rose scent enveloped him; all he had to do was dip his head just the slightest bit . . .

"Nay, you are no longer a child." At the husky rasp of his voice, Rand started.

Wheeling his horse around, he shouted, "Move out, men!"

He glanced at Rose. "You and your lady are to ride in the middle of the party. The pace shall be grueling, but we'll stop regularly for breaks," he informed her and then rode to the head of the party as it crossed over the drawbridge.

Chapter Three

Sitting atop her black palfrey, Rose arched her lower back trying to loosen the painful knot, and groaned beneath her breath. Their party had ridden from dawn to dusk for two days straight with only brief breaks to rest and care for the horses. Despite Rand's relentless pace, she did not dare complain.

They received a slight respite from the relentless sun when the road cut through a wooded area. The rhythmic creaking of saddle leather and jingling tackle created a gentle melody.

Rand rode in the front of the party beside another knight, Sir Justin. The auburn-haired knight was polite and respectful, but when he was not riding beside Rand he was flirting with Lady Alison. Rose's attendant, with her brunette hair and vivid, laughing brown eyes, easily attracted the attention of the male species. But at that moment, Alison, riding on a mule behind Rose, grumbled in irritation.

Suddenly, a jagged pain shot down Rose's spine. A sharp groan escaped her lips. Up ahead, Rand raised his hand and called a halt to the group. Rose stiffened when he turned around and came directly toward her.

Beside Rose, Alison murmured with evident relief, "Blessed Lady Virgin." Then sighing loudly, she slid from her brown mule and rubbed her posterior.

Before Rand could help Rose dismount, she swung her right leg over Evangeline's rump and, clutching the pommel of her saddle, wiggled down, her stomach pressed against her horse. In the process, her skirts bunched up, exposing her legs. She landed with a jolt and quickly rearranged her clothing. When she turned to greet Rand, he shot her a wide grin, his lips quirked in obvious humor at her ploy to avoid his touch.

Rose gritted her teeth. The buffoon. She did not appreciate his amusement at her expense. The man was incorrigible and had an unnerving tendency to goad her temper. She relaxed her tense shoulders and smoothed her face of irritation.

Having removed his gauntlets, Rand tossed them to a passing man-at-arms, and then ran his fingers back through his dark blond hair. With lighter streaks of gold threaded through them, his locks fell loose to graze broad, well-defined shoulders— shoulders that carried his suit of mail with apparent ease. Over his hauberk, or coat of mail, he wore a simple azure knee-length surcoate. His heater shield, hanging from a strap down his back, completed his accoutrements.

Sir Justin took her palfrey's reins at a nod from Rand and led Evangeline and Alison's mount to a small clearing off the road fifty yards away.

Gray-green eyes twinkling, Rand swept his arm before him. "After you, my lady."

She shifted her gaze away from his and followed the others into the grassy clearing.

Rand kept his pace steady with her slower, measured gait. "I pray the journey has not been too taxing upon you or your attendant."

Jolted, Rose met Rand's gaze. His solicitous regard continued to surprise her, though she supposed it should not. Despite his flirtatious, irreverent wit, Rand was not unkind. But years of Bertram's self-absorbed, self-indulgent behavior had engraved in her an expectation of wretched treatment.

"Aye. I have naught to complain about. Though I don't understand what is so imperative about this audience with the king that we could not take an extra day to make a brief stop at Lichfield?"

"As I said yesterday, Edward instructed me to deliver you to Westminster with all due haste. It is not common knowledge yet, but in a few days he will be departing for his territories in France in order to raise troops and money for the upcoming war with Wales."

Rose's hand flew to the stone hidden beneath her wimple and gown. "So the rumors are true? We are to war with Llewelyn?"

Rand dropped his gaze to her, and his smile dimmed a fraction. "Aye. It would appear so, Rose. Since Edward became king, he has shown unusual restraint in his dealings with the prince. Numerous times Llewelyn was to meet with King Edward to pay homage for his principality, and each time the prince has not shown as promised."

"You knew this was possible and you forced me to leave Jason behind? We have to go back for him." Rose lifted her skirts and made to retrieve her horse. "I can't leave him unprotected when war with Wales can erupt at any moment."

"Rose, stop." Rand caught her arm and pulled her around to face him. "Jason is in no danger. It shall be many weeks before Edward calls his council to discuss the merits of the war and get his magnates support for it."

Rose shook her head, and clutched her hands in her skirts to keep a tight rein on her emotions. "I can't take that chance. You cannot guarantee me that hostilities will not break out sooner. I need Jason with me. I must protect him."

Rand crossed his arms over his chest, his gaze shadowed. "We are not going back for Jason, Rose. I have my orders and I will not disobey them. To set your mind at ease, though, I shall send two of my knights back to Ayleston for Jason's protection."

A bead of sweat rolled down Rose's forehead. She wiped it

away with the back of her hand. She exhaled slowly. "Very well. But I would complete this journey as swiftly as possible so I can meet with the king and then return to Jason."

"Agreed." Rand hooked his arm in hers and led her down the path.

Though Rose was anxious to have her audience with the king, the uncertainty of his intent was troubling. She could only surmise that King Edward had made a decision regarding wardship of her son's estate. When Bertram had died over two years ago, Jason inherited the Ayleston title, and all the coin and vast lands it entailed. But until Jason reached his majority, Edward could grant wardship of the land to anyone.

As they approached the clearing where the others had already settled in the grass around a cold fire pit, Rand held back the low-hanging branches of a birch tree shading the narrow path. Rose gave Rand an absentminded smile of thanks. Deep in her thoughts, she did not see his startled look of pleasure.

After Rose settled on a log next to Alison, Rand sauntered away from the group and into a copse of trees.

Rose's contemplation returned to her son. Last spring, as lady-in-waiting to Queen Eleanor, Rose gained the influence of the queen and finally won custody of her son. It was unusual, though not unheard of, for a woman to be granted guardianship of her son.

But the upcoming audience with the king complicated matters for Rose. She did not like the uncertainty that bloomed in her chest. She despised change and she had a feeling this change was not to the good of either her or her son.

Back near the shallow, rocky stream, in a daze, Rand crouched down and cupped water into his hands. A quiver of pleasure raced in his blood, thrumming in places he dared not think about, or he might embarrass himself. He took several deep drinks to soothe his parched throat, and then splashed some water over his heated face; neither sensation was the result of the unbearable weather.

Rose's smile, rarely bestowed, touched him deeply. He chastised himself. It was just a smile, for God's sakes, Rand thought, and one she did not even intentionally direct toward him.

Rand stood and wiped his hands on his surcoate. Sheltered by the trees, he gazed at Rose. Beside Lady Alison, who was dressed in amethyst silk, Rose looked drab in comparison, with her simple woolen brown surcoate and concealing headdress. But her garments, obviously meant to detract unwanted male attention, had the opposite effect on Rand.

The wimple and veil delineated her exquisite heart-shaped face, vivid blue eyes, and narrow, sloping nose. And her lips, plumper in the middle and turned up on the outer edges, were so temptingly kissable.

Throbbing heat shot to his shaft. He grumbled beneath his breath, pressing his erection down and willing it to subside. A warm breeze wafted across his face, carrying the scent of warm moldy earth and greenery.

The sooner he completed his assignment, the sooner he could return to his more pleasant duties, like hunting and fighting. Until then, he would stay as far away as possible from the beauteous Rose, given that close proximity in their daily interactions was necessitated by his duty to escort her safely to Westminster.

As dusk approached, the armored party and the two ladies they escorted on the ride southeast were sweaty, dirty, hungry, and exhausted. For two nights they had slept under the stars with only a small tent for the ladies.

Rand shouted back to those in the party, "Beyond the bend

ahead lies a monastery! Tonight, we shall have warm food in our bellies and a roof over our heads!"

An exuberant shout went up. Rand, laughing, spurred his horse forward in anticipation of a hot meal and a soft pallet to rest his head upon. He pulled Leviathan up on the road before the gates and allowed the rest of the party to pass him. Sir Justin and young Will were in the rear, following Rose and Alison.

Rand surreptitiously observed Rose as she approached him. Her face was lined with fatigue and her shoulders drooped. Then, all of a sudden, a hare darted across the road in front of Rose's horse. Evangeline reared up, kicking her white forelegs in fright. Rose slipped sideways. The mare came down with a hard jolt—Rose hanging precariously onto the saddle—and bolted past Rand before he could respond.

Rand's heart plummeted to his toes, then bounced up into his throat. He spurred Leviathan, shouting to Justin, "I've got her!"

He bent over his gelding, his heart pounding in his ears as he galloped at full speed after Rose. He could just see her in the distance as the sun disappeared over the horizon.

If aught happened to Rose, he would never forgive himself.

Rand closed the distance between them. Rose still clung tenaciously to her speeding mare. His eyes bore into Rose's narrow back, willing her to hold on a little longer. The fabric of her veil and full tunic skirts flapped behind her. Close enough now, Rand reached out to grab the palfrey's trailing reins.

But at that moment her mare veered sharply to the right, throwing Rose. She screamed, the high-pitched sound a dagger thrust into Rand's heart. She landed with a sickening thump. Rand jumped off Leviathan and rushed to her, feeling as though stone weighted his body down.

Rose lay crumpled facedown and unmoving at the bottom of the muddy roadside ditch.

"Noooo!" A scream of agony ripped from his throat.

He climbed down into the ditch, slipping in the mire in his haste. Falling to his knees, he lifted Rose into his lap and cradled her like a baby. She was not breathing. Nay, she was not dead, he would not let God take her.

Rand stared down at her pale, drawn face. There was a long shallow gash on her forehead. Blood poured down her temple, mixing with the mud covering the left side of her face. Rand slapped her cheek gently, but she did not respond. He called her name over and over and clutched her to him, willing his warmth and strength into her limp body. He prayed beneath his breath, his lips moving in fervent supplication.

"Help me! Someone, help me!" he shouted, his desperate plea echoing in the silent woods like a ghostly lament.

Suddenly, he was aged ten and three again, and was lying on the muddy bank of the river Garonne. His slender arms clutched his sister and he stared down at her face, a nearly exact though more feminine replica of his own. Her beautiful, long gold curls were matted to her head and her gray-green eyes stared blankly up at him in reproach.

She was so wet and cold and lifeless. But he kept holding her, refusing to let her go. Or believe she was dead.

Rand shook her hard, so hard her head snapped back, and called out her name over and over, "Juliana, Juliana!"

A great gulping inhalation seized her abruptly, making her chest rise and fall violently as she brought air into her lungs.

Rand, blinking, stared down as Juliana's small face faded away and Rose's eyes snapped open. A sudden euphoria filled him and made him light-headed with relief.

Rose's clouded, pain-filled gaze searched his. Her voice scratchy, she asked, "Who is Juliana?"

Rand stiffened and shuttered his eyes to keep her from delving too deeply and discovering the pain he carried inside. But her eyelids drooped down and slowly closed. Her breathing slowed.

The pounding of hooves on the road behind him reminded him they were alone in the countryside at night. He needed to get Rose back to the safety of the monastery and have someone examine her. He had yet to know how seriously injured she was.

"Sir Rand!" Justin shouted and pulled his roan gelding up beside the other horses grazing alongside the road.

Rand lifted Rose gently in his arms and stood up, his mail clinking. "Over here, Justin. Rose took a spill from her horse and needs immediate care."

Rand scrambled up the bank and handed Rose up to Justin so Rand could mount his horse.

Once mounted, Rand sidled up next to him. "Give her to me."

Staring intently at Rose, Rand did not see Justin's startled gaze at his leader's possessive tone. Rand was oblivious to everything but seeing Rose safely into the care of the monastery infirmary.

Rand sat on the stool in the small austere cell and stared at Rose. She lay in the narrow bed, chest rising and falling in shallow breaths. A bulky bandage was wrapped around her forehead, and her hair trailed loose down her shoulders.

Not again, he swore. It could not be happening again. First Juliana, then his mother, and now Rose, too?

He lunged up and swallowed a groan as his lower back twinged from sitting so long on the stool. He paced away, swung back and stared down at her. A single candle on the chest beside the bed glimmered on her pale complexion, and delicate eyelids. His gaze bore into her, willing her to wake, to move, to do something to assure him she was going to be all right.

As if hearing his plea, Rose moaned softly and her eyes flickered.

Rand took two steps to the door and called out, "Sister Margareta!" He ducked his head out the short, narrow door frame and hollered again, "Sister Margareta!"

"Hush, my son." The rosy-cheeked sister hustled inside the chamber. "'Tis loud enough to frighten the dead."

He turned back and gestured to Rose, his voice a whisper. "Lady Ayleston. She's waking."

Rose clutched her head, patting the linen bandage. She tried to sit up and then fell back on the bed with a groan.

Sister Margareta sidled around him. "Easy, milady." The nun's pale, slender hand gently touched Rose's shoulder. "Don't try to move. You took quite a blow to your head. We have been very worried about you."

Rose murmured, "We?"

"Aye, your young knight. Sir Rand Montague."

"He is not my—"

Rand rubbed his chest. "Rose, you are awake. God be praised."

Rose stared up at him in bewilderment with her crystal blue eyes. "Oh, God, my body aches. What happened to me? Where am I?"

He frowned. "Do you not remember?"

"Nay." Her dark red eyebrows dipped down in puzzlement. "The last thing I recall was eating a repast of bread and cheese when we stopped for dinner."

"That was earlier today. We arrived at the gates of the monastery to stop for the night, when your horse bolted. I caught up to you but your horse threw you into a roadside gully. You must have hit your head on a rock or branch or something." Rand moved to her side and touched her bandaged head. "How do you feel? Are you in much pain?"

Rose turned away from his touch. "My head is pounding, my eyes are blurry, and my body aches everywhere."

Rand tried not to let her rebuff offend him. She had not always despised his touch.

"Any dizziness?" Sister Margareta chimed in.

"Aye. When I sat up."

"It is as I told your young knight. The blow you received to your head shall cause you some discomfort and pain. I'd like you to rest for about a sennight before you resume your journey."

A ripple of concern lodged in his chest. "I don't understand, Sister. I thought you said she was going to be all right. Need I be worried? How serious is her injury if you wish to keep her here for a sennight?"

"I don't believe there is cause for alarm, my lord. But just to be sure the blow to her head caused no serious, lasting harm, I would like her to remain here for a few days. Also, her fall caused severe bruising on her hip and shoulder. As soon as her headache and dizziness subside, and she feels well enough, you may continue on your journey."

Rose whispered, "You need not worry I shall delay the journey any longer, Rand. I shall not give Edward a reason to reprimand you for failing to do your duty in a timely manner."

When she made to rise, Rand gently eased her back down. He could not believe she thought his concern was because of the journey's delay and not worry for her good health. "Don't move, Rose. You are going nowhere till the good sister grants you permission to leave this bed. I'll send Edward word of your injury. He'll understand that our late arrival is unavoidable." Rand understood her distrust of men, but Rose had known him for a long time and knew him better than that. How could she ever believe him capable of doing aught to endanger her welfare?

"I shall leave you to your rest now, Rose. As soon as you recover, we leave for Westminster."

Rose looked so lost and vulnerable. Guilt reared its twisted, ugly head, mixing with Rand's feelings of disappointment and regret. He wanted Rose, but it could never be. His duty was clear. Golan was soon to be her husband and responsible for her welfare.

Rose's eyes blurred again, so the brief shadow she caught in Rand's gaze must have been an illusion, for that roguish grin appeared, dimples deepening. Rather, two ridiculous grins, her vision doubling his image. She eased her eyes closed, her pounding head a misery she would not wish on anyone. Sister Margareta, bless her, gave Rose a hot chamomile infusion sweetened with honey for her aching head. Then the nun slipped out of the cell, leaving the candle alit on the table by the bed.

As Rose drifted off to sleep, a memory surfaced of Rand leaning over her, his voice agonized, calling out for a woman named Juliana.

Chapter Four

Five days later, Rose sat on a bench in the monastery's ornamental garden. Flowers of every color filled the garden with their heavenly aroma. The musky scent intertwined with sweet-smelling honeysuckle, which hung on a lattice on the garden wall at her back. Rand sat opposite her, propped against a bench made of a grass-covered earthen mound. An illuminated book lay open in his lap.

At Sister Margareta's instigation, Rand was practically forced to keep Rose company by reading to her. The nun chose a French romance from the scriptorium about a brave knight who rescues his ladylove—a woman he has loved from afar for many years—from the tyranny of an evil baron.

Other than the occasional birdcall, Rose heard naught but the husky timber of Rand's voice. The deep, vibrating tenor resonated within Rose like a forgotten caress. Enthralled, she searched his face. His firm lips moved in a breathless whisper, his high cheekbones prominent with the intensity of some strong emotion.

An ache surged up inside Rose's chest, yearning for what could have been. The heroic story and Rand's reaction triggered in her a memory of the girl who once adored him. Before he left for the Crusade and she met and married

Bertram Harcourt. Before her husband revealed his true depraved nature and shattered her innocence.

Now only bitterness resided within her heart. There were no gallant knights in this harsh world, such as the fictional Sir Lance in the story Rand was reading. Women were mere chattel to be used by greedy, ambitious, lecherous men. Except men treated their chattel better than their easily expendable wives.

Rand was an example of the lechery of men. He used one woman after another in the pursuit of his lusty appetites. A secret part of her realized she was being too harsh, but then she'd have to acknowledge her own complicity in succumbing to a night of temptation in Rand's arms.

Rand's voice in the background, Rose drifted back into the past. It was several months after her marriage, and Rand had returned from the Crusade to inform her Alex was dead—though later it turned out Alex was instead imprisoned in a Mamluk fortress.

She was devastated at the news, and still numb from learning her husband's true evil nature. Feeling lost and vulnerable, she desperately wanted to discover what it was like to be cherished as a woman. And Rand was there for her, their shared grief a bond that only drew them closer. They made love, one night of passion and surrender. But there was no love involved, only grief and animal lust.

As she returned from her reverie, her eyes alighted on Rand. They never spoke of that night. But she did not doubt that, to him, she was just one more of his countless conquests, like the pretty servant at Ayleston Castle. Rose's face heated as she remembered his torrid embrace of Lisbeth the night before their departure.

But what of the other woman whose name he called out when he pulled Rose from the ditch? The agony in his voice had been palpable.

"Who is Juliana?" The question slipped out before she could contain it.

Oh, God. I pray you did not hear me, she thought desperately.

Rand stopped reading and slowly closed the leather-bound manuscript. He cocked his head. "What do you know about Juliana?"

Since she had awoken from her fall, Rose had been unable to stop thinking about the woman. Surely it was not jealousy that tightened in her breast? Nay. The feeling was simply curiosity.

Rose shrugged. To keep from twisting her hands, she clutched the seat of the bench tightly. "You called out for her the other day when I tumbled from my palfrey. Do you not remember?"

He did not answer but asked her another question. "How can you remember aught when you were rendered insensible?" His right eyebrow arched in lazy inquiry.

"I don't know. The memories are hazy. But I remember feeling as though I were watching from a distance as you held me in your arms and cried out for Juliana. So who is she?"

Rand leaned back against the grass seat. "Mayhap it was just a dream."

"Nay. It was not a dream. The memory is too vivid to be something I conjured in my dreams."

Rand stared at her, not answering, his gaze speculative.

For some reason Rose persisted. Normally she avoided confrontation and used cunning to get what she wanted. "Why do you avoid answering my question, Rand? Are you embarrassed for some reason? Is she a woman you bedded?"

Rand flinched as though shot with a barbed arrow, and his voice was as sharp. "Enough, Rose." She watched his green eyes dim to a muted gray. "You know not of what you speak. Juliana was my sister."

Rose gasped aloud in horror. "Oh, Rand. Forgive me. I did

not know. I mean, Alex told me you had a twin sister who died. But I never knew her name, or the circumstances of her death."

She reached her hand out to touch Rand's arm in commiseration, but she caught herself and dropped it back to her side.

With his free hand, Rand pushed himself up from the bench and stood. "Alex told you about Juliana?"

Uncomfortable with Rand looming over her, Rose lurched to her feet. Only a slight twinge in her hip indicated her bruising was nearly healed.

She lowered her lashes, hiding her gaze. "Not exactly. It was many years ago. It was the first visit you made to Briand Castle with my brother. Curious to know all about you, I pestered Alex until he told me about you and your family." She jerked her gaze up when he chuckled.

His mouth curved up, smile rueful. "I remember how persistent you were when you wanted something. So what did Alex tell you?"

Chagrined, Rose felt a slight flush heating her cheeks. As a young girl she had been spoiled and indulged, so she usually got whatever she wanted, be it a pretty silk dress for a celebratory feast, or extra sweet pudding for dessert, or intimate details about her brother's handsome best friend. Her voice dropped, soft with sympathy as she replied, "He told me how your mother and sister died a year apart shortly before your father sent you to foster with your grandfather in England. Alex mentioned Lady Montague died in a fire. But he never spoke of how your sister died."

Rand stared down at the top of Rose's head. The wimple and veil he despised were gone, destroyed by the slimy mud. Parted down the center, her hair was braided. The warm afternoon sunshine shimmered within the silky red locks, creating copper and gold streaks.

"You never speak of your sister. Will you tell me how she died? Was it illness?"

He did not know why, but suddenly the words were torn from him. "Juliana drowned." The anguish of his loss seeped into his voice without volition. Grief for his mother and sister surged to the surface.

Her questioning eyes softened, a warm glow of sympathy alighting upon him. Unable to bear her gaze, Rand turned his back on Rose and paced away. He did not deserve her sympathy. If not for him, Juliana would be alive today, married with children of her own and chatelaine of her own household.

It had been his idea to go to the river that summer day six and ten years ago. They were playing near the riverbank when Juliana lost her footing and was swept out to deeper waters. Rand jumped in to rescue her, but he was tugged underwater with her and nearly drowned. So he let Juliana go to save himself.

He should have died that day instead.

It was his duty to protect her, but he had been careless and inattentive. They were extremely close and practically inseparable, as if being twins they had been of one soul. With her death, he had felt as if a piece of it had been ripped from him and lost forever.

No amount of penance could relieve him of his guilt.

Rose's soft voice penetrated his reverie. "Rand, I am so sorry. Would you care to tell me what happened? How she drowned?"

Rand could feel an internal struggle, wishing to confide in Rose. But he could not bring himself to reveal his secret shame and see the pity or, God forfend, accusation in her eyes.

Rand fixed his countenance in his usual teasing grin and spun around. "There is nothing to tell, Rosie, truly. It happened so long ago." He tweaked her chin. "Now, I need to check on my men and make sure they are ready to resume our journey. We depart for Westminster at dawn. I'll see you in the refectory for supper."

He turned around and walked jauntily away.

Rose slumped her shoulders, disappointed Rand did not wish to confide in her. Something did not feel right about his glib response. To lose his sister in a drowning accident when he was ten and three, then his mother in a tragic fire a year later, must have had a deep impact on one so young.

As Rand neared the garden gate, he began whistling a ribald tune. Oh, what was she thinking? This was Rand. He much preferred the flippant attachments of loose women and could not be bothered with expressing deeper emotions of substance. He was a shameless rogue to the core.

Six days later, Rose sighed in relief when Rand halted their party at the top of a hill north of Westminster. In the wide valley below, men in short braies and long shertes were busy cutting fields of wheat, barley, and rye, with the women and children following behind gathering the grain into stalks. Beyond the fields lay Westminster Abbey and the adjoining palace. The muddy serpentine Thames River hugged the palace to the south and east and glimmered with the last rays of the rapidly descending sun.

Rand proceeded forward, and a while later they entered the north gate of the palace. Several castle attendants approached to take their horses. Before Rose could dismount, Rand came to her side, clutched her waist, and lifted her from her palfrey.

A sudden breathless sensation quickened in her chest; confused, she frowned. Rand released her and stepped back.

Sir Justin led Alison away to give Rose and Rand privacy.

"Rose, I shall give you my leave now. I doubt I shall see you again before you leave court and return home."

Her heart thudded. "You are leaving?" Rose bit her tongue to still a sudden rush of nervous blathering.

An awful sensation of being abandoned shuddered through her. Which was ridiculous, because Rand was only doing his duty. Yet during the journey, she had felt oddly safe in Rand's protection. Now, fear of the unknown would not release its grip on her. She clutched Jason's stone, her son never far from her thoughts. She would endure whatever the king had in store for her—for Jason's sake.

"I assumed you would stay long enough to discover what the king intends of me. Are you not even a little curious?"

His eyes shone with an emotion she was unable to interpret. Was it regret? she wondered. Disappointment?

"Of course," he said, his voice oddly strained. "But I have other business that I have been neglecting that needs my immediate attention. Sir Justin—"

The clatter of horse hooves erupted as a party of brightly dressed ladies on horseback entered the courtyard. One woman with hair the color of flame, dressed in a jewel-toned blue silk surcoate, and riding an elegant bay mare, left the group and approached them.

Lady Elena Chartres held her arms out for Rand to help her dismount, drawing attention to her voluptuous bosom. "Rand, my dear, I am sooo glad you are back. Court has been a veritable desert without your delicious presence." A smile of seductive promise graced her lips.

Rand hurried to her side like an excited puppy. His strong, masculine hands clasped her waist and lifted her from her perch. The woman blatantly leaned into him and, her breasts cushioned against his arm, whispered into his ear.

Rand threw back his head and laughed, glints of sunlight catching in his dark blond hair. "Elena, you need not flatter me. You are not a woman to remain lonely for long."

Rand made no move to extricate himself from the woman's possessive hold.

"You reprobate. You know me too well." A slender finger caressed his cheek.

Flushing with embarrassment, Rose clenched her fists in her gray wool skirt. "If you will excuse me, Rand." She took a step to go around them.

Elena turned to Rose, her gaze arch. "Why, Lady Ayleston, welcome back to court. 'Tis always a pleasure to see you."

Rose spun back to Lady Elena. "Likewise, I am sure." The woman's patronizing tone irked. Her gaze shifted to Rand. "If you will excuse me, I have *business* that needs tending," she said mockingly.

Rose did not doubt Elena was the "business" Rand had been neglecting. She flounced away and headed toward the residential ward of the castle, a three-story building with round towers at each corner. Alison and Justin, deep in conversation, stood before steps that led to a large double-door entry.

"Rose," she heard Rand call out a moment before his strong grip caught her arm and stopped her headlong flight.

She shook his arm off. "What more is there to say, Rand? I believe we've said our farewells."

Crossing his arms, Rand caught her gaze. "Before Elena arrived I was saying that Sir Justin is staying at court. If you have need of me for anything, inform Justin. He will know where to get word to me."

She harrumphed. "I shall have no need of your help."

He bowed, his eyes shifting away. "I wish you well, Rose. Till we meet again."

Did she detect a shadow of regret in his gaze? Nay, it was probably a trick of her imagination.

"Sir Rand. Lady Ayleston." A tall, distinguished man with gray-streaked brown hair came down the stairs and stopped before them.

The king's household steward bowed to her. "I see you have recovered fully from the fall from your horse, my lady. The journey was not too taxing, I hope?"

Rose lightly touched the gash on her forehead below her wimple. "Aye, my lord. My headache and dizziness have subsided. I have no lasting effects from my injury."

He smiled with relief. "The king shall be pleased to hear it. He was quite concerned for your welfare. If you will follow me, I shall escort you and your attendant"—he nodded to Alison—"to your chamber so you may refresh yourself before supper. After supper, I'll take you to an audience with the king.

"Sir Rand, the king will have your report on the morrow."

Rand bowed to the steward his acknowledgment. "On the morrow."

His gaze lingered on her. "Fare well, Rosie." Then he pivoted and walked off, Justin on his heels.

Following behind the steward and Alison, Rose glanced back just before she entered the palace. Lady Elena skipped up to Rand, her softly sculpted lips lifted for a kiss.

Rose averted her gaze. As she entered the cool shadows of the Great Hall, her fear unerringly returned.

How I despise being at the mercy of a man, whether he is king or not!

Escorted into a sumptuous private chamber, Rose curtsied deeply before King Edward, who lounged upon an elaborately carved throne in the middle of the audience chamber. "I give you good greeting, Sire," she said, voice soft with deference, her eyes shadowed by her lowered lashes.

"Rise, Lady Ayleston," Edward intoned with regal flare, a gold crown upon his leonine head.

She straightened, folding her hands demurely before her, and braced for his pronouncement.

"Welcome to court, my lady. I summoned your presence here to inform you of decisions long overdue. I have neglected conferring upon Ayleston a suitable guardian. But neglect my duty I shall no more. I have chosen an honorable knight of great esteem to bestow the honor upon. Sir Golan, come forward."

Rose jerked her eyes up. From the shadows a man of extreme elegance, masculinity, and handsome features walked forward. His dark green silk surcoate flowed gracefully from broad shoulders and was belted with a jewel-mounted sword belt.

"Lady Ayleston, I present to you Sir Golan de Coucy."

A tremor of recognition coursed through her blood like ice in her veins. He was the man she spied staring at her throughout supper, for whom snippets of rumors abounded concerning a dead wife and child.

Sir Golan, stopping beside her, bowed, his dark brown hair sweeping along his broad cheekbones. "My lady, 'tis indeed a pleasure." He smiled, his eyes crinkling pleasantly, but the possessive light that sparked within his gaze shot to her gut like a barbed quarrel.

"Sir Golan, I am pleased to make your acquaintance," she said, her heart thundering. This was the man who would administer her son's estates. She had no wish to antagonize him.

Edward waved to a servant, who came forward with a tray with three chalices. Edward plucked the more elaborate jeweled vessel from the tray. Rose took the chalice the servant proffered her, Golan following suit.

Edward raised his chalice. "'Tis indeed a moment to rejoice. Sir Golan, for your dedication and exemplary service to our realm, we salute you." Then he drank from his cup.

Not wishing to offend, Rose lifted her chalice in tribute and drank a deep draught.

Sir Golan stared at her over the rim of his chalice as he downed several drinks. "Sire, you do me great honor. I shall give you no cause to regret your generous reward."

Edward nodded and turned to her. "Lady Ayleston, your widow status is of great import to me as well. Sir Golan has made an offer for your hand in marriage. And I have accepted."

A rush of blood roared in her ears. Rose froze with her cup halfway to her lips. Her gaze swung to Sir Golan. He was watching her closely, his sensual lips curled up in satisfaction.

Trepidation shuddered down her spine. She could not help feeling an instinctual distaste for the man. His eyes were too possessive and his manner too suave.

She lowered her hand and smoothed her expression. "Sire, I admit to some surprise. I don't wish to disappoint, but I have a prior commitment that precludes marriage. I have vowed chastity to God. Bishop Meyland—"

"Neither Bishop Meyland nor any other bishop in this realm shall receive your vow, Lady Ayleston. You shall marry Sir Golan at my command. My will shall not be gainsaid." His stern voice and fierce scowl promised dire punishment if she did not accept.

Rose sucked in a deep breath, stunned. By his words, Edward confirmed her suspicions about the bishop's postponement of her vow. "Aye, Sire." Rose closed her hand over the round stone at her neck. *Jason, how I miss your uncomplicated, laughing exuberance and loving heart. Soon, very soon, I shall return to you.*

The king leaned back in his chair, his forearm braced on the chair arm and wine cup dangling from his hand. "In three days' time, here in the chapel at Westminster, we shall celebrate the nuptials, with a grand feast to follow."

"Sire, that does not leave much time for wedding preparations. And what of the reading of the banns?" She knew delay was fruitless but could not help a last attempt to slow the proceedings so she might discover a way to escape the shackles of matrimony.

Having received his way, the king bestowed upon her a benevolent smile. "I shall wave the banns so you need not wait two weeks to marry. And the queen is quite fond of you. She intends to gift you with cloth from the royal wardrobe and grant her ladies leave to help you make the necessary arrangements."

How typical of the king to switch from arrogant despot to

magnanimous benefactor in the space of moments, she thought bitterly.

Golan had remained silent and still during this exchange. Now he turned to her. "My lady, I know this is very sudden, but I promise I shall give you no cause to regret marrying me." His voice grew gruff. "My precious wife died giving birth to a stillborn son a year ago. If you would allow it, I'd be proud to raise your son, Jason, as if he were my own blood."

The man spoke eloquently, yet . . . She'd felt a subtle sinister air of speculation swirling around the knight at supper concerning his wife's death. Now the king wished to shackle her to this man, this stranger? She tried to read de Coucy's face. He had a smooth, wide forehead, straight eyebrows over a pair of wide-set, nearly black eyes, a long narrow nose that curved slightly to the right, and a shallow cleft in his chin. It was impossible to glean anything from his dark, impenetrable eyes.

Edward handed his chalice to the servant, stepped down from his throne, and approached them. He clasped his hand on Golan's shoulder. "'Tis a most gracious pledge, Sir Golan." The king turned his gaze on Rose and cocked his head. "You can have no better knight as husband and stepfather to your son."

She chose her words carefully. "Sir Golan, I am overwhelmed. Jason would be fortunate to have such a noble influence in his life."

The king laughed heartily. "You shall make a fine match. Indeed, I do not doubt that before long you shall be busy producing heirs to carry on the proud de Coucy lineage."

A cold sensation slithered across Rose's flesh and tentacles of fear took root. Her face paling, Rose mumbled a response. Golan's intense dark gaze held hers. His smile was firmly in place, but his eyes reflected . . . what? Pride, offense, indignation?

Finally dismissed, Rose hurriedly returned to her chamber.

Thoughts and emotions roiled inside her like a violent storm at sea, making her sick with worry, fear, and indecision. She did not know how she was going to survive being forced to lie beneath Sir Golan as he violated her body, no matter that it was considered her conjugal duty to submit willingly to her husband.

Elena's warm breath bathed Rand's chest as she fell into a deep sleep. Rand slowly lifted her hand from his chest and slid off the bed. He padded across the rough floorboards, plucking up his clothes as he moved toward the fireplace, the blaze now extinguished. After piling his garments on the settle, he dressed as swiftly as he could.

Chagrin filled him as he skulked out of Elena's town house, retrieved Leviathan from the stable, and made his way back to the castle.

He was uneasy. His head was hazy with drink, and dissatisfaction consumed him. The usual relief he achieved upon gratifying his carnal needs eluded him tonight. He felt empty and more alone than he ever had before. Usually he could stave off the feeling with various duties performed for the king, and by overseeing his thriving wine-trading business.

But neither gave him a sense of fulfillment as they had in the past.

Rand called out to the palace guard at the gate. In the stable yard, he dismounted and led Leviathan into the vaulted, wide-aisled structure. There were thirty stalls on each side of the aisle and a sliver of moonlight shone into the darkened building through a high round window above the stable door.

It was silent except for the occasional rustling of hay and neighing horse. He led his horse into an empty stall and removed the saddle and bridle. Leviathan dropped his head and made a huffing sound of pleasure as Rand began grooming his back with the comb hanging on the stall wall.

Rose's upcoming marriage to Sir Golan had exacerbated his growing discontent with his life. All night he had been trying without success to forget about her, first with drink and then in Elena's arms.

With every passing day he desired her more, her unique essence seeping into his blood and bone and sinew—a potent concoction. His normal regimen of exhaustive pursuit of pleasure no longer could suppress his rising appetite to possess her, body and soul.

He refused to contemplate offering Rose the choice to marry him instead. Even if the king would accept him, Rand would never inflict himself upon Rose, for death seemed to follow him. The two people he loved most had died before his eyes because he couldn't save them. Once he married Rose, he would have to "love, honor, and protect" her. But he feared he was incapable of protecting her. The past had born out how inept he was when it came to those to whom he was closest. He could not bear it if Rose was harmed due to his inability to shield her from danger.

Rand placed the horse comb on the stall wall, swung open the stall door, and left the stables. The only thing he could think to do was seek the quiet sanctuary of prayer in an attempt to find the absolution he desperately craved, but forever eluded him.

Chapter Five

Before dawn of the next morning, as Rose knelt in front of the chapel altar in prayer, biting cold from the flagstone floor seeped into her knees. The elaborate carved rood screen guarded the chancel of the palace chapel dedicated to St. John. Before the screen was the simple stone altar, atop which stood a forlorn lit candle. Very little light illuminated the area directly in front of her. She clasped her hands tightly to still their trembling.

The silence in the chapel could not calm the debilitating fear that coursed through Rose. The solace she sought in prayer eluded her. Her thoughts kept returning to the audience with the king. When Edward demanded she marry Sir Golan, her first instinct was unmitigated terror and then outright defiance. But one did not defy a king, and especially not one as capricious as Edward.

If Rose defied him, he could revoke her custody of Jason as easily as he had given it. The only alternative was to flee, but she would never leave her son behind. She would have to return to Ayleston and retrieve him. There was no doubt in her mind, though, that the king would seize Jason before she could. If by some miracle she did succeed, how could she protect Jason? A woman and child on the road without the protection of a man would be at the mercy of criminal and scoundrel alike.

Nay. She loved Jason so much she would do anything to protect him.

Perhaps she was overreacting. Sir Golan was a handsome man, but that was no proof he was anything like her cruel husband. She pulled the stone out from beneath her bodice and rubbed its smooth surface, seeking to ease her anxieties. It made her feel closer to Jason. At least Jason was legally in her custody and care. Golan would have no part in arranging his education, fostering, and marriage settlements.

Rose dipped her head again and prayed for guidance. A shiver lifted the hairs on the back of her nape. She shuddered and looked over her shoulder. The enveloping darkness of the barrel-vaulted nave no longer exuded a sense of solemnity.

Rose said a final prayer, crossed herself, and with one hand levered up off her aching knees. She hurried through the nave, her gaze moving back and forth to the arcade columns. Surely someone could not be watching her from the darker concealment of the aisles?

She entered the small vestibule when a large masculine hand reached out from the shadows. A shrill scream emerged from the back of her throat but was quickly cut off by his hand over her mouth.

"Don't scream, Rose. 'Tis just me." He released her immediately.

Her heart was palpitating so hard it felt as though it would burst. Stunned, she allowed Sir Golan to lead her back into the chapel. The moon shone through the clearstory windows—windows high in the second story above the arched columns—giving subtle illumination.

"Sir Golan, I was just returning to my chamber to retire. I pray you excuse me."

He blocked her exit. "Rose, we have yet to speak privately

about our upcoming marriage. Now we are alone, it would be a shame not to take this opportunity to discuss it."

"My lord—"

"Prithee, call me Golan." He smiled, baring his straight teeth. "We shall be married soon."

"Golan," she said after a slight pause. "The king made clear I am to marry you in two days' time and I shall obey him. What more is there to discuss?"

"I can see you are troubled. How may I allay your concerns about marriage? Or is it me you object to?" A dark shadow passed over his eyes.

Disturbed by his blunt question, she looked away. "'Tis not you . . . Golan," she lied. "My objection is to marriage, to any man. I had intended to dedicate my life to a vow of chastity."

He stepped closer, reached out and cupped her cheek. "Beauty such as yours should not be squandered on chastity."

She recoiled, but his other hand came up to clutch her head. He slowly drew his lips down toward hers. "Let me kiss you. I mean to convince you that you were meant for me, to bear my children."

Cringing away from him, she brought her hands up and pressed against his chest. He did not budge. "My lord, Golan, you do not want me. You want my lands and vast wealth."

His breath wafted across her lips. "Aye, but I want you more. And I shall have you."

Rose shivered at the dark current of possession in his voice. "Golan, we are not yet wed. Prithee, release me," she babbled desperately.

"One kiss. You shall not be disappointed," he vowed.

"I do not want—" His mouth covered hers, cutting off her denial.

The moment his cold, thin lips touched hers, a shudder of disgust traveled down her body. Wrapping his arms around her, he groaned in satisfaction and plunged his tongue into her mouth. Rose whimpered, trembling uncontrollably. He ravaged her mouth, his tongue nearly gagging her as it thrust inside exuberantly.

He raised his mouth, and then trailed a wet path down her neck, mumbling, "Oh, God, you cannot deny it. I can feel you trembling with desire."

She squirmed to escape his embrace. "Nay, release me. I do not want you. We are not yet married. Shall you dishonor me in the Lord's house?" Her voice grew shrill.

He ignored her protests. "You need not be coy. I know what you want. You need to be coaxed and taught how to please me." His thick fingers clutched her breast and squeezed hard.

Sharp pain seared her breast. Rose cried out, "Let me go! You are hurting me!"

His black eyes blazed with possessive determination before he crushed his mouth over hers. Rose moaned in misery and appalled disbelief as nausea churned in her stomach.

She began to struggle harder, but Golan shoved his big muscular body against hers and pressed her up against a stone column. He thrust his hard member into her shuddering belly. Terror struck a dagger into her heart. She froze as humiliating memories from the past tormented her—memories of Bertram's forced seduction of her while Lady Lydia watched; of his braying laughter and her feelings of shame and degradation. Rose could not breathe. She gasped, trying to gulp air into her constricted lungs.

Tears of pain and humiliation blurred her vision. She bucked against him, and finally tearing her mouth free, she cried out, a desperate plea in her voice, "Stop, prithee!"

A roar of savage fury erupted in the chapel. Golan turned in stunned surprise. Rose flung away from the knight's hold and huddled against the column. Her eyes grew wide when Rand flew at the man and pummeled him in the face. With a final punch, blood erupted from Golan's nose and he flew backward. He landed on his arse on the chapel floor, clutching his nose and groaning in agony.

Fury pumping through him, Rand drew his sword, pressed the sharp tip beneath Golan's chin, and glared down at him. "How dare you assault my betrothed. I could slay you where you lay." After seeing Golan force himself on Rose, Rand could never let the marriage proceed. With that in mind, he knew of only one way to convince the king Rose was ineligible to marry Golan.

Golan scrambled to his feet, blood splatters on his tunic. Rand kept the steel blade steady and shoved Golan's chin higher.

"You, Sir Rand, are a liar. Lady Ayleston is my betrothed." Golan's eyes glared with a hatred that bordered on madness. "The king just confirmed it this day."

Rand curled his lip. "Then I pity you. The lady and I have a prior claim. With unimpeachable witnesses who will swear we were betrothed last spring."

"I do not believe you. Rose swore she intended to take a vow of chastity." Golan spun around and headed for the chapel exit. "The king shall hear of this!" he shouted.

Rand strode over to Rose, crouched against the stone column with her veil pulled over her face. "Oh, God, Rose. Are you all right? Did he hurt you?" He reached out to hold her.

Rose flinched and whimpered like a wounded animal. He swallowed a growl of frustration and clenched his bruised knuckles to keep from touching her.

Rand knelt on his right knee before her, bending his other knee up and resting his forearm on it. He had wanted to kill Sir Golan. And he would have were it not a sacrilege to commit homicide in the consecrated edifice.

Rand spoke in a soft, soothing voice. "Rose. It's all right. Sir Golan is gone. Prithee, remove the veil and show me your face so I know you are not unduly harmed."

Cautious not to frighten her, Rand reached out slowly, caught the tail end of the fabric, and eased it out of her hand and away from her face. Though she didn't resist, she drew her knees up against her chest and wrapped her arms around them tightly.

He searched her face. Skin usually soft and clear with good health was mottled and streaked with tears. And her eyes appeared dazed with a deep and unimaginable pain.

Feeling as though a fist squeezed his heart, Rand gasped. He inhaled deeply, trying to get a breath into his lungs.

"Speak to me, Rose. Did the bastard—? Did he touch you in a sordid manner?"

She shook her head violently. "Nay. He tried to convince me that I would enjoy his kisses, but I cannot. I pleaded for him to stop—" she stopped short, exhaling with a shudder.

"'Tis my fault." Rand frowned. "I heard rumors about Golan, but I did not believe them. I thought you would be better—" He stopped midsentence when he realized Rose was still ignorant about his part in this travesty.

She raised her gaze, clouded with confusion. The moon silvered her heart-shaped face with a luminescent glow. "What are you talking about, Rand? How could you be to blame? You could not know that Golan would force his attentions on me. Or that he would believe he had a right to do so."

"Rose, I pray you—"

She ignored him and continued, "You see, the king has given Sir Golan wardship of Jason's estates." Her voice dropped to a shuddery whisper. "And giving me no choice in the matter, Edward has demanded I marry the man in two days' time."

Rand dropped his gaze. Flexing his stiff knuckles, he stared at them, unable to look her in the face.

Though he was not looking directly at her, he saw her entire body stiffen in sudden suspicion. "Rand? Why do you not look surprised that King Edward ordered me to marry Sir Golan?"

When Rand hesitated, she dropped her arms from her knees and shoved up from the column awkwardly. He clutched her arm gently to help her rise and released her as soon as she was on her feet so that she did not feel threatened.

"Rand? Why will you not answer my question?"

"I am sorry, Rose. I could not disobey my king."

"Sorry for what? Unless you . . . Tell me the truth." Her voice grew louder, almost shrill. "Did you or did you not know Edward was going to force me to marry when you came to Ayleston and escorted me to court?"

Rand braced himself for her contempt. "Aye. The king told me of his plans."

The stiff mask of her face crumpled and she shrieked in despair. Surprising him completely, she launched herself at him. Her hands arched like the claws of a cat.

Rand, reflexes amazingly quick, caught her hands before she could gouge his face.

Rose tugged on his grip wildly, her body wiggling like a captured eel trying to get free from a trap. She wailed, "How could you? How could you do this to me? You knew I never wanted to marry again."

"Stop, Rose. Calm down. I could not tell you. Edward made me swear to keep the knowledge to myself."

"But you knew. You knew I was going to take a vow of chastity. Now it is too late. I'm trapped. How could you betray me like this?"

"Rose. Stop struggling. You're going to hurt yourself."

"Nay! Let me go!" she hollered.

Rand released her wrists. Not yet spent, she began hitting him in the arms and chest. Rand let her land a few blows he thought were well deserved and then wrapped his arms around her. He held her till her fury elapsed.

Rose slumped against him. Her tears wet his tunic and her heavy breathing penetrated the cloth, bathing his chest with warmth.

"Why, Rand?" she begged, her voice thready. "Why did you not warn me when you came to the castle?"

"I could not. The king swore me to secrecy. As his loyal and sworn man, honor bade I keep my word."

Rose pulled out of his arms with a violent tug. "What of your loyalty to me? We have been friends for a long time. And once were much more to each other. Have you forgotten so easily the night we made love? Where was your honor then? I deserve better treatment from you. I shall not forgive you for this betrayal."

"Are you speaking of that night we made love? Or that I could not tell you of King Edward's plan to marry you to Golan? Because you know that night was a mistake on both our parts. You made me swear never to speak of it."

Rose clutched her hand over her heart. "Aye, I do not want to be reminded of what a fool I was. Twice. I cannot believe I actually trusted you."

"Believe me, I wanted to warn you."

Her eyes widened with sudden terror and her body tensed as though she were a frightened doe about to bolt. "Oh, Lord, how shall I survive marriage to Sir Golan? He will be furious now. I fear what he will do to me."

"Do not be afraid. I'm not going to let him hurt you. I promise."

"How can you make such a promise?" Rose shuddered, blue eyes haunted. "The man will be my husband in two days' time. No one could protect me from Bertram, and no one can protect me now."

Rand clutched her head between his hands and forced her to gaze into his eyes. His eyes blazed with conviction. "Listen to me. I know I failed you before, but I am going to make it right. I swear to you, Sir Golan will never have the opportunity to hurt you again."

"Why should I believe your promises after you lied to me?"

"Because despite what you think, I care about you. I do not wish to see you forced to marry a man I now know is a danger to you."

"What are you saying, Rand? Edward insists I marry; there is naught you or anyone can do to sway the king when he has decided upon a course."

Rand took a deep breath. "I am going to see that your betrothal to Golan is discredited, and then to appease Edward, I shall marry you instead."

Rose's temples began to throb and her palms dampened as Rand laid out an elaborate scheme based on the rocky foundation of a preposterous lie. She shook her head, refusing to accept Rand's plan. It was madness. It would never work. She would absolutely not be a party to such absurd machinations.

Chapter Six

The following afternoon in the king's private reception room, Edward towered over Rose with a piercing stare. "Answer me honestly, Lady Ayleston. It is imperative that you tell me the truth of the matter."

She clutched her hands behind her back to keep them from trembling. Surely all in the chamber could hear the pa-bum pa-bum pa-bum of her wildly beating heart.

She shifted her gaze to her father. Philip de Beaumont, Baron Briand, gave her an encouraging smile. His blue eyes, darker than hers, were soft with love.

Avoiding direct eye contact with Golan, Rose noticed his face was now marred with a black-and-blue eye and swollen nose. Satisfaction stirred in her breast.

Finally, she regarded Rand.

His gray-green eyes held hers—willing her to answer in the affirmative. Rose took a deep breath and lied to the king of England. "Aye, my lord. Sir Rand and I vowed to marry when I was at court last spring."

At Golan's deep inhalation, Rose looked at him at last. A fierce light flared in his black eyes and pierced her with a promise of retaliation. She shuddered.

Upon seeing Golan's stare, Rand moved to Rose's side and fixed a frozen glare on Golan till he jerked away.

Lord Briand added, "When my daughter informed me of her and Rand's betrothal, I gave them my blessing. Though as a widow, Rose need not have my permission to marry."

When Rose's father arrived at court early that morn, Rand had apprised him of Rose's betrothal to Golan and the events that had transpired in the chapel. Lord Briand had been incensed, not only because Golan had attacked Rose, but also because Edward had given Sir Golan permission to marry Rose without consulting him. For those reasons, when Rand had laid out his plan to concoct a former, secret betrothal, Lord Briand had been quite willing to swear falsely that he knew of it.

"Sire, surely you don't believe this nonsense," Golan thundered, a purple vein bulging at his temple. "Last night Lady Ayleston claimed she intended to take a vow of chastity. Yet we are to believe she and Sir Rand had a prior betrothal agreement, which we are only hearing about now?"

Lord Briand, his voice soft yet lethal, inquired, "Are you calling me a liar, Sir Golan?" He frowned fiercely at the younger man.

Lord Briand stood tall and robust, his black hair silvered at the temples. Though not in his prime, he was still a powerful man. He had once been King Henry III's champion.

Rand watched Golan squirm. The barrel-chested knight held up his hands in acquiescence. "Nay, my lord. But I believe I have the stronger claim."

King Edward chose that moment to intervene. "Lord Briand, you have put me in a difficult position. I granted Sir Golan permission to marry your daughter, and when I give my word I don't rescind it. The prior betrothal between your daughter and Sir Rand was verbal, not a written contract."

Sir Golan looked smugly at Rand.

Edward continued, "Yet verbal agreements are as valid as

written ones in the eyes of the Church. And it would appear that Rand does have the prior claim."

Though the whole plot to fabricate a betrothal with Rose had received Edward's tacit approval when Rand spoke to him this morrow, the king was ever unpredictable. Rand would not put it past him to alter the secret agreement they made between one another, which included a sizable coin payment from Rand.

Rand flexed his fists with the urge to repeat last night's thrashing. "Sire, I demand to prove my rightful claim to Lady Ayleston in trial by battle." He smiled at Golan in anticipation. "Dare you accept my challenge, Golan?"

Golan pushed his chin out. "I accept your challenge, Rand, and when I defeat you, all shall know I am the rightful claimant of the lady."

Brushing his hand over his chin repeatedly, Edward's eyes narrowed with a thoughtful gaze. "Very well. Sir Golan, Sir Rand, this will be decided on the field of combat. A joust will be held in two days, the winner of it shall claim Lady Ayleston's hand in marriage and wardship of her son's estate."

A soft gasp escaped Rose. Rand wondered if it was out of concern for him, or if she realized there was no going back and she would have to actually marry one of them in the end. Rand grinned at Golan. He was going to make the other knight regret he'd ever laid a hand on Rose.

Nor did he doubt he would win. And when he did, he would deal with Rose then. He needed his complete attention fixed upon the upcoming battle. Afterward, he would be able to contemplate the ramifications of marriage to Rose.

Rand swore a solemn vow. *Golan will never claim Rose as long as I am alive.*

A twig snapped in the cover of the dark, impenetrable woods. Golan jerked this way and that. "Who goes there?"

The wind sighed, the rustle of leaves whispering a ghostly chant as moonlight cast eerie shadows through the tree branches. His heart pounded; his palms grew damp with sweat. At that moment, three large forms moved into the small clearing. One carried a mace, one a flail, and the other a war ax.

Hand on his sword, Golan swallowed down his trepidation. He had been informed that he was to parlay alone or there would be no negotiations. These men were ruthless and unpredictable outlaws. For a price they'd perform any nefarious service.

The leader, Golan assumed, and the largest of the outlaws, stepped forward while the other two stood guard behind him. The leader stood with his feet spread apart and his arms crossed over his chest.

Golan cleared his throat. "I came alone, as you requested."

The man laughed, a gravelly sound that sent a shiver down Golan's spine. The black cloth covering his face from the nose down puffed with the exertion. "My men ascertained you were alone."

Golan was startled by the aristocratic tone of the speaker.

"I am a cautious man," the outlaw said. "Betray me, and I will kill you."

The man with the mace grunted and ran his hand across his neck to indicate cutting a man's throat. Golan gulped, but his mouth was dry and his tongue stuck to the roof of it.

"I am not here to betray you. I wish to hire you to remove a rival."

Silence. Long, intimidating silence. Golan's chest rose and fell rapidly, his puffing breath loud to his ears.

The leader smiled with a baleful gleam in his eyes. "Do you have a plan to eliminate your rival?"

Golan nodded. "In two days there will be a joust at Westminster. I and another knight shall be the final combatants. I intend to be the victor, and to the victor go the spoils."

Revenge upon the lying, deceitful pair added sweetness to the plot, so much so that Golan could almost taste it. Rand had humiliated him. Golan let no one make a fool of him and live. His first wife, carrying a bastard in her belly, had discovered her mistake before Golan smothered her in childbed.

He smiled, his lips twisted in anticipation.

The next day in the palace garden, Rose sat on a turf bench leaning back on her hands. She threaded her fingers through crisp blades of grass, her face raised to the sky, and her ankles crossed before her. She sighed, basking in the warmth of the sun's rays.

Behind the bench, which lined the hedge wall, were raised herb beds planted with rosemary and thyme, their fragrant scents saturating the courtyard. She smiled, remembering the afternoon she and Jason had spent gathering herbs in the woods. His infectious giggle and mischievous grin could always cheer her when she was feeling troubled. She missed him so much her heart ached.

"Rose. Here you are. I've been looking for you."

She jerked and sat up, her gaze alighting on a tall woman who entered the small square courtyard surrounded by six-foot-high yew hedges. Gravel crunched beneath her bright-yellow-slippered feet. Wearing a yellow long-sleeved surcoate over an embroidered lavender tunic, Lady Katherine, her sister-in-law and best friend, smiled warmly and approached with her hands outstretched. Rose got up and greeted her.

"Kat. I'm so glad to see you." Clutching Kat's fingers in her hands, Rose kissed her cheek and then pulled back to look at her. "You look positively radiant."

Her golden skin and gray almond-shaped eyes were glowing, and yet a new serenity seemed to permeate her whole being. Rose reached out and touched her rounded belly with both hands. "How is my little niece doing?"

Kat's smile grew wider. "What makes you think the baby is a girl?"

"What else would it be with two headstrong people such as you and my brother insisting it will be a girl? I am certainly not going to gainsay either one of you."

Kat burst into laughter, an infectious, sparkling sound. Her long black hair, covered with a veil and circlet, rippled to her waist when she threw her head back. Rose laughed and pulled Kat down beside her on the turf bench.

"Tell me. How are you and Alex faring? Though I have received all your letters, now that you are back at Montclair I would hear it firsthand."

"Of course, I shall tell you everything. But I want to know how you are doing. Alex and I spoke to Rand when we arrived at court. I cannot believe Edward would arrange for you to marry Sir Golan without consulting your father. Now Rand and Golan are to joust to determine your rightful betrothed? This must be awful for you!"

Rose tried to keep a brave smile on her face, but it was impossible. Her emotions—revolving from fear to anger to disbelief to doubt—hammered away at her till her head ached with the relentless bombardment. It was why she had decided to come to the garden for a few moments of peace. Now, her brow creased and she rubbed her thumb over a wrinkle in her gray gown along the top of her thigh.

Kat covered Rose's hand to still the nervous gesture. "Oh, what am I saying? You don't need to worry that Sir Golan shall win. Rand is one of the fiercest and bravest knights in Christendom. He shall trounce the man and make him wish he'd never dared to aspire to marry you."

"Rand can rot for all I care!"

Kat's mouth dropped open and her eyes widened. "Rose! Surely you do not want Rand to lose to Sir Golan?"

"Aye, I do. I mean, nay, of course not. The truth is I don't want to marry anyone. You know how I feel about marriage.

What you don't know is that before I arrived at court, I was on the verge of taking a vow of chastity. Then Rand arrived at Ayleston to escort me to Westminster."

"Why are you angry at Rand? He was only doing his duty."

"Because he knew. The dastard knew I intended to take a vow of chastity." Rose withdrew her hand from Kat's and broke off a sprig of thyme from a nearby bush and jerkily plucked several small dark green leaves from the stem. "Yet still he escorted me to the king, all the while knowing Edward meant to betroth me to Sir Golan. And Rand said not a word to warn me."

"But can you not understand the difficult position he was in?" Kat clutched Rose's shoulder and squeezed. "It must have been very hard for Rand considering his divided loyalties."

The thyme slipped from her fingers to the ground unheeded. "Aye, but it does not change the fact that he lied to me. You of all people should understand how I feel. Alex abandoned you on your wedding night without a word to go on Edward's Crusade."

"Verily, I do not deny it. But I forgave Alex eventually. I know Rand cares for you and feels terrible he can't do more to protect you."

"Rand did protect me. When Sir Golan attacked me." She shivered, crossed her arms over her chest, and rubbed her upper arms. "If Rand had not intervened—" The thought was too terrible to contemplate.

"So 'tis true?" Kat's soft voice was riddled with sympathy. "Rand discovered you before the fiend could violate you?"

"Aye. Rand arrived with no time to spare." Remembering Golan's repugnant flesh pressed against her belly made nausea churn in her stomach. "Except for the humiliation I endured, I am unscathed."

Kat reached for her right thigh and caressed the hidden

dagger Rose saw outlined beneath her gown. "I would dearly love to geld the bastard for daring to touch you."

Having grown up training with her father's knights, Kat was skilled in the art of combat and always carried the dagger for protection. The habit had saved Kat's and Alex's lives when Lady Lydia, Alex's vengeful ex-lover, sought to murder them with the help of an accomplice.

"I just wish everyone would stop meddling in my affairs. I need no husband to manage Jason's estates. Under my stewardship, Ayleston has grown and prospered. Bertram had allowed it to become derelict from neglect. I repaired the walls and outbuildings, reclaimed land for crops, and expanded the cattle grazing lands. There is still much I wish to do, but now Edward has declared I must marry. Once married, I shall have no say in ordering my life or the estate. My husband shall have all the power," Rose said grimly.

"I understand why you did not wish to marry again after Bertram's cruelty. But surely you don't believe Rand is even remotely like your dead husband?"

"Of course not. But I shall be forced to—" Rose cut off her confession and lunged to her feet. "Oh, how can I explain my fears to you? You and Alex have an enviable marriage based on love and respect. You can never understand what I endured as Bertram's wife."

"Rose, I may not understand, but you know you can tell me anything and I would never think less of you. What is it you are afraid of?" Kat's gray eyes beseeched Rose.

She walked a few steps away. "You know Lady Lydia was Bertram's mistress, but there is much more I never told you." Her voice dropped to a whisper. "Bertram forced me to do vile, despicable acts to please him. I dare not speak them aloud. But now I cannot endure the intimate side of marriage. The shame and humiliation is too much to bear." Her voice cracked with pain.

Kat came up behind Rose and wrapped her arms around

her. "Oh, Rose. I am so sorry. You are right. I can never know what it was like for you. But I care about you, just as Rand does. You must tell him what you told me. He will understand. With time I am sure he can help you overcome your fears, and you and he can have a loving relationship."

"God forfend. I intend no such thing." A deep shudder shook Rose and then she pulled out of Kat's arms and spun around to face her. "If I am going to be forced to marry, I insist it shall be a marriage of convenience. Rand may continue with his *affaires de coeur* as long as he does not parade his mistresses before me. And I shall tell him so. If I can ever get him to stop avoiding me."

That evening, on the night before the tournament, Rose sat at the dais table between Rand and Sir Golan. Her thoughts moved counter to the festive atmosphere that filled the vast lesser dining hall. Whenever Sir Golan "accidentally" brushed against her hand, or arm, or thigh, it sickened her and she inadvertently moved closer to Rand.

Keeping her head and eyes down, she avoided conversation and remained silent. A crisp white linen cloth covered the table, which was laden with meat, fish, and vegetable dishes along with wine from Bordeaux, Burgundy, and the Rhine.

She reached for her wine and, at the same moment, Sir Golan picked up his napkin and slyly stroked her wrist. Rose recoiled. Burgundy sloshed over the rim of her chalice. A dark red splotch of wine spread on the tablecloth.

She stared at the stain, her eyes growing wide with horror. Memories of the night her husband died flashed in her head. Oh, God, the blood was everywhere. It matted Bertram's shining gold hair, while his vacant green eyes stared up at her coldly in accusation. Abruptly, Rose excused herself and climbed over the bench.

Rand turned from speaking with Edward just as Rose

spilt her wine. She bolted as though she were a sinner fleeing a phantom from Hell. When he rose to follow her, he noted Sir Golan's smug grin. Rand realized the knight had said or done something to disturb Rose. Before he left the table, he clutched the top of Sir Golan's shoulder and squeezed it very hard.

With a smile on his face, Rand bent down to Golan's ear and whispered, "Never, I repeat never, are you to say or do anything to hurt Rose again. Or I shall kill you. Do you understand?" When he didn't respond, Rand squeezed harder. "Nod if you understand me." Golan nodded. Rand released him. "Good. On the morrow, I am going to enjoy squashing you like the little bug you are."

Rand left the candle-filled dining hall for the darker, torchlit hallways. Directed by an observant palace guard, Rand followed Rose to an herb garden not far from the kitchens.

The stars were bright in the night sky, yet a light breeze brought with it the fresh scent of a recent rain shower. Rose sat on the edge of a raised planter bed, digging in the wet earth and removing weeds from the base of a marigold.

A look of sadness etched her face. She did not acknowledge him as he approached.

"Rose? What are you doing out here?"

She tugged sharply on a particularly stubborn root. "I enjoy digging my fingers into the earth, removing weeds and such. Nurturing plants and caring for them gives me great satisfaction."

"Will you tell me what Sir Golan did to upset you in the dining hall?"

"I'd prefer not to discuss the cur." She cocked her head, looking up at him. "Except . . . do I need to worry about the outcome of the joust? What are the chances he will defeat you on the morrow?" The weed gave at last. Rose yanked it from the earth, yet she pulled so hard that part of the marigold came with it. Consternation marred her brow as she stared at the plant in her hand.

Rand sat down across from her and eased the greenery from her white-knuckled grip. She did not resist. A look of surprise arched her elegant eyebrows as she stared down at her hands within his. Then Rand brushed the damp earth from her fingers and used the bottom of his surcoate to remove the rest of the sticky mud.

"I don't want you to worry about tomorrow, Rose. Sir Golan is a worthy foe, but your father taught me well."

She lurched up and stepped away from him. "Yet you cannot guarantee that you shall be the victor. What will happen to me if Sir Golan wins? I will not survive marriage to another brute like Bertram. I cannot do it. I simply cannot." Hands shaking, she covered her face.

At seeing her so cowered, Rand felt a lump lodge in his throat. He lunged to his feet, withdrew her hands from her face, and locked his gaze on hers so she would see the fierce determination in his eyes. "I swear to you, Rose, I shall be the victor. Yet if for some reason I fail to win, I shall make you this promise: I will personally make sure you never marry Sir Golan. I vow it."

"But—"

"Have I ever broken a vow to you, Rose?"

"Nay," she answered, her lips barely moving.

Rand's gaze riveted on the velvety flesh of her full lips, which were the color of strawberries misted with dew. He loved the taste of strawberries. His gut wrenched. His mouth tingled with the overwhelming desire to kiss her. But he did not want to frighten her. He needed to gain her trust so she would not fear him when it came time for them to marry.

He shook his head to recall what he had been trying to say. She was a distraction to his good intentions. "I have never broken a vow before, nor do I intend to start now. So I ask you, do you believe me when I say I shall never let Sir Golan have you?"

Chapter Seven

Rose stared into Rand's eyes. At his intense regard, a shiver raced down her arm. It was not desire or pleasure she experienced. She was numb to such things. It was as though a reckoning was upon her that she could not control, and it frightened her. Unable to withstand his penetrating stare, she finally dropped her eyes.

Rand touched her pointed chin lightly, guided her gaze back to his, and repeated, "Do you believe me when I say I shall never let Sir Golan have you?"

She nodded. "Aye. I do believe you." Shock rippled through her. She had not lied. She truly believed Rand would do as he said, in this instance at least. He would see to it that she never married Sir Golan. But that brought back to mind the weighty issue of what marriage to Rand would mean. She was terrified of the marriage bed. Where once Rand's touch had thrilled her, Rose was cold to feelings of pleasure and felt only shame and humiliation at the act.

"I believe you, Rand." Rose took several steps over to the next raised planter bed and plucked a sprig of rosemary from one of the plants. She pinched it, sniffing the sweet fragrance. With her back to Rand, she inquired, "But you still intend to marry me, do you not?"

"Aye, Rose. War with Wales is imminent. Edward wants one of his household knights in charge of Ayleston and its resources. He sees wardship of Jason's estate and marriage to you as an opportunity to reward one of us, while also protecting the vulnerable borders from Welsh raids."

"I have been managing Jason's estate since his father's death. I don't see why I need some man in charge. I can protect Ayleston as well as any man with the help of the castle guard."

"You have been an able administrator for Ayleston, Rose—"

She spun around. "Aha. So you agree."

"You did not let me finish. Since Bertram's death there has been relative peace between England and Wales. But I have been worried for your safety for some time now. As a wealthy widow, you are prey to abduction by any ambitious knight who wishes to enrich himself. You would be raped and forced to marry to recover your reputation." He raised his hand when she opened her mouth to protest. "'Tis not fair to blame the woman and vilify her character, I know, but, unfortunately, that is how society and the Church perceive such cases of forced abduction. So far you have been lucky to avoid such a fate. Then, too, when war is declared, it shall become even more dangerous."

"I must disagree—"

"You may disagree as much as you like, but it shall not change the king's decision. Or mine either, for that matter. Come, the hour grows late. I'll escort you to your chamber. We can discuss these and other issues after we wed."

Realizing the futility of the argument, Rose acquiesced, but not happily. "Very well. But there's one thing I wish to settle before we marry, and it cannot be delayed a moment longer." Rose flicked her knuckles over her collarbone.

"What is so important it cannot wait till the morrow?"

Rose took a deep inhalation and expelled her words in a

rush. "I will marry you on one condition. That ours be a marriage of convenience."

"Very well, I shall agree to your condition."

She saw not even a flicker of surprise or disappointment. Her brows dipped down sharply at his easy capitulation. Rand was the most lustful male creature she knew. So why would he agree without hesitation to forego the marital duty a wife and husband owed one another? It made no sense. Unless he did not understand what she was insisting upon.

"You do understand that if I am to give my wholehearted consent when we wed, I insist that we never consummate our vows?"

"Of course. I understand very well. I have no objection to abstaining from carnal intimacy."

"By agreeing to my condition, you shall never have an heir of my body. Never have a legitimate male heir to carry on your name. And yet you are still prepared to marry me? Why?"

"I am now one score and nine years of age and have never been married. Have you never wondered why this is so?"

Rose could not admit to Rand that she had indeed wondered why he had never married. But she decided he enjoyed his blithe womanizing existence too much to give up his freedom.

"Why have you never married?"

Rand shrugged. "I vowed long ago never to marry. The reason no longer matters. If Edward had not betrothed you to Sir Golan, I would not have offered to marry you."

"But you escorted me to court knowing Edward intended me for Sir Golan. You could have offered for me then instead of creating a fake prior betrothal. You admitted you were aware of Sir Golan's reputation before he attacked me. So what changed your mind?"

"I have several reasons. 'Tis complicated."

She rubbed her upper arms. "Go on. I would hear them."

Rand smiled grimly. "When I came to Ayleston to escort you to court, I admit I heard a rumor that Golan had murdered his wife. But his wife died in childbirth. Too, I knew Golan personally and his reputation was beyond repute, so I did not believe the rumors. Then when I learned how much you abhorred marriage, I considered offering for you in Golan's stead. But I thought you would dislike marriage to me as much as to any other man.

"But what convinced me was that night in the chapel." His eyes glittered. "When I saw him forcing himself on you despite your protests, I wanted to rip out his throat. I realized then I could never let him touch you like that again. Marrying you, despite my vow never to do so, is a small price to pay for the debt of gratitude I owe you and your family. Your parents have treated me like a son since I came to England long ago."

An odd emotion punctured Rose's heart and her breath caught. She was sure Rand did not mean to insult her, but disappointment flooded her. She had no reason to be disappointed. She did not wish to marry him, either.

"This is your last chance," she said. "Are you sure you don't wish to give more thought to your decision?"

Rand crossed his arms and leaned back on his heels. "I have given it plenty of thought, actually. I need no more time to realize you cannot abide my touch. I'd never force you or any woman to my bed. Our marriage would simply be a mutual exchange of benefits to us both. You shall receive my protection from Edward's machinations and Sir Golan's unwanted advances. And believe it or not, as my wife, I shall receive your protection from fathers who wish to betroth their daughters to me for my connection to the king."

She did not despise his touch. She was just dispassionate in general. Passion was reserved for whores; her husband had taught her that lesson well.

Sudden heat flushed her cheeks and she dropped her eyes as her heart thudded with embarrassment. "Of course, I shall not begrudge you satisfying your desires with other women. I realize you must assuage your lustful appetites. I promise I shall not object or act like a termagant whenever you take other women to your bed."

Rand stepped closer, his breath moist in the air between them. "That is very commendable of you, Rose. But how can I trust that you shall not change your mind once we are married? *Now* you say you do not mind me bedding other women." Rand's voice dropped to a dark, seductive whisper. "But what if you change your mind?" He ran a finger down her cheek, a soft caress that neither repulsed nor seduced. Shock held her immobile.

"Can you swear to never become a jealous shrew? That you won't come to resent me or the other women I shall surely bed?" A dangerous current thrummed beneath his voice, which sounded suspiciously like anger.

Rose frowned. She was positive Rand was mocking her. She searched his face, framed by long golden hair. His smile was wolfish, deepening his dimples, and gray-green eyes appeared almost feral in the moon's glow. But it must have been a trick of the moonlight, for a teasing light sparked in his eyes.

She shook her head. "You need not fear I shall change my mind. All I ask is for you to be discreet. That you not humiliate me by flaunting your mistresses or fornicating while you are in residence at Castle Ayleston. I will not have you bedding my own servants and undermining my authority as chatelaine."

Rand kept his smile pasted on his face, unsure why he was so angry. Her crystal blue eyes made his stomach flip. Eyes wide and almond shaped, the corner of her outer lashes curling up together. Her sharp white teeth chewed on her plump bottom lip.

"So you don't mind if I have mistresses. You just do not want to be confronted by them. Fair enough. I believe I can agree to that." Rand forced the words past his lips. As comprehension dawned on him, he inhaled sharply.

He could have any woman he wanted, yet the one woman he desired—with a desperation that cut like a blade to his heart—did not want him. Rand rubbed his chest where it hurt. He nearly laughed at the irony. Married to the one woman he could never possess.

The justice of it was brilliant. When his mother died in the fire, Rand swore to atone for her and his sister's deaths for the rest of his life. God was now reaping the ultimate penance Rand owed Him.

Ayleston Castle, Chester County
In the year of our Lord 1272, September 12
Fifty-fifth year in the reign of King Henry III

In the bridal chamber, Rose stood naked before Bertram and about fifty guests who crowded into the chamber to get a glimpse of the happy couple. Her modesty was barely preserved by her waist-length red-gold hair, which she draped in front of her shoulders to conceal her small breasts. She covered her hair-covered groin with her hands as a chill gust of wind whistled through the shuttered windows. Goose pimples rose on her skin all over her body. She shuddered.

The bedding ceremony was a humiliation every virgin had to endure to prove to the groom he was getting an unmarred bride. Bertram, not looking at her exposed body, grabbed her chamber robe from one of the female guests, Lady Lydia, Rose realized. Lydia and Bertram exchanged a brief look, which Rose could not interpret, and then Bertram wrapped the robe around Rose's shoulders. She smiled shyly at her new husband, grateful for his considerate gesture.

Since the day they had met at court last Christmas, his gallantry and charm had entranced her. He was ever spoiling her with his caring and generous heart.

Bertram quickly escorted the guests out of their bedchamber

*and poured her some wine to ease her fears. But her curiosity
and excitement was greater than any virginal fears.*

*The spiced wine went down her throat in one smooth gulp.
Then Bertram took her chalice from her hand and set both
their cups on the bedside table. Without preamble he pulled
her into his embrace and captured her lips with his mouth.
His tongue delved deep and hot, probing her with lashing
strokes. Rose whimpered, her lower body gyrating against the
hard bulge of his desire. She grew damp, her nether lips tingling with swollen heat.*

*Bertram pulled back and said, his voice hoarse, "Take off
your robe and lie down on the bed."*

*In a blaze of desire, Rose did as he bid. She removed the
robe and smiled when he turned away, no doubt wanting to
preserve her modesty. She climbed into bed and pulled the
covers up. An odd smile on his face, Bertram stared at the wall
across from the bed, where a tapestry of a stag hunt hung.*

"I'm ready, Bertram."

*He came over to the side of the bed and stared down at her.
"And now I am ready too," he said, his raspy voice a caress.*

"What do you mean?"

*He smiled slyly. "You shall find out soon enough." When he
dropped his robe, she caught a quick glance of his erect shaft;
then he slid into bed and on top of her.*

*He kissed her again, his mouth and tongue ravaging her.
Her desire became a tempest, his heat and hardness driving
her hips to rise up to seek a connection. His shaft probed between her legs and slowly eased inside her.*

"You're wet," he spat out, disgust tinging his voice.

*"What?" Rose squirmed, prickly sensations making her
feel like she was going to explode if he did not shove inside
her and complete the union of their bodies.*

*His emerald green eyes, usually creased with laughter,
burned with condemnation. "You are wet between your legs."*

Rose's face flushed. "I'm sorry, did I do something wrong?"

"Only whores get wet. My wife is not supposed to enjoy what is meant for procreation purposes alone."

Rose moved, trying to escape her humiliating predicament. But she was pinned beneath him.

Bertram groaned. "It's too late. Just lie still and keep your mouth shut." Then he pumped inside her, grunting and groaning until his body shuddered and he collapsed on top of her.

Hot tears of misery leaked from Rose's eyes as she lay trapped beneath him. Her face burned with shame, yet her whole body felt as though it had been dunked in a cold stream.

She was reeling with confusion at Bertram's sudden shift in mood. It was not like him at all, and she wondered if she were unnatural. Somehow she had ruined everything, and she didn't understand how. She had enjoyed his initial intimacies, but when her body had excreted wetness, he had become repulsed.

"That was an amazing performance, my love." A seductive feminine laugh echoed in the chamber.

Rose jerked and scrambled to cover her breasts with a sheet when Bertram left the bed to greet the woman who entered the bedchamber.

"Oh my God, Bertram. What is she doing in our chamber?"

Bertram just laughed, grabbed Lady Lydia to him, and proceeded to kiss her thoroughly. Without shame, Lydia kissed him back and reached her hand down to stroke Bertram's shaft.

Rose shot up in bed, her heart pumping rapidly. A shrill scream in the back of her throat was cut off. As her chest rose and fell, her panting breath sounded loud in the darkened chamber. She looked around, realizing she was not in her bedchamber at Ayleston Castle. In bed beside her, Alison slept soundly, her soft snores penetrating the quiet.

A sigh escaped Rose, her eyes damp with unshed tears. It was just another dream. Beads of sweat coated her face and chest, making her shiver. Rose crept slowly from the bed so as not to wake Alison and moved to the washstand, where she splashed cold water on herself to rinse off the perspiration. With a clean linen towel she dried off, rubbing her face briskly to try to erase the lingering remnants of her dream.

That night of her wedding was just the beginning of one humiliation after another she'd endured at the hands of her husband. Later, she learned she was so physically repugnant to him that he could bed her only with the titillation of having his mistress or cousin observe them. Behind the tapestry was a squint in the wall for the lord of the castle to peer into the chapel to observe Mass in privacy. But Bertram had corrupted it for his perverse lecherous proclivities.

With time the memories had faded, but with her upcoming marriage her nightmares were becoming more vivid. Rand had sworn to her he would not expect her to share a bed with him as man and wife, but what real guarantee did she have? Once they were married, as her husband he could demand anything of her and she would have no recourse to deny him.

But first he must defeat Sir Golan in the lists. Rose shuddered at the thought of what would happen should Sir Golan win the joust competition. She returned to the bed, got down on her knees, folded her hands before her, and began to pray fervently that Rand would prevail this day.

Rose, Kat, and Lady Alison strolled among the makeshift booths set up south of the Abbey Almonry. Next to the practice field where the lists were situated, wooden stands had been hastily erected over the last two days. Rose was distracted, unable to enjoy various festive entertainments and merchant offerings. The joust between Rand and Sir Golan would be the last of the day and would be celebrated later that evening with a grand feast.

In front of a booth protected from the elements by a black-and gold-striped tent, Kat and Alison were looking at some brightly hued scarves spread out on a board. Kat chose a sheer yellow silk scarf with blue embroidered roses on it. As Kat paid the mercer for her scarf, Rose gazed north past the lists where twenty-some-odd competitors' pavilions were erected. Banners and pennons flew from the top of the various round- and rectangular-shaped tents. She spotted Rand's banner, a golden lion rampant on an azure background, waving in the brisk breeze.

When Rose turned back, she caught Kat staring at her with a speculative look in her eyes. But Kat did not say a word. She smiled, wrapped the scarf around Rose's neck, and tied it loosely over the dark blue cloak she wore.

"Kat, 'tis a lovely scarf, but I cannot accept your gift." She touched the delicately woven silk.

"Of course you can. Every lady has to have a favor to grant the knight of her choice so he may proudly display it during battle."

"I had not intended giving anyone my favor."

"I know. Why do you think I gave it to you? When Rand requests a token, surely you do not wish to embarrass him by denying him?"

Alison sighed and clapped her hands before her chest in girlish infatuation. "Aye, my lady. Sir Rand is so handsome and gallant and brave. You cannot deny him your favor."

Rose rolled her eyes and answered Kat. "What makes you think Rand will even ask me for one? He is marrying me only because of the loyalty he feels toward my family."

"Because I know my cousin very well. He shall ask for your favor, and you must be prepared to accept." Kat cocked her head and stared at Rose. A teasing light flared in her silver-gray gaze. "And to prove that I am right, how about we make things interesting by wagering on it?"

A bloom of caution unfurled in Rose's chest. "A wager? What kind?" When Kat's eyes glowed with mischief, as now, Rose knew to be wary—very wary.

"I am willing to wager that if Rand does not request your favor, I shall kiss a mule's arse before a crowd of spectators. But if Rand does, then you must—"

"Aye? If you are correct, I must what?"

"Then you shall have to kiss Rand before the crowd when you bestow him the scarf as a token."

Rand sat on a bark-denuded portable tree stump outside his round pavilion sharpening his dagger on a whetstone. His nostrils flared at the scent of wood smoke emanating from a number of lit fires in the makeshift encampment. The unusually hot weather had broken and been replaced with a cool, crisp autumnal day.

The whetstone in his left hand, Rand scraped the blade at an angle over the coarse, dusky yellow sandstone. He did it twice, then turned the dagger over and repeated the process on the other edge of the blade. By rote, he sharpened the blade, as his thoughts returned to Rose and the upcoming joust.

Sitting beside him, Will, his squire, polished Rand's gauntlets with a pumice powder and wet cloth. When the youth had both gloves done, he buffed them thoroughly with a dry cloth. A dark-haired knight shouted a greeting as he passed the tent. Rand had accompanied him on a couple of missions for the king.

On the ground nearby lay three sturdy lances, having been thoroughly checked by his squire for strength and durability. It would not do for a defect or weakness in the wood of the lance to be discovered. Should a lance break too easily upon impact with his opponent's shield, it could spell injury or even death for Rand. Rand would not—nay, could not—allow Rose to be left to the not so tender mercies of Sir Golan. Her very life, Rand was sure, depended on him defeating the vengeful knight.

Sir Justin approached the tent, leading Leviathan by the reins. "'Tis one more joust before your match, Rand."

Rand stood up, tucked his dagger in the sheath at his waist, and took the gauntlets Will handed him. He moved to Sir Justin, who passed him the reins.

Shifting his gloves to the hand that held his mount's reins, Rand patted Leviathan's neck with his right hand and spoke softly. "Well, my friend, I have placed my faith in you numerous times in the past, and I know you shan't fail me now."

Leviathan dipped his head and shoved his nose against Rand's chest, snorting a snuffling sound of puffed air from his muzzle. "Good boy." Rand stroked his horse's neck beneath its black mane. "Let us go show Sir Golan what happens when he crosses me, so he never forgets whom he is dealing with."

Chapter Eight

In the raised wooden stands overlooking the lists, Rose, with Kat and Lady Alison by her side, sat to the left of Queen Eleanor. Lord and Lady Briand sat next to the king. A great purple silk canopy with golden fringe shaded the party.

Kat leaned over and whispered, "Rose, the next joust shall be Rand and Sir Golan. Don't forget our wager. If Rand requests your favor for the joust you must kiss him for all to see. 'Tis too late to turn back now."

Rose plucked her skirt, cursing herself for letting Kat goad her into that ridiculous wager. She did not like bringing attention to herself. The mood of the crowd grew more volatile as the main event approached.

Rose returned her attention to the joust in progress.

Alex and Rose's cousin, William de Beauchamp, Earl of Warwick, and Henry de Lacy, Earl of Lincoln, couched their lances as they charged forward. Their destriers' hooves pounded loudly, churning up dirt. With a sudden spurt of speed at the last moment, the two mounted warriors met with a resounding clash. Lord Warwick's lance blow was a direct hit to the younger lord's shield. Lord Lincoln jolted backward, then slowly slid to the side of his mount before falling to the ground.

The crowd in the stands roared with excitement. The tournament herald announced Lord Warwick the winner of the joust. But the main draw of the competition anxiously anticipated by everyone came next. Rose tried to relax her tense shoulders, her eyes fixed on the entrance to the lists. Rand entered first, followed by Golan. A second roar rose from the crowd.

Rand wore over his hauberk a surcoate emblazoned with his coat of arms. Leviathan was caparisoned in the same bold colors. Golan also wore his coat of arms: black and white chevron, or checked pattern, quartered by a white cross.

Rand reined in Leviathan, and Golan proceeded to the far side of the field.

The herald read a list of great feats and the rank of first Rand and then his opponent. All the accolades were announced and pageantry was performed according to the joust rules. The crowd grew suddenly silent as Rand approached Rose in the stands.

Sidling up to the railing, he bowed at his waist before her. "Lady Ayleston, will you do me the great honor of bestowing upon me a token of your esteem so I might do battle in your honor this day?"

Rose felt her face brighten in consternation and embarrassment. Her pulse beat at the base of her throat.

She had little choice but to honor his gallant request, not only because of the wager, but because she refused to dishonor him before the crowd. Sir Golan watched the spectacle with a fierce glare. She perceived the evil menace in his stance, and even in this crowd, it threatened to suffocate her.

She gulped, drawing deep breaths into her chest. Rand shifted in his saddle at her silence. Gray-green eyes dimmed, and his broad smile slipped infinitesimally. She got up from her cushioned seat and stepped down to where Rand waited on his destrier.

After removing the scarf from her neck, Rose leaned over

the railing and knotted the silk material around his upper arm. She looked back at Kat nervously. Her friend gave her an encouraging smile.

Rose leaned closer to Rand; his eyes widened.

A shiver raced down her spine as his intense regard held hers with a heat that scorched them both. She pressed her lips to his smooth cheek. The sensation of warmth penetrated her lips and his pleasant scent filled her nose. Gasping, she jerked back in shock.

A jolt of heat speared Rand. He touched his cheek briefly where Rose's soft lips had ventured. She appeared surprised. But surprise could barely begin to describe what Rand felt at that moment. Wonder and amazement beat in his breast. He tried to tame it, without success.

Rand bowed again. "Thank you, my lady. I shall wear your token with pride and honor." Then he turned Leviathan around and returned to where his squire awaited him.

"Your shield and helm, my lord."

Rand pulled on his metal helm first, tied the laces to his hauberk, and then slipped his left arm through the braces of his leather-covered wooden shield. The first horn blew, calling the participants to take their initial positions. The spectators cheered. Rand maneuvered Leviathan into position, reached down and took his lance from Will. He tested the weight and balance, and, deeming it perfect, tucked it under his arm.

Silence reigned over the crowd, the only noise the jangle of horse tack as their restive destriers shifted in anticipation. Rand stared at Sir Golan in fierce concentration.

He could not let Rose down. She was counting on him to rescue her from a life of servitude and humiliation as Golan's wife.

The horn blared, and Rand spurred his mount. Leviathan shot out, and Rand lowered his lance and couched it next to his chest. Hooves pounded. The crowd roared. Golan came closer and closer, racing toward Rand on the left. The blunted tip of Rand's lance smashed into Golan's shield, and at the same moment Rand absorbed Golan's lance blow. Rand jerked back, pain vibrating through his shield arm at contact. He turned around and made his way back to his station.

In that first round, neither gained an advantage, each scoring a point. Two more rounds remained. Before the next one could commence, though, a commotion broke out behind Rand. He spun around on Leviathan and stared in horror as flames curled up the wall of a large pavilion, a billow of smoke rising above it.

Inside the tent, a horse screeched with fear. A squire, heedless of his safety, ran into the burning pavilion. Rand jerked his reins. Leviathan sidestepped nervously, kicking up his forelegs. The spectators in the stands scrambled from their seats. Several charged toward the fire while others sought to flee from the threat. But Rand was oblivious. His heart seized in fright as he was plunged back to the day of the stable fire, when he'd rushed into the building and tried to save his horse.

Flames all around him, Rand charged toward Caesar's stall near the back. He swung his hand before his face, dispersing the smoke impeding his vision. His eyes stung, but he did not turn back. Then, suddenly, he tripped over a large bulk on the floor. Lunging headfirst, he landed with his hands outstretched, scraping his knees. He looked back, and upon seeing the giant stable master's eyes open wide in death, he yelped. His heart thundered in his chest.

Puny little brat, you are a disappointment to the Montague lineage, his father's voice echoed accusingly in his ears. "Nay!" he shouted in denial. Determination to prove to his father he was not weak and ineffectual imbued him with steely resolve.

Groaning in pain, he lurched to his feet and continued. As

he approached Caesar's stall, he noticed the fire enveloped the entire back of the building and crawled across the ceiling beams. The left divider wall of the stall and one wooden column were ablaze. Caesar reared up slamming against the other wooden divider in an attempt to avoid the blaze. His large dark brown eyes rolled back in fright.

Overhead, timbers groaned heavily. The intense heat and thick black smoke seized Rand's lungs. He choked, falling to his knees. He coughed uncontrollably. Time was running out; he needed to retrieve Caesar and get out of there quickly, before the ceiling collapsed. With his last ounce of strength, he pulled himself up by the stall door and flung it open.

Rand entered the neighboring stall and slapped Caesar on the hindquarters. The panicked palfrey shot out of the stall and toward the stable exit.

"Rand?! Where are you?! Can you hear me?! Rand?!" A shrill feminine voice called out.

Rand heard his mother's shout a moment before she appeared through the smoke.

"Mother, get out of here! The ceiling is about to collapse!"

Holding a handkerchief over her nose, she held out her hand. "I am not leaving without you, son! I refuse to lose another child!"

Stricken with guilt, for she did not know the truth of his cowardice when he'd let his sister drown, Rand grabbed her hand and they turned as one.

There was a sudden booming clap. Rand looked up. A beam above them plummeted straight down. He shoved his mother toward the entrance a moment before a heavy, crushing pain seared his back. As he was pinned beneath the burning beam, bright white pain struck him and his world went black.

He woke, choking. The section of the beam lying on his back was no longer aflame. Wheezing, his mother dipped a bucket into a nearby barrel of water. She hurried back and tossed the contents on the fiery beam, extinguishing it. Then she bent down and tugged on the heavy timber. He blinked, his wet hair straggling in his eyes.

His mother's ethereal, frightened countenance blurred before him.

"Mother, I pray you, go, save yourself," he begged, his voice weak and thready. "The beam is too heavy. You cannot lift it. 'Tis hopeless."

Staring down at the beam, a sharp V etched between her blond eyebrows, his mother concentrated on lifting and tugging the beam off him. At his words, her head suddenly shot up. She stared into his eyes, her soft hazel gaze darkening with conviction. "Naught is ever hopeless, my darling boy. Do not *ever* believe otherwise. Do you promise me?"

Knowing better than to disagree with his mother, Rand croaked out, "I promise, Mama." He bravely gulped down tears in the back of his throat.

She nodded her approval and gripped the beam again. Grunting and straining, her breath harsh, she gave a mighty heave. A long, torturous groan expelled from her throat. The beam shifted. But she lost her grip and stumbled backward.

Another thunderous crack rumbled above them. Several more beams came crashing down. He yelled hoarsely, "Mother, run!" and then a paroxysm of coughs overtook him.

The beams missed her, but her body jerked up short. She twisted around. A heavy beam trapped her long, trailing velvet skirt, flames catching it ablaze.

She screeched, batting at the flames with her hands.

"Mother, jerk your skirts free and douse yourself in the water barrel."

But the fire jumped and spread to her lower back. The long end of her braid caught aflame.

His heart beat in his throat and his eyes grew wide in terror as her screams rent the air. Rand struggled beneath the beam, desperate to escape and help his mother, but it was useless.

As she frenziedly twisted and turned, the fabric finally

tugged free. In panic, though, she ran instead of dousing the fire. Her whole skirt was ablaze, and soon the flames engulfed her head. Rand wailed, watching as she crumpled to the ground and writhed in agony as the fire consumed her.

"Naaay, Mother!" His cry ended on a hoarse croak.

Blessedly, a great agonizing pain seized his back and blackness descended on him.

"Rand, are you coming to put out the fire?"

Rand started, and stared at Justin. The knight gazed at him oddly.

Disoriented, Rand glanced around. Only moments had passed. The crowd was running in all directions in panic, and cries of fright filled the air. Having dismounted Leviathan without realizing it, Rand clutched the destrier's reins in his white-knuckled grip and sweat beaded his brow. His shield, gauntlets, and helm were on the ground beside him.

Where is Rose? He searched for her in the crowd. The king was calmly assisting the queen and the rest of the royal party from the stands. Rose was not among them.

His heart fluttered in panic. Rand swung his head this way and that, searching the chaos. People ran with buckets of water from the Abbey Almonry to put out the fire. Merchants were loading their wares in carts in case the fire spread. At a booth not far from the stands, a group of women were collecting linen for bandages, one of whom wore a wimple and veil headdress.

Rose stared at him, but he was unable to read her expression. Rand shuddered in relief.

"My lord?" Justin queried.

His gaze jerked back to his friend. "Aye, Justin, I shall be right behind you," he said gruffly, embarrassed. He prayed his friend did not guess at the secret depths of his fear of fire.

Justin hesitated, then nodded and headed for the tents.

Rand threw back his shoulders and followed Justin. By the time he reached the burning tent, a fire line had formed. He joined in next to Justin about a third of the way down the line.

He gritted his teeth as bursts of flame shot into the air. Ignoring the heat blasting his face, Rand passed the buckets down the row. Sweat trailed down his temple and his heart pounded.

While the fire distracted everyone and the crowd dispersed, a dark-clothed man waited till the lists were deserted. He quickly switched Sir Rand's lance with one made of a piece of defective ash. The exchange happened in moments, with none the wiser. The outlaw Golan had hired returned to the tents and joined the men in the fire line.

When the fire was extinguished, Rand handed the bucket to a liveried page as King Edward approached Rand. A fierce frown marred the king's face. Could the king have seen him freeze with fear in the lists when he'd first spied the fire? Rand braced himself, expecting the king's reproach for his cowardice.

"Well done, Rand. The fire could have caused great harm if it had spread. 'Tis a miracle no one was hurt."

Rand breathed an inward sigh of relief and wiped his moist brow with the sleeve of his surcoate. "Aye, Sire. We are blessed indeed. I wonder what could have started it, though?" His gaze shifted to Sir Golan, standing not far away. The man's hard, menacing glare did not shift or waver.

Hands on hips, Edward nodded to a nearby fire, which was now sputtering from the recent dousing. "Probably a spark from that fire. It is somewhat gusty today."

"Aye. No doubt you're right."

Edward turned and addressed Sir Golan. "Come, Sir Golan. Now that the fire is put out, the joust shall proceed."

Rand looked over and saw Rose examining the back of a young man's hand for burns. She glanced up at Rand, her gaze worried. Rand lifted his hand to half-staff to assure Rose he was unharmed. She looked away swiftly. He dropped his hand, feeling like a fool. Of course, her concern was not directed toward him specifically. She was a healer and never liked to see either man or beast injured or hurt. To believe she had special feelings for him was to head down a path that could only end up hurting them both.

His unconscionable actions today proved his unworthiness. The memories of the cruel deaths of his loved ones would haunt him forever—and remind him of the dangers of loving anyone.

Rand grabbed his destrier's reins and vaulted into the saddle.

Across the lists, Golan raised his great helm in mock salute, his lips twisted with contempt. Rand ignored him and put on his gauntlets, helmet, and shield. Will handed a lance up to him. Rand tested it, frowning. The balance of the lance felt distorted. But it was too late to check it; the first horn blew, signaling them at the ready.

A second blast of the horn sounded and Rand spurred Leviathan forward. The thunder of the crowd echoed in his ears, his gaze intent on Golan. The tip of Rand's lance slammed against Golan's shield and shattered as easily as a brittle stick. The force of Golan's lance jarred Rand's shoulder, excruciating pain shot through him, and he flew backward off his horse. Rand landed on his back, the breath pushed from him. White spots danced before his eyes. His vision blurred.

Rose screamed. Rand had landed with a sickening thump on the packed earthen floor, his head bouncing with the impact. Hands over her mouth, she watched in horror as Sir Golan dropped his broken lance, dismounted from his destrier, and drew his sword, all while Rand lay unmoving in the middle of the lists. Leviathan nudged his fallen master, and

Kat slipped her arm around Rose's shoulder. They huddled together, shaken and in shock as Sir Golan approached him. "Rand!" Rose shrieked.

Suddenly, Rand groaned, then rolled away before Golan could press the sword to his throat. He staggered to his feet, bringing up his shield to block Golan's downward strike. Quickly recovering, Rand went on the offensive and landed several strong blows to Golan's shield. Their grunts echoed in the palpable silence pervading the field. Rand slashed at Golan's unprotected legs. The knight jumped back.

Engaging once more, they fought back and forth across the lists until Rand caught the larger knight off guard. He rammed his shield into the knight, swung his right leg behind the man's legs, and shoved the larger, unwieldy knight over, tripping him so he fell backward.

Chest heaving, Rand thrust his sword at Golan's exposed neck. "Cry craven," he bit out.

When Golan did not answer, Rand pressed the sharp point to his throat. "Yield, I say."

"Craven," Golan's voice came thick with fear from behind the perforated steel helm.

Rose released a deep breath she'd not known she was holding. It felt as though a great energy was sucked from her body, draining all her pent-up fear for Rand since she'd learned of the trial by battle.

Rand untied his helm and removed it. "Did you hear him, my lord?"

"Aye, Sir Rand." Edward rose from his seat and proclaimed, "Sir Golan, with your defeat, God has judged your claim to the betrothal of Lady Ayleston invalid."

Rand is the victor. Rand is the victor. The voice inside Rose's head repeated the refrain over and over as relief flooded her senses. Golan could never hurt her again. She was safe at last.

Rand sheathed his sword and backed away from Sir Golan.

The knight rolled to his feet, removing his helmet and revealing his disgruntled, red-hued mien.

"On the morrow, Lady Ayleston and Sir Rand Montague shall be joined together in Holy Matrimony." Edward's tone had turned jovial. "Come, all"—he raised his arms up to encompass the crowd—"to the hall, where we shall feast and dance to celebrate the conclusion of the joust, a most worthy and chivalrous affair."

Rose's thoughts inevitably switched to marriage with Rand.

Would Rand keep his word and not demand his marital rights? Could she truly put her trust in someone who kept so much of himself hidden behind a lethal charm that easily persuaded women to his bed with but a smile and a kind word?

She knew firsthand of his persuasive abilities. Had not his intriguing dimples and sensual lips once proved irresistible to her? Did he not exude a wicked charm that had coaxed her to sinful fornication?

But she was immune to such carnal temptations now. Her humiliating experiences with Bertram became so unbearable she learned to remove herself from all feeling when he bedded her. Eventually she became cold to sensual stimulation. But that happened after she spent one amazingly passionate night with Rand.

Now, she knew better than to let base passions rule her ordered existence. Surely she and Rand could find a way to coexist as man and wife so they could both be satisfied. 'Twas how most dynastic marriages were conducted.

Rand, still wearing the mail coif over his head, shifted his gaze to her. A slight, though enigmatic, smile curved his lips. Then, with a wink, he flicked the scarf tied around his arm and dipped his head in her direction.

Blushing, Rose looked away, to see Kat studying her. Her gaze warm, Kat squeezed Rose's hand in encouragement.

Edward held his arm out to Eleanor. The queen, a gracious

smile on her olive-tinted face, rose as her ladies straightened her trailing green sarcenet skirt.

Rose popped up from her seat, not making eye contact with anyone. The curious, probing stares of the scandal-hungry court would get no concession of weakness from her. The royal couple left the stands for the palace. Rose and her companions followed in their wake.

Rose could not believe this moment was upon her. It all seemed unreal even as heat from numerous candles and frankincense smoke swirled around her in a dreamlike eddy.

Rand's nudge jolted her back from her thoughts. The priest, in his red-trimmed chasuble, repeated, "Rosalyn Harcourt, Lady Ayleston, do you want this man?"

She swallowed, moistening her lips to speak. "Aye."

Rose had slept poorly. When she had woken, the mirror above her washstand had reflected the lavender shadows beneath her eyes.

The priest continued, "Do you wish to serve him in the faith of God as your own, in health and infirmity, as a Christian woman should serve her husband?"

"Aye."

"Sir Rand Montague, do you wish to serve her in the faith of God as your own, in health and infirmity, as a Christian man should serve his wife?"

"Aye."

Lord Briand took her gloved right hand and transferred it to the priest's, who then placed it in Rand's, saying, "On this condition, I give her to you."

The warmth of Rand's larger hand seeped through her glove.

Rand received the blessed ring from the priest, a beautiful gold band engraved with runes. Reciting the Trinity, he slipped it over her thumb, then index, and finally middle finger, where it remained. "With this ring, I thee wed, this gold and silver I give thee, with my body I thee honor, and this dowry I thee give."

She looked up into his eyes, which darkened to green with calculation. What was going on behind those dark orbs? she wondered. Did he now regret rescuing her from the clutches of Sir Golan?

After the priest gave the Raguel blessing, joining them together, Mass began. Rose was lost in a sea of thoughts. Hot, her face flushed, she lifted her collar in an attempt to cool herself.

When Mass concluded, the priest blessed the couple and a common cup, from which they then drank. Rose shuddered at the finality of the ceremony. The dark red wine slid down her gullet. Rand stared at her neck as she swallowed. Feeling exposed, vulnerable, she fluttered up her hand, and clutched her bare throat. At Kat's insistence, she had dispensed with the wimple and veil, wearing the more traditional linen barbette and fillet headdress. A rapid pulse beat, hot and hard, in the hollow at the base of her neck. A shivery sensation surged in her blood. 'Twas just anxiety, she told herself, not . . .

The small party in the chapel surged forward toward the altar before the carved rood screen and congratulated Rand and Rose. Lord and Lady Briand embraced her first.

Her father clutched her face with both hands and kissed her forehead. The creases at the corners of his dark blue eyes deepened in concern. "Rand is a good man, Rose. He will treat you with respect and decency. I pray you will give him a chance to prove it."

Alex, blue eyes nearly as dark as their father's, approached next. A tall man with long black hair, he hugged her and whispered into her ear, "I love you, sprite. Rand's a very lucky man. I hope together you find the love you deserve."

Rose's gaze moved to where Rand was talking to his cousin. He smiled down at Kat, shaking his head, his hands on her shoulders. The priest had proclaimed Rose and Rand joined together forever in Holy Matrimony. But Rose felt as though shackled, the weight of the marriage yoke a burden that could not be broken except by death.

Rand turned. Their gazes collided. Green-gray orbs flickered with interest. One corner of his mouth lifted in a wicked grin, though, for the first time, she realized it did not reach his eyes.

Frowning, she prayed she had done the right thing for herself and for her son. She desperately missed Jason and could not wait to return to him. Her heart fluttered in sudden distress; she clutched Jason's stone. God forfend Rand discovered the truth about the boy. The truth Bertram had discovered the day of his death.

It was Lady Rosalyn Montague's wedding night. Lady Rosalyn now, not Lady Ayleston. She exhaled loudly, pacing before the massive canopy bed in the center of the room, which was illuminated by several sconces.

Rose sat on the edge of the bed and crossed her arms. The bed was covered in lush red-and-gold brocade bed curtains and coverlet, and stacked with a bolster and gold pillows. An elaborate carved washstand, a large mirror above it, was situated across from a window. Agatha, the housekeeper, had told her it overlooked the ornamental garden the previous lady of the house had nurtured and cared for until she became too old to tend it. Rand had bought the house, which was situated on the Strand not far from court, when he'd learned they would wed.

Now, Rose tapped her foot on the floorboards, restless. She surged up from her seat, unpinned her veil and barbette chin piece. She tossed the headdress and strips of linen onto the washstand, then moved across the room to the window and opened the shutters. Cool air inundated her senses and soothed her flushed cheeks. She exhaled and began unbraiding her hair, combing through it with her fingers and massaging her aching scalp.

The long red tresses fell over the front of her shoulders, rippling slightly in the breeze. She closed the shutters and turned toward the washstand.

Rand stood at the foot of the bed, gazing at her, his expression rapt.

She let out a gasp as her mouth dropped open in horror.

She clutched her collar, her pulse pounding at her temple. "Rand, what are you doing here? You swore we would not share a bed as man and wife. Are you not a man of your word?" Accusation hung heavily in the air.

His cloudy gaze cleared and he propped himself against a laurel leaf–carved bedpost. "Aye, 'tis true I agreed we would not have carnal relations. And I shall keep my promise. But it would be best if we shared a bed so there will be no undue gossip."

"Nay." Her voice was shrill. "I shall not spend a single night in the same chamber, let alone same bed, with you."

Rand sat down on the bed and tugged off his boots. He spoke slowly as though to a child. "Be reasonable, Rose. If it became known we did not consummate our union, we would be forced to do so, or our marriage could be overturned. I know Sir Golan would seize any chance to thwart me and have you in his power once again."

His tone infuriated her. Men were vile, selfish creatures who were quite capable of lying to achieve their dastardly ends.

All she could think of was the humiliation and torment she'd suffered at Bertram's hands. She watched Rand's lips move, but could not hear him. Her ears buzzed as images from the past began to flash before her eyes. Of Bertram, laughing at her for naïvely believing for a moment he wanted her boyish body; kissing and fondling the voluptuous Lady Lydia; striking Rose for anything he perceived as defiance of his authority.

With a cry of despair, she dashed past him to the door. She lifted the latch and tugged, but it did not budge.

She spun around. Bertram loomed over her, his arm poised to strike. She screamed and crouched to the floor, her arm raised to ward off his blows. "Don't hurt me, Bertram. I beg you, don't hurt me. I promise never to defy you again." Her entire body shook with fear and her heart pounded as she waited for a blow to fall.

Rand gazed down at Rose, his heart in his throat. A boiling rage welled up inside him at the bastard who had reduced the once spirited and cheerful Rose to a quivering woman fearful of men. His fists clenched till his knuckles whitened. If Bertram were alive today, Rand would hurl the man down the stairs himself.

Relaxing his fists, he reached down and gently lifted Rose into his arms. Surprisingly, she did not resist. Her eyes were blank, appearing opaque, as though she were in some sort of trance. He placed her on the bed and removed her slippers. She lay rigid, her arms straight down at her sides as he pulled the brocade coverlet over her.

He stared at her—lost in a world he could not reach. Her chest rose and fell in shallow breaths. Tears slowly seeped from eyes stark with torment.

Rand rubbed the back of his tense neck. His temples pulsed with pain as frustration gnawed at him. He desperately wanted to heal the wounds the monster had inflicted on her and continued to haunt her despite the bastard's death. Yet he was unsure how to reach her, to prove to her he was not remotely like her first husband.

He shoved his hands through his hair and paced away. Discovering a brazier in the corner beside the bed, he added some coals and stoked the fire to warm the suddenly chill room. He found extra blankets and a gray fur throw in the wardrobe. After he covered Rose with the fur, he made up a pallet beside the bed for himself.

When he turned back to check on her, her eyes were closed and she was snoring softly. The tight knot in his chest loosened as relief flooded him. Reaching out, he stroked her cheek with the back of his fingers. Her skin was exquisite, its texture velvety soft, and her complexion delicately luminous. Ethereal.

Very lightly, he kissed the healing gash on her forehead. "Sleep peacefully, my wife."

He removed his sword belt and surcoate, but kept on his sherte and braies. If Rose awoke, he did not wish to alarm her.

Once he lay down on the pallet, he began to notice his throbbing shoulder. He shifted the opening of his sherte and stared at the black-and-blue bruises, realizing he must have wrenched it again when he lifted Rose. Mayhap she had an ointment to ease his bruised muscles, though he would not count on it after this disastrous eve.

He had only wanted to protect her. But no matter how hard he tried, he always ended up hurting those he loved. He sat up, startled at that thought. Nay, he did not love Rose. She was just his best friend's sister, someone he cared for very much. But in love with her? A scoffing laugh escaped his lips.

That ridiculous notion settled in his mind, Rand laid back down and closed his eyes. And dreamed . . .

Rand jerked awake, a deep groan echoing in the chamber. He looked around, disoriented, unsure where he was. He lay upon a disheveled pallet in the bedchamber at Strand House. It was his wedding night. And he'd just woken from a dream, a memory from the past so vividly real his skin still hummed with quiescent pleasure and his aroused cock throbbed painfully. He'd dreamt of the night he had made love to Rose. When she'd pushed her way into his bedchamber at Ayleston Castle so she could tend the knee wound he'd received on the Crusade that had festered.

Pulling up the right leg of his braies, he idly smoothed his fingers over the three-inch-long jagged scar above his knee.

After Rose had dressed his wound, she'd begged him to remain at Ayleston a few days until it healed. He'd stared down at her, her body cushioned between him and the bedchamber door. Her soft blue eyes and erotic scent had lured him beyond his resolve. Her lips were a hairsbreadth away. A moan, a sigh, a whispered plea wafted. Then she'd kissed him or he'd kissed her. No matter who started it, he'd finished it, their breaths shivering with delight, their bodies pounding hot and heavy with a desire that could not be denied.

Moments ago, at his remembrances, a long, deep animalistic groan had erupted from his chest.

Disquieted, he surged up from his pallet. The sound of bedclothes rustling drew him to the bed. Rose was asleep, restlessly shifting beneath the blankets.

Her exquisitely molded lips parted, expelling a soft moan.

His cock twitched. He groaned again. This time in carnal frustration.

Disgusted, needing to exorcise his demons in mindless physical exertion, Rand dressed, gathered his sword and scabbard, then exited the chamber.

Chapter Nine

Rose gasped, waking from a dream—a dormant memory from her past. Her lips tingled. Her femininity was engorged and quivering. She touched her mouth in shock. She had forgotten what passion and its aftermath felt like and marveled at the sensation.

Then her recollection of last night returned. Rand. The last thing she remembered was Rand laying her down on the bed. Her heart beat a painful staccato. Had it only been a dream, or something much more sinister? Surely Rand had not violated her while she had been senseless?

She peeked beneath the coverlet and saw that she was fully dressed. Nor did she feel a sticky residue between her thighs. Relief rushed through her tense body and she relaxed.

She gazed around the room. Light shone through the partially opened shutters. She was alone in the chamber. Rubbing her puffy eyes, she wondered where Rand was.

She fluffed the pillows behind her back and reclined against the headboard. As she noticed the gray fur blanket, her thoughts returned to last night. The fur had not been on the bed then, for she had perused the room thoroughly. Had Rand covered her with it after she blanked out all sensation and thought? It was a mechanism she had learned to use in order to escape the painful degradations her first husband had forced her to endure.

What must Rand have thought of her violent reaction, and her subsequent spell? She could not bear that he had seen her in such a state. He must think her a raving lunatic or perhaps possessed by demons. She had no idea how she was going to face him again.

But face him she must, Rose thought, as she climbed from the bed to ready for the day.

Returning from court, where all the talk was of the inevitability of war with Wales, Rand looked around at the peacefulness and beauty of the garden with a greater appreciation for nature. The musical call of birds in the trees was a reminder of halcyon times romping in the vineyards on summer days with his sister.

He found Rose seated on an exedra. The U-shaped bench overlooked a bend in the river's winding course. Her lips were curved in a soft smile as she watched the boats traveling up and down the Thames.

"Positively breathtaking."

Rose jerked in surprise, her willowlike torso snapping upright. Shielding her eyes with her hand, she gazed up at him. "Rand, I'm sorry I was not waiting for you in the Great Hall. I'm afraid the hour advanced without my knowledge."

She made to rise, but Rand motioned her to sit and sat down opposite her. "You need not apologize."

"But you must be hungry."

"I am hungry and the weather is mild, so I asked Agatha to serve the midday meal in the garden. I hope that meets with your approval?"

"Of course, whatever you wish."

"But do you wish it so?"

Surprise registered in her eyes and she cocked her head. "Do you truly wish to know my desire?"

"Of course. Why would I ask you what you wanted if I did not care to know the answer?"

Rose looked down and rubbed her thumb over a wrinkle in her gown on top of her thigh. "I am sorry. Our marriage is new and 'tis difficult to know what to expect from you. My only experience is with Bertram, and he cared for naught but his own wants and desires. 'Tis a surprise you would defer to my preference."

Rand raised her chin with his forefinger so that she looked him in the eye. "I am naught like Bertram at all. The bastard is where he belongs. I'd never hurt you the way he did. I made a vow to protect you, and I mean that in every way."

Even from myself, he thought.

Rose nodded her understanding. "The day is lovely. I would be pleased to dine alfresco with you."

Rand waved to the housekeeper waiting at the kitchen door for Rand's order to serve them dinner. Two servants brought a trestle table and sat it between him and Rose. Then Agatha and two servers brought out a trencher for them to share, a number of hot meat dishes and vegetables, a basket of bread, and a flagon of wine, then set the meal before them. Rose remained silent while Rand filled their chalices with an excellent burgundy he specifically chose to have stocked at Strand House.

When Rose drank from her chalice, his gaze dropped to her throat, once again covered by her wimple headdress. But his imagination conjured up pictures of her bared throat, the supple muscles working as she swallowed, a pulse beating at the base of her neck. He wanted to press his lips there, to feel the throbbing beat beneath warm, silky flesh.

His lips tingled at the thought.

"Oh, God, that is absolutely delicious."

"Whaa . . . ?" For a moment, the seductive images merged

with Rose's words, and he thought she was referring to the imaginary kiss.

Rose gazed at him oddly, her eyebrows pitched upward. He took hold of his wayward sensibilities.

Rand cleared his throat and tried again. "What's delicious?"

"The wine. It tastes wonderful."

"I am glad you like it. I stocked Strand House's cellars with several casks, along with the white wine we had for dinner last night."

"'Tis obviously a very high-quality wine. You always did enjoy an excellent vintage."

Was that a slight smile he detected? he wondered.

"Indeed. I enjoy my wine. I don't mind paying an exorbitant price for such quality."

Rand took another bite of his lamb. "How do you like the gardens? I hope they meet with your approval?"

She put down her spoon and knife. "I have never seen more beautiful gardens," she said, using her hands to express herself. "The kitchen garden has a number of herbs I would like to take and plant at Ayleston Castle. The townhome's former owner must have been very knowledgeable of the healing herbs."

A quiver of excitement emerged in her words, triggering Rand's memories of when she was younger—vibrant and full of life.

"I bought it for you. For its privacy and because I thought you would appreciate the beauty of the magnificent gardens." He took a gulp of wine.

"Thank you," she said softly, touched by his thoughtful gesture. He'd always been kind and considerate to her, despite his infuriating teasing. And unlike her first husband, Rand had never treated her cruelly, so it was unfair to continually expect Rand to behave in such a manner. It would take time to adjust, to accept her new position as Rand's wife.

To that end, she wanted to learn why he was the man he was. She clutched the stem of her chalice and cocked her head. "Your older brother inherited the Montague vineyards, did he not? Tell me about growing up in Gascony."

Rand leaned his forearm on the table. The sun behind his head created a glow around the edges of his long blond hair. "When I was a lad, Juliana and I would sneak away from our nurse to traipse about barefoot in our family's vineyards. We always played with the tenant's children, building forts and exploring along the banks of the river. Mother always bemoaned the fact that she could not tell us apart from the peasants whenever our nurse dragged us back home."

Rose's heart did a flip at the image he presented. She could easily imagine Rand as a mischievous youth, getting into one scrape after another, his adoring twin sister gamboling at his side, eager not to be left behind. She was touched that he shared a glimpse of his life before his sister died.

She sipped from her wine to wet her suddenly dry mouth. "'Tis where your love for a good wine flourished, if I am not mistaken?"

A huge grin spread across his face. "I have business in London that I must see to, and I would like you to accompany me."

Her heart beat uncontrollably. Confused, she said more sharply than she intended, "Surely you don't need my presence to conduct your business?"

Rand merely quirked his brow; the crease between his eyes deepened so much it appeared as though a sharp V was carved there. "Come, I want to show you something very few people know about." He stood up and reached out a hand to help her to her feet.

Never a slave to curiosity, like her friend Kat, Rose felt an odd tremor of that very emotion shimmer through her.

Without hesitation, she placed her hand in his.

Rand's gaze widened with surprise and pleasure as he

stared at her hand clutched in his. Shock held her immobile. For the first time, she reacted without forethought and voluntarily touched Rand. Warmth flowed from his bronzed hand into her smaller, more delicate one, his pleasant scent enveloping her, enticing her.

Rand smiled with gentle reassurance. His eyes—more green than gray, with gold flecks—softened. She shook her head to regain her senses and followed him down to the water stairs.

After debarking from the barge, Rose clutched Rand's forearm as he guided them off the lane and heading east crossed the wharves behind the stone buildings that fronted Thames Street.

"Have you ever visited the wharves of London before?" Rand inquired, a half smile on his face.

"Nay, I have only seen the riverside from coach or boat." Her gaze darted back and forth at the teeming wharf.

"This is the ward known as the Vintry. 'Tis mainly inhabited by wine merchants and their families. The vintners live above the warehouses and cellars where their wines are stored."

Raucous shouts of mariners vied with calls coming from the handful of cookhouses interspersed among the buildings and warehouses.

"See those ships?" Rand indicated with a sweep of his arm.

Several ships lined the wharves, which swarmed with activity as ships' cargos were discharged onto the quays and revetments along the riverbank.

"Aye. What are in those sacks and barrels being laded onto the vessels?"

"Grain, wool, and salted herring mostly. Many of the ships are bound for Bordeaux, where their cargos will be traded for the new vintages, which in turn will be brought back to England in time for Christmas."

A beggar dressed in rags, a boy not much older than Jason, reached out a dirty hand to them. Rand's muscles tensed beneath her hand, the strength and heat of him reassuring.

Rose's heart contracted at the poverty and misery of such an existence. She was grateful her son would never know such degradation and was touched when Rand retrieved a farthing from the purse hanging at his sword belt and tossed it to the boy.

The black-haired child grinned at them, revealing two missing front teeth. "Thank ye, milord," he said and then rushed off to the cookhouse nearby to purchase hot food with his recent fortune.

"That was generous of you, Rand."

Rand shrugged, his cheeks reddening at her praise. "I have seen many such scenes at every port and city I have ever visited. I would never wish such an existence upon a child, especially not a child of my own."

"You do not regret you will never have a son?" Rose cringed inwardly. The words came out unbidden. Perhaps she wanted to torture herself with imagining the impossible. For she had secrets, secrets she could never share with anyone, and *especially* not with Rand.

Rand shrugged. "If you will allow, I would be honored to stand in as father to Jason."

Rose swallowed, her eyes rounding.

"Do not answer that now. Give it some thought," he said gruffly.

He hooked his arm through hers and they continued walking.

A cart loaded with casks containing pitch and tar trundled past them. Her nose wrinkled at the sharp odor. A gust of wind off the river whipped her skirt around her legs, drawing her gaze out to the ships anchored in deeper waters. River traffic was brisk, with the smaller oar-powered fishing boats and cargo boats giving way to the larger, single-mast, square-sail cogs, keels, and hulks. The ships' colorful banners flying from their sterncastles identified their owners.

At the fourth building along the wharf, Rand stopped and Rose released his arm. Less than a hundred yards away, the door to the back entrance of the large, two-story stone house was open. Not far from the door was a bench beneath a grapevine-covered arbor. A gravel walkway led down to the waterfront, where porters were loading sacks of wool and grain into the open hold in the middle of a large cog. A forecastle rose upon stilts at the ship's bow and at the back of the ship a sterncastle was built right into the hull. Rand's banner, a gold lion rampant on an azure background, flew from the sterncastle.

Rose glanced up at Rand, curious. Slowly, it began to dawn on her where his wealth came from—she guessed it was connected somehow to the vineyards his family owned in Bordeaux.

A plump gray-haired man, who had been supervising the loading of the ship, approached them. "Sir Rand!" he shouted, waving as he weaved his way past several dockworkers.

Rand smiled at the man. "Harwood. Have any trouble on the voyage back from the Baltic?"

"Nay. Storms delayed our departure for five days, but otherwise the journey was uneventful."

Rand slapped him on the back. "Glad to hear it. Your timing is impeccable. The first vintage this season promises to be very profitable." He turned to Rose.

"Harwood. I want you to meet my wife, Lady Rosalyn. Rose, meet Master John Harwood. Harwood is my factor here in England and Bordeaux and master of my ship, the *Argo*."

Rose blinked, startled by the name of Rand's ship. The *Argo* was the ship sailed by the mythical hero Jason in his quest to retrieve the Golden Fleece, which Rose had read about in the Greek epic poem *Argonautica*.

Could it be . . . ?

Harwood bowed deeply. "My lady. I'm honored to make your acquaintance."

The raucous caw of a gull blared above Rose's head. Spikes of fear shot down her lower limbs. Suddenly her knees buckled. She grabbed hold of the bench and lowered herself before she fell flat on her hindquarters.

As Rand spoke to Harwood, she worried her lower lip, wondering if the ship's name had any special significance. But there was no way Rand could suspect . . . Surely he had no idea of the secret she had nearly died trying to protect.

Fear of discovery had been Rose's constant companion for many years. Swiping her arm over her moist forehead, Rose stared at Rand's broad back, noticing the subtle play of muscles beneath his dark red tunic as he gesticulated toward the *Argo*, giving Harwood instructions.

She'd thought her worries were over with the death of her husband's greedy cousin, Sir Stephen. Stephen had never guessed her deepest, most shameful secret, and fortunately, Bertram had never shared the knowledge with his cousin. Not that Bertram had had proof of the accusation he'd leveled at her the day of his death.

But now, with her marriage to Rand, her fears came rushing back like a river surging over its banks at flood tide. For Rand would never forgive her for keeping Jason's paternity from him.

She clutched Jason's stone beneath her bodice, shaking. It was for Jason's own protection that she had kept it secret. And she had protected him. From Bertram and his vile threats.

She remembered it as though it happened yesterday.

Chapter Ten

Ayleston Castle, Chester County
In the year of our Lord 1274, January 2
Second year in the reign of King Edward I

"Milady. I tried to stop him, but he made me leave him alone with the boy."

Rose stopped outside her bedchamber. Her son's nurse was pacing before the closed door. "Who, Edith? Who is with Jason?"

"Lord Ayleston, milady," she said, wringing her hands, her raisin eyes bright with fear.

Rose gasped in surprise. Not once in the two months since Jason's birth had Bertram shown an interest in his son. When he was born, Bertram simply inquired if the baby was the male heir he desired and returned to the bed of his whore.

Worried herself now, Rose rushed into her bedchamber. When she saw the room was empty, she entered the adjoining chamber. Her husband, his golden hair elaborately curled, stood over Jason's cradle, staring down at the sleeping baby.

Bertram's handsome, pale chiseled features were pulled down in a fierce glower.

A pulse jumped in Rose's throat. She moved subtly toward

the cradle, her eyes cast down. "Milord, is there something you need of me?" She had learned well the role of docile, submissive wife Bertram required.

She reached into the cradle to pick up Jason, but Bertram shoved her aside. His milk-white slender hands, which she had once thought elegant and refined, grabbed the boy and lifted him to his chest awkwardly. Jason's head lolled to the side.

"Milord, his head. You must be careful to support his head."

Dark ire flared in his jewel-green eyes. "Never think to instruct me as though I'm one of the castle pages."

Rose dropped her gaze, nodding obsequiously.

But he did as she asked and cupped his hand around Jason's head, which had a strip of wispy blond curls on top.

"He does not look very much like me."

"He is still too young to look like anyone."

"His eyes are blue."

"I have blue eyes."

He grunted irritably.

"Milord, may I take him? 'Tis time for his feeding."

"Not yet. Lydia mentioned that the boy was very big for a two-month-old baby born a fortnight early."

"He's nearly three months old."

Bertram clutched Jason tighter; the baby whimpered. "Correct me one more time and I shall deny you visitation of the boy for a fortnight." His eyes narrowed with the threat.

Rose gasped. Lydia was a viper in the nest.

The ease with which Lydia manipulated Bertram was diabolical. Rose could not understand the hold the woman had over her husband. He treated Lydia with more respect than his own wife. Ensorcelled by Lydia, Bertram seemed willing to do any vile deed at her behest. Indeed, Bertram's marriage to Rose had been plotted with great care by Lydia. A vendetta for the perceived insult Rose's brother, Alex, dealt Lydia when he rejected her.

Yet Rose could never tell anyone of the humiliating situation in which she found herself. Married to a man who despised her, who'd wed her to please his mistress, a mistress who'd schemed to destroy Rose simply because she was Alex's sister. Lydia's vindictive tentacles could no longer reach Alex, for he was dead, buried in the rocky soil of Palestine.

Bertram put Jason back in the crib and began jerking the swaddling off the baby. Jason began to cry, his scrunched-up face turning bright red.

Her heart jumped into her throat, so her words came out as a croak. "Milord, what are you doing?"

His hands searched all over the baby, rolling him over, checking his back and bottom and limbs. "I'm checking your son for blemishes or marks of the devil or of witchery."

Her heart stopped and a hand flew to her throat. *What non-sense is this?* "Milord. Prithee, have a care with your son. You are frightening Jason."

He spun around and grabbed her shoulders. She winced in pain. A light flared in his eyes, his gaze intense, fevered, and held her frozen in its grip. "Is he? Is he really my son? I say I do not know."

"Jason is your son and no other's." Drawing Bertram's wrath upon her and away from Jason, Rose added, her lip curled in utter contempt. "'Tis all Lydia's doing. That whore put these ridiculous notions into your head. And you are a fool to believe that viperous slattern."

Bertram shoved her hard. Rose fell to her hands and knees. Splinters jabbed into her palms and her hair flew down into her face. Unable to see, she shoved it out of her eyes and got up. But a long hard object struck her. Pain seared her back and she fell onto her knees again. She cried out, protecting her belly and face as repeated blows—with a broom, she realized—struck her back and buttocks. Her cries filled the room, begging him to stop.

Then the blows ceased. Bertram's heavy breathing smothered

the air around her and her lungs worked like a bellows to staunch her fear.

"That disapproving bastard Sir Rand was here last year and could very well be the father. I saw the way his eyes followed you when he thought no one was looking. Did you let him touch you? Did you?"

Rose gasped and stared up at him, her hands clenched before her in supplication. "Nay. I have never let him or any man touch me. I have lain with no man but you." She prayed God would forgive her for the lie.

He raised the broom again. "Liar."

She gazed up at him, her eyes open, innocent. "Nay. I swear. You are Jason's father."

His intense jewel, fever-bright eyes held hers. "Swear it on your brother's soul."

"I swear on Alex's soul Jason is yours." She cringed inwardly upon her blasphemy. But Jason's very life depended on her sacrilege.

Bertram's shoulders relaxed. "You'd better pray Jason begins to look like me. I shall be watching Jason as he grows. If it begins to appear the boy has even so much as a single feature of Rand Montague's . . . Well, know that I shall not have a bastard bear the Ayleston title and let you make a fool of me. There are many ways for children to, shall we say, languish in childhood, either by accident or by illness."

Rose clutched her arms around her stomach as her entire body began to shake. "You would not dare do such a wicked deed as take the life of your own son."

Bertram clutched her hair and snarled in her face. "I will do whatever it takes to ensure a child of my own loins. Either through you, or another wife, should you continue to defy me. Children are easily begotten till the mother either dries up or dies in childbirth. Wives are easily replaceable," Bertram spat, and then, releasing her, marched from the room.

Rose jumped up, grabbed Jason from his cradle, and

clutched him protectively to her. She rocked back and forth, soothing the infant, her mind reeling with anxiety.

Then a bolt of intense clarity shot through her like lightning and dispersed the fog clouding her reasoning. It was at that moment Rose decided to flee her husband. To seek the safety and shelter her powerful father could provide. Until this moment she had been too ashamed to tell her parents of her husband's abuse and perfidy. After all, it was her fault Bertram could not perform his husbandly duties without the stimulation of knowing others watched. It was her fault she was too passionate and spoiled and unruly.

Now Jason was in danger because of her weakness: her sinful passionate nature. So she must flee. Because she could not risk that Bertram would one day see Rand in the boy and retaliate.

London wharfs
In the year of our Lord 1276, October 22
Fourth year in the reign of King Edward I

"Rose . . ."

The sounds of the city by the river, shouts of seamen and rumbling cart wheels, seemed far distant as Rand tried to get Rose to answer him.

"Rose," Rand said again. He knelt before Rose and patted her icy hand. She rocked back and forth, gazing through him as though he were a phantom. Her crystal blue eyes were dull with pain and her skin awash in a pale alabaster hue. "Rose, answer me," he said sharply, his heart palpitating.

Her eyes cleared. She stopped rocking and gazed around.

They were alone. The porters and ship's crew had been discharged for the day and he'd sent Harwood to check the cellars.

"Rand, what are you doing?"

Rand cocked his head. "I was concerned for you, Rose.

When I returned from speaking with Harwood you were rocking and humming softly beneath your breath. You stared blankly through me and would not answer me when I addressed you."

Rose blanched, growing paler. She pulled her hands free and rubbed them up and down her upper arms. "I am sorry. I'm not mad, if that is what you think."

"I do not know what to think. Obviously something was troubling you. You seemed distraught and fearful for no apparent reason. Care to tell me about it?"

"I am fine, Rand, verily."

"You can talk to me. I know Bertram was a . . . a difficult man to be married to, but you can confide in me. I shall not judge you."

"How did you know I was thinking of Bertram?"

"We have not spoken of it, but last night you had a similar spell. You cried out for Bertram not to hurt you. Obviously, you were not cognizant. You were locked in a nightmare where I could not reach you."

Rand understood her demons more than she knew. He wanted her to confide in him, but how could he expect her to when he was not willing to reveal his own inner torment?

"Will you not tell me about it? You need not fear my censure. Unlike Bertram, I shall not condemn you for exhibiting an honest emotion."

Soulful blue eyes evaded his. "What do you know of an honest emotion?" she said with a sad sigh. "You can charm a lady to do your bidding with your laughing eyes and seductive smile. But you have no deep feeling for her beyond animal lust."

The insult cut deep. Rand stood up and stared down at her. He could not refute her accusation. To do so would reveal the means by which he allowed his emotions to be subsumed beneath a charming exterior in order to protect those he cared for.

Rand laughed. "You are right. I enjoy women and they

know better than to expect me to fall in love with them. 'Tis good you realize that, because I would not want you to fall in love with me," he said with a devilish grin.

Her gaze snapped, blue eyes glittering. Good. He much preferred her anger to her fear and pain. He felt helpless before her when she exhibited the effects of her abusive past. It brought back memories of his own ineffectualness to prevent his father from hurting his mother and sister.

"Help!" A terrified shriek pierced the sound of splashing water.

Rand turned and saw a black-haired boy bob in the river, his arms flailing as he tried to stay above water. Running toward the river, he watched the lad disappear beneath the surface.

Rand slid to a stop near the bow of his ship. Frozen, his heart pumped in agitation. A cold sweat broke out over his body.

Rose followed Rand to the river's revetment. She expected Rand to jump in and rescue the boy, but he just stood there staring, trancelike. "Rand, don't just stand there. The boy is drowning. Save him."

He shuddered. Mumbled what she thought was "I can do this" and then tore off his tunic and boots.

Rand dived in and swam to where Rose last saw the child. His buttocks and feet surfaced as he dove down into the depths of the river. Twice he came up for air and went under again. Suddenly, Rand's head popped up, the black-haired boy held in his arms. He swam toward her with one arm back, grunting with exertion.

Harwood emerged from the cellar, and Rose turned at his approach. "The boy almost drowned."

Gaze troubled, the shipmaster nodded and knelt down, then grabbed the unconscious boy from Rand's arms. Rose gasped. It was the beggar boy whom Rand had given a coin to earlier. Rose knelt over the child as Rand shoved up onto the revetment with both hands. She checked the boy's pulse. It was steady but weak.

"Is the boy going to be all right?" Rand flipped his dripping wet hair back, staring down at the lad, his eyes dark with fear.

His gaze moved to hers and Rose realized it had been a trick of the light. For his green eyes were clear and untroubled. It had likely been a shadow created by his thick, dark eyelashes.

"I believe so. Is there a bed where he can rest till he wakes up?"

"Of course. He can stay in the apprentice's bed off the kitchen. Harwood can show you where it is." Harwood picked the boy up.

Rose followed Harwood through the back door and down the stairs to the kitchen. Before she descended the steps, she turned back. Rand, his fists clenched at his sides, stared out over the river, a lonely sentinel.

Rose sat on a stool beside the narrow bed situated along the fireplace wall in a small chamber off the kitchen. The boy now lay in a clean, dry sherte. As she waited for him to rouse, Rose could not help replaying in her mind Rand's hesitation to rescue the boy.

She had always considered Rand extremely brave and strong and afraid of naught. It reminded her of the afternoon at the abbey when Rand revealed his sister had drowned. Had he been there when Juliana died? Had he watched helplessly as she gave her last breath before surrendering to death?

Watching the boy struggle in the water must have brought back feelings from that day, causing Rand to hesitate. It was the only explanation for his odd behavior.

With sudden insight, Rose realized there was more emotional depth to Rand than he let show. Juliana's death had had a profound effect on him. Rose had seen the devastation and guilt etched on Rand's face when he'd spoken of his sister's death. Nor could she forget Rand's enraged defense of her in the chapel when Sir Golan assaulted her.

Then today, when he revealed his concern for her, she'd accused him of being a heartless womanizer, and he'd responded with a provocative quip and an irreverent laugh.

'Twas not the first time he had retorted in such manner. Always she had negated the emotion he expressed as an aberration, and pounced, perhaps unfairly, on his blithe rejoinders and infuriatingly glib remarks.

Now she could not help wondering, could his irreverent wit be a mask he used to keep people at a distance? Could it have anything to do with Juliana's death? Rose got the feeling there was more to his sister's death than he disclosed.

The shield she wielded to protect herself from being hurt slipped a little and her heart softened toward him.

The boy moaned on the bed, blinking, and opened his eyes. Rose left off her musings to assure him he was safe.

Upon returning to Strand House, Rand entered the bed-chamber and quickly completed his ablutions. Afterward, he tossed his soiled sherte in the wardrobe, grabbed a clean one, and returned to the bedchamber. A feminine gasp brought his head up.

Rose stood at the foot of the bed, a hand to her throat, staring wide-eyed at his bare chest. "Forgive me. I didn't know you were in the bedchamber. I thought you were with Will in the stable."

With a teasing wink, he spread his arms wide. "As you see, I'm here, hale and whole before you." When he rose his arm too high, a streak of fire shot through his shoulder, and a groan escaped him.

Rose hurried to his side, a frown of concern on her flushed face. "Not so hale and whole. Where did you get these bruises and why did you not tell me you were in pain?" she asked as she examined his left shoulder, her soft hands gently probing the black-and-blue areas.

He stared down at her, her scent, her touch, her nearness enticing him beyond distraction. She bit her plump lower lip. His gaze drifted down to her lips. They were so near all he had to do was dip his head and press his mouth to hers. He wanted to thoroughly explore the delectable flesh with his teeth and tongue. He groaned.

"I am sorry. I didn't mean to hurt you." She went to the wardrobe and returned with a glass vial. He deliberately kept his back, and hence his scar—which rose a few inches above his braies—from her gaze. "You should have told me you injured your shoulder. Sit on the bed, and I can rub this oil onto it. It should help heal the bruises and ease your pain."

Rand sat down on the bed and laid his sherte over his braies and his hands on top of the sherte to hide his embarrassing predicament. "'Tis just bruised. I did not wish to bother you for such a minor nuisance."

Rose removed the glass stopper from the vial and poured a small quantity into her palm. He caught a whiff of clove. She closed the vial and handed it to him. Then she spread the oil over her hands evenly before she began massaging it into his bruised shoulder.

She shook her head. "I do not know why men insist on never admitting to any pain or illness. 'Tis not weakness to recognize a problem and seek help for it."

"And women tend to coddle, fretting about every inconsequential bruise or ache. 'Tis any wonder men are cautious not to seek help unless absolutely necessary?"

A small smile curved her lips. "I shall concede your point, on condition you concede mine."

His heart flipped, and he could not keep the smile from his voice. "Very well. I agree there is some truth in your statement. What is in the oil?"

"Saint-John's wort and arnica oil for healing the bruises, clove for the pain. I also use the ointment to reduce swelling of the joints and muscles. You never said how you got the bruises."

"Jousting. When my lance broke on the last pass, I received the blunt force of Golan's lance blow to my shield. My shoulder received the worst of it." He did not mention he suspected that Golan had tampered with his lance, that the tent fire was likely a diversion to accomplish the deed. He had naught but suspicions and did not want to worry her.

"I remember it." She shuddered. "For a moment I was afraid you would not rise. That you were de—" she stopped, her big eyes wide, haunted.

Rand dropped the vial on the bed and clutched her smaller, more delicate hand in his larger one. "Rose, I am not so easy to kill. You may be sure I have no intention of leaving you vulnerable to Sir Golan. The bastard shall never hurt you again. Whatever it takes, I shall protect you."

Rose looked into Rand's warm gray-green gaze, the amber flecks like tiny candle flames. Warmth from his calloused hand seeped into hers. He smelled of clove with an underlying essence unique to Rand, of warm skin, leather, and clean, fresh soap. Her hands still retained the imprint of his firm muscles and silky skin.

Nervous, she licked her lips. His eyes dropped to her mouth; amber flecks sparked and her lips caught on fire. Her heart constricted, making it difficult to breathe. Rand's mouth inched closer toward hers. He was going to kiss her. Panic fluttered in her chest, or was it anticipation?

Those beautiful, full sensual lips of his touched hers, a breath of a touch. A soft moan, hers, she thought. He brushed her lips again and again, the velvet caress melting her from the inside out. Her right hand flitted up and landed delicately on his chest.

With a hoarse groan, he tugged her into his embrace and

slanted his mouth over hers with fierce abandon. His tongue flicked out, rough and wet, probing the sensitive inner recesses of her mouth. Tingling heat throbbed. On her lips, and shooting straight to her moist feminine center. She trembled in his arms, wanting to rub her loins against him and ease the ache.

Just as suddenly, shame engulfed her. She was weak, immoral. Passion had led her to destruction twice before, and she was blissfully following the path of old wanton behaviors with only a heated look and coaxing touch of his lips and tongue.

Chest rising and falling, Rose cried out and yanked away. "You kissed me." She flung the words at him like a curse, breath heaving. "How dare you. You promised our marriage would be chaste."

Rand stood up and Rose stumbled back farther. That wicked twinkle in his eye returned. *Blast him.*

"Indeed. But you can't expect me to abide by my promise when those soft blue eyes of yours were begging me to kiss you."

Rose gasped, appalled. "I did no such thing. And I'll thank you never to kiss me again."

Rand crossed his arms over his chest. Distracted, she dropped her gaze. She stared, enthralled at his bulging chest muscles. "Very well. I promise never to kiss you again. But heed me well. I will take whatever you willingly offer. Don't expect me to deny you when you weaken and want me to thrust my manhood between those beautiful thighs of yours to slake—"

Her eyes flew up. Her hand swung out. The slap rang out in the ensuing shocked silence.

The red imprint of her hand rose on his cheek.

"I made that mistake once," Rose cried out. "But I swear by no means shall I ever do so again." She flung away and stormed from the room, the crude boast repeating a refrain in her head. The man was an incorrigible rogue, lecher, libertine.

She could not believe how quickly she'd succumbed at the

first touch of his lips. How easily the allure of his masculine scent and potent kisses had weakened her knees and drawn forth a passionate response from her. She'd thought she was no longer susceptible to the pleasures of the flesh.

The rhythm of her heart came in short, rapid beats, in time with her echoing footsteps down the outer stairs.

Rand had an uncanny ability to provoke her ire . . . She jolted to a stop. Blast the man. Once again she had let him goad her temper with his lewd boasts. He did it apurpose, she was sure now, when he wished to create a wall between them that in-depth feelings and emotions could not surmount. Rose whirled around and marched back up the stairs.

She swung the door open silently.

Rand stood where she'd left him, gripping the carved bed-post. A ripple of emotions swept across his face—an odd combination of desire and poignant regret.

A tender, indefinable feeling clutched her heart. "Why do you do that, Rand?" she asked, her voice a soft plea.

He jerked his gaze up. Rose stood not far away, her head cocked. Catching him unaware, her glare intent, she saw his pupils contract and then close off all emotion from her probing stare.

"Do what?" Rand straightened and tugged a dark green surcoate over his head.

"Every time it gets too emotional you say something to push me away. Why? What are you afraid of?"

She saw a pulse beat in his throat.

"I don't know what you are talking about, Rose."

"I think that you do. And that it has something to do with your sister's death. That day in the garden, I heard the anguish in your voice. Your refusal to speak of Juliana and your hesitation to save the boy from drowning made me realize how deeply her death affected you."

She took two steps and stopped. A hairsbreadth from him, she felt a sensual tension shimmer betwixt them. Rand grasped the bedpost once more, his white knuckles straining and jaw clenching.

She cupped his cheek, his whiskers tickling her palm. "By the river today you asked me to confide in you, and I responded thoughtlessly, hurting you, I believe, and then you lashed out. Deny it, but I know better now." She stood on tiptoes, clutched his shoulders, and kissed him, gently, tenderly.

Rand's velvety soft lips clung to hers, his sweet breath mingling with hers for an instant before he clutched her waist and drew her against him. Cushioned against the heat and strength of his hard, muscled chest, her nipples throbbed and pulsed with desire.

Her soft moan merged with his deep groan. Someone rapped on the chamber door. Rose jerked away, startled.

"Enter," Rand called out, voice hoarse with arousal.

Agatha entered. She glanced first at Rose, then Rand, an amused smile lifting her lips. "My lord, a messenger from court has arrived. The king requests your presence at court anon."

"Thank you, Agatha. I shall leave straightaway."

Rand turned to Rose, made a swift farewell, and beat a retreat. She stared at his departing back, unsure whether it was relief or regret thundering in her blood.

Chapter Eleven

At the palace the following night, servants broke down the trestle tables to clear the room for dancing, while Rand stared across the dining hall at Rose. She leaned close, in an intimate conversation with the attractive, dark-haired Henry de Lacy, the Earl of Lincoln. Despite Rand's resolve to remain distant, a flare of jealousy erupted and his smile broadened as though he was amused. But inside ire clamored. His grip on his chalice tightened. Leaning against a column in pretend negligence, he caught her gaze, tipped his wine cup to her, and then took a fortifying gulp.

She turned from him and then laughed at something the earl said. Smile still in place, Rand tensed. That did it. He could not remember the last time Rose had laughed like that at anything he'd said or done. Rand lurched from the column, but a voice stopped him short.

"Never say that the man known for the legions of broken hearts he has left behind is jealous of the attention his wife's showing another man."

Rand spun around and glared at Alex. If any other man had spoken thus to him, Rand would have laughed and acted as though the comment were in jest. But Alex knew him better than any other person and Rand did not bother to hide his disgruntlement.

"Your sister has the most unusual ability to twist me into knots despite my restraint." After their interrupted conversation the other night when she'd delved uncomfortably close into his heart, he'd made it a point to return from court after she fell asleep. He'd made up a pallet on the floor again and left before she woke. He had to keep up the pretence of a real marriage, but he need not suffer the torment of forced intimacy when he could not touch his wife.

"Which is not a bad thing, in my opinion. But you are overreacting. Knowing Rose's previous marital woes, do you seriously believe her interest in the earl is of a prurient nature?"

Pausing to reflect, Rand realized Alex was right. "Nay, I do not." His gaze returned to Rose. "But now my curiosity is piqued to discover what she is speaking to the earl so intensely about."

Rose smiled up at Henry de Lacy. "My lord, I believe you will agree that my son, Lord Ayleston, would be an agreeable candidate as husband for your young daughter, Lady Alice. The parties are of the same age. But, more importantly, the honor of Ayleston goes back to the time of William the Conqueror, and is rich in titles, honors, and lands. Such a match would greatly benefit both Lincoln and Ayleston. Do you not agree?"

Rose tried to strike the right tone of flattery, yet not be deferential. She needed to reinforce the belief that they were equals, or he would see no benefit to the marital alliance.

"I agree it would be an excellent match for your son. Through my daughter, upon my death, he would inherit the title of earl and all its inherent lands, privileges, and honors."

"The chances of that are very unlikely. You and the countess are still young and may yet produce a male heir. In which case, it stands to reason that Lady Alice, and thus Lincoln, shall benefit more from the alliance than Ayleston."

Lord Lincoln waved over a servant carrying a flagon of wine. The slender young man refilled their chalices.

Lincoln continued once the servant left. "Lady Rosalyn, I cannot deny a betrothal would be financially more beneficial for Lincoln. But I have higher aspirations for Lady Alice. She is my sole heir and deserves no less than an earl or even a prince for husband."

"Princes are few and far to come by. Lord Alphonso, King Edward's only surviving male heir, is already betrothed. And though there are two earldoms in England that your daughter could marry into, neither is as wealthy as Ayleston. Obviously you must weigh the merits of a title versus financial gain. But I believe if you were to see the details of the contract I wish to advance, you would agree that your daughter shall be amply rewarded."

A new look of respect entered his dark brown probing eyes. "I see you have done your research."

She allowed a small smile to grace her lips. "I have, which is why I know you wish to increase your presence and influence in Wales. An alliance with Ayleston would be advantageous in that regard with its backing and support."

"You bring up an excellent point. But will not your husband have a say in the betrothal arrangements?"

"Lord Ayleston is my ward. My husband has no rights to arrange a marriage for my son. He will not be a factor in the decision process."

Lord Lincoln crossed his arms and tipped back on his heels. "Of course. But with his recent wardship of the Ayleston estate, his decisions will have an impact on whether I wish to proceed with betrothal negotiations. As you pointed out I wish to expand my base in Wales. If Sir Rand does not approve of the match, he could deny material support of Ayleston.

"Is that not correct, Sir Rand?"

Rose jerked toward the direction of the earl's gaze. Rand swaggered toward them wearing an azure tunic decorated with black bands of silk on the square neck and wide cuffs. The sword belt cinched at his waist emphasized his powerful shoulders.

Rand stopped next to Rose and nodded to the earl in greeting. "Lord Lincoln, my dear," he said, and proceeded to kiss her cheek as he wrapped his right arm behind her back and squeezed her shoulder in a brief embrace.

Rose cleared her throat in embarrassment.

Amused, Lord Lincoln winked at her. "Sir Rand, your lady wife and I were just discussing the possibility of a betrothal between Lord Ayleston and my daughter, Lady Alice. What are your thoughts on the matter? Is this a match you would support?"

"I am sure my husband has no opinion on the matter. He has little concern for the boy's welfare and can have no stake in the outcome of the negotiations. Am I not correct milord?" Rose smiled to soften the dismissal.

"Actually, as guardian of Lord Ayleston's estate, I am concerned with his welfare."

"What concern is it of yours if I arrange a marriage for my son? Need I remind you, Jason is *my* ward?"

Though Rand was smiling, Rose noticed a small frown appeared on the bridge of his nose between his eyebrows. "I was not aware you were considering a marriage for Jason. If you ask my opinion, I think he's a little young yet for you to be making marriage arrangements for him." He continued, turning to the earl, who was watching their byplay with fascination, "But of course, as guardian of the boy, my wife needs not my approval to conclude a betrothal agreement."

Rose smiled up at Lord Lincoln. "There, you see, my lord. I hope I have erased all doubts you may have had, and you will consider my proposal."

"Very well. I shall consider it. Have your steward's clerk send the documents to mine and I shall go over the proposed betrothal." After handing his chalice to a passing servant,

Lord Lincoln bowed and bid them good eve. "Sir Rand, Lady Rosalyn."

The king's musicians, having finished setting up their instruments, began to play a lively country dance. Rand pressed his hand against the small of Rose's back and, leaning in, whispered in her ear, "Come, wife, let us dance," then led her onto the dance floor.

Heat seeped through the fabric of her dress. Breathless from her negotiations, Rose assured herself. She acknowledged his bow with a curtsy.

Holding hands, they jumped, shuffled, and swirled in a circle, then parted to dance with other partners. When they met again, the shock of his warm hands swirled up her arms. Her face flushed. The fool just grinned and gave her a teasing wink. They repeated the pattern of dance steps twice more before the music stopped.

Rose, her chest heaving, could not help smiling, the excitement of the dance thrumming in her blood. She stared up at Rand, whose gray-green eyes blazed with desire. The heat in his intense gaze kindled her blood. He tugged her off the floor and out of the dining hall. She followed, unresisting, heart pumping excitedly. When he pulled her into a secluded alcove, her lips met his hungry mouth as it came down on hers.

Strong arms pulled her against his hard, unyielding body and molded them together chest to chest, thigh to thigh. His tongue thrust into her mouth, hot and wet and rough. He sought her tongue with bold slashes, sending shivers down her back, one ripple at a time, like waves upon a shore.

Silky breath shimmered across her neck at his whisper, "God, you make me so hot I want to rip off my clothes."

He kissed her again, long and hard, slow and soft. Then his lips shifted, slowly trailing down the long column of her neck, and settling at the base, where her pulse leapt. He licked her there and then pressed his lips to her neck and sucked the soft flesh into his mouth. It tingled and throbbed, making her crazy with desperation.

Hooking her leg beneath her thigh, he wrapped her quivering limb around his hip. His hand gathered up her tunic skirt to her waist, skimmed up her exposed thigh, and gripped her bare buttock. A shivery caress shot straight to her core. She recoiled.

The combination of desire and shame made her stomach roil.

"Nay, this is wrong." Her voice hoarse with desire, her plea came out too softly. She was weak, wicked, and wanton. Everything Bertram had accused her of.

She bucked against Rand to push him off, but he pressed harder into her and his mouth returned to hers, cutting off her denial. Her mind blanked all emotion. She went completely stiff and closed her lips tight.

Desire, thick and sluggish, pounded through Rand. His phallus was hard to the point of pain. But in his arms, Rose had stiffened and clamped her mouth shut. He dropped her leg and lifted his head to stare down at her in confusion.

The sudden cold withdrawal where once burned a seething inferno withered his desire like an unexpected early frost on the vine. "Rose, what's wrong?"

"Prithee, release me," she mumbled, staring down at her toes.

Rand stepped back immediately.

"I am sorry. My behavior was wanton and I regret inflicting my licentious behavior on you. It won't happen again," she said, her voice quivering. Her eyes flickered briefly to his. The big blue centers were glazed with shame and a glossy tear slid down her cheek.

Rand reached out to comfort her, to deny her contention, but she slipped away and headed toward the dining hall.

He fisted his hand and slammed it into the stone wall. Pain radiated through his knuckles, the skin scraped raw and bloody. Frustration coiled in his gut and gnawed at his innards. He felt useless in the face of Rose's emotional pain.

The depth of abuse she'd received from Bertram had been both physical and mental. Now he suspected it had been much more flagitious. What had the man done to her to so warp her thinking and repress her passions, her spirit for life? He must have derided her passionate nature as wicked and wanton. Her own words hinted at such.

Rand wanted to heal her and prove to her that her desires were natural and beautiful, not amoral and wicked. But he realized that was impossible. He'd have to be satisfied with the knowledge that with his marriage to her, she'd never have to endure again the physical intimacies she so abhorred.

·

Lady Rosalyn returned to the dining hall and slid along the fringes of the crowd to slump into a darkened alcove. But her attempt not to draw attention to herself failed. One man in particular followed her progress from the moment she entered the vaulted chamber. He'd been waiting for the opportunity to get her alone for days. Since the day she rejected him and humiliated him before the whole court.

Sitting on a bench, Lady Rosalyn stared down at her hands folded in her lap. Golan smiled with evil intent as he slipped into the alcove. Her head jerked up at his entrance, her eyes going wide with fear. Excited, his cock stiffened as straight as a pike.

When she attempted to get up, he blocked her exit and she was forced to remain seated.

"Lady Rosalyn, 'tis a pleasure indeed."

"W-what do you want?"

"Like all women, you are corrupt and amoral. I merely wish to warn you that I shall take my due pleasure from you in good time." He reached out and caressed his finger along her cheek. She flinched, drawing her head back to escape his touch. "You shall not always have a horde of people to protect you."

"If you dare harm me, my husband will kill you. I know you have not forgotten the beating he gave you the last time you touched me. Your face still bears the marks of your insolence."

Golan touched his bruised cheek. "Your *husband*," he snarled, "will not be safe from my wrath either. I shall make you both pay for your impudence and cheating me of my rightful claim."

He leaned down and pinched her chin between his finger and thumb. "I shall see you all pay. Even your precious heir shall suffer for your defiance."

At the threat to her son, a hand squeezed Rose's lungs and cut off her breath. She pulled her chin free of Golan's grip and hissed, "If you harm my son, I'll cut out your heart and shove it down your throat."

His hate-filled gaze burned into hers. "Tsk, tsk, you are a bloodthirsty wench. Mayhap the rumors are true and you did kill your husband."

She gasped, her heart pumping with a mixture of rage and fear. "I suggest you leave. *Now!* Before I create a scene in front of the whole court. Then I would be forced to tell the king what precipitated it. Rand is his cousin and one of his most valued knights. Edward would not be best pleased to learn that you threatened him."

"Go ahead, make a scene. I shall just tell the king you mis-understood me."

"So be it. You leave me no choice." Rose lurched up from her bench and opened her mouth to say loudly, "Sir Go—"

A young lord and lady who had their backs to the alcove turned their heads to stare.

Golan hissed, "Very well. I am leaving. But this is not over." He slunk away quickly.

Rose plopped back down on the bench. Releasing a deep breath, she pressed her hands to her knees to stop them from knocking together in belated fear. Then a slow smile of satisfaction graced her lips and her chest puffed up with pride, for standing up to Golan, and not cowering as she'd done so many times in the past.

Men of Golan's character were secretive and duplicitous, their vile and vengeful nature concealed from society by their respected positions as knights or barons of the realm. The last thing Sir Golan would want to do is incur the wrath of the king. He'd seek his revenge in a way that would not draw suspicion upon himself.

Rose needed to warn Rand, but she was afraid he would challenge the knight to a trial by battle, this time to the death, and she knew Rand was not yet healed from the injury he received in the joust. That would play right into Sir Golan's hands.

But what frightened her the most was the threat to her son. Would Sir Golan really go so far as to harm the boy? Rose jumped up, a flutter of panic in her chest. She had to speak to Rand, find a way to warn him without revealing that Golan had threatened her.

If it were not for Jason, she would have died long ago. When he was born she'd found a reason to live despite the abuse Bertram heaped on her. Now Bertram was dead and she was married to Rand. But one thing had not changed: her love for her son. Jason was her whole life. She would protect him with her last breath if need be.

Rose began searching the crowd. Her eyes jumping from man to man, finding very few blonds.

"Lady Rosalyn," someone called.

Rose turned. Will sidled past Lady Lynette, one of the queen's ladies-in-waiting, and stopped before her. "My lady, I have been looking everywhere for you. Sir Rand—"

She grabbed Will's arm. "Is he all right?" Will started, gazing at her in surprise. "Pray, answer me."

"Fear not." He patted her hand. "My lord asked that I escort you back to Strand House. The king has called an emergency session of his council, and Sir Rand expects it shall be very late before it is over."

Rose floated, wrapped in a warm cocoon, her cheek cushioned against a hard yet warm yielding surface. A comforting, safe feeling enveloped her, but a nagging sense that she was supposed to do something important kept pulling her back to wakefulness. Her eyes were heavy, and she struggled to open them. Then she was falling, falling until she landed on a fluffy mattress, a blanket pulled up to her chin. She blinked, once, twice.

Rand stood over her, a finger to his lips. "Shhh, go back to sleep."

She'd been sitting on the bench at the foot of the bed waiting for Rand to return from court. Apparently, she must have fallen asleep, and when he'd found her he had carried her to bed.

She closed her eyes, about to drift asleep, when that persistent feeling of doom pricked her again. Rolling onto her side, she pillowed her hands beneath her cheek. Rand stood before the washstand, his back in shadow and his front gleaming golden in the candles' glow. He was naked except for a sherte tossed over his shoulder as he washed.

Rose swallowed a gasp. Her eyes grew wide. She'd never seen Rand naked. Though they made love once before, theirs had been a brief, swift, furious coupling against the chamber door, with only minimal adjustments of their nightclothes to satisfactorily accomplish the deed.

The branched candle stand on the washstand glimmered across every ripple and indention of his muscular chest, stomach, and thighs. He rinsed the linen cloth in the basin again. When the cloth made contact with his face, he gasped. His stomach muscles flexed. The fleshy member between his legs jumped.

The hair at his groin was darker than the hair on his head, and springy. Were all men as large? Rose was amazed, for he was not even distended with desire, and he was huge.

The moisture in her mouth dried up. Her breath grew ragged. She made a small sound. Rand pulled on his sherte, spinning toward her. She snapped her eyes shut.

"Rose, are you awake?" Rand moved closer to the bed and gazed suspiciously at her. Her eyes were closed, but he'd heard a mewling cry and swore she had been watching him.

"Rose?"

Her eyes fluttered open. "Rand. You have returned." She peered around, taking in her surroundings as though confused, but her cheeks were flushed with what he thought was embarrassment.

The suspicion that she'd been watching him had a predictable effect on him. But he kept a tight rein on his wayward lust. He would not inflict any more pain on Rose because he could not stop wanting her. "You should go to sleep. 'Tis very late," he said, voice gruff with restraining his desire.

He flicked a blanket out and laid it and a pillow on the pallet he'd placed on the floor earlier.

Rose scooted up in bed, pulling the coverlet up to her chest and placing her hands in her lap. "I would speak to you first. About Sir Golan." She paused, her words hesitant, then said, "I do not trust the man and fear he means to do us harm."

Rand frowned. "Has the man done something to upset—"

"Nay," she said quickly. Too quickly? he wondered? "I am just concerned Golan means to retaliate against you. He does not seem like a man who takes kindly to being thwarted."

"Though I am flattered you are worried about me, you need not be. I shall not underestimate Golan's character again. To that end, I have made arrangements to have him watched. He will not make a move that I do not know about."

She plucked the coverlet on her lap. "You cannot have the man watched forever."

"Certes. One day there will be a reckoning between us, but for now it will have to wait. The king's council declared war on Llewelyn."

A hand flew to her throat. "Lord have mercy. Why did you not tell me sooner?" Rose flipped the covers off and threw her legs over the side of the bed.

Distracted by her bare toes and slender ankles, he said, "It was very late and I did not want to worry you when it could wait till morning. There is naught you can do anyway."

Rose jumped out of bed. "There you are wrong." She dashed into the wardrobe and returned carrying an armful of drab widow's clothes. "I must leave for Ayleston Castle immediately. Jason is in danger. With war declared, raids will increase and preparations must be made to increase the guard."

She returned to the wardrobe and dragged out an iron-bound chest.

"Rose, 'tis the middle of the night. Aside from the fact 'tis too dangerous to travel on the roads at night, arrangements must be made for the journey."

Grabbing the gowns from the bed, she tossed them into the chest. "Nay. 'Tis imperative we leave now." Her words came out muffled and breathless as she bent over, her hair hanging loose to the floor and shrouding her face.

His eyes flicked to her rounded bottom, her sheer chemise molded to her bare skin. The shadow between her bottom cheeks stoked his senses and lured him into temptation. He wanted to reach out and run his hands over the soft firmness, to grab hold and clutch her to him as his fingers dipped into the indentions that separated the cheeks of her buttocks from her thighs.

His cock surged hard and erect. The sherte tented embarrassingly, and he prayed she would not look up and notice.

"There is no need for panic," he said. "Edward is sending the Earl of Warwick immediately to secure Chester and begin raising an army. But the bulk of the troops shall not advance into Wales and fight Llewelyn till next summer. We will leave for Ayleston in a day, two at most," he said adamantly.

She straightened, turning and pulling a wisp of loose hair from her mouth. Like a tug on a string, his gaze shot up from her bottom to her pinkened, wet lips.

"Naught you say can sway me. I am leaving tonight."

Entranced by her lips, the soft curve of the corners, the plump, fleshy sweetness, he did not hear her words at first. Then she slammed the chest shut and turned the key on the lock.

His jaw clenched at her stubbornness, and he crossed his arms over his chest. "On the morrow, I am to meet with Harwood to give him some final instructions before the *Argo* sets sail with the evening tide. Meanwhile, preparations for the journey to Ayleston are already under way. We leave the day after tomorrow. Together."

"I understand you must stay. But—"

"Nay, you do not understand. You are not going. You'll only endanger yourself, and I will not allow it."

A stubborn glint lit her crystalline eyes. "I'm going. You cannot keep me here."

"I can and I will." He lifted the chest and carried it into the wardrobe. He returned to the bedchamber. The room was empty. The door was open.

Swearing, he ran after her. She dashed down the stairs, her chemise billowing out behind her in full sail. The silvery glare of the moon illuminated her like a ghostly specter. He grabbed for her and clutched her linen shift. She screamed. He reeled her in, lifted her in his arms, and carried her back to their chamber.

"What is wrong with you, Rose? Where do you expect to go in your nightclothes?"

She flailed in his arms, shrieking, "You don't understand! Jason is there alone without me! He is in danger and I must go to him!"

Rand set her down and dropped the bar over the door. "You

cannot go to him in naught but your chemise, without an escort. You are acting like a lunatic."

She flipped her hair out of her eyes and tugged her night-dress down to straighten it. She glared, her eyes narrowed, and her breath coming in pants.

"You are right," she gritted out between her teeth. "I am sorry. But you don't know what it's like to have a son whom you love so much you will do anything to protect."

A fist to the gut knocked the breath from Rand. Envy and sadness rocked him to the core. Rose's selfless defense of her son brought to the surface a well of emotions he kept buried. He envied Rose her son. If he had a son, he would be a loving and protecting father, the kind of man his own father had never been.

The old Lord Montague insisted his son marry the heiress who would bring her wealthy dowry of Bordeaux wine estates to the marriage. But Rand's father was a proud and vain man. When his peers ridiculed him for marrying a woman who came from peasant stock, despite her royal father, he became resentful and hateful as the years passed. That hatred mani-fested itself into an emotionally and physically violent man.

Now Rose and her son were his family. The fear of failure was a burden that weighed heavily on him. He despised his weakness but could not relinquish the doubts that assailed him. He felt like that helpless adolescent who'd let his sister drown because he saved himself, then a year later watched his mother burn to death as he lay trapped beneath a collapsed beam. Yet he hid his fears from Rose.

Rand skimmed his fingers through his hair, pushing it back off his face. "I understand you wish to protect Jason. I com-mend you for it. But we must proceed rationally. Though we cannot leave for another day, I'll send a messenger immedi-ately to Ayleston with instructions for the castellan to increase the castle guard and check everyone entering the castle gates. Jason will be safe until our arrival."

"You cannot know that. Anything could happen to him. Children are susceptible to all kinds of illnesses and accidents." Rose began to pace, her hand clutched to her throat.

The truth of the statement cut Rand raw. He winced inwardly, his guilt over Juliana's death never far from his thoughts.

Outwardly, he exuded confidence. "That is even true when we are not at war, Rose. Let us not borrow trouble," he said and clutched her shoulders to still her agitation. "I do not suspect to see unrest in the northeastern Marches for weeks yet, but it can't hurt to be cautious if it will help ease your mind. I will go now and send a messenger on his way with orders for the castellan at Ayleston to make the changes we discussed and to inform him of our imminent arrival."

Rose nodded her acceptance, even as a residual murmur of disquiet echoed within her. Rand could not know of her fears that Sir Golan intended harm to them all, including her son. The threat of hostilities with the Welsh increased her anxiety twofold. It was stressful and worrisome because, despite his assurances, Rose could not put her trust in Rand. Rand was the only thing standing between Sir Golan's intent to retaliate and Rose. She knew better than to put her faith in anyone other than herself. No one had protected her from Bertram, and her brief, sinful liaison with Rand had only endangered her more.

In the end, she had protected Jason. And she would do so again. At first light, she would send a message to her steward to put a guard on Jason.

Rand need never know the truth. What was one more secret when she'd already kept from Rand the devastating facts surrounding Bertram's death and her son's paternity?

Shivering, Rose crawled into bed and pulled the bedclothes up. She drew Jason's necklace off over her head and stared down at it, rubbing her fingers over the smooth, oval brown stone. And prayed Rand never discovered he was Jason's father.

She could not bear his hatred.

Chapter Twelve

The following evening, Rose opened the spice cupboard with a key from the chatelaine's ring of keys hanging from her girdle. A variety of long boxes lined the shelves. She opened the lid on a box containing saffron and measured out a small amount. She gave the cook the spice and precise instructions on how to prepare the sauce for the fish. Her family would be arriving soon for supper to bid them farewell before she and Rand departed for Ayleston on the morrow.

Everything had to be perfect. She did not want her family to know of the unusual arrangement she and Rand had made to keep their marriage chaste. By serving them a wonderful meal and keeping up an appearance of a normal marriage, she hoped to prevent her parents from worrying about her happiness. After Bertram died, she'd revealed hints about their marriage difficulties, and she knew her father especially blamed himself for agreeing to the marriage.

But Rose knew where the blame truly belonged. It was her impulsive, reckless, passionate nature that had led to her disastrous marriage. The moment she'd laid eyes on Bertram, she had wanted him for her husband. Her father's one true weakness was in loving her too much. So much so that he had given her everything she ever wanted. And that included Bertram.

"Milady. 'Tis late. Your guests will be arriving soon and you have yet to dress. Go, now. I promise everything shall be prepared exactly as you ordered," the cook said.

Rose looked down and saw a splatter of grease on the tip of her slipper and a caking of flour on the skirt of her work dress. Her hand fluttered to her headdress. It was askew and wisps of hair had come free. "Oh my, you are right. I must go and clean up."

She rushed out of the kitchens and up the outer stairs to her bedchamber.

Rose stopped abruptly at the threshold. Rand sat on a bench at the foot of the bed pulling on his boots. Dressed in a calf-length surcoate of a green hue found in peacock feathers, he glanced up at her entrance.

The back of her hand flew to her cheek in embarrassment. "Good Lord, I must look afright. I pray you will pardon me while I dress in proper attire to receive our guests."

Without saying a word, Rand walked loose-limbed, predator-like the short distance to her. His eyes, holding her transfixed, appeared extremely gray against the green of his tunic. In a slow, melting caress, his gaze moved over her face, down her breasts, hips, and thighs, and then returned to her face. A rush of heat settled in her cheeks.

He tapped the end of her nose with his forefinger, brought his finger to his mouth, and licked the white substance that had transferred from her nose to his digit.

"Hmmm." An amused yet tender smile quirked his lips. "Flour."

Reaching out his hand, he pushed a strand of hair off of her face. Strong, masculine fingers grazed her cheek. A shiver curled down her spine.

His smile slipped, and an odd light appeared in his gaze. "For what 'tis worth, I think you look absolutely lovely as you are. But I understand you would wish to refresh yourself before your family arrives. I'll go now so you may dress." He walked around her and opened the bedchamber door.

"Rand," she called out before he left the room.

He spun around, his hand still holding the latch. "Aye, Rosie, what is it?"

For the first time the hated nickname felt like a caress rather than a childish endearment.

She had no idea what she meant to say. There were so many things she could say.

That she was sorry he was forced to marry her. Sorry that she was not like normal wives who willingly bedded their husbands to bear children. That he deserved a bride of his choosing—a woman whom he could love, admire, and respect.

Instead she blurted out, "Thank you."

His brow puckered. "For what?"

"I never thanked you for preventing my marriage to Sir Golan. Though you didn't wish to marry me, you did so to protect me. You even braved battle with Sir Golan to accomplish it. I know I've seemed ungrateful for the sacrifice I made, but I do thank you."

"I do not deserve your thanks. I should have done more, so much more, and a long time ago. I shall never forgive myself for that." A fierce frown on his face, he closed the door behind him as he left.

Rose ambled into the wardrobe puzzling over Rand's enigmatic words. He should have done what and how long ago? The comment was very vague. What could he possibly be sorry for? Surely he was not referring to her marriage to Bertram? Rand was in the Holy Land when she met and married her first husband. And after Rand returned from the Crusades there was naught he could do.

Without thought, she plucked a surcoate and tunic off a peg and selected a matching pair of slippers. She returned to the bedchamber and tossed them onto the bed. She removed her outer garments and washed her face, chest, and hands at the washstand as her thoughts returned.

The Church considered marriage sacrosanct. A husband had authority to do what he would with his wife. Even beat her for any reason. He was lord and master. And though some churchmen might abhor wife beating, a marriage could not be dissolved on such grounds.

Furthermore, a woman who left her husband could be dragged back to him unwillingly and without recourse. Rose's powerful father could have protected her. But she had been too afraid to leave Bertram until he threatened Jason.

So there was naught Rand could have done. As such his comments made no sense to her.

She changed into a clean chemise and stared down at her choice of gown. It was the only colorful one she owned. The light blue surcoate was embroidered with red rosebuds at the flared cuffs and rounded neck. She refused to consider that she had unknowingly chosen it to please Rand.

It was the perfect choice to convince her parents she was content with her new marriage. She had changed her dull widow's attire for that of a happily married bride. They need never know the marriage was a pretense and, therefore, there would never be children from the union, or at least none that they knew of.

She squelched the tremor of guilt that rattled her and began dressing.

Savoring a glass of wine, Rand sat in one of two chairs in the corner next to the fireplace. Alex was sitting beside him in the other. When Rose entered the Great Hall, his friend's voice faded to a distant hum. Rand blinked. His eyes grew wider at the loveliness of his wife. She wore a shimmering surcoate of a bright blue hue akin to a clear summer sky, which made her almond-shaped eyes brighter. Embroidered red rosebuds around the cuffs and neck enhanced her delicate wrists and long, graceful neck.

But what shocked Rand the most was that Rose had decided to forego the hated wimple and veil headdress. Rose's vibrant reddish-copper hair hung down to her waist and was held back with a simple veil and circlet. As she made her way to the dais table, where Kat, Lord Briand, and Lady Briand conversed, she waved to him and Alex, with a brief flutter of her hand.

Rand was so stunned he could do naught except nod his head, to the back of hers, because his reaction was slow. The glow of the chandelier highlighted shimmering streaks of gold in her hair.

How fanciful of her! She was never fanciful. Mayhap farcical, but never fanciful.

"You might want to close your gaping maw, friend. You look utterly ridiculous."

Rand snapped his jaw shut, jerked his head around, and glared at his gloating friend.

Alex chuckled, a huge grin on his face. His black shoulder-length hair was pulled back in a leather thong. The hand not holding a chalice moved to his chest and patted over his heart several times. "My, my. I believe thou heart is smitten. With my sister, no less."

"Absolutely not," Rand said. "You cannot possibly surmise such a thing."

Alex waved his hand at Rand's head. "'Tis writ all over your face."

Rand's hand flew to his face. He searched his facial features—wide-set eyes, bold cheekbones, dimples, and lop-sided grin in place—naught unusual there.

Alex chuckled again. "You won't find the truth of your heart in that way. 'Tis the way you look at Rose with your eyes." He cleared his throat. "Anyway, I cannot describe it except that as you stared at her, 'twas as though you were pouring out your soul to her."

"Do not be absurd. You simply read pleasant surprise in my eyes. 'Tis nice to see her wearing more flattering attire rather than her usual drab widow garb."

Alex scoffed. "Does your heart beat rapidly out of control whenever Rose is near you? Do you find your thoughts inexplicably drawn to her during the day when your mind should be on the important duties you must fulfill for King Edward? Does she frustrate you and challenge you at every turn, yet your heart still misses a beat whenever you see her smile, or laugh, or cry?"

Shock held him still, and then he blurted out, "How could you know all that?"

Alex stared at him with a look only a friend could muster that said, "Did you really just ask me such a stupid question?"

"Forget I said that. But your relationship with Kat is different, your—" Rand could not even tell his best friend that his marriage was not consummated and he never intended to copulate with his bride.

"Aye, you were saying?"

Rand shifted in his chair. "You and Kat love each other. Neither I nor Rose ever intended to marry, yet duty on my part and sheer desperation on Rose's has bound us together forever in holy wedlock."

"Certes. But I did not love Kat when we married. Our marriage was arranged, like that of most other couples of our station." Alex turned his gaze to his bride. Kat threw back her head and laughed at something Lord Briand said. A besotted smile spread across Alex's face. "Now I cannot imagine my life without her."

"You are missing the point. Rose and I both vowed never to marry, for reasons you are very well aware of. 'Tis not an auspicious way to begin as man and wife."

Alex swung back to Rand. "I understand why Rose never wished to marry again." His eyes narrowed. "But surely you did not intend to punish yourself for your mother's and sister's deaths for the rest of your life?"

Rand took a deep draught of wine. Alex could not know that it was fear more than aught else that kept him from making theirs a true marriage.

Alex persisted despite Rand's silence. "There is naught keeping you from having a fulfilling marriage with Rose now it is a fait accompli. You just have to find a way to persuade Rose to trust you, to convince her that you are the man she needs despite her bad experience with Bertram."

But how could Rand persuade Rose to trust him when he did not trust himself to protect her? 'Twas better for all concerned that their relationship remained chaste and loveless.

After supper, Rose sat with Kat by the fire. A great clap of masculine laughter rang out in the Great Hall. Rose's gaze swept across the room to the dais table. Rand, grinning, sitting at the table opposite Lord and Lady Briand, shoved his fingers through his hair and pushed it back off his cheek. His dimples twinkled at her like distant stars in the northern sky. The tugging sensation low in her belly caught her unawares and took her breath away.

In the chair beside Rose, Kat murmured, "Good God, you love Rand."

Her head jerked back to her friend, whose gray gaze was open wide in disbelief and pleasure. "I do not love Rand. What would make you say such a thing?"

Rand's handsome goldenness was a constant distraction despite her attempt to ignore him. But she certainly did not love him.

"I have never seen you look at another man that way before."

"What do you mean? How do I look at Rand?"

"'Tis difficult to explain, but your eyes light up like candle flames when you look at him."

"How remarkable. I've never known you to be so poetical. Whatever you think you saw, 'tis certainly not love. Love is a manifestation of the poets that men use to their advantage and to the detriment of women."

"So you do not believe in love? Then you must believe that Alex does not love me, nor I love him."

"I believe you and Alex love each other. And that Mother and Father love one another. But you're the exception. The love I have to give is completely reserved for my son."

"Rose, you have the most generous heart I know. With more than enough love to give. Will you not open your heart and give Rand a chance, give love a chance? He is a good man and I believe he has feelings for you that he keeps deeply buried."

"I'm sorry to disappoint you, Kat, but Rand does not love me. Why, he did not even hesitate when I made it a condition of our marriage that we keep it chaste and in name only."

Strangely, that still hurt. Though she got exactly what she wanted, Rose wondered why Rand had been so quick to accept the condition when it was within his right to bed her.

"You mean you and Rand have never—"

"Aye, we have not consummated the marriage and we never shall," Rose interrupted. "Our marriage is one of convenience only."

She could never reveal even to her best friend that she had committed adultery with Rand. She was ashamed of her weakness. And, obviously, Rand had no desire to repeat the experience. Aye, he'd kissed her twice since their marriage, but her wanton behavior provoked him.

Kat reached out and squeezed Rose's hand. "I have no idea why Rand agreed to such a condition."

Because he does not desire me, Rose thought silently. She need only look at the women he bedded in the past to know why. He preferred the voluptuous curves and ample breasts of women like his current mistress, Lady Elena Chartres. It was the only explanation that made sense to Rose. If Rand truly wanted her in a carnal way, naught would stop him from trying to bed her again.

"But I do know this," Kat continued. "Ever since you were a young girl, you and Rand have had an unusual relationship. He was always teasing you, and you were forever seeking his attention. Then Rand left on the Crusade and you met and married Bertram."

Rand leaving on the Crusade had devastated Rose. Secretly, she'd hoped one day they would wed. Feeling lost and vulnerable when he left, Rose found solace with an adoring Bertram. He was gallant and charming and very attentive. It was only later she'd realized what kind of man he truly was.

"Have you never wondered why Rand teased you so relentlessly? Why he enjoyed calling you Rosie when he knew it annoyed you?"

Because Rand was an inveterate tease and enjoyed tormenting her, she thought.

Kat did not wait for an answer. "I shall tell you why. Because beneath all the teasing, I believe Rand has feelings for you. And despite your disavowal, I believe you feel something for him too. As a wise woman once told me, you owe it to yourself to discover what underlying feelings you truly have for your husband. If you do not, you will regret it for the rest of your life."

Rose shifted in her chair, uncomfortable having her words turned against her.

Only a few months ago, when Alex had returned from captivity in the Holy Land to win back the bride he'd abandoned, Rose had encouraged Kat to give Alex a second chance. To explore the feelings she still had for her husband despite his betrayal, or she'd regret it forever.

"I know you wish the best for me, Kat. But my relationship with Rand is nothing like yours and Alex's. Certes. Rand and I are content just as things are. So you need not worry about me or your cousin."

Kat opened her mouth to speak, but a shadow fell upon her. Rose and Kat looked up at Alex. Placing his left hand on the back of Kat's chair, he bent down and kissed his wife on her pale golden cheek. He smoothed the palm of his other hand over Kat's slightly rounded stomach.

A tender smile spread over Alex's wide lips. "This one hasn't given you any trouble tonight, has she, my love?"

Rose had spoken truly. Kat and Alex's relationship was different from hers and Rand's. The love radiating between Kat and Alex was blinding.

As Rose watched them, a wave of emotion swelled up in the back of her throat. She swallowed, shocked to realize how envious she was of their love. No matter what she'd told herself, deep down she wanted what they had. She wanted Rand's love—wholehearted and unwavering.

Sadly, even if Rand could love her, she did not know who she was anymore. She was just a cold, hard shell of her former self. Bertram had molded her into the perfectly biddable, passionless wife he wanted. And she didn't know how to find the woman she once was, the woman who enjoyed life to the fullest, who never suppressed her emotions and feelings.

Chapter Thirteen

"Oh, and to soak my body in a hot, scented bath. Heavenly," Lady Alison said with a dreamy smile on her face.

Riding atop her mount, Rose listened with half an ear to Alison's excited ramblings about having a hot bath and soft bed to sleep in this eve when they arrived at Ayleston. Tired, wet, and cold, Rose was just as happy to have those things, but her excitement was reserved for her son. She missed Jason desperately and wanted to assure herself he was safe and unharmed.

As they approached the last stretch of woods south of Ayleston, a ray of sun broke through the clouds and the drizzling rain of the last two days ceased. Holding on to her reins with one hand, she slipped the hood of her cloak back and raised her face to the warm sun.

After traveling several miles into the woods, the men riding in front of Rose surged forward on their horses. Sir Justin and Rand's squire, Will, came to Rose's and Alison's sides protectively and made them halt.

"Sir Justin, why have we stopped? Where are Rand and the rest of the men going?"

"A cart was attacked on the road up ahead by some outlaws.

Sir Rand ordered us to remain behind to protect you while they hunt down the bastards."

Rose gasped. "Was anyone hurt?" Without waiting for an answer, she kneed her palfrey into a trot.

Sir Justin groaned. Alison moaned.

"My lady," Sir Justin pleaded, voice raised, "Rand made it clear I was to protect you—"

"I am not stopping you from protecting me," she hollered back over her shoulder. "Merely going to the aid of some travelers in need."

"But, my lady, you don't understand. They are dead. Sir Rand did not wish to expose you to the bloody carnage."

Rose caught sight of a cart tipped sideways on its broken front wheel, an assortment of wool cloth strewn across the ground. A merchant and his rotund wife clutched one another in the driver's seat, a single lance run through them both, holding them upright together in a grotesque parody of a lover's embrace.

Rose halted and stared aghast. Her hand flew to her mouth as her stomach rumbled with nausea. A sudden moan echoed from somewhere within the trees.

"Sir Justin, Will, did you hear that?" Rose dismounted.

She cocked her head and listened. The wind rustled the canopy of leaves. Sir Justin stepped up beside her, while Will helped Alison dismount from her mule.

The moan, louder, came again to the right of the downed cart. Rose grabbed her basket of medicinal supplies off the pack mule and made for the trees.

Justin stepped in front of her. "We don't know if they are friend or foe." He turned to Will. "Stay here and guard Lady Rosalyn and Alison." To Rose he added, "Once I determine it is safe, then you may see to the care of whoever is in the forest." Rose nodded and then watched Justin brush past a bush and enter into the trees.

Moments later Justin returned and waved her forward.

Less than a hundred yards in, Rose saw a lad with short, curly dark hair sprawled facedown on the ground in the wet, moldy leaves.

Kneeling down beside him, she placed her basket nearby and then checked his limbs for broken bones. "Justin. Gently, help me turn the boy over."

They turned him over onto his back.

The boy moaned, opening his eyelids and blinking. His gaze shot to Justin. Fear flared in his eyes and he cringed away.

"Easy there. No one is going to hurt you. I'm a healer and want to help you." She reached over and held up her basket. "See. I have medicine in here."

The boy sat up, groaning. "Who's he," the boy asked, suspicious, pointing to Sir Justin.

"He protects me. Now let me take a look at your head. You have a nasty cut on your temple."

She leaned forward and gently probed around the wound. "You don't appear to have any other injuries. Does it hurt anywhere else?"

"Nay, just my head." His voice was soft and raspy.

"Can you tell me what your name is?"

"Of course. I'm not daft. My name's Geoffrey."

She tipped his chin up and stared into his eyes. They were unusually blue, the lashes curled on the end, but they appeared clear and focused. "Are you dizzy? Do you have blurry vision?"

He pulled his chin away and tried to stand up, but groaned and sat back down. Clutching his head, he moaned, "Oh, my head hurts."

Rose lifted the lid on her basket and retrieved a linen bandage. She ripped a small strip off and doused it with water from the flask she carried in her purse.

She dabbed the wet cloth against his temple. As she wiped

away the blood she asked again, "Do you have any dizziness or blurred sight?"

He crossed his arms over his chest. "Nay. I see fine."

Next, she dabbed an all-heal ointment on the cut, and wrapped the linen bandage around his head to cover the wound.

Her voice gentle, she probed, "Can you tell us what happened to you, Geoffrey?"

"Mother, Father, and I—" He gasped and staggered to his feet. Short and somewhat stout, the boy appeared to be about four and ten. "I need to get back to my parents. They'll be worrying about me."

Justin stepped forward and stopped him. "Not yet. We need to ask a couple more questions. How did you get your injury and end up in the forest separated from the cart?"

"When the brigands attacked, Mother ordered me to hide in the trees. I ran, but one of the men caught me and hit me in the head with a club." A stubborn glint entered his eyes. "Now, I answered your questions. I want to see my parents." He dashed past Justin and back toward the road.

"Geoffrey, wait—" Rose hollered, wanting to stop him from seeing the horrific sight of his slaughtered parents.

Rose and Justin followed quickly. To the rear of the cart Will had his arms around Alison, giving her comfort.

The boy stood beside the driver's seat staring at his parents in disbelief. A single tear ran down his small dark-skinned face. "They're dead. The bastards killed 'em."

"Aye. I am sorry, Geoffrey. I wanted to spare you seeing them this way," Rose said.

Silence, except for the rustle of the leaves and dripping water from the trees.

"Get it out!" the boy shouted suddenly.

"What?" Justin asked.

He ran to his mother's side and tried to pull the lance out.

"Get it out! Get it out!" he screamed in a high-pitched voice over and over. "I want it out! *Now!*" His voice cracked.

Seeing the boy's grief, her heart thumped painfully. Rose nodded to Justin.

Justin went to the boy and pulled him aside, then waved Will to the opposite side of the cart. "You pull, I'll push. When the lance is free, we'll put them in the back of the cart."

Lady Alison kept her back to the gruesome sight. Grunting and groaning, the men pulled the lance out, lifted the pair up and over the driver's seat, and laid them down in the flat bottom of the cart. The boy climbed in next to his parents, and after closing their eyes shut, he covered them with a dark woolen cloak that had spilt from a broken chest.

When he scrambled down, Rose noticed his right hand was clenched so tightly into a fist that his knuckles were white.

"What have you got in your hand, Geoffrey?"

The boy opened his hand. In his palm was a small gold cross on a delicate chain. A pointed edge had punctured his palm and a bead of blood ran down his hand.

"'Twas my mother's. A gift from my father."

Horse hooves and jangling tack pierced the dense silence.

Geoffrey swiveled his head back and forth as though looking for a place to hide. "Run. They're back."

Will and Justin drew their swords.

Rose turned her gaze down the road to the sound of the approaching horses. Rand, a black surcoate over his hauberk and his shield at his back, rode at the head of his men. He sat straight and proud upon his mount, sunlight glinting off his mailed coif.

"Be easy, Geoffrey. 'Tis my husband and his men. You have naught to fear from them."

Will and Justin sheathed their swords. Rand dismounted, pulled off his gauntlets, then pushed back his mailed coif and ran a hand back through his hair. Sir Justin and the squire approached Rand. Though Rose was unable to hear their exchange, she assumed they were giving Rand an account of what had happened.

Rand lifted his head sharply and pierced her with his green-gray gaze. His smile never wavered, but Rose got the impression he was struggling to control his anger.

Rose clutched the boy to her, wondering whom she thought she was protecting, the boy or herself.

Rand made straight for her. She looked away, and taking Geoffrey's hand in hers she examined the shallow wound.

"We'll need to clean and bandage it to prevent it from becoming infected."

A shadow fell on Rose. She released Geoffrey and gazed up at Rand, her chin raised stubbornly.

Rand clutched her shoulders tightly and pulled her to him. "I gave my men strict orders to stay behind to guard your safety." She swore she saw fear glimmer in his eyes, but realized she was mistaken when he added, "Why must you," exasperation creeping into his voice, "continue to defy my attempts to protect you?"

She jerked free of his grip. Defensively, she said, "I was in no danger. Besides, as you can see, we found Geoffrey alone and injured in the woods. Who knows what would have happened to him if we had not found him."

Rand's gaze shifted to the lad. Staring at him for a moment, Rand cocked his head, eyes narrowing.

The boy shifted nervously. Rose put her hand on his shoulder to ease his fear.

Rand turned back to her. "'Tis not the point. I do not give orders arbitrarily. When I do give them, I expect to be obeyed. 'Tis my duty to safeguard you—"

"Verily, we all know how greatly you have sacrificed by marrying me for duty's sake," she said bitterly.

His lips froze. "Exactly, so next time I expect you to follow my orders. Understand?"

They stared at one another, a tense silence between them.

The lad groaned, pressing his hand to his forehead. "My lady, do you have something for my head? It hurts."

Relieved at the interruption, Rose turned back to Geoffrey. "Of course. But we'll have to wait till we arrive at Ayleston. I'll need to brew a tincture to give you for the pain."

Rand, his fear slowly receding, inquired, "Geoffrey, where was your family traveling to when you were attacked?"

It was getting late and they needed to continue on their way if they were to make Ayleston before nightfall. But first he had to decide what to do with the boy.

"We were traveling to Chester to sell wool cloth to the soldiers who are going to be arriving soon for the conflict with Wales."

"Can you tell us about your family and where they reside?" Rand thought the boy looked familiar but could not be sure.

"I have no family, except Mother and Father. And they are dead now," he said sullenly.

"You may stay at Ayleston if you wish," Rose said before Rand could respond. Her gaze, demure and sweet, met his. "Of course, 'tis up to my husband whether you can remain with us or not."

Who did she think she was fooling with her feigned solicitousness? Or did she really believe him so heartless that he would leave the boy to fend for himself? There was only one choice. The boy had nowhere else to go and was too young to be left behind. Rand was sure he could find some position for him at Ayleston, mayhap in the mews or stables.

"Of course, you are welcome at Ayleston, Geoffrey." Rand shouted to his men, "Will, the lad will ride with you! Mount up, men! We must make haste if we are to arrive at Ayleston before dusk!"

To the boy he said, "When we arrive at Ayleston, I'll send someone to come back for your parents so they can be buried properly."

Geoffrey mumbled his thanks and went to Will.

Rand led Rose to her palfrey.

His hands settled on her small waist. The warmth of her body flowed into his hands, her flowery scent, and the luscious feel of her, taunting him. He quickly lifted her and set her on her mount.

"Never disobey me again, madame," he said sternly.

Rand spun around, returned to his gelding, and mounted. "Let's ride!" he called out, spurring his horse forward into a canter.

Immediately, his thoughts returned to the moment he had realized Rose had disobeyed his orders and put herself in danger. It was his greatest fear that she would get into a dangerous situation and he would not be able to save her. A shadow of his fear still hounded him, though he hid it well from Rose. He would rather she believe him domineering than discover his secret failings.

Emerging from the woods, Rand gazed up at the soaring crenellated walls of Ayleston Castle. The shadows of dusk crept westward over the castle. Rose rode beside him. He'd wanted to arrive together as a united front to allay any fears or anxieties the people of Ayleston might have now that they had a new lord ruling over them.

Evangeline shook her head, snorting. "Easy, girl, we're almost home," Rose said.

Five miles southwest of the city of Chester, the castle, surrounded by a moat, lay nestled in the Dee River Valley. The eighty-foot-high stone curtain wall was D-shaped and encompassed an inner and outer bailey, which included the stone Keep and Great Hall, adjoining chapel, stables, gardens, orchard, fish pond, and various outbuildings.

Serfs and freemen alike stopped their work and watched curiously as their party wound through the village toward the western gated entrance. The horses' hooves clip-clopped loudly over the wooden drawbridge and cobbled passageway beneath the darkened castle gateway. They continued through the outer bailey, riding under an arch in the stone wall between the two baileys, before entering the inner courtyard.

Jason's nurse, Edith, stood before the Keep's steps holding her charge's hand. Rand helped Rose dismount. Jumping in place, the boy suddenly broke free.

Rand smiled seeing Jason run to greet his mother.

"Mama! Mama!" The boy's blond curly hair bounced with each step.

The boy collided against her knees. Rose laughed, then knelt down and hugged him. "I missed you, too, darling."

Jason proceeded to ramble as quickly as he could talk about all he had done in her absence.

When he took a deep breath, Rose expertly steered him toward Rand. "Jason, do you remember Sir Rand Montague? He's the knight King Edward sent to escort me to court."

"Of course, Mama." The little boy bowed, grinning. "Welcome to my home, Sir Rand."

Rand marveled; for one so young, it was an elegant and graceful bow.

"The king ordered Sir Rand and me to marry. He is now my husband and guardian of Ayleston."

His big, blue-green eyes, so much like his mother's, grew wide with excitement. "So he truly is my papa now?"

"Nay. He is not your papa. Remember we spoke of this? Your father is dead and no one can ever replace him."

His smile dimmed.

Rand knelt before him, the pointed tip of the shield on his back scraping the ground. "I can never replace your father, Jason, but I'd like us to be friends." Rand pulled a crudely carved toy out of the purse hanging from his sword belt. "Here. I made this for you. 'Tis a replica of my ship, the *Argo*. This carved one floats in the water like a real ship."

"A ship, for me?" His incredulous face tore straight to

Rand's heart. It was not a grand gift—just a simple toy he'd made from a piece of old driftwood he found on the riverbank near his London warehouse.

"Thank Sir Rand, Jason."

"Thank you, Sir Rand," Jason said, then promptly plopped onto the ground and began examining the boat.

Rose smiled tenderly at the boy.

Now that it was just the three of them in the courtyard alone, Rand pulled Rose aside out of Jason's hearing. "For the nonce, I must see that my men are settled and then speak with the castellan of Ayleston about the castle fortifications. But later, Rose, I'd like to have a frank discussion with you about Jason."

Rose stiffened, her gaze wide and incredulous. "What can you possibly wish to speak to me about concerning Jason? You may be the ward of his estate, but you have no authority over *my* son."

Rand noted the odd emphasis on the possessive and stored it away for further insight. "In principle, you are right. But as guardian of his estate, I cannot ignore the boy's welfare. I'd like to be kept abreast of your care of Jason—"

Her face flushed. "Surely you are not suggesting I am incapable of caring for my son properly?"

"Rose, I cannot discuss this with you now. As I said, there are other duties that need my immediate attention. We'll speak further regarding this later," he assured her and marched away quickly to the stables in the outer bailey.

Beneath her gown, her foot tapping, Rose fumed as she watched the arrogant lout walk away.

How dare he question the care and attention she gave to her son. Rand had no idea of the extreme depths she would go to in order to protect Jason. Everything she did, her whole existence centered round doing what was best for her son. And she would certainly not let Rand dictate to her how to be a good mother. Especially since he could not possibly know what it was like to be a parent.

A sudden stab of guilt bloomed in her chest. She walked over and crouched down beside Jason.

"See, Mama. This straight thing in back moves."

"Aye, son, 'tis called a rudder and steers the ship upon the seas."

Seeing Rand with Jason, his kind words and gift for the boy, Rose could no longer pretend to herself that Rand was not Jason's father. He deserved to know he had a son. But Rose was terrified what he'd do if he ever found out. Nor did she know what would happen if it became common knowledge that Jason was not Bertram's son. Might King Edward strip Jason of his inheritance?

As Jason was an adulterine bastard, or an illegitimate child born to a married woman, the barony could not be seized by legal measures. But Edward had a reputation for acquiring lands through underhanded means in order to enrich himself or the queen.

Nay. Rose would never let that happen. She had suffered too much to allow her son to lose his rightful inheritance. Long ago she vowed to see he received the best education and training available for when he gained control of the barony.

Even more disturbing, though, was the thought Jason would be labeled a bastard. She could not bear for him to know that shame. Especially since it was her fault she had selfishly given free rein to her passionate nature, regardless of the consequences. She could not let her sweet, innocent boy bear the blame for her sinful transgression.

In that moment, she realized their vow to have a chaste marriage was the right course. She must never again waver to passion's onslaught.

She gazed at Jason. Her heart turned over at seeing the joy upon her son's face.

"Son, I have something for you."

Reaching under her wimple, she removed his stone necklace and placed it around his neck.

"Did it help you 'member me?"

She hugged him and kissed him. His small arms squeezed her back. "Aye, son, it gave me great comfort. But I'm home now. Come," Rose said, then clasped Jason's hand in hers and pulled him up. "I want to hear about everything you did while I was away."

Jason chattering beside her, she entered the Keep, her heart full of gladness to be home with her son once more.

Chapter Fourteen

At the dais table during the celebratory supper later that evening, Rose sat next to Ayleston's steward in deep discussion about this year's abundant harvest.

David, his dark auburn hair shining in the candles' glow, was handsome in a rugged way.

"What of your husband?" he asked, nodding toward Rand, sitting next to the castellan at the opposite end of the dais.

Rand's sensual lips quirked and his eyes twinkled with laughter. Her breath caught and her gut quivered with desire. Tingling warmth pooled between her legs. Oh, she was wicked, wanton. She must resist her lascivious attraction.

She gave herself a mental shake. "What about him?"

"Will he not wish to see to the day-to-day administration of the manor now that he is your husband and the estate's guardian?"

That still rankled. Though Ayleston had prospered greatly under her stewardship since her husband's death, by the king's decree control was stripped from her and given to Rand. Reminding her how little she controlled the ordering of her existence, unless . . .

"Sir Rand has been commissioned by King Edward to recruit a contingent of men-at-arms and archers for the upcoming war with Llewelyn. He will be away from the castle for much of the time traveling through the countryside, but he will also be busy seeing to increasing the castle defenses. He shall not wish to be burdened with the manor's daily operations. You shall continue to receive your orders from me and report back to me," Rose hedged.

Upon Bertram's death, Rose had removed all those she could from positions of power in the household who were loyal to her husband. She'd handpicked David to replace the old steward and did not doubt his loyalty to her. Prior to Rand being named guardian, the king's escheat—the man responsible for the management of Jason's estate during King Edward's wardship—had been quite willing to allow Rose to see to the management of the barony. While she did the work, the escheat's liege, King Edward, received the benefits of her labors.

But now that Rand was the guardian of Ayleston, it was only to be expected that David would question his role and who was in charge. Rose meant to cling to her power for as long as she could, but she knew it was only a matter of time before Rand would seize control from her. Mayhap she could implement the improvements she wished to make to the estate before he took charge. Once they were established, she hoped Rand would see the merit in the changes and not care to override them.

A seductive giggle drew Rose's gaze to the other end of the dais. Lisbeth, the pretty, dark-haired servant whom Rand had previously fornicated with, brushed up against Rand as she set a flagon of wine on the board. Rand gave her a teasing wink, then turned back to speak with the castellan.

Razor-sharp jealousy scraped along Rose's flesh. She clutched her chalice tightly and swallowed several mouthfuls of wine.

Preoccupied with her thoughts, she did not see David stare entranced at her wine-moistened lips on the rim of the chalice.

Staring across the board, Rand saw Rose turn and smile

at the handsome steward. Rand's smile froze and his eyes narrowed.

Forbidden to touch his beautiful wife, he'd contemplated bedding Lisbeth. But he knew it would not assuage his need for the woman he truly wanted. Besides, he would not humiliate Rose by bedding anyone associated with Ayleston now that they were married.

Yet he was too virile to remain celibate forever. One day he would no longer be able to suppress his appetites and would seek out a willing woman to bed.

Suddenly, Rose reached out and touched the steward's wrist. A touch so brief Rand would have missed it if he'd blinked.

Like a punch to the gut, jealousy seized him. Rand growled beneath his breath.

Beside him, the castellan said, "My lord, did you say something?"

Until now, he had not considered that Rose might contemplate a carnal liaison of her own.

"A salute!" Rand blurted out.

Standing up, he walked to the other end of the dais table and stood between Rose and the steward. He helped her rise with his right hand and raised his chalice high in his other. "In honor of my new bride. The gracious and beautiful Lady Rosalyn Montague. No man could ask for a better wife. To Lady Rosalyn," he said, then gulped down the contents of his chalice.

A roar of approval climbed to the wooden ceiling.

Beneath the noise of the crowd, Rose whispered, a hint of hurt in her voice, "We both know how untrue your words are. 'Tis cruel to mock me so before the people of Ayleston."

One by one the residents in the Great Hall began to chant. But Rand was oblivious.

He stared at Rose, his eyes searing with sincerity. "I am not mocking you, Rose. I mean every word." His eyes hardened. "But do not think I shall allow you to bed the good steward. If I cannot have you, no one can. Understand?"

Rose gasped. Her eyes widened in disbelief, then narrowed. "How dare you accuse *me* of harboring thoughts of adultery. I saw you shamelessly flirting with Lisbeth," she whispered back heatedly.

His heart beat faster. Rand was thrilled at her jealous reaction. "Ahh, but by our bargain to keep our marriage chaste, you gave me leave to sleep with other women. Or have you had a change of heart and wish to be a wife in *every way*?"

A stiff smile formed on her face. "Nay, of course not. Bed whomever you wish. All I ask is that you be discreet and not rut with anyone in the household. I shall not be humiliated or pitied in my own home."

His pleased smile slipped. Euphoria rapidly withered.

Disheartened, Rand finally heard the chant. "Kiss her. Kiss her. Kiss her."

Rose blinked and looked around.

The moment could not have been more opportune. He desperately wanted to kiss her. To give her a small taste of what she was missing. It conveniently ignored his own reasons for not wanting to bed Rose. But at the moment logic was the furthest thing from his mind. Passion ruled him and he would not be denied.

Rand seized her in his arms, pressed his lips to her ear, a feathery imprint on her intoxicatingly scented skin. "Kiss me, Rose." Voice low, husky, desperate. "If we don't, someone might begin to suspect our marriage is not valid. God forfend word gets back to King Edward and he decides to delve into the matter, mayhap even order a public bedding."

When her body relaxed, he kissed her.

He slashed his lips over hers. Slowly. Thoroughly. Heatedly. He explored the soft, sensual contours of her full lips.

The crowd roared its approval. But it could not drown out the moan he drew from Rose. Her palms skimmed up his stomach and chest, the exquisite pressure of her caress scorching him wherever she touched. She threaded her fingers through his hair behind his neck, and clung to him.

Oh, God, he was falling, slipping, losing all sense of command. He grabbed for control, but instead . . .

He deepened the kiss, thrusting his tongue inside the silken cavern of her mouth. Their tongues tangled in a moist caress. His cock surged to poker hardness.

It lasted a moment. He wanted an eternity.

They broke apart, breathless and avoiding eye contact. Rand gazed around the crowded Great Hall. All eyes were upon them, the smiling, laughing countenances of the people of Ayleston thrilled at the lusty display between their lord and lady. Except the steward, who had left the Great Hall, Rand noted. To distract attention away from himself and Rose, Rand hailed the entertainment to commence.

Soon the castle folk were laughing uproariously, completely absorbed in the antics of the tricolored tumblers and acrobats. Rand joined a group of his men at the back of the vaulted chamber and avoided Rose for the rest of the evening.

Later, after the trestle tables and benches were moved against the walls, the musicians played sprightly dance music.

One by one the castle knights requested a dance from Rose. She graciously accepted each one. Sir Justin took his turn. Their hands met and they spun in a circle. Justin grinned down at her and winked. Rose laughed like a giddy girl, smiling up at the dark, handsome knight.

Rand's gut clenched. Jealousy, unwarranted as it was, consumed him. He trusted Justin with his life. But Rand wanted to be the one to make Rose laugh. Wanted her to come to him and confide in him what her fears were and how he could help her overcome them. But how could he help her when he could not triumph over his own fears?

He watched the festivities from a distance, wearing a smile on his face yet brooding in his heart. His inner demon was tearing him apart.

He wanted his wife. Desperately. Wanted to sink his body deep into hers, to revel in the delights of her carnal flesh. But once he made love to Rose, he knew he would fall under her spell and never recover from her enchantment.

With every knight she seduced with her warm smile and gentle praise, the deeper Rand's jealousy and obsession grew.

And the more wine he imbibed.

Rand relaxed, breathing a sigh of relief when Rose and Lady Alison left the Great Hall for the private chambers above stairs.

In the solar after supper, Rose and Alison were weaving in companionable silence on stools pulled up before the fireplace. Between them, sitting on the floor, Geoffrey sorted the various colored yarns they were using to weave the pattern on the cushion tapestries.

Jason was asleep in his bedchamber. An occasional burst of laughter drifted up the stairs from the Great Hall, but Rose was oblivious.

She could not stop thinking of Rand's salute. *In honor of my new bride. The gracious and beautiful Lady Rosalyn Montague. No man could ask for a better wife.* But the truth was she was no wife at all. Rand truly deserved someone better than her. His praise of her deepened her consuming guilt at the secrets she kept from him. She owed him her loyalty and trust. But she could not bear to see the hatred and disgust in his eyes when she told him Jason was his son.

She raised her fingers to her mouth. Nor could she forget his kiss. Her lips still throbbed intermittently like an echo of a memory.

The door to the solar suddenly slammed open against the wall, shattering the silence. Geoffrey jerked, startled. Lady Alison, eyes wide, put down her needle slowly as though afraid she'd startle a wild beast.

Rand's gaze caught and held Rose's. His gray-green eyes, as dark as a stormy sea, never wavered when he ordered, "Leave us."

Rose stood up and set aside her tapestry frame and needle on the stool. "Lady Alison, Geoffrey, you are excused for the night."

She knew now Rand would never harm her, emotionally mayhap, but not physically. No matter her provocation, he had been patient and understanding. In her heart she had always known it was not his character to strike out in anger, but after years of Bertram's abuse it was difficult to release her fear.

Alison and Geoffrey hastened from the room, closing the door behind them. Flames flickered over Rand's face— golden light and dark shadows—creating an illusion of the two sides of his conflicted personality she was coming to recognize. The smiling, laughing, genial man who always found humor in the mundane, and the man who deeply mourned the death of his mother and twin sister, yet masked his sadness behind the persona of a charming rogue.

She surmised he hid his true feelings because if he opened up and explained what happened the day his sister died, he might expose an unforgivable weakness; unforgivable because a warrior was trained to be strong, brave, and above all, fearless. To expose a vulnerability to your enemy could lead to certain death.

Rand broke the silence. "I tried to sstay away from you. To abide by our voww to keep our marriage in name only. But you're soo damn irr . . .irresisiistible."

Rand weaved slowly, unsteadily toward her. He stopped a hairsbreadth away from her; his breath smelled strongly of wine.

She stiffened. "My lord, are you drunk?"

He clutched her hips and hauled her up along his hard, muscled body.

Heat and hardness pressed against her belly. Breath, hers and his, grew erratic.

"I need you sooo mush it hurts." His silky voice caressed her ear, sending a shiver down her neck.

The desperate plea melted her resistance, and she clutched his waist to keep from pooling at his feet.

Rand cupped his hands around her face. His eyes dipped to her lips. "Your mouth is so lusscious and sweet, I could kiss you for hours without end."

His mouth came down on hers. A delicate brush of his lips, like the flutter of a butterfly's wings, raised a tingle on the plump flesh of her mouth. He kissed her for long, luxurious moments, while his hand removed the brooch at her neck, spread the split neckline of her surcoate, and delved beneath her bodice to loosen the drawstring neck of her tunic and chemise.

"I can't help wishing to explore your perrfect breasts in my palms."

His right hand clasped her bare breast. A deep groan vibrated against her moaning lips. He circled his palm round and round her breast, the friction searing her nipple to a hard, throbbing point.

Bertram had convinced her she was ugly and undesirable. Rand's words were like a balm to her wounded heart. At that moment, her reasons for why it was best to keep their marriage chaste eluded her and she kissed him, her tongue penetrating deep and wet into his mouth.

She squirmed against him, wanting more, unable to verbally articulate her desire.

Yet Rand had no difficulty expressing his need and she gloried in her ability to make him lose control.

"I want to lick and . . . and tasste the sweeet nectar of your breast's rosy bud."

Lowering his head, he lifted her breast and clamped his hot, wet lips around her nipple. Tingling heat shot directly to her intimate core. She gasped in surprise, panting loudly as she clutched his head to her breast like a baby's.

Slowly, inexorably, he sucked the tip deep into his mouth. She moaned. "Oh, God, what are you doing to me?"

Though married for more than a year, she'd never experienced aught like it. And the one time she and Rand had been together, their coupling had been swift and brief with no preliminaries to speak of.

He lifted his head from her breast, his sensually molded lips damp with desire. Gray-green eyes, as deep and fathomless as the sea, caught and held her gaze. "What I have yearned to do for the last three seemingly endless years. I cannot live without you."

Shock gripped her. During the same three years, Rose had believed Rand had indulged his lust in her willing body and then left her to her shame with no more feeling for her than for a slattern walking the streets. Could he truly not live without her? she wondered.

His mouth came back to hers. He kissed her, deep thrusts of his tongue, even as he lowered her onto the fur before the fire. He tasted of Mediterranean wine, seductive and full-bodied. On his knees, he removed his sword belt and set it against the wall next to the fireplace.

Then lying down beside her, he bunched up her skirts in his hands and pulled them up past the garters holding her hose at her knees. The golden glow of the fire flickered over her pale, slender thighs. He stared down at her lower body, his eyes blazing with desire. Rose shivered at the intensity of his need. The same need pounded inside her.

As he gazed deep into her eyes, he skimmed his hand up her leg and spread her quivering thighs. She licked her lips, breathless with anticipation. When he entered her with one finger, she moaned. Adding a second digit, he stretched her, swirling around her inner walls with delicate brush strokes. The intensity of his eyes enthralled her. The desperation of his need endeared her. The thrust of his hand seared her.

Teasing, taunting. Tormenting. His hand moved with

exquisite strokes in and out. All sensation concentrated between her thighs. The pressure built, expanding, coiling, tightening. She clutched his back, holding on to him for dear life as she approached the summit. The sensation was too intense; she could not prevent her hips from lifting to meet him as his hand thrust to the hilt. In a sudden onslaught, pleasure washed over her feminine folds in a hot tumult. Tingling heat suffused her damp delta. In ecstasy and torment, a hoarse cry tumbled from her lips. His mouth covered hers, swallowing her cry.

Rose stared up at Rand. She was stunned, unable to think of the repercussions while she tried to regain her breath. His own gaze was a combination of tenderness and pained desire.

Rand fumbled with his braies, unlacing them. When he shoved them down, his shaft sprang free. He slid on top of her. Instinctively, her legs spread and she cradled his body between her thighs. He groaned, his hard ridge sliding persistently against her core heat. Her breath hitched, his shaft slickened with her wet arousal.

As though doused with cold water, her senses returned. Her heart began to pound harder, this time with panic. She should have realized where all this was leading. A latent shame at her wanton behavior burning her face and clutching her heart, she shoved against him.

He was drunk, out of his senses, and looking for a willing receptacle to assuage his lust. Any woman would do; she just happened to be the easiest at hand.

"Get off me! I'll not be your vessel for lust again. Once was more than enough!"

Rand, panting heavily, stopped his mouth just inches from hers. His voice a hoarse caress, he said, "Aye, you are right. This is wrong." He rolled off of her and flopped onto his back.

Rose lay there, trying to calm her rattled nerves, her heart aching at his easy capitulation. Oh, she was perverse. She wanted him to want her, but when he acted upon his desire she condemned him. *What is wrong with me?*

After a long silence, she looked over at him. His eyes were closed and his breathing was slow and even. He was asleep, or so she thought.

Suddenly, he rambled, "I told myself . . . to stay away. I've wanted you for, umm, foorever. I ssswore . . . when Mother died—" A great choking sob burst from his mouth. "'Tis my fault she is dead."

Shocked, Rose leaned up on her elbow and stared down at him. "Rand, what are you talking about? Your mother died in a fire. How is that your fault?"

His eyes blinked open; dark gray shadows lurked within. A single tear pooled in the outer corner of his right eye. Rose brushed it away with the pad of her right thumb.

Rand swallowed visibly and clasped her hand in his. His thumb stroked her palm, a tender, gentle caress that melted her heart. "'Cause sshe came into the burning barn . . . to saave me. I survived. She didn't."

"Oh, Rand. I am so sorry. How awful for you. But you cannot blame yourself. I am a mother. I would make any sacrifice to save my son. I know your mother in heaven rejoices that you are alive and does not begrudge her sacrifice."

"And Juliana? Is her death justifia . . . ble? I had her in my arms . . . but let her droown to save myself. I was weak. Nay, I should be dead . . . not Juliana. Sshe was the good, dutiful twin."

He closed his eyes, shuddering. His face twisted with misery and guilt.

Tears blurred Rose's eyes. He hid such a great well of sadness because he did not want to appear weak; her heart bled for him. She was glad Rand survived drowning and the fire. If he had not, Jason would never have been born. But she could not tell Rand that.

"Swore . . . never to love you. I'm cursed." He released her hand and turned his head away. "Don't want to hurt you. Like everyone elsse I've l . . . lo—"

Her heart jolted, then beat uncontrollably. Surely he did not mean that he loved her? "Rand. What were you about to say?" No answer.

She brushed back his hair from his face. His eyes were closed. "Rand, can you hear me?" She nudged him.

A loud snore was his response.

Rose groaned and collapsed onto her back. Unable to stop thinking about what his muddled words meant, she stared at the beams of the ceiling. He said that he was cursed, that he'd sworn never to love her. That he did not want to hurt her like everyone else he ever loved.

Like he loved her?

Of course not, she answered her own question. It was ridiculous to think he could ever love her. What was there to admire in her? He may desire her, but he had no deeper feelings for her.

Oh, what did it matter anyway? Rose wondered. Hot tears slid slowly down her temples. Angrily, she swiped them away with the heels of her hands. Even if somehow he did love her, she could never lie with him as man and wife. Not when she was incapable of getting past her feelings of shame and humiliation at her lewd desires.

Chapter Fifteen

Sunlight penetrated Rand's closed eyelids, waking him. At the sudden sharp pounding in his head, he groaned. His buttocks and back ached where he'd lain on the hard floor all night. He rolled onto his side and awkwardly got to his knees. He glanced down. His braies and hose were bunched around his knees. Sudden images from the night before flashed in his head—of him storming into the solar, taking Rose into his arms, and kissing her. Of her convulsing in his arms.

Dropping his head into his hands, he groaned again. This time at the drunken fool he'd made of himself. He did not remember everything, except Rose had stopped him from making a colossal mistake with only moments to spare. He prayed he had not said anything too revealing.

He rubbed his hands over his face. His stubble was rough, his mouth was rank, and he smelled of stale wine. He did not want to contemplate what the stains were on his tunic.

Carefully, he eased to his feet, pulling up his braies, and tying the laces at his waist. He went to retrieve the sword and scabbard he'd removed last night, his movements slow as he tried to loosen the stiffness in his muscles and joints. Buckling his sword belt, he headed for the bedchamber he intended to share with Rose, at least for the first few months of their marriage, to allay any suspicions it was not consummated. Later it would not seem odd if they did not share a chamber. It was not uncommon for married people of their rank to live separately. Marriages were arranged by parties who were interested only in dynastic purposes and did not consider whether the couple even liked one another or whether they could live peaceably together.

Now he needed to freshen up, shave, and change his clothes. The coming days and weeks would be hard and grueling and there was not a moment to linger. He had to start by gathering up all the males in the village between the ages of ten and four, and three score. It was imperative they receive extensive combat training so they could defend the manor from Welsh raids when the large body of Ayleston knights was absent fighting. Not only that, but Rand had to recruit more knights to increase the castle guard. It was a temporary situation, and he'd hire mercenaries for that purpose.

Those were the responsibilities he owed Ayleston as its guardian. But the king had also charged him with raising paid troops from the western regions of Chester County for when the major offensive began next year.

The door to Rose's bedchamber was open. Rand entered and closed the door behind him. Never having been inside her bedchamber before, he looked around, curious. Except for the massive, carved canopy bed, he saw Rose's feminine touches everywhere. The counterpane was gold and cream damask and the bed curtains were a matching gold silk. Tapestries of garden scenes hung on three walls. A delicate, painted pitcher and basin stood on the washstand.

Rand leaned forward and pressed his nose against the insubstantial linen nightshift hanging on a peg. Closing his eyes, he took a deep whiff. Lavender and rose inundated his senses, entranced him with the delicate fragrance of Rose.

A giggle and a splash shattered the quiet. Rand jumped in

embarrassment. He jerked his head left and right, sheepish. He gazed into the shadows by the bed. Empty. Then he checked behind a carved screen in the corner opposite the hall door, but all he saw was a large empty bathing tub. No one was in the chamber.

That left only one other place to check. As he was moving toward the curtained doorway of an adjoining chamber, more exuberant splashing came from inside it. Rand shoved the curtain divider aside, and peered into the room.

Rand jerked back in surprise. Next to a narrow bed in the far left corner of the small chamber, Jason sat naked in a round, shallow tub. He was giggling and splashing in his bath water. Edith, kneeling beside the tub, was trying to rinse the last of the soap off the squirming little boy's shoulders.

Jason looked up from his play and saw him. "Papa, Papa."

Rand's heart twisted at the word "papa." It was difficult to describe what he felt each time he heard it, but he was positive he did not wish to acknowledge the sensation.

"Good day, Jason. Edith." He nodded to the nurse. Edith must have been some two score summers old, and had a streak of gray running through her dark black hair.

"Have you come to play with me?" The boy raised his arm, dripping with water. In his hand he held up a small object for Rand to see.

It was the carved ship he'd made for Jason.

"Oh, my lord. Praise be you are here," Edith said, brushing back a strand of hair from her face with her arm. "Jason has not stopped talking about his boat. I always give him some time to play in the tub after his bath. But I forgot to get the lad's clean garments from the laundry. Can you show him how the boat works while I go below stairs for a moment?"

Rand glowered, a look he reserved for recalcitrant squires in need of a scolding. "I am not a nursemaid, Edith. I only came for a change of clothes." He indicated his soiled, smelly tunic, and then crossed his arms over his chest.

She did not even glance at him as she climbed to her feet. "Of course not, my lord. I have already bathed him. You need only keep him occupied with the toy you gave him till I return."

Rand turned to Edith when she passed him and headed for the hall door. "Wait. I don't know how . . . What . . . do I—"

"Just make sure he does not slip and hit his head, or let an accident of the like befall him. We do not want the little lord drowning."

Rand blanched and his stomach dropped to his knees. She opened the door and hurriedly left, and so did not see his reaction. Rand glanced at the open door, his entire body tense, yet vibrating with the urge to bolt after her.

He'd not asked for, nor ever wanted, the responsibility as Rose and Jason's protector. He had a terrible record of failure in his role as such. He'd failed to protect his sister, his mother, Alex, and even Rose, when he made love to her four years ago, then left her to the mercy of her cruel, vindictive husband. But as always, he knew where his duty lay.

Warily, Rand glanced back into the chamber.

"Papa, it floats. Look." Jason put the ship in his bath and held it as he hollered, "Raise anchor, mates! Unfur' the sail!" Then he gave the ship a slight push and it floated to the other side of the tub. Rand smiled at the lad's mispronunciation.

Could he deny the child's simple request?

Rand had sworn to never let his own father's abysmal treatment and hatred toward him influence how Rand treated others. He could never resent Rose and Jason, or blame them for his own deficiencies.

So despite his initial instinct to flee, he could not leave Jason without supervision.

Footsteps hesitant, Rand made his way to the tub, wiping a bead of sweat from his upper lip.

"It's sailing, Papa. It's sailing." A huge grin became evident on Jason's face, a shallow dimple appeared in the boy's cheek.

Despite his apprehension, Rand chuckled at the child's enthusiasm. "Aye, Jason, you are sailing it. You would make a wonderful shipmaster."

"One day I wanna sail a ship like you."

"I do not sail the *Argo*, Jason. I just own it. Master Harwood sails it for me, shipping cargo from all parts of the world."

Jason slapped his arms in the water, spraying droplets into his face. He giggled. "I shall own my own ship, then."

Rand ruffled the boy's hair. "When you are older, certainly you can. Now then, let me show you something." He knelt down beside the tub, plucked the boat from the water, and pointed to the back of the miniature cog. "Do you know what this is?" A thin, nearly rectangular piece of wood extended straight off the back of the stern like a dolphin's fin.

Jason nodded his head up and down vigorously, gold curls bouncing against his cheeks. "A rudder. Mama told me."

"Very good. Now, the rudder helps steer the ship. And this lever is the helm, which moves the rudder back and forth, allowing the rudder to maneuver the ship in the sea." Rand pointed to the appropriate parts of the carved ship as he gave each term. "Would you like to see how?"

The boy's blue-green eyes, the color of the Mediterranean Sea, shone brightly. "Will you show me?" He clapped excitedly, splashing water over the tub's edge.

"Certes. But first you should know a few terms. Now then, the front, back, and both sides of the ship each have special names. The front of the ship is called the bow and the back of the ship is the stern." Again pointing to the parts of the ship. "And when you're on a ship facing the bow, the right side of the ship is starboard and the left side is larboard."

Rand stopped and looked up. The boy stared at him, his eyes wide and engrossed in his instruction. But Rand realized he did not know if Jason knew his left from his right.

"I didn't think, but do you know the difference between right and left?"

Jason scrunched up his nose, offended. The gesture reminded Rand of the boy's mother. "Of course. I am very smart. Mama taught me. Right. Left." He held up his right hand, then left hand for emphasis.

Rand laughed. "My pardon, Jason. Shall we test how smart you are? Can you tell me what the front of the ship is called?"

He grinned from ear to ear. "The bow."

After Rand pointed to the parts of the ship and Jason answered correctly, Rand showed the boy how to shift the rudder with the helm. The toy rudder was attached to the ship's sternpost by bowstring to allow the rudder to shift slightly from side to side.

Rand commanded, "Helm astarboard."

"Helm astarboard," Jason repeated, then shifted the helm to starboard, the rudder moved opposite, and the lad put the toy in the bath. The boy's smile lighted up as he watched his toy ship "sail" in the water, veering left.

Jason clapped excitedly. "Once more. Can I? Can I?"

"Go ahead, Jason. How 'bout we try turning the ship in the other direction?"

Jason laughed and scooped the ship into his palms under the water beneath the hull.

"Helm alarboard," Rand ordered in a stern, shipmaster voice.

"Aye, sir! Helm alarboard!" he gleefully shouted. After pushing the helm larboard, he put the ship in the water with a shove. They watched as it floated, veering right this time.

Rand continued to play with the boy, his anxieties forgotten in the moment.

Until . . . Rose suddenly came storming into the chamber breathing heavily, her cheeks flushed. "Rand . . . I pray you . . . forgive Edith her impertinence. I shall see to Jason now. I promise you shall never be burdened with the care of him again." In her hands she held a stack of folded garments.

Rand got to his feet. "'Twas no burden. Jason and I are having a fine time."

"Mama," the lad spoke up, "Sir Rand was showing me how to sail."

Startled at the formal address, Rand gazed back down at Jason. The lad's expression did not alter, but a conspiratorial gleam lit up his eyes. A burst of laughter escaped Rand at their secret.

A frown marred Rose's brow. "Would you care to share with me what you find so humorous?"

No, he would not. Rose would not be amused that her son was disobeying her command not to address Rand as "Papa." Rand did not understand her stubborn insistence that the boy not call him so because she wanted Jason to honor the memory of his father. It made absolutely no sense, for she'd despised the man. It made more sense that she'd want Rand to fulfill the role of father to Jason. It was obvious the boy desperately wanted a fatherly presence in his life. Not only was he constantly seeking Rand's attention, but he was as stubbornly persistent about calling him "Papa" as Rose was that he should not.

Rose laid the clothes on the bed and retrieved a linen drying cloth. "Bath time is over, Jason. Sir Rand must be about his duties now," she said, coming around to the side of the bath next to Rand.

Nose wrinkling, she stared purposely at his chest. He glanced down. A dark greasy stain smeared his tunic, and he smelled odorous—reminding him he still wore his clothes from last night.

'Twas not all he remembered. A sudden disturbing memory of his drunken confession in the solar lashed him.

It all made perfect sense now.

She knew his deepest fear and failings and did not believe him capable of being a good father to her boy, or of protecting him. She'd seen deep into his heart and judged him lacking. Just as Lord Montague, Rand's dead father, had.

Raw disappointment, rising thick and virulent, stuck in the back of his throat. Rand stumbled back, giving her room to finish Jason's bath.

Rose held up the large towel, and when Jason got out of the tub, she wrapped it around him and rubbed his whole body vigorously.

The mundane chore sparked a memory from when he was a child that he'd forgotten. But it returned vividly back to life, menacing him like a skeletal specter refusing to stay buried . . .

Chapter Sixteen

Châteaux Montague
Gascony, Bordeaux countryside
In the year of our Lord 1253
Thirty-sixth year in the reign of King Henry III

"Oh, my son," Lady Montague said. An exasperated laugh escaped her. "How do you manage to always find yourself in such messy straits?"

Rand raised his arms high above his head, giggling as his mother removed the last of his muddy garments and tossed them on a chest at the foot of her bed. He knew his mother did not truly expect an answer, but he replied, "A pirate never gives away the secrets of his brethren. You shall get no answers from me."

His mother's voice dropped to a deep, craggy tenor. "Very well, then, milord Pirate. You leave me no choice. If you do not divulge all your secrets to me, then I shall have to," she paused, drawing out the suspense of what she intended to do to him, "torture you till you do."

Her fingers reached out like claws, and then she caught him in her arms and ran her fingers lightly over his ribs. A feathery tickle skimmed over his flesh. He burst out laughing, wiggling in her arms to get free of the torturous tickles. Breathless, eyes watering, he cried out, "Craven, I say, I cry craven."

His mother released him. "Good decision, milord Pirate." Her voice had returned to the soft melodic tones familiar to him. "Now into the tub you go, son. You stink."

She grabbed him beneath his armpits and lifted him into the tub of water. Rand sat down, the hot water soaking into his skin and loosening the caked dirt that covered him.

Wearing a faded blue tunic dress, his mother knelt down and scrubbed his chest and shoulders with a cloth she'd lathered with soap. The water quickly turned muddy brown. The front of his mother's dress became splotched with dirty spots of water, and strands of her golden hair, having come free of her braid, hung in her face.

He giggled. "Mama, you are dirtier than me now."

After brushing her hair back from her face with her arm, she gazed down and laughed. "So I am, Rand. Juliana needs a bath next, but I do believe I shall have to perform my ablutions afterward."

Juliana, playing quietly in the corner with her wool-stuffed doll, piped up, "I don't need a bath, Mama."

Rand scoffed. "If I have to bathe, Juls, so must you." He pointed to the mud from the riverbank spattered on her dimpled cheek and in her golden hair.

She stuck her tongue out at him. "But I do not stink like you do."

"You do too stink," he shot back.

"I do not," she whined.

"Lady Montague?" They all froze at the faint call. Then it came closer, deeper, darker, angrier. "Lady Montague?"

"Where is she?" a gruff, masculine voice demanded from the antechamber.

Rand clenched his body tight to still his sudden shaking. His father always made him afraid. He was a mean man who said hateful things and enjoyed bullying them. Rand avoided his father whenever he could because he was quick to beat them for any wrong he felt they'd committed.

"Who, my lord?" Lady Montague's maidservant replied.

"Your mistress, you fool. Tell me where she is."

His mother, her gaze wide and fearful, ordered, "Get out of the tub, Rand. Hurry." She helped him out of the tub, then grabbed a linen towel off the stool and handed it to him hurriedly. "Dry off, Rand, and put on your clean sherte. 'Tis lying on my bed."

Rand obeyed.

Juliana sat clutching her doll tightly, her small face frozen in fright.

Lady Montague, the wet washcloth in her hand, knelt before Juliana. "Darling, let's get you cleaned as best we can," his mother spoke softly, slowly.

Her calm voice fooled Juliana, but not Rand. It was the voice she used every time their father came from his town-home in Bordeaux to visit them at their country manor.

"Get out of my way, you old crone," Lord Montague swore. A sharp slap followed. "I shall find her myself," his voice grew louder as he neared the bedchamber.

Rand, wearing the clean sherte, turned toward the doorway. Footsteps pounded.

In tempo with each step, Rand's heart thumped.

His mother whispered, "Children, stay here. Rand, protect your sister." Rand nodded, knowing his duty. The curtain swished closed behind his mother, her edict reverberating deep inside him.

"My lord. You called for me?"

Juliana stood with her doll dangling from her fingers, her eyes glossy with fright. Rand went over and wrapped his arm around Juliana's narrow, shaking shoulders. He held his breath, listening.

"Aye. What were you doing? How come you did not answer me immediately?"

"I am sorry," she said, voice deferential. "Just about to bathe, I was undressing and could not hear you."

"Never mind. I've come to tell you we have—"

His father stopped abruptly. Footsteps echoed. "What is that appalling dress you are wearing? And what is that stain on it?" His voice cracked like a whip, "'Od's blood, woman. How many times have I told you to dress in a manner befitting your rank as lady of Montague?"

His mother's voice dropped to a thready whisper. "Forgive me, my lord. As I said, I was just about to bathe and change into appropriate attire. If you'll excuse me I shall do so now."

"Churl." A scuffle ensued and a startled shriek sounded. "Get in your chamber and remove that garment."

Rand's fists tightened in anger, and then he hustled into motion.

"Hide, Juls," he ordered and shoved his sister beneath the bed. "Don't come out unless Mother or I call you."

From the other chamber, fabric ripped. Iron curtain rings scraped along the rod and his mother came tumbling through the curtain and into the room. She landed on her bottom and scrabbled back on her heels as Lord Montague came in and towered over her.

Rand fell to his knees beside her. "Mama, are you all right?" He pushed her hair back from her face.

She appeared unharmed, except for her usual pale, gaunt face. The front of her tunic was ripped open to the waist and gaped open, revealing her chemise beneath.

She glanced around quickly, and seeing Juliana hidden, gave him an infinitesimal nod of approval. "I am all right, darling."

Rand clutched her arm, as thin as his own, and helped her get to her feet.

His father exploded in anger. "What are you doing in here?"

"Son, you should go to your chamber," his mother said, no

doubt trying to protect him from his father's temper. "Your father and I have things we need to discuss."

Rand was about to refuse when Lord Montague gazed about the room. Rand saw what he saw. The tub of muddy water, the damp linen towel hanging over the side of it, Rand's pile of dirty clothes on the chest nearby. Lord Montague's eyes narrowed on Rand.

His eyes snapped green fire. "You worthless whelp."

A large, beefy hand came out and smacked Rand upside his head. Pain exploded in his cheek and his ears buzzed.

Lady Montague cried out, "My lord, prithee, don't hurt him!"

"I told you not to cavort with those filthy serfs, Rand. I shan't let you embarrass me and remind people of your tainted blood."

Rand glared up at his father. "I am not tainted. I have the blood of king's running through me. Mama said so."

"You may have royal blood in you, but your grandmother was a dirty peasant. She contaminated the pure blood of your mother and that same blood runs through you and your brat sister. Now begone."

Rand opened his mouth to speak. But Lord Montague grabbed his wife's braid, wrapped it around his wrist, and yanked her against him. A yelp of pain escaped Rand's mother. "Not another word, or I shall make your mother pay for your insolence."

Eyes glittering with pain, his mother spoke, "Go on, Rand, leave us."

Rand, gut churning with fear, frustration, and guilt, backed from the room. His father was bigger than him and knew exactly how to hurt Rand by hurting the ones he loved. No matter what he did to try to protect his mother, Lord Montague found ways to retaliate for Rand's defiance.

Lord Montague released her. As she backed away from him, Rand's father glared, scorn contorting his aquiline features. "You are a disgrace, Mary. Your peasant roots run deep in the brats you bore me."

An ache in his heart, Rand left the chamber. But he remained nearby, crouched down in the hall listening to make sure his mother was harmed no more.

"I received word that Lord Montclair and your sister will be arriving soon." The wooden lid of the clothes chest creaked open, rustling of fabric sounded, and then the lid slammed shut. "Here, you'll wear this. I expect you to be on your best behavior while Lord Montclair is here. He brought his wife so you two could visit. But the purpose of his stay is to negotiate a new wine trade agreement for the Crown of England.

"I've brought the best entertainment and a chef from the court of Aquitaine to preside while our guests are here. You'd better pray you do not embarrass me. I need not tell you how important these negotiations are."

"Nay, my lord, you do not. I assure you I shall behave exactly as you wish."

"See that you do." He grumbled. "And keep the brats out of my sight. I want naught to go wrong while Lord Montclair is at Châteaux Montague."

"As you say, my lord."

Over the sharp rap of footsteps, he said, "I'll inform the housekeeper to bring fresh water for you to bathe. Do not ever demean me by reverting to your peasant roots again. We have servants to do the menial tasks."

Rand scrambled down the hall and hid in a wardrobe chamber. When the door to his mother's chamber slammed shut, he ran back inside her bedchamber.

Lady Montague was helping Juliana out from under the bed. His sister's golden curls hung in her face and two tracks of tears trailed down her dusty cheeks. A pallor of subdued sadness invaded everyone.

"Take your sister to your chambers, Rand."

"Aye, Mama. Juls and I shall stay in our chambers and not bother anyone while Lord Montclair is visiting."

"You heard everything?"

"Aye."

"Your father does not mean the things he says, Rand. He's just . . . a bitter man who is prideful to a fault. Do not take his words to heart."

"Of course, Mama. I know you are right," Rand lied and wrapped his arm around Juliana's shoulders and led her out of the chamber. Feet dragging, shoulders slumped, Juliana looked up at him with her big, sad, gray-green eyes, an exact replica of his. "Why, Rand? Why does father hate us so?"

Rand sighed, his heart a tangled knot in his chest. "I don't know, Juls. I don't know." For the second time, Rand lied.

Ayleston Castle
In the year of our Lord 1276, November 3
Fourth year in the reign of King Edward I

The haze of childhood memories evaporated and Rand stared at another bath scene, in another country, in another time, at another manor, with different people. Rose pulled Jason's tunic on over the lad's raised arms.

Rand blinked, for Jason looked amazingly like Juliana, down to the golden curls—though his were shorter—and the dimples in his cheeks. Blinking again, he discharged the absurd thought. His imagination was overreacting. For a moment, he'd actually wished Jason were his son.

Slowly, devastating thoughts swirling inside his head, he backed away toward the curtained doorway. Jason was not his son and never would be. The pain clenching his chest shocked him, made him realize deep down that he wanted to be a father. To be the kind of father he'd never had—who would teach him how to ride and fight and swim and to be respectful toward women. One who would even play with him at his bath.

But sadly, he had no happy memories of being with his father as a child. What few he had of Lord Montague he preferred to forget. Seven years after Lord Montague stormed from the bedchamber, Rand's sister and mother were dead.

Because he was cursed to hurt the ones he loved.

He stared at Rose and Jason, mother and child. His heart began to palpitate and blood drained from his face. *I cannot love them. I will not love them.*

But he feared it was too late.

Nay. It was never too late. Distance would cure him.

"I must go. I have to get out of here," Rand blurted out.

"Very well, my lord. Shall we see you at dinner?"

"Nay. I am leaving Ayleston. I think it best if we keep separate households. Rest assured, I shall give you authority to settle estate affairs as you wish. But I'll leave Sir Justin in charge of the castle forces and for your and the boy's protection. I have a home in the port of Chester and shall be recruiting in the surrounding countryside for the next several months, so I shall stop on occasion and check to make sure your needs are being met. If you should need me for any reason before then, have Justin send word to Chester and I can return in no more than two days' time."

Rose stared in stunned surprise as Rand practically ran from the chamber. A huge lump lodged in the pit of her stomach. Rand was gone, and she had no idea what she'd done to make him flee from her as if she were a fire-breathing dragon. Dazed, she reached down and retrieved Jason's ship, bobbing in the water.

She stared at the crude toy made from Rand's own hands. She did not understand the man. One moment he was professing he could not live without her, was kind enough to occupy a little boy hungry for some male attention, and the next he was declaring his intention that they separate before their marriage had barely begun.

Beside her, Jason tugged on her skirt. "Mama? Did I do something wrong?"

Rose looked down at Jason. As he gazed up at her, his aquamarine eyes were wide and hurt.

She knelt down before him and clenched his arms. "Nay, darling. Of course, you didn't do anything wrong. Why would you think such a thing?"

"Because I made Papa angry, and now he is leaving us."

"Jason, you did not make Rand angry. Aye, he is leaving, but 'tis not your fault. Sometimes 'tis best if a husband and wife live apart. The king arranged our marriage. But Sir Rand did not want to marry me. He only did so out of loyalty and respect for your grandfather."

"Why would he not want to marry you?" His voice quavered with childish indignation. "You are more pretty than any girl I know."

Her smile slightly quirked, Rose said, "Thank you, dear. But it does not matter whether I'm pretty or not. People of our rank do not get to choose whom we marry. Marriages are arranged between two people so families can acquire more wealth and prestige. One day when you are older, you'll understand."

"But why can he not live with us? Doesn't he want to be my papa?"

"I am sorry, Jason. I know you want a father. But we have always just had each other. Cannot that be enough?"

He pushed out his lip. "Aye, Mama. I am glad he is leaving. I don't want no silly father anyway." Suddenly, his face crumpled. He grabbed the toy from her hand and hurled it to the floor, shouting, "I hate him and his ugly boat!" It cracked—the mast and sail breaking off from the hull—and skittered across the floor.

Rose gasped. "Jason!"

But he ran from the room, leaving her staring at the shattered remains, her heart aching for her son. Rose collapsed on Jason's bed, dropped her head into her hands, and wept.

Wept for a lonely boy who wanted a father. Wept for the naïve girl who'd married for love and then discovered her husband was a cruel brute. Wept for the deception she was forever a slave to, for fear of Rand's hatred.

Rose, her basket of medicinal herbs, oils, and salves in the crook of her arm, exited the cramped cottage. A cold, brisk breeze ruffled her cloak collar and she clutched it tightly around her.

Beside her, Robert, a reed-thin boy with light brown stringy hair, age ten and nine years, asked, "What am I to do, my lady?" The lad was the eldest of Widow Grayson's nine grandchildren. "'Tis my responsibility to provide for my family now."

A thin layer of snow covered the spiky golden grass along the path they followed around to the side yard. Here, a fenced garden plot next to the cottage was protected from the two small boys who kicked a leather ball back and forth. Sir Justin stood sentinel inside the gate by the road keeping a vigilant eye on Jason, the smaller of the boys.

"The cottage and land will be yours when—"

"Aye. You can say it. When Grandmama dies."

"With land to inherit, you can now marry the miller's daughter you fancy."

He blushed to the roots of his hair. "'Tis so obvious?"

"You have my permission for the marriage and I will speak with Sara's father. She has a respectable dowry, which shall be indispensable to start your married life. 'Twill just be up to you to convince Sara to accept your offer."

Robert grinned and winked. "Oh, she'll accept my offer. Sara cannot resist aught I ask of her when I do it sweetly."

She bid Robert good day and walked to the gate, where Sir Justin stood in full armor waiting. Justin was diligently taking his responsibility of guarding her and Jason whenever they were not within the safe confines of the castle walls. She was relieved. A number of travelers had brought reports of Welsh raids west of Ayleston. Then there was Sir Golan's threat. That the man had not tried to retaliate yet did not mean he had forgotten. She knew Sir Golan was not the type to forgive an insult, especially when he had been so publicly humiliated.

"Come, Jason!" she hollered. "We must be getting back to the castle!" The sky was dark with impending snow.

Jason picked up the ball, waved to his friend, and ran to Rose's side. Sir Justin took Rose's basket, opened the wooden gate onto the main village road, and stepped out onto the dirt road, where he'd tied up the horses. She and Jason followed. Having secured her basket to her saddle, Justin gave her a hand up onto her black mare and then lifted Jason to sit before her.

"How does the Widow Grayson fare?" Sir Justin asked as they followed the meandering road.

Clutching Jason to her tightly, Rose shook her head sadly. "I am afraid she is not long for this world."

"Is Widow Grayson going to die, Mama?"

"Only the Lord knows, son. But Widow Grayson has had a long and fulfilling life. We shall pray she gets better."

"Aye, I will pray for her," Jason said, sniffling.

"It must be burdensome for you when you cannot save the poor souls you seek to heal."

Rose glanced over at Justin, riding beside her. "Aye, 'tis difficult when someone I am caring for dies. But I have a special calling for healing. For those I do have a small hand in saving, their lives make up for the pain and suffering I see every day."

As they approached the last bend nearing the lowered drawbridge, a loud clattering of horses' hooves came up from

behind them. Tack and armor jingling, the party of soldiers
came upon them rapidly, forcing them off the road. Rose
cried out, clutching Jason to her. Sir Justin guided her horse
safely off the road, but in the process, his horse stumbled and
went down. Rose screamed. The destrier rolled over Justin,
crushing him, then staggered to its feet, limping and shaking
its head.

Helping Jason down first, Rose slid off her mare and ran
to Justin's side. She skidded to a stop, nearly slipping on the
snow-covered grass, and dropped to her knees.

First, she carefully removed his mail coif. He lay pale and
still. Her lips moved as she prayed beneath her breath that
he was alive. She patted his face, but he did not respond. She
checked his pulse. It was weak, erratic. Next, she checked
his limbs.

She grimaced upon seeing the bone of his lower leg poking
through his mail chausses.

The party of riders entered the castle except one man, who
turned around and approached on a large black warhorse.

"You fool!" Rose blasted the miscreant. "What were you
thinking? Your reckless disregard has endangered my knight."

The knight in the black tunic and cloak who'd led the party
slowly removed his hood. "I was thinking you would give
way to your betters, as is custom."

The breath ripped from her lungs. "*You*. How dare you seek
hospitality within the walls of Ayleston. Do not dare to think
you will be given such. Especially after this day's deeds."

Sir Golan smiled, a gloating smile so evil she shivered.
"I'm afraid you have no choice, *my lady*. King Edward has
awarded me the position of lieutenant-justiciar for the Earldom of Chester. Surely you do not wish to offend me or the
king by denying me hospitality?"

He sneered, knowing she had no choice but to allow him
to stay. Rose glared at him in impotence. As an officer in the

earldom's administration, Golan held a position of power and no doubt intended to wield it to their detriment.

Several of the castle guard rushed out. She gave them instructions.

Sir Golan had dismounted and approached Sir Justin's horse, behind which Jason had been hidden during their exchange. "Who is this, my lady? Mayhap this is your son? Lord Ayleston, am I correct?" His hand came down on Jason's shoulder.

Rose, her heart palpitating in fear, rushed over and grabbed Jason from him. "Stay away from my son."

Two men of the castle guard came forward with a stretcher to carry Sir Justin inside. "Take him to the chamber next to mine."

Another knight helped her and Jason mount Evangeline.

Staring down at Sir Golan, Rose said, "By all means, you may stay at Ayleston for the night. But I'm afraid we have no private chambers available for your use." She smiled, pleased to deny him this small comfort. "You may sleep in the Great Hall with the rest of the household, or with your men in the west tower. I doubt you shall see me before you leave on the morrow. Good day."

Sir Golan sneered, ignoring her dismissal. He would have the last word. "Where is the ever valiant Sir Rand?" he asked snidely. "I hear he has been away for some while and now resides in Chester. You do not have him to protect you anymore."

Her eyes grew wide, fearful. He thrived on her fear. She was just like his first wife—a whore to the very core, he thought.

But in some ways, he hated Lady Ayleston more. For she'd humiliated him before the whole court, by choosing Sir Rand and no doubt whoring with him, also. She was going to pay for rejecting him. And he knew exactly the means by which he was going to achieve his revenge.

Chapter Seventeen

Sitting on a stool beside Justin's bed, Rose wrung out a linen cloth in the basin, folded it neatly, and pressed the cool cloth against the knight's forehead. She was very worried for him. He'd not awoken since his accident. Not even when she set his broken leg bone and put it in a splint. She piled on extra blankets and now waited to see if he would awaken.

Jason sat quietly on the window seat on the other side of the bed, scratching out his letters on a wax tablet. The sun had yet to set on the day, and a heavy snow had begun to fall.

"Edith, Jason and I shall be sleeping in this chamber while Sir Golan is in residence. I do not trust the man. He is a pestilence determined to infect us with his evil presence. Prithee, send David up. I need to speak to him about posting a guard at our chamber door for the night."

Edith picked up the last bloody towel on the floor and put it in the basket she carried on her left hip. "Aye, my lady." She huffed, breathless, and brushed a loose strand of graying black hair off her face. "Should I have him send word to Sir Rand about Sir Golan's arrival and what has transpired?"

"Absolutely not. Sir Rand wishes to maintain separate households. I shall not burden him every time a crisis arises.

I am perfectly capable of managing the situation," she said stiffly, wounded.

"But surely he'd wish to be informed about Sir Justin's injury."

Rose chewed the corner of her lip in thought. She did not want Rand to think she needed him in any way. He'd easily rejected her and she did not want or need him. She and Jason were perfectly happy to rely only on each other. But Edith was correct. Rand should learn that his friend was hurt and that Rose did not know whether he would survive or not.

"Of course, you are right. When you return, bring my writing accoutrements from my chamber and I will prepare a message for David to have delivered."

Edith nodded and left the chamber. She soon returned with Rose's writing box, which contained ink, a quill, parchment, a bag of sand, and sealing wax. Rose wrote Rand a brief message, sanded it, and then sealed it with wax. A few moments later David arrived.

He bowed, his gaze dark and unreadable. "My lady. Edith said you wished to speak to me?"

"Aye, David. As you know, Sir Golan and his party will be staying at Ayleston for the night. But I do not trust the man. He's threatened to harm me and my son, yet I cannot afford to offend the new lieutenant-justiciar by denying him hospitality."

"I understand, my lady. Tell me what it is you would have me do."

"As I need to watch Sir Justin through the night, Jason will sleep here in the chamber with me. I need you to have the captain of the guard send me his ablest knight to guard the chamber door until Sir Golan leaves. The man is quite capable of harming us in our own beds while he pretends to seek our generosity."

"Of course. I shall go speak with the captain now and have him send his best knight immediately."

"Wait, there's more. I do not intend on leaving this chamber all night, so I will not be dining with you in the Great Hall this evening. I spoke with Lady Alison. She will entertain our visitors in my place. Despite my suspicions, give our guests every courtesy and treat them graciously. I do not wish to give Sir Golan any reason to accuse me of inhospitable treatment."

"Very well, my lady. Is there aught else you wish me to do?"

She hesitated, then turned and picked up the sealed missive on the washstand beside Justin's bed. "There is one more thing." Handing the letter to David, she said, "Have this message delivered to Sir Rand in Chester. 'Tis imperative he get it with all due haste."

David stood staring down at the message in his large, bronze hand. He cleared his throat as if he wished to speak.

"That will be all, David."

He suddenly raised his gaze to hers, his eyes feverish with yearning. "My lady, there is no need to send for Sir Rand. You know I will do whatever it takes to protect you from Sir Golan."

The sudden intensity of his emotion made her uncomfortable. "I trust you will. But Sir Rand needs to know Sir Justin is gravely injured."

"My lady, forgive me. I've not said a word since Sir Rand left, but I can no longer contain myself." He drew closer and clutched her hands in his. "I love you, Rose. It seems like I have loved you forever. Yet I never dared to confess it because you were so intent on taking a vow of chastity. Then you married, and your husband abandoned you."

"David, pray do not say another word." She pulled her hands free and stepped back. She glanced over at Jason. He was preoccupied and could not hear their discussion.

"How can I? I see the way you look at me. Tell me you love me as much as I love you."

"I do not love you, and I have certainly given you no reason to believe such."

A surge of anger heated his face and his next words. "Do you love him? Are you in love with Sir Rand?"

Rose lurched back in shock. "You go too far. It is none of your concern what happens between my husband and me. I appreciate the loyalty and expertise you have provided Ayleston since my first husband's death, but if you wish to continue on as steward, you will refrain from such intimate discourse in future."

He dropped his head. "Forgive me, my lady, if I offended you. 'Twas not my intent. You need not fear I shall overstep my bounds again."

"Very well. You are dismissed."

He spun on his heel to leave.

"Do not forget the letter." Rose picked it up off the bed, where he'd dropped it when he held her hands. She handed the missive back to him.

This time his cheeks flushed in embarrassment. "Of course, pardon my lapse. I'll send that guard for your protection straightaway."

"Naaaay!" Rose cried in denial. She jerked awake, sitting upright on the stool, heart pounding. The echo of a nightmare suffused Rose as she stared around the room. Light from the hanging oil lamp next to the washstand penetrated the suffocating darkness. She was in Bertram's former chamber, but he was dead. Now, Sir Justin lay in the bed, his raspy breathing the only sound in the bedchamber.

She rubbed her face. Wrinkles from the bedclothes lined her cheek where she'd rested it on the bed. Getting up from the stool, she checked on Jason, sleeping on a pallet at the foot of the bed. He was lying on his back, his curls matted on the right side of his head.

The door suddenly rattled. Rose jumped, startled. She heard a deep groan outside, followed by a heavy body slumping to the floor. A second loud thump jarred the door, then silence.

Her hand flew to her throat and her pulse pounded. She went to the door and leaned against it. "Sir William? Are you all right?" she asked the guard who'd been posted at her door hours earlier.

When he did not respond, she spoke louder. "Sir William. Answer me if you can hear me."

She knew better than to open the door. It could be a ploy by Sir Golan to draw her out from the safety of her barred chamber. But she had to check to make sure William was not hurt or gravely ill. She could not live with herself if William was hurt while trying to protect her and she didn't do anything to help him.

But she would not open the door unarmed and defenseless. She grabbed the basin off the washstand and shoved the bar on the chamber door aside. Then she leaned her back against the wall beside the door and threw it open. William's upper body, having been slumped against the door, fell inside the chamber. A dagger was embedded in the paneled door piercing a piece of parchment. Rose gasped, her eyes widening.

Stepping forward, she gazed down the corridor both ways. She saw no one and bent down to check William's pulse. It throbbed beneath her fingers. An icy quiver ran down her spine. She could feel a malevolent presence in the shadows, watching her.

Alarm racing through her, she yanked the dagger from the door, the parchment still stuck in the tip. Hurriedly, after she set the basin down, but still clutching the dagger, she hooked her arms beneath William's and hauled him inside. She groaned with exertion, and sweat broke out over her skin.

Once he was inside, she slammed the door shut and shoved the bar back in place.

She checked William for injuries but found none. She lifted his eyelids. His eyes were unfocused as though he was drugged. Assured he was safe for the nonce, she pulled the parchment free and studied the dagger. It was plain and non-descript with no special markings to indicate its owner. She moved to the hanging lamp next to the washstand, unfolded the parchment, and held it up to the light. Written in French, it read:

> *I know your secret. One hundred marks buys my silence. Leave the coin at Lord Ayleston's tomb in the chapel crypt at the hour of Lauds. Tomorrow.*

The parchment fluttered as her hand shook. Someone knew her secret. But which secret was the extorter referring to? She was hiding two damning secrets: that she'd killed her husband and that she'd committed adultery and as a result Jason was not Bertram's son.

Rose paced before the fire, unsure what to do.

It would be disastrous if either secret was to become known. But if someone knew her secret, why did the person wait till now to expose her? And how could the person possibly know the truth? Which led her to wonder who had left the note. Was it just a coincidence that the extorter surfaced the very night Sir Golan, her hated enemy, arrived at the castle?

It made more sense that someone who resided in the castle at the time of her husband's death had seen her struggle with Bertram at the top of the stairs that night. And, for reasons that eluded her, had kept silent. But very few of her first husband's retainers remained at Ayleston.

One particular person came to mind, though. David. She would not believe it. The seneschal was her most trusted servant. Why would he wish to harm her? Unless . . . could he wish to punish her for rejecting her? His passionate confession that he loved her had completely taken her by surprise.

Whoever the perpetrator was, if she did as demanded, she might as well confess her guilt.

What if she did not leave the money? A fist squeezed her chest, making it difficult to breathe. Light-headed, she stumbled to the bed and sat down, the questions going round and round inside her head.

Her gaze landed on her son, lying on his pallet at her feet, his sweet, beautiful countenance softened in sleep. Her heart did a flip-flop, her love for her son an unceasing gale force emotion. She knelt down and brushed his matted curls back off his face. She had less than a day to decide what to do. Whatever her decision, it would be in Jason's best interests, no matter the cost to her.

Nor could she rely on anyone but herself to protect him.

Upon returning from Beeston Castle, Rand stomped the snow from his boots as he entered the Great Hall of the house he leased in Chester. Will followed him inside, wiping the snow from the collar of his squirrel-lined cloak. The porter, John, took their cloaks and hung them on pegs inside the Great Hall entry.

"My lord, 'tis good you are back. You have—"

"Bring us some spiced wine, John," Rand interrupted. "Ballocks. 'Tis as frigid as a witch's teat out there." A fire was blazing in the hearth, and Rand sought its warmth.

"But, my lord—"

A large, looming figure emerged from the tall-backed chair by the fire. Rand veered back in surprise, his hand going to his sword. When he recognized Amaury de Valence, he dropped his hand. The man he'd hired to follow Sir Golan's every move.

Rand waved Will away. The squire turned on his heel and went and sat down at the dais table.

"Amaury, what are you doing here? Is aught wrong? Pray,

tell me Rose is all right?" Rand could not suppress the anxious quiver in his voice. Amaury usually sent one of his underlings to keep Rand informed of Sir Golan's movements. The switch in routine was disconcerting at the least, but he feared the worst.

"Lady Ayleston is fine, Rand."

Rand exhaled with relief.

"To the best of my knowledge, that is. But that may change. That's why I wanted to speak to you. I have some disturbing news to report," he said, and then his lips pinched into a taught, grim line.

"Go on, man. I am listening."

"One of the men following Sir Golan was found strangled in the alley behind a brothel Golan frequented. I have no proof Golan was the culprit, but I think it would be prudent to assume he discovered he was being followed and killed the man as a message to you."

"Murdering bastard," Rand swore. Jaw clenched in frustration, Rand paced before the fire. A sudden disturbing thought struck him and he stopped, his body as rigid as a lance. "Do you know where Sir Golan is now?"

"Aye. 'Tis another reason I wished to speak to you personally. Fortunately, I had posted two men to follow Sir Golan. I received word from my other spy that Sir Golan was last seen headed in the direction of Ayleston Castle on his way to his new post at Chester."

A sharp pounding pain pulsed at Rand's temple and his palms broke out in a sweat. "Will!"

His squire started. Wine from the chalice he held splashed over the rim and onto the board.

Rand blanched. A foreboding shiver skimmed across the back of his neck, raising the small hairs there.

"Aye, Sir Rand."

"Have my horse saddled and readied. I head for Ayleston posthaste."

Will set his wine on the table and stepped down from the dais. "But, my lord, 'tis too dangerous to travel now. The blizzard shall make the trip impossible. You could become stranded and get lost in this storm."

"Do as I say, Will. *Now*," he thundered, his fear a living, breathing beast crawling beneath his skin and making him itch to be in motion.

Will nodded and raced from the Great Hall. Unable to remain idle, Rand decided to gather some viands for the trip himself. He turned on his spurs and headed for the kitchen. Then, remembering something Amaury said, he spun back.

"You mentioned Sir Golan was on his way to Chester to take up his new position. What position?"

"Have you not heard?"

Rand growled beneath his breath. "Would I ask you if I had?"

"The king appointed Sir Golan lieutenant-justiciar of the earldom of Chester. He shall pose an even greater adversary now that he holds such a prominent position of power."

In that moment, Rand knew he had to kill Golan. Rose would never be safe till the man was buried and residing in Hell with Bertram. The revelation warred with his strong sense of loyalty he owed the king. To kill a sworn official of the king was a breach of the king's peace.

Thunderstruck, his heart palpitated faster than a speeding quarrel. It was then he realized he had fallen in love with Rose. Mayhap he always had loved her.

That he would go against his deep-seated beliefs in order to protect Rose made it impossible to deny his feelings for her anymore. And struck him with near mortal terror.

Rand, atop his mount, dipped his head down into the biting wind and flexed his frozen fingers and toes. Huge icy snowflakes hit his face with a stinging impact. His horse trudged through foot-deep snow, the well-worn tracks in the road long having been eroded by the blanketing snow. Not a single star guided his way.

Riding for hours, he should have arrived at Ayleston by now. He could deny it no longer. He was lost.

Shivers overtook him. He tried to keep his attention focused ahead for any familiar identifying marker, but his thoughts were tangled. And his eyes kept drifting closed. He released a stiff hold on the reins and slapped his face to force himself awake.

Riding another mile, he saw a dark lump in the snow up ahead. A hand stuck up out of the mound. In amazement, Rand realized it was a man buried in the snow.

He jumped from his steed to the ground, stumbled to the man, dropped to his knees, and began clawing him out of the snow. The young man lay faceup, eyes open, body stiff and frozen. The man was obviously dead. Rand saw no wounds and surmised the man had died from the elements. If Rand did not reach a settlement soon, he would succumb to the same fate.

Even as the thought penetrated his befogged mind, a wolf howled. Startled, Leviathan bolted. Rand cursed, jumped to his feet clumsily, and staggered after his steed. But the animal disappeared rapidly in the distance. Rand stumbled to a stop and dropped to his knees. Icy snow penetrated through his tunic and cloak into his flesh where he knelt.

Breathing heavily, heart racing, Rand moved his numb lips in prayer, asking God to give him the strength to continue.

Chapter Eighteen

Rose kissed Jason on the forehead and pushed herself up from the floor with a hand to her knee. Legs wobbling, she moved to the fire. After reading the extorter's note once more, she tossed it into the flames and watched it burn to ashes.

Just as her heartbeat returned to normal, a ferocious pounding shook the door again.

A cry of alarm skewered her throat.

Oh, God, what now?

Paralyzed by fear, she stood staring at the door with her eyes open wide. The iron hinges rattled with the force of the blows. "What do you want?! Why don't you leave us alone?!" she cried out in despair.

"Mama?" Jason whimpered, wakening. He sat up in his pallet trembling in fear.

Rose rushed to Jason and dropped onto her knees. She clutched him to her breast, stroking his cheek.

"Jason, darling, I want you to listen to me. Crawl under the bed and hide beneath it. Don't come out till I tell you to. Understand?"

He nodded. His wide blue-green eyes flooded with tears and her chest constricted. "Go then." She got up, and once he'd crawled beneath the bed, she grabbed the dagger and raised it high, blade thrust outward.

Suddenly, the pounding stopped.

She waited. Her heartbeat pulsed at the base of her throat.

"Rose, are you all right? Open the door."

As she recognized Rand's voice, though it sounded slightly hoarse, relief shuddered through her. She dropped the dagger on the washstand, unlocked the door, and threw it open.

Rand stepped into the chamber. After a brief glance at the drugged guard on the floor, his gaze sought hers. It glittered with the flame of relief.

She launched herself at him, saying, "Praise God 'tis you."

Rand stumbled, but clutched her to him tightly. "Aye 'tis me. I promise never to leave you again."

Her head pressed to his chest, she felt him shivering. His cloak was stiff from the cold. She pulled back and looked up at him. He teetered on his feet, his lips were lavender, and his eyes were dazed. She recognized the signs of being exposed to the elements too long.

She clutched his icy-cold hands between hers. "We need to get you out of those clothes and warm you up."

That he did not make some lewd jest at her words told her the seriousness of his condition.

"What's wrong with Justin? And why is Sir William lying on the floor in your chamber?"

"Did you not get my message?"

"I didn't receive any message."

"Then why are you here?"

"The man I hired to follow Sir Golan came to Chester and informed me of Golan's latest movements. I came as soon as I learned he was headed for Ayleston."

Then Rand swayed on his feet and stumbled.

"Ahhhh!" she cried in alarm, dipping her shoulder beneath his arm and wrapping her arm around his waist to keep him from falling. But his heavy weight pulled her down and she landed on her knees.

Driving pain shot straight up her knees. Breathing heavily, she clutched his waist tightly. Rand's head dipped warily to his chest, his golden hair concealing his face. The snow encrusted on his cloak melted and dripped onto the floorboards. Plop, plop, plop. It formed a puddle of water.

Exhaustion sapped her body, but she needed to garner enough strength to tend to Rand. So she closed her eyes, inhaled deeply, and tugged Rand up onto his feet. "Come. Let's get you out of your damp clothes and into bed."

A thump emerged from under the bed.

"What was that?" Rand asked.

"'Tis all right, Jason. You may come out now," Rose said, her voice softly encouraging.

Jason crawled out from under the bed bottom first. When he stood up, he glared at Rand, his small mouth pursed in a disgruntled pout. Rose knew Jason was still angry with Rand for leaving him and was not about to forgive him easily.

Rand's eyebrows arched in inquiry. "What was Jason doing under the bed?"

"When you were pounding on the door so forcefully, I was frightened it was Sir Golan and he might gain entry. I made Jason hide for safety's sake."

Beneath her arm his body tensed. "What are you talking about? I never pounded on your chamber door. I rapped once and then called for you when you did not answer."

She led him out of the occupied chamber and into the corridor. "I can only surmise it was Sir Golan then."

"What has been going on here tonight, Rose? The gatekeeper said Sir Justin was injured. Now I find the man who was ordered to guard you is unconscious and in your chamber."

"I'll explain everything when you are warm and dry. I am worried for you. You are in danger of becoming very ill if we do not warm you up quickly."

Jason scuttled in front of them and opened her bed-chamber door.

"Jason, prithee pull the bedclothes down for me and then seek your bed for the night."

After he did as she bid, Rose turned and set Rand down on the side of the bed. She helped him pull off his cloak, tunic, and sherte. When the tight sleeves of his sherte came free of his wrists, she stumbled forward. Cradled between his rock-hard thighs, she clutched the muscles of his chest to stop her momentum. Her face dove into his neck, her lips brushing silky-soft skin. She caught a whiff of snow, pine, and his unique masculine scent.

Inadvertently, her fingers flexed, testing the heat and strength of him. His tautly rippled stomach clenched when he sucked in a deep breath. Warmth bathed her neck on his exhale. Goose bumps rippled down her side.

Feeling a rush of heat up her neck, she jerked backward.

Avoiding his gaze, trying to regain her emotional distance, she said gruffly, "We need to remove your damp underclothes." She reached for the tie at the rolled waist of his braies.

He brushed her fingers aside, saying, "I can remove them myself. I am not infirm."

Rose gasped. Rand looked up into Rose's wide, stunned eyes. He read recognition at his inadvertent words. He'd said those very words many years ago when Rose treated his infected knee wound. The same night he and Rose made love.

"Rose—"

But Rose turned away. "I'll get some extra blankets to warm you."

Sighing at her continued refusal to discuss that night, he reached down and tried to untie the cord at the waist of his braies, but his fingers, stinging with numbness, fumbled with the knot.

At the foot of the bed, Rose delved into the clothes chest she had opened.

He groaned in frustration and flopped down on the bed in exhaustion.

Conversely, his cock was alive and pumping with blood, a reaction to Rose accidentally brushing her fingers and lips over his bared upper body. The offending member tented his braies.

Her lavender and rose scent lingered in the bed pillow, an exquisite torment to his self-control.

His teeth began to chatter. "I cannot . . . untie my braies. My fingers . . . are numb."

After she retrieved a fur and two woolen blankets from the chest, she tossed them on the foot of the bed and moved to his side again.

"Stubborn fool," she mumbled. Her fingers worked quickly untying the knot. With her gaze turned away, she pulled his braies and hose down to his knees as he raised his hips.

Aye, stubborn fool, he cursed his erection. He wanted to seize her and make her his own in the most elemental of ways. But he must resist temptation.

He had assumed responsibility for protecting Rose when he married her. Failure was not an option. But what did he do at the first sign of his deepening feelings for Rose? He abandoned her, and as a result, Sir Golan seized the opportunity to retaliate.

On the long ride to Ayleston, Rand had realized it was time he stopped running away whenever he wished to avoid unpleasant situations. Since he was a small boy escaping his father's abusive control, it had become the way he dealt with personal dilemmas he did not wish to confront.

He would do so no more.

He meant what he said to Rose earlier. He was never going to run away from her again. But to succeed, he'd have to rein in his carnal impulses. He would not subject Rose to his unwanted advances again. It was the one thing she had ever asked of him and he meant to keep his promise. No matter the temptation.

Rose's fingers brushed his thigh. Rand groaned. He gritted his teeth and reiterated in his head, *No matter the temptation. No matter the temptation. No matter the temptation.*

Though Rose turned her face away, it was impossible not to give a brief glance at his member.

Amazingly, he was semiaroused.

With a flush of embarrassment, she pulled both hose and braies down to his ankles and tugged them off his feet. Stopping in surprise, she stared at his toes. The two smallest toes of one of his feet were webbed like a duck. The oddity made her smile. She'd always considered Rand perfect in face and form, and this slight imperfection made him less intimidating.

Once more Rand began shaking with shivers and his teeth chattered. Inwardly cursing her distraction, she flipped the coverlet up over him and tossed his undergarments on the mound of clothes on the floor beside the bed. Then she piled the wool blankets and fur she'd retrieved from the chest on top of him.

Next she moved to the fireplace and added more kindling and logs. A spark caught. Flames flared and roared to life, their hungry fingers reaching out to tease and caress the logs like a fiery lover.

"'Od's blood, I am cold," Rand swore.

Rose turned back to Rand, frowning. Curled on his side, Rand reached out his shaking hand and clutched the fur tightly to his chin.

It was difficult seeing Rand so weak and vulnerable. He could have died out in the storm, yet he'd braved the danger to travel to Ayleston to protect her from the vengeful Sir Golan.

Rose could not bear watching him suffer anymore. Indeed, there was one more way she knew to get him warm. She could not let her fears prevent her from using every means she knew as a healer to reverse his symptoms. Hesitating but a moment, she hurriedly removed her garments, then lifted the blankets and crawled into bed with Rand.

Rand stiffened, saying between gritted teeth, "What do you think you are doing, Rose?"

Rose huddled up behind him and wrapped her arms around him. Her body touched his back, buttocks, and thighs. "Being exposed to the cold so long made your body heat drop dangerously. Our bodily contact is the only thing that can make you warm again."

Long, silent moments passed, except for their breathing and an occasional pop from the fire. A thickening tension built as they lay skin to skin—like sultry waves of heat given off by a roaring fire. Rose felt open and vulnerable. Breathless.

"'Tis working," Rand said, his voice a raspy caress. "I'm warming up already."

She could feel it too. Her naked breasts pressed against him—heat from her body seeped into his supple, muscular back, making her colder. But she barely noticed. His thighs were impossibly thick and strong. She inhaled deeply, taking air into her lungs, breathing in his pine scent. It was redolent and extremely alluring.

Rose clutched him tighter, frowning as she felt a rough, uneven patch of skin near his lower back. "Rand, what is this on your—"

"Tell me what happened here tonight," Rand suddenly blurted out.

When he rolled onto his back, she snuggled up to his side and laid her head on his shoulder. Eager for the distraction, she explained everything that occurred yesterday, beginning with the arrival of Sir Golan.

"The bastard," Rand swore. "I shan't rest till Sir Golan pays for harming Justin. I should have killed the man on the jousting field."

Rose could not have agreed more heartily. Instead, she

finished describing the events that unfolded right up to Rand's return.

Rand shifted, stretching his legs. "'Tis all my fault. If I had been here, the bastard would not have dared to attack you. In the morning, I shall remove Sir Golan from Ayleston. If he knows what's best, he shall not gainsay me."

She bit her lip and rested her hand on his chest. "Dare you risk insulting him? He now has great authority to do us harm." The thud of his heart beat a rhythmic tattoo against her palm.

"I don't want you to worry about Sir Golan."

"How can I not when he seems determined to destroy us?"

"Now that I have returned he will not challenge me face-to-face. The man is not a fool." His hand came up and covered hers. "He knows I have King Edward's trust. As such, Sir Golan can't risk going against me without drawing the king's wrath upon him."

"Aye, but he shall use every devious means at his disposal to claim retribution. This night is proof of his determination to do so." Rand did not even know about the extortion threat she'd received. "And you can bet if he was to succeed, there would be no evidence to point to his involvement." His thumb massaged her sensitive palm; her breath grew uneven.

"Don't worry. I am going to take care of Sir Golan. The man believes he is too clever by half. But I have a man looking at Golan's wife's death. I don't doubt he shall dig up a witness or evidence to convict Golan. And if that fails, well, I have no qualms about disposing of Sir Golan by under-handed means in order to protect you and Jason."

Despite Rand's assurances, Rose could not suppress the overwhelming feeling of impending doom that engulfed her. Without volition, she clutched him tighter. Heat radiated between them, stirring her emotions into a stew of fear, excitement, and longing.

Rand groaned, long and deep. The vibration rippled through her breasts, peaking her nipples into hard nubs.

She jerked, and then clutching the sheet to her chest, she leaned up on her elbow and caught his gaze. "I am sorry, Rand. Did I hurt you?"

A bark of laughter erupted. "Nay. You did not hurt me." He rolled over to face her. He traced the crease in her brow with his finger. "The opposite actually. Surely by now you must know the effect you have on me?"

He took her hand in his and pressed it on top of the fur covering his groin area. He was aroused. The long, hard ridge of flesh seemed to burn into her palm. Her stomach quivered. With fear? Or could it be something more pleasurably elemental? Her heart wanted it to be more.

But her instincts won out. She dropped her gaze and curled her fingers into a fist. He released her hand immediately. "I don't understand why you desire me. My body is too slender and bony, and my chest too flat to appeal to a man's carnal urges."

"Why would you ever think such a thing?" Rand growled beneath his breath. "Was that what Bertram told you?"

"Bertram did not have to tell me so much as show me by whoring with Lady Lydia in my own abode," she said bitterly. She despised how weak she sounded. No matter that Bertram was dead these many years, he continued to influence her thoughts and decisions to her detriment. Continued to make her feel small and unworthy.

He stared into her eyes, his gaze darkening with lust. "Your husband was a fool for desiring Lydia over you. If I were your husband, I would not need to seek others to fulfill my desires."

Her heart jumped into her throat. "But you are my husband," she said softly.

Rand blinked at her wistful tone. In the months since they'd wed, did Rose have a change of heart? Did she now wish their marriage was one where they expressed their desire for one another without shame or regret? "Of course.

I am your husband, but you must admit our marriage is not conventional in any sense. You wanted a chaste relationship, and I swore to abide by your desire."

With his forefinger, Rand skimmed down the side of her neck, dipped into the hollow where her pulse throbbed, and continued down her chest to the edge of the sheet she clutched. "Have you changed your mind in that regard? You need only say the word and I shall gladly show you how much my body aches to join with yours." His voice thrummed with desire, and his member stiffened hot and hard.

Rand held his breath, waiting—nay praying—Rose would give him a signal that she wanted more from their marriage.

He watched as several emotions flashed in her big, almond-shaped blue eyes. Indecision, need, yearning, and finally, despair.

She shook her head, misery in her voice as she said, "I can't. I want to. But 'tis hopeless."

Rand reached up and tenderly brushed her red-gold hair back off her forehead. "I don't believe that. Naught is ever hopeless." The words shocked Rand, reminding him of the promise his mother had drawn from him before she died.

Rose's mouth twisted with bitterness and disbelief. "Do you truly believe that?"

An ache deep in his chest flared; nay, he did not. Not in his case anyway. But he could not bear to disappoint her, or see the pain in her eyes, so he lied through his teeth. "I do. Now tell me. What is holding you back?"

Indecision flickered in her eyes, then deep sadness. She dropped her gaze and lay back down. "You can never understand. How could you? You're a man. Men wield all the power and never question or concede that that power should not be abused."

Rand clutched her fist on top of the fur. "You speak of your husband, Bertram. Not me. I, of all people, understand abuse of power."

"How? How can you truly understand? You have never been at the mercy of a man who has all the power, who has the physical strength to overwhelm any resistance you might dare to conjure, or who thrives on hurting the people you love because it hurts you—"

At each revelation of Bertram's cruelty, it felt as though someone twisted a dagger in his gut. He knew firsthand what kind of toll abuse took on a person, had experienced the fear and pain, along with the feelings of shame and unworthiness he could not dispel.

That he'd done naught to protect Rose from Bertram shamed him.

That night over three years ago when he'd returned to Ayleston to tell Rose of Alex's death, he'd suspected something was not right with her marriage. It was not long before he began to see the signs of abuse. Bertram controlled Rose's every movement, and kept constant vigilance of her during the visit. Additionally, the change in Rose from the spontaneous and open young lady she was when Rand left to go on the Crusade, to the listless and obedient wife when he'd returned was dramatic.

The night Rose tended his infected knee wound was seared into his memory. She'd begged him to make love to her. It was obvious she wanted to wipe away the taint of her husband's touch. But afterward she'd been unable to look at him, so totally ashamed of what to him had been beautiful and precious that she refused to see him again before he left. Angry and confused, he'd gone, and forever regretted leaving her to the merciless bastard.

All these thoughts now sifted quickly in his mind.

"Rose," he interrupted her. "I do understand what it feels like to be powerless, to be the victim of someone stronger than you, more powerful than you. I understand exactly how you feel. I do. More than you can possibly know."

Beneath the words, Rand heard the pain and hurt he had

tried to deny but had carried since boyhood. He never could understand why his father hated him. Perhaps it was what convinced Rose of his sincerity and had her eyes gazing at him with sympathy and understanding.

His hand was still clutching hers, and she laced her fingers through his. "I see that you do understand. But how?" Her gaze was steady, and encouragement gleamed in her eyes. "Who was it who hurt you?"

A huge lump formed in his throat. For so long, he'd hidden the pain so deeply inside him it was as if the abuse happened to someone else. He'd convinced himself it was better if the past remained buried and forgotten. But Rose deserved to know the truth.

Rand swallowed. "I have never told anyone of this before. Never spoken of it to a living soul since my sister's and mother's deaths."

Rose said naught, but completely surprised him when she slid her arm beneath his neck and laid her head on his chest. The sheet remained a barrier between their bodies. "Go on. I am listening," she said softly.

Slowly, in stops and starts, Rand delved into the memories of the past and told Rose the tale of a father who despised his wife and children for their tainted peasant bloodstock. How that hatred and resentment metamorphosed into a violent, unforgiving man who emotionally and physically mistreated them. How Rand had tried to protect his mother and sister from his father's fists but was too small and powerless to defend them.

"The day my father disowned me and sent me to England, I swore that I would never become like him. That I would never let his hate and resentment infect me. I may have his blood running through my veins, but my English blood, peasant stock though in part it be, is stronger than his precious Gascon blood."

"Nay, Rand. You are not your father." Rose breathed

against his neck; her warmth seeped into him, a balm to his ragged memories.

Rand exhaled slowly. It felt as though an obstruction in his chest broke up and was released from his lungs with the exhalation. He breathed easier and felt lighter, less burdened by the pain of the past.

But soon a heavy weight pressed on his eyelids. He could not keep his eyes open. Rose caressed his face and hair, the soothing motion lulling him asleep.

"Sleep, Rand. You need your rest. Don't fight it."

His eyelids fluttered open again. He wanted to finish their conversation, to discover if there was a chance she could ever let him show her how she deserved to be worshiped, body and soul. How he wanted to erase every bad memory of Bertram's ill treatment with tender caresses and gentle devotion. But exhaustion tugged and blackness engulfed him.

Rose stared down at Rand, a soft smile on her face as his eyes closed and his breathing grew deep and even. She'd never felt closer to Rand than she did at this moment. The shared experience of abuse enabled her to see beyond the portrait Rand wished to portray of himself and realize there were depths to him she wished to explore and plunder.

With her forefinger, she traced his strong blade of a nose, nostrils slightly flared. She continued along his broad cheekbones and into the hollows created below them. His lips, top and bottom, had been perfectly sculpted by a sensual hand. The beauty of his face did not intrigue her half as much as the man himself who hid the painful memories of his childhood behind a genial mask.

Tremendous sadness filled her as she formed a mental image of Rand as a youth craving his father's love. It was not difficult, for the face she imagined was nearly identical to Jason's.

Indeed, Rose marveled that no one had recognized the

resemblance between father and son. They had the same shapely lips, engaging dimples, and wide-set eyes.

Though she wanted to explore more deeply the complex depths of Rand's inner self, she realized it would be courting danger. She was becoming too emotionally attached to Rand. She could feel this growing need to confide in him. It was terribly tempting to unburden her conscience and tell him the truth of Jason's paternity. To tell him of her culpability in Bertram's death and, as a result, that someone now threatened to expose her.

But she could not risk losing her son. She could trust no one but herself and, therefore, a true marriage with Rand was out of the question.

Chapter Nineteen

Before dawn was a glint on the horizon, Rose crept out of the chamber and down the passageway to the family's private chapel. Ayleston Chapel was a three-story stone structure connected to the Great Hall. It consisted of a stone-vaulted, ground-floor crypt; the first-floor chapel for the servants; and the second-floor gallery for the family's exclusive use.

Hanging from her girdle, she carried the chatelaine's ring of keys. She found the key to the private gallery entrance, inserted it in the keyhole, and turned it. The iron key scraped loudly in the wooden lock, and then she pushed open the aged oaken door.

When she locked the chamber upon her husband's death, she never expected to set foot inside again. It was her attempt to lock away the debaucheries Bertram had committed in his quest for an heir because he was unable to perform his husbandly duties without the titillation of having his cousin or mistress observe them. He'd taken a perfectly benign occupation, gazing through a squint from his bedchamber into the chapel to observe Mass in privacy, and instead used the secret spy hole for his illicit games. Rose still carried the shame and humiliation of having been forced to participate.

But her degradation was in the past. Now, she inhaled

a deep breath for courage and stepped into the back of the chamber. In her haste, she did not close the chapel door completely.

Before her were two benches. On the wall to her right was a mural of a scene from the Bible, the paint peeling from the face of Jesus ministering to the poor. She remained in the shadows and waited in the hushed silence. Her gaze was riveted to the altar on the floor below, which was situated beneath the large carved crucifix hanging on the rood screen. Behind the pedestal stone altar and rood screen was the entrance to the family burial crypt.

After Rand had fallen asleep, Rose had decided not to respond to the extorter's threats. Doing so would only give credence to her guilt. Or it might be a trap by Sir Golan to get her alone with the intention of exacting vengeance on her. Instead, she had decided she would try to discover who the perpetrator was by observing the crypt entrance from the secret vantage point of the private chapel.

There was no back entrance to the chapel, so whoever entered or exited the crypt would be fully visible from where she was watching.

A whoosh and sudden scraping of wood erupted behind her. Startled, she clutched a hand to her speeding heart and spun back toward the door. The door was closed—a draft most likely had drawn it shut. More cautious now, she locked the door and returned to her vigilant post to catch the villainous culprit.

As the first fingers of dawn beamed through the high round window opposite her, someone entered the chapel below. A slender figure wearing a hooded cloak approached the altar with slow, hesitant steps. But instead of passing the rood screen and heading to the crypt, he made the sign of the cross and knelt in prayer before the altar.

Rose, afraid that the man would frighten away the extorter, sat in tense silence, waiting for him to rise and leave the chapel. She could not remain here indefinitely; she had duties that needed tending. Soon someone would begin searching for her.

The man in the chapel suddenly rose to his feet. After crossing himself, he turned and started walking toward the chapel entrance. Rose was sitting in the shadows above him, but at that moment, he tipped his head back and stared up into the gallery. His hood slid back on his head, revealing Geoffrey. A flicker of surprise jolted her. A brief frown marred the boy's face, but he continued walking and exited the chapel.

Rose released her held breath and waited. And waited some more.

Hearing the door to the bedchamber close, Rand woke suddenly. Rose was gone. He jumped out of bed and hurriedly dressed. Until he evicted Sir Golan from the castle, Rand did not feel it was safe for her to be roaming the castle grounds unprotected. With one boot on, he raced to the door, opened it, and looked down the corridor. She was not in the hall. Jumping up and down while he tugged on his other boot, he made his way to the stairwell. He was just about to descend the spiral staircase when he noticed the door to the private family chapel was cracked open.

He pushed the door open farther and peered inside. Rose, her slender back to him, sat on a bench with her head dipped down in prayer. Rand could not help smiling. He'd missed her terribly and been on the verge of making an excuse to visit Ayleston before he'd received word of Sir Golan's movements.

Not wanting to disturb Rose at prayer, knowing she'd be safe for the nonce, Rand closed the door and went to check on Sir Justin and William. He had many questions that needed answering.

William was still unconscious on the floor. Sir Justin was

awake and alert, though his eyes were dim with pain. "Rand, 'tis glad I am that you have returned. Pray, tell me Lady Rosalyn is all right." His voice quivered anxiously. "I hope she fares well with Sir Golan in residence."

"You may rest easy on that score, Justin. Rose nursed you through the night and is now at prayer in the chapel. But William is another matter. With you injured, he was posted at your chamber door last night to guard Rose and Jason. But someone managed to slip him a sleeping potion."

"Who would do such a thing? And why? Surely Golan would not be so brazen as to try to assault Lady Rosalyn when he was a guest here." His eyes lifted up to the canopy above him in thought. "Yet, who else could it be?"

"Aye, who else? I shall not rest till I discover the answer. One thing I know for sure, whoever it is, he is very cunning. He managed to drug the very formidable Sir William—a man who does not trust easily."

Rand shifted his gaze to William, lying on the floor. His voice hardened. "'Tis past time I find out who."

He knelt down beside the still knight. At that moment, a narrow beam of sunshine penetrated an arrow-slit, and a flash of light flickered in the corner of Rand's eye. He turned toward the source—the light glared off a metal object on the floor beneath the washstand.

Curious, he reached beneath the washstand. His fingers grazed a leather-covered handle.

"What is it, Rand?"

He grabbed the weapon and rose to his feet. Standing over William, Rand stared in surprise at the dagger clenched in his hand. "'Tis a dagger," he replied. He'd never seen it before. Mayhap it was William's?

"Eeeeck!" A screech like that of a wounded gyrfalcon reverberated in his ear. Rand spun toward the door. Edith stared in horror at the dagger and raised her arms before her as if to ward off a blow.

William, rising onto his elbow, groaned and clutched his head.

If possible, Edith screamed even louder. Her face became as white as a shroud and she made the sign of the cross.

Rand tucked the dagger into his belt, realizing Edith thought he'd fatally wounded William. "Easy, woman. I assure you I did not harm William."

Rand grabbed William by the elbow and helped him to stand. The man staggered and Rand led him to the chest at the foot of the bed.

William sat down and dropped his head into his hands. "Oh, my head. What happened to me?"

"It appears you were drugged. Can you tell me what you remember?"

William stiffened and shot straight to his feet. He winced in pain, then inquired, "Lady Rosalyn? Is she all right, my lord?"

"Your lady is well. No harm came to her. But someone tried to force his way into the chamber last night. Had I not arrived when I did . . ." Rand could not continue. Rose had come to mean more to him than his own life.

Edith wrung her hands. "Verily, my lord? Are Lady Rosalyn and the little lord unharmed?"

"Aye, your lady is in the private chapel and Jason is asleep in his bed."

The nurse's eyes grew wide. "In the private chapel, my lord?"

"Aye. What's wrong, Edith? You seem surprised."

Her expression shuttered. "'Tis naught really. After Lord Ayleston died, my lady closed up the second-floor chapel and never stepped foot in there again."

Rand frowned, puzzled by the extreme measure. The locked chamber must have some special significance to do with Bertram. But why would she broach the chamber now? The timing so soon after someone had tried to gain entrance to Rose's chamber disturbed Rand. Had aught happened last night that she did not tell him about? And the mysterious dagger—could it be of some significance?

"William. Edith. I found this dagger under the washstand," he said, drawing it from his belt. He held it up for their inspection. "Do either of you recognize it? Or know whom the dagger belongs to?"

William stared at the wide pointed blade, his brow puckered. "Nay, my lord. I know no one who owns such a dagger."

Edith shook her head. "I've never laid eyes on the weapon before."

"'Tis not your lady's dagger then?" Rand asked her.

"Nay, my lady has naught but an eating knife in her possession."

"Very good. You may go, Edith."

"I'll send a servant to bring food for Sir Justin." Edith bowed her head and left.

William's eyes beseeched him. "My lord, forgive me. I failed in my duty."

But it was not William's fault. Rand should have been here to protect Rose. He'd underestimated Sir Golan, but he did not intend to do so again.

Rand clutched William's shoulder. "Nay, for there is naught to forgive. I am to blame more than any other. Instead, we shall work together to discover the culprit who did this."

"What would you have me do? Whatever you wish I shall gladly do it, my lord."

"For now I need information. Whoever drugged you had to administer it in your food or drink. When was the last time you ate or drank?"

"I had supper and a pint of ale before I came on guard duty."

"Did you notice anything strange about it? Anything unusual about the taste or odor?"

His eyes grew wide. "Aye, now that you mention it I

remember my ale tasted slightly bitter. I did not drink the whole pint, thinking it was past its prime."

"Were you served alone, or did you dine with others?"

"I supped alone at the gatehouse. When the steward informed me I was to guard Lady Rosalyn, I ordered one of the castle pages to bring me a repast to sustain me through the night."

"Which castle page?"

William's eyes narrowed. "I don't know his name. 'Tis the lad your lady brought home with her upon your return from court."

"Geoffrey?" Rand's voice rose on a note of surprise. "Is that who it was?"

"Aye, sir." William stiffened and his brow drew down in a fierce frown. "Do you think he drugged my ale?"

"I don't know. But I intend to find out. That is all for now, William. You may go."

William nodded and left, still a trifle unsteady.

Rand was having difficulty believing the lad had had a hand in last night's events. Rose had rescued the boy and taken him in when he had nowhere else to go. And he seemed to be thriving in his new position. Yet what did they truly know about the lad except what he'd told them? He remembered that when he'd first met Geoffrey the boy had looked familiar to him.

"What are you thinking, my lord?" Sir Justin spoke up from the bed. "Do you believe Geoffrey could have drugged William?"

"I do not know, Justin. Anyone in the buttery would have had access to the ale. There are some who are willing to do anything for a price."

"Do you truly believe someone from Ayleston could have done this?"

"I do not want to believe so. But I shall discover who is responsible if I have to question every person in the castle."

Rand clenched his jaw and a tic flared in his cheek. "Most likely it was Sir Golan, though. If you'll excuse me, 'tis past time I remove the vermin from Castle Ayleston."

Rand exited the chamber in long strides. First he stopped at the chapel entrance. He tried the door latch, but it was locked. He continued down the stairs and entered the Great Hall. Many of the castle residents were sitting at trestle tables breaking their fast, but Rose was not among them.

"Sir Rand." Father John hailed him over to the dais table.

Rand approached the stern-faced older man. "Father," he greeted him, nodding.

"We were not aware you had returned to Ayleston."

"I arrived in the night."

"'Tis good you have returned. Your place is here at Ayleston. With your wife," he said pointedly.

"I could not agree more. Do you know where I can find her?"

"Where she is at this time every day. Lady Rosalyn is with the steward in his office. She is a very diligent and devoted mistress."

Rand stiffened and glared at the priest. "What did you say?"

The priest, realizing his gaff, reddened. "My . . . my lord," he sputtered. "Forgive me. I meant mistress of Ayleston. I did not mean to imply any impropriety."

"Pray you do not make the mistake again. I shall have no one disparage my wife or her reputation." With a dark glower, Rand spun on his heel and headed for the estate office.

The priest's poor choice of words had brought a surge of seething jealousy in the pit of Rand's stomach. He'd seen the way the steward looked at Rose. He was sure the man was in love with her. Rand could not help wondering if she returned his feelings. During his self-induced exile from Ayleston Castle, he had been tormented by visions of Rose in the man's arms. His suspicions were baseless, but his growing obsession with his wife, a woman who was forbidden to him, was making him laughably foolish.

As he approached the chamber door his footsteps slowed. The mist of anger began to recede; he could not let the fact that he was a jealous fool cause him to charge in there and accuse her of an improper relationship with the steward.

Looking down at the parchment in her lap, Rose tapped her fingers on the arm of her chair across from the steward's writing table.

David read from his list to make sure their records were duplicated. "Of livestock, we have one bull; eight plow oxen; twenty-three grazing oxen and cows, with two lost or stolen this winter; five dairy cows; five yearling bulls and calves; and five heifers."

"On to the next order of business, then." Rose leaned forward and tossed the parchment onto the table. "I wish to discuss the conditions of the betrothal between my son and Lady Alice that Lord Lincoln and I settled upon. When I was looking over the contract the earl's clerk sent me, I discovered an error regarding the *maritagium*. The gift of land by the bride's parents to the couple upon their marriage should stipulate that the *female* heirs begat by my son and his wife are to inherit the grant of land upon Lady Alice's death. I am sure 'tis a simple error. But I wish you to write the earl and inform him so he may remedy the discrepancy immediately."

"I shall draft a letter addressing the matter and send it posthaste, my lady."

"Very good. I'd like to have all the arrangements completed come summer when the Earl of Lincoln is to travel to Chester with King Edward. The king, joined by the queen and a large party of nobles, is to lay the foundation stone of the altar at the new abbey of Vale Royal. Afterward, Edward intends to visit Ayleston Castle for several days. 'Twill be the perfect opportunity to sign and seal the betrothal contract." Rose climbed to her feet.

David stood up behind the table, his gaze clear and innocent.

Rose had purposefully delayed discussing with David her suspicions. It was an uncomfortable subject, bringing up as it did his painful confession that he was in love with her. If David had misrouted the message, he certainly showed no signs of guilt.

She stared him directly in the eye. "You have no doubt heard by now that Sir Rand returned to Ayleston late last night."

He nodded solemnly. "I did, my lady."

"I imagine you were surprised by his arrival."

"Surprised? Of course I was not. Surely you remember I sent his lordship the message you wrote telling him of Sir Justin's injury."

"Then why did Sir Rand never receive my message?"

"I am sorry. I don't understand. If he never got the message, then what is he doing here?"

She waved away his question. "That is not important. What is important is that I discover what happened. Can you swear to me you sent Rand the message?"

"I do so swear, my lady. I would never lie to you or do aught to hurt you. You know my feelings for you." His mouth twisted in disappointment. "But if you cannot take my word for it, ask the page, Geoffrey. I gave him the message. Or ask the head messenger—he'll tell you who delivered the missive and when."

Outside the steward's office, Rand clenched his fist tight to keep from drawing his sword and challenging David to a duel. But he kept a tight rein on his anger and remained to hear more. Not only had David confirmed Rand's suspicions about the steward's feelings for Rose. But Rand also now knew David had supposedly given Rose's missive to Geoffrey. Was it just coincidental that Geoffrey was involved in this bit of intrigue too? With the clues pointing more and more to Geoffrey, Rand was extremely skeptical that the lad was innocent. But what could he possibly have to gain by the deception? And who was he really? Something was not adding up here.

Inside the chamber, Rose's steps tapped on the floorboards as she approached the door. Rand backed down to the end of the hall and hid in the shadows. Rose exited the chamber, but suddenly turned back and clutched the door frame. David's heavier footsteps sounded, then stopped.

Rand strained to hear Rose's softly uttered words. "David, there is one more thing. 'Tis about the night Lord Ayleston died." Rand sucked in a deep breath in surprise. "We never spoke of it, but you alone knew I was going to flee my husband that night. You left a horse for me in the nearby woods for my escape."

Shock at this revelation sent hot blood pumping through Rand's veins. Bertram had fallen down the Keep stairs that night. Did Rose know more about his fall than she claimed?

"Aye, my lady. Lord Ayleston was a cruel lord. You were always kind to me, and when you asked for my assistance, I was more than willing to oblige you."

There was a brief pause, then a deep inhalation. "David, I must ask you if you told anyone I was leaving my husband that night. Anyone at all?"

"Nay, my lady." His voice betrayed utter hurt and dismay. "I would never divulge your confidence to a living soul. Why are you asking now?"

Why, indeed? That she was asking David if anyone knew about her escape plans led Rand to believe Rose was keeping a secret. His hand clutched the handle of the dagger at his waist. Did it have aught to do with the dagger he found? He remembered there was a moment when Rose had opened the chamber door to drag William into the bedchamber. Had whoever drugged William left the dagger as a warning to Rose?

"I cannot say. I must go now."

"My lady?" It was more a desperate plea than a question.

"I know you asked me to never speak of it again. But I cannot remain silent now that your husband has returned. Sir Rand does not love you. He'll never love you as I do. If you give me a chance to prove how much I lo—" David reached out and cupped her cheek in his hand.

"Do not say such things, David," Rose interrupted, her voice appalled.

Rand stepped forward to rip away the man's trespassing hand, but when Rose jerked back, he froze in midstep.

"What you speak of is impossible. I told you last night that I do not love you. I am sorry you misconstrued our innocent friendship for more. Rand is my husband and naught can change that." It was hardly a declaration of love for Rand, but at least he now knew she did not desire the steward.

"I would hardly call our friendship 'innocent.' These last few months have been wonderful without your husband making a nuisance with his presence." A flash of light exploded in Rand's brain. He could throttle the pair for playing him false. "You trust my advice and know—"

"I trust your professional advice," she said, voice slicing like steel. "There is no other relationship between us, nor will there ever be. If you cannot accept that and continue to perform your duties as steward, I shall have to terminate you from your position and ask you to leave Ayleston."

A heavy silence rife with desolation pervaded the atmosphere. Rand gloried in the man's heartbreak. The man had dared to possess that which was Rand's alone. But the upstart would learn there was an extreme price to pay for his audacity.

Finally, his voice devoid of emotion, David said, "That shall not be necessary. I will not burden you with my feelings ever again."

"Good day." Rose spun away and headed up the spiral staircase at the end of the corridor near the castle entry.

Rand charged into the office. The steward, his back to Rand, was walking to the table. Rand spun David around and grabbed the front of his tunic in his left hand. As he shoved him up against the stone wall, Rand withdrew the dagger from his belt and pressed the sharp blade against David's neck.

"So you think to poach another man's wife without retribution? I could kill you for bedding my wife."

The man struggled, but when Rand drew blood with the cold caress of the blade, he stilled. David spoke, his voice a hiss. "She is hardly your wife."

Rand stiffened and his eyes narrowed. Surely Rose had not confided in David about their unconsummated marriage. Images of the two entwined among tangled bedclothes whispering intimate confidences tormented him. "What are you talking about? I can certainly attest that Rose is my wife."

"According to the Church, mayhap. But a true husband would not have abandoned his wife mere days after their wedding. You do not deserve her."

Rand breathed an inward sigh of relief that the chaste status of his marriage was still secret.

David's lips lifted in cool satisfaction. "Obviously she needs more than you can give her, because she fell into my bed not long after you departed."

A surge of rage like a tidal bore washed over Rand. He shoved his forearm up against David's throat and cut off his air passage. David, choking, clawed at Rand's arm. His face reddened. "Never shall you speak of my wife in such lewd boasts or I shall kill you. Understand?" David nodded, gasping for breath.

Rand grabbed him by his tunic again and threw him against the table with a roar of disgust.

The steward caught himself on the edge of the table, jarring the pot of ink, which tipped over and spilled onto a parchment scroll.

"Pack your bags, David. Your services are no longer required. I want you gone from Ayleston within the hour."

His face went from red to pale in a matter of moments. "You cannot do that. Lady Rosalyn will not allow you to discharge me."

"I can do whatever I want. I am lord here." Rand shoved the dagger into his belt, watching for any sign of recognition by the steward. "I suggest you leave now on your own power, or I shall remove you forcibly." His cold glare indicated he preferred the latter method.

Charcoal eyes simmered with hatred. "You shall live to regret this," David grumbled beneath his breath, then marched out of the chamber.

Rand followed him out of the Keep and watched him make his way across the inner bailey to Hill Tower, where his private chamber was located. Drifts of snow were piled against the castle walls. Not far away a party of men and their horses gathered before another tower. Golan's shield was propped next to the tower door. But there was no sign of Golan.

Rand made his way to the squire with short blond hair standing next to the shield. "Where is your lord?" Rand inquired, his jaw clenched.

"Ahh, Sir Rand. Good morrow. 'Tis a pleasure that we meet again," Golan said pleasantly as he exited the tower, though his wide-set dark eyes reflected animosity.

Rand drew the dagger and drove it into Golan's shield. "You forgot your dagger!"

The ring of steel being drawn from several scabbards sounded behind him. Golan raised his hand to stay his men. "I do not know whose dagger that is, but it certainly is not mine."

Rand had watched him closely for signs he was lying. He saw none.

Golan removed the dagger from the wooden shield and held it out to him handle first.

Rand ignored it. "You are not welcome here, Golan. You

may be able to fool King Edward, but I know what a conniving bastard you are."

Golan shrugged and handed the weapon to his squire. His genial smile was as false as his next words. "I'd hoped we could put our past disagreements aside for the king's sake, but I see you have no desire for peace between us." Golan slung his arm around Rand and spoke under his breath. "I shall leave for now. But next time you see me, I shall have taken everything you hold dear away from you. Including your wife." Teeth bared, Golan's smile was a rabid snarl.

Rand threw off his arm. "Get off of my land," he said, his voice dark and lethal. "And don't return. You're not welcome within these walls."

Golan's eyes narrowed to black pinpoints of hatred; then he turned and shouted, "Mount up, men!"

Once upon his mount, Golan accepted his teardrop-shaped shield from his squire. He slipped his arm beneath the shield's leather strap and slung it to hang down his back. Spurring his horse forward, he left without a backward glance.

As Golan's party made its way to the castle's outer gate, Rand crossed the courtyard and mounted the steps to the top of the curtain wall to observe from the wall walk Golan's departure.

Chapter Twenty

After ensuring Edith had Jason well in hand, Rose exited the castle Keep to find Geoffrey. Her gaze was drawn inexplicably to the castle wall walk where a lone figure loomed. Tall and broad shouldered, Rand stood staring northward with his arms crossed over his chest and his legs braced apart as though at the bow of his ship. The dark cloak he wore whipped and undulated against his legs in the cold, brisk wind, shaping against his firm, muscular buttocks.

Rose shivered, from the cold, she told herself, and clutched the collar of her fur-lined cloak closer about her. The cold air cut her breath in half and her breathing grew heavier. A seductive force stronger than her will conveyed a message to her legs and she suddenly found herself climbing the steps up to the battlements.

Rand turned toward her as her boots crunched on the snow-packed wall walk. His gaze, burning with an odd combination of anger and desire, slowly drifted down her form then back up before settling on her face.

"My lord, what are you doing up here? 'Tis ill advised for you to expose yourself to the elements so soon after your recovery."

Rand stepped back and swept his arm beyond the battlements. Rose followed the gesture with her eyes; through the crenel, between two merlons, she spied a party of men traveling away from Ayleston on the road north.

"I wanted to see for myself that Sir Golan departed Ayleston."

"Surely another could have verified Golan's departure and informed you. Do you wish to have a relapse?" she accused him, frowning.

"That would please you, would it not? *Should* I relapse, that is?"

Rose jerked at the sudden unprovoked charge. Where was his anger stemming from? What had she done wrong?

"Of course not. I have never wished ill upon another man." Rose winced; except for her deceased husband, she thought. But he'd threatened her son, and she would commit any deed to protect Jason. "What would make you believe such a thing?"

His gaze bore into her, as though he were trying to read deep into her long-dead heart. Uncomfortable with his intense regard, afraid he would see too much, she looked swiftly away.

In the bailey below, her gaze landed on David. He carried a satchel over his shoulder. A groom from the stable brought out his saddled horse. David raised his arm and gave her a wave of farewell.

Rose frowned in confusion. "Where is David going?" she wondered aloud. "Forgive me, Rand. I must go and see where David is headed."

Rand reached out to stop her, but she slipped away and made her way down the steps. He followed her, and when he reached the bailey, he sped up and caught her by the arm to stop her advance. "You, madame, are going nowhere near the man. David is no longer your concern."

She stared down in dismay at his hand clutching her arm.

"What is wrong with you? Surely you do not mean to prevent me from speaking to my steward?"

"Your *former* steward," he gritted out. "And, aye, I have every intention of doing so."

Her eyes widened in disbelief. "Former steward? Whatever are you talking about?"

"I have decided to take up my duties as lord of Ayleston. In that capacity, for my first act, I dismissed David. I have no need of his services anymore."

She planted her hands on her hips and her eyes blazed with fiery indignation. "How dare you get rid of David without consulting me. He has ever been a loyal servant of Ayleston and does not deserve to be treated so foully."

Rand bent down and whispered in a cold, silken caress, "I know exactly the kind of *loyalty* the steward extended toward you. If you believe I shall turn a blind eye while it continues, you, madame, are mad."

Rose lurched back. After a brief stunned silence, she whispered back in a painful rasp, "Are you accusing me of lying with a man not my husband?"

But he did not hear the hurt disbelief in her voice. While on the wall walk, the pain of her betrayal with the steward had festered and putrefied inside him like diseased flesh. It hurt so badly he wanted to cut the pain out and never feel again. But ever since he'd acknowledged his love for Rose, his normal defenses no longer seemed capable of protecting him, and he lashed out without thought. "Do not pretend you are incapable of betraying our marriage vows. Marriage to Bertram did not prevent you from fornicating with me."

A shrill moan split the air; Rose clutched her stomach and her whole body seemed to collapse inward as her shoulders slumped. Her soft blue eyes rounded with shock and pain.

Rand regretted the words the instant they tripped from his mouth. Guilt, razor sharp, ripped him to shreds. "Oh, God. Rose, forgive me. I did not mean—"

Rose cast her eyes down. "You meant exactly what you said. And you are right." She spoke so softly Rand leaned down farther to hear her. "Coupling with you was a sin and unforgivable. One day I shall pay for my transgression." Her head snapped up and her eyes held his steadily. "But whether you believe me or not, I would never betray our marriage vows. Pardon me, I must check on Jason."

Her face paler than the snow on the ground, she turned and hurried across the inner bailey and up the Keep steps.

Oh, God, what did I do? Rand cursed himself. *I am a fool, an insensitive, bungling fool.*

The moment he flung the accusation at her and saw her devastation he realized he'd misconstrued the conversation he'd overheard. He'd let his jealousy get the better of his sensibilities.

In a stupor of disbelief, Rand gazed around the bailey. Castle folk looked abruptly away and continued with their various duties. A woodsman in a green hooded wool cloak collected an armful of logs from the pack mule's panniers and headed toward the Keep. The blacksmith turned back to his forge, plunging the half-formed rounded steel blade into the hot coals.

David, sitting atop his mount, glowered at him with seething hatred. With a mock bow of deference, he spun his horse around, kicked the gelding into a walk, and entered the passage leading out the castle gate.

Rand, needing a private moment to regain his faculties, had sought the armory to check on Ayleston's inventory of weapons and armor. A sudden blast from the horn at the castle gate announced an important arrival. Exiting the building, he brought his hand up to block the bright glare of the sun reflecting off the snowy ground. Melting snow dripped from the roofs of buildings and landed in puddles.

Rand stopped before the raised portcullis at the castle gate. The clip-clop of horses' hooves on cobbles reached his ears. Will emerged from the darkened passage. Behind him on the rump of his horse, facedown, was the man Rand had encountered frozen in the snow last night.

His squire called out, his arm raised in a salute of welcome. "My lord, 'tis glad I am you survived the storm. I can't say the same for this unfortunate soul. When I found your horse wandering lost, I followed its trail to this man."

"Indeed, Will." Rand grabbed Leviathan's reins from his squire and stroked his gelding's cold, silky neck. "It would seem one man's misfortune is another's saving grace. I was lost in the storm when I came upon this man. Then Leviathan here, spooked by a wolf, bolted and left me stranded. I was fortunate that enough of the dead man's tracks in the snow remained, which led me to Ayleston." Rand stiffened. It was at that moment he realized the man might be the missing messenger.

Will dismounted. "I feared the worst when I discovered you were without your mount. But I was greatly relieved when I followed your trail here."

Rand handed Leviathan's reins to a groom who approached him. "See that you take especial care with him."

Knowing his horse was in good hands, Rand pulled the dead young man off Will's horse and laid him faceup on the ground. He searched his clothing, finding a small pouch attached to his girdle. Several letters were inside it. He sorted through them and found Rose's sealed missive addressed to him.

Hearing voices behind him, Rand looked up. A crowd had gathered around him and Will, whispering and pointing at the body.

"You there," Rand said, motioning to one of the guards who checked all those who either entered or exited the castle. "Do you know this man?"

The scruffy guard grimaced in recognition. "Aye, 'tis

Owain Fychan, son of the head messenger. Last eve he left to deliver messages in Chester."

A loud wail pierced the stunned silence. A middle-aged man rushed forward and flung himself over the dead messenger. "*Na my fab*. Nay, not my son. You can't take my son from me."

The wail of grief reverberated achingly inside Rand's chest. He was envious of the untenable grief this man expressed for his son. Rand wondered how different his life would have been if his own father had loved him even a minor portion of what this man felt for his son.

Rand perused the young man once more. After he searched the messenger's belongings, he checked his body but found no marks to indicate foul play. Which meant Geoffrey was innocent, in this at least. It did not explain who had drugged William. Or how it had been accomplished.

Where was the new castle page? Rand realized he'd not seen the boy since his return to Ayleston. His earlier encounter with Rose had distracted him from his quest to find Geoffrey. Rand wanted to ask the lad if anyone else had had access to William's drink—the most likely source of the sleeping potion.

The crowd parted. Rose strode through the gap in her drab garb, an unusually frazzled Lady Alison following behind her. Rose glanced at him, and then her blue eyes darted away from his steady regard.

His gut clenched at her chariness, for he knew he was at fault.

She knelt beside the grieving father and covered her hands over the older man's white-knuckled grip on his son. "Owain, I pray you, release Owain Fychan into my care. I promise to ready him for burial with the respect and dignity he deserves."

At her earnest appeal, Owain's shoulders shook with grief. "Aye, he was a good boy. A man could not ask for a more loyal son." He released the lad.

Rose waved over two men holding a stretcher. "Take him to the scullery *lavar* so I can wash his body for burial."

The crowd dispersed when Owain followed the men carrying his son.

"Alison, inform Father John of Owain Fychan's death. Afterward, I'll need your assistance in the scullery." Lady Alison rushed to obey her mistress's commands.

Rose began to walk away, but Rand caught her hand and pulled her to a stop. A spark shivered over Rand's fingertips at the touch of her soft skin.

Rose gasped. Her breath ruffled the gray fur on the collar of her cloak. He released her slowly, reluctantly, wondering if she had felt it too.

But her gaze was closed to him and her voice sharp from impatience. "What is it you want, Rand? There is much I have to do to prepare for Owain Fychan's burial."

Rand patiently inquired, "Have you seen Geoffrey today? I have seen no evidence of the boy in the castle. I thought you would know where I could find him?"

Irritation flared hot and brilliant in her usually soft blue eyes. "I know not where the lad is. David could tell you Geoffrey's whereabouts, had you not dismissed him. He was always in charge of the castle pages' duties and assignments."

"Rose, I shall not apologize for dismissing David. He had an inappropriate affection for you. But I wish to apologize for accusing you of infidelity. When I spoke with David earlier, he inferred an intimate knowledge of you, and I let jealousy cloud my judgment." He did not reveal he had spied on her conversation with the steward. He wanted her to confide in him of her own free will, not because he coerced her. "I know now 'twas just prideful boasting meant to provoke me. Will you forgive me?"

Her eyes grew wide at his reversal. "Certes? You wish my forgiveness?" Her voice cracking.

"Aye." He nodded solemnly.

"Then, of course, I forgive you." She paused, then asked, "Why are you looking for Geoffrey?"

Rand debated whether he should inform Rose of what William had told him about the page. In the end, he decided to tell her what he'd learned. He wanted to see if she might inadvertently reveal anything more about what occurred last night when someone tried to break into her chamber. He sensed she was not telling him the whole truth about the incident.

"I wish to question Geoffrey. When William revived this morning, I interrogated him to see who had the wherewithal to drug him. It seems Geoffrey served him supper last night before William went on guard duty. Upon reflection, William remembered the ale he drank with his meal tasted bitter."

"Are you suggesting Geoffrey slipped William a sleeping potion in his drink? He is but a boy."

"A boy nearly on the verge of manhood."

Rose stuck her hands up the sleeves of her cloak. "I do not believe it. What possible reason could Geoffrey have to drug William? We took him in when his parents were murdered and provided him with a new home and position. It defies common sense." A brisk wind gusted, blowing Rose's hood off her head.

Rand hooked his arm through hers and led her back toward the Keep. "What do you really know about the boy? You must admit he has not provided very much information about himself. Indeed, he is practically a stranger to you. How do we know he is not lying?"

"I know the boy has done naught to merit your suspicion. So Geoffrey served William the bitter ale prior to William's guard duty—that proves nothing. Any number of people could have secretly slipped a sleeping concoction in William's ale before the boy served it to him."

"If that is so, then the most likely opportunity to mix it in his drink would have been when the ale was being prepared in the kitchen buttery. That means one of Golan's servants could have bribed the kitchen help to administer it. Which would you rather believe, that one of Ayleston's trusted servants is corrupt and duplicitous, or a boy you have known for a matter of months?"

"There is one other possibility you have not considered. It makes more sense that one of Golan's servants gained access to the buttery and slipped something in the drink with none the wiser. Have you questioned the servants to see if anyone other than Ayleston folk were in the kitchen areas?"

"Nay. Not yet. I wanted to speak to Geoffrey first. He is the main link between the kitchen and William. Afterward, I intend to question every retainer if necessary to find the bastard who did this. But I have not seen Geoffrey."

"I refuse to believe Geoffrey is the guilty party. And I intend to prove it. But first I need to see Owain Fychan properly prepared for burial."

"What exactly do you intend to do to prove he is innocent?"

"I'll simply question all the kitchen servants and see if one of Sir Golan's party gained access to the kitchens during his stay."

"Absolutely not," he said with a fierce frown. "I forbid you to question the servants. If you are wrong and someone from Ayleston is culpable, there is no telling what lengths they may go to keep their involvement secret."

She jerked back in disbelief. "You forbid me?"

He crossed his arms, his stance adamant. "I do not wish to resort to such tactics, but it is for your own safety."

She bowed her head. Whenever Bertram had forbidden her from doing anything, he'd used the excuse that he was doing it for her protection. But what his commands were truly meant to do was to keep her under his overbearing control.

He tipped her chin up with his forefinger. "Rose, you understand I'm doing this for your own protection, don't you?" His warm breath a shivery caress upon her lips, she stared deeply into his green eyes. The cold receded and a tingling heat suffused her.

Aye. Rand was not Bertram. She understood he wished to protect her, but that did not mean she was happy to have her activities curtailed. Or that she intended to docilely abide by his dictates. "Of course, Rand."

In the scullery, Rose stood over a long table sewing the last stitches on the shroud that enclosed Owain Fychan. The lad held a plain, unadorned silver cross in his folded hands. He appeared surprisingly peaceful, as if he'd simply fallen asleep and never woken again.

"My lady," Edith called out, stomping the snow from the bottom of her wooden pattens as she entered the back entrance to the scullery.

"Edith," Rose said, glancing up at her, "Praise God you are back." Then she inserted the needle in the linen shroud, pausing in her chore. "I'm anxious to hear what you have discovered. Were you able to discreetly question all the kitchen servants?"

"I did, my lady, but I am afraid I don't have much to report. No one saw Sir Golan or any of his men in the kitchens during their brief stay."

Rose's shoulders slumped with disappointment. She had been so sure Edith would find someone who had witnessed a henchman of Golan's skulking around where he did not belong on the day in question. "That leaves then the likelihood that Sir Golan paid one of the castle servants to dose William's ale. I do not want to believe Geoffrey capable of such deceit."

"There is another possibility," Edith said hesitantly.

"Go on, Edith. I am listening."

"'Tis possible someone saw something but denied it because they are afraid they shall be punished."

Rose cocked her head. "Hmmm . . . I never thought of that.

Was there a particular servant you questioned whom you suspect was lying?"

"When I questioned Lisbeth, she said she did not see anyone, but her cheeks turned bright red. Initially, I thought it odd but not suspicious, until later when I remembered seeing Sir Golan's squire flirting with her last night in the Great Hall. Now I wonder if he could have slipped into the buttery feigning interest in her and dosed the ale without her knowing."

Rose braced her hands on the board. "If it were anyone other than Sir Golan, I might believe the plot far-fetched. But Sir Golan has no scruples. 'Tis exactly the kind of under-handed scheme he'd perpetrate in order to achieve his ends."

"Lisbeth may now suspect she was used but may be too afraid to admit it because she does not want to get in trouble."

She exhaled deeply. "We have no proof, merely specula-tion. I need to speak to Lisbeth to discover the truth. Bring her here so I can interview her in private."

Edith rubbed the bump on her forearm. "Is that wise, my lady? Sir Rand forbade you to question the servants. Since I was the one who questioned them, you have yet to defy him. What if he discovers you spoke to Lisbeth?"

Rose smiled with assuredness to ease her trusted servant's fears. "Sir Rand shall not find out. Ask Lisbeth to come to the scullery through the back entrance. I will speak with her alone and make her understand our conversation is to remain between us. If she did neglect her duties to ren-dezvous with the squire, she will surely not wish to tell anyone of our discussion."

"What if the maid is innocent? She will have no cause to keep quiet."

"And what reason would she have to discuss it? As her mistress, 'tis not unusual for me to instruct her. Now go, Edith. I am almost finished here." Rose picked up the needle and continued to sew the last stitches. "I don't want anyone to come looking for me before I can speak with Lisbeth."

"You may go now, Lisbeth," Rose ordered. "And remember, this is just between you and me. I am pleased you told me the truth when confronted. But I cannot predict what Sir Rand would do if he found out you met Sir Golan's squire in the buttery for a tryst."

"Thank you," the maid said, her voice suffused with gratitude.

Rose felt a stab of guilt, but firmly ignored it.

"You are very kind, my lady. Especially when I tried . . ." She cast her eyes down and bit her lip, while a delicate flush painted her cheeks. "I promise it shall never happen again."

"You tried? You mean you and Sir Rand never—"

"Nay, my lady," Lisbeth hurriedly supplied. Her face grew brighter. "He could not . . . well, you know, do it. And since your marriage, he has shown no interest in me."

Pleasure suffused her at the knowledge Rand had not bedded Lisbeth. Rose watched the tail end of the maid's blue woolen tunic swish behind her as she left through the back entrance.

Edith came back in, her eyes raised in question.

The smile slipped from Rose's face. "'Tis as we suspected. Lisbeth confessed the squire was persistent in his pursuit of her, and she even consorted with him when he followed her into the buttery. It was she who gave Geoffrey the ale intended for William."

Edith wrung her hands, a nervous tic when she was agitated. "That is a relief to know. But soon enough Sir Rand will interrogate the servants. What if somebody mentions I already questioned them? And Sir Rand suspects your hand in the inquiry?"

"I have already considered the possibility and have devised a plan that shall guarantee he never knows of our inquiries."

"Oh no. I am afraid I am not going to like this."

"You worry too much, Edith. My plan shall work. I will have Lady Alison tell Rand that one of the servants confessed to her that they saw Golan's squire in the buttery, but that she cannot tell him who because she promised to keep their identity secret."

"I don't know, my lady. What if—"

Rose clutched her former maidservant's hands in hers. "Do you not see, Edith? 'Tis perfect. Rand need never question the servants, and hence learn of my involvement, and at the same time he will be convinced of Geoffrey's innocence and of Golan's perfidy."

"But what if he does not believe Lady Alison and insists on questioning the servants himself?"

"Sir Rand is too chivalrous to believe a woman of Lady Alison's character would lie to him. It would not occur to him to question the verity of Lady Alison's confession. Besides, she is not going to lie about how Sir William was drugged, merely about how she learned the information."

Brow wrinkling, Edith said in surprise, "I believe it just may work, my lady. But are you not concerned that you are going behind his lordship's back and defying his orders?"

"Like my first husband, Sir Rand has left me no choice," she said stubbornly.

When she was a young girl, she had been innocently dutiful. She would *never* have thought of defying an express order from someone who had authority over her. Then she'd married Bertram. On their wedding night, Rose learned he expected complete obedience to his dictatorial rule. And he had no compunction about beating her if she defied him.

So she became the dutiful, abject wife he wanted—despite how helpless and inept and unworthy she felt at her easy acquiescence. Then Bertram forbade her to heal the castle and village inhabitants. He thought it was undignified for his wife to associate so closely with the dirty peasants.

It was after that moment that she secretly began to defy him. She could no more stop healing people than she could take a knife and stab it through her heart. Healing people was her lifeblood. Nor could she watch the sick, injured, and dying suffer needlessly when it was in her power to use her gift to ease their pain.

Hence a deception was born. Edith would do the hands-on care of the people—at Rose's direct instruction. And Bertram never discovered the truth.

Now it was ingrained in Rose to use every manipulative and devious weapon at her disposal to achieve her ends. This trait was not something she was proud of, but if she was ever to have any sort of control over her life, she knew of no other way to act.

Edith interrupted her thoughts. "But surely you do not believe Sir Rand is like your dead husband. I have found the new master to be quite fair, honorable, and just in his dealings at Ayleston."

"Have you forgotten his unfair dismissal of David?"

"Perhaps it was harsh, but the steward's feelings for you were inappropriate. I believe it was past time he found a new position elsewhere."

Rose would never admit it, but she was relieved David was gone. Still, she wished Rand had consulted her. She would have liked to provide David with a letter recommending him for a position at one of her father's or brother's estates. His loyalty to her over the years had been invaluable and anyone would be extremely lucky to have such a talented steward working for him.

"If you have no more need of me, my lady, I shall relieve Lady Alison of her care of the little lord. Shall I tell her of your plan and have her seek out Sir Rand now?"

"Nay. I do not wish to involve you any more than I must.

Now that I have properly prepared Owain Fychan for burial, I shall inform Lady Alison—"

The rear door burst open. Rose jerked back, startled, afraid she'd been caught conspiring. A chill wind brought in a blast of snow, the white flakes swirling in the air like a whirlpool before floating back down and settling on the brick floor.

When Lady Alison stepped into the scullery Rose exhaled in relief.

They spoke simultaneously.

"Lady Alison, I was about to come find you."

"My lady, praise God I found you."

Alison's frantic voice sent a shiver down Rose's spine. She looked behind her attendant expecting to see Jason's small blond head peep out from behind Alison's tunic skirts.

When Rose did not see him, her breath hitched and panic fluttered in her chest.

"Where is Jason, Alison?" she asked, her voice trebled.

Chapter Twenty-One

Rose raced across the bailey to the castle gatehouse. Her lungs burned from exertion. Alison's condemning words kept replaying inside her head.

"I was praying in the chapel, waiting for Lord Ayleston to finish his lessons with Brother Michael. Somehow, after his lessons, Jason was able to slip out of the chapel unbeknownst to me. I was not worried initially. You know how he is forever sneaking away to play with the other children. But I looked everywhere for him on the castle grounds, and he is nowhere to be found."

When Rose reached the imposing castle gatehouse, she stopped before the door leading to the guardroom on the upper floor and pressed her hand to the pain in her side. Bent over, she tried to catch her breath to give her strength to climb up the tower stairs.

On the wall walk above, the castle porter called down to her. "My lady, is aught amiss?"

Between gasped breaths, she called out, "Sir Rand. I was told . . . I could . . . find him here. 'Tis imperative . . . I speak with him. Now!"

"Of course. I'll get him right away." He entered the gatehouse through a small arched door nearby.

Alison, panting heavily, pulled up beside Rose. Tears streamed down her pale cheeks. "I am sorry, my lady. I should have been more attentive. 'Tis all my fault Jason is missing."

Nay. Rose knew exactly who was at fault. She was Jason's mother. She should have protected him. Especially after everything she knew about Sir Golan, she should have been more vigilant watching over her son. But once Sir Golan had vacated the premises she'd thought Jason was safe.

Was it a fatal mistake she'd live to regret?

The aged oak door swung open quietly on well-oiled hinges but slammed against the stone castle wall with great force. Rand exited the gatehouse and stood before her.

They spoke simultaneously.

"Rose, what is wrong?"

"Rand, Jason is missing."

Rand's chest constricted at the terror written on Rose's face. "What do you mean Jason is missing?"

Rose clasped his hands and squeezed so hard he winced. "He is gone. Vanished. We have to find him. I have to find him. He is all I have. I cannot lose him. I cannot. Don't you understand, he is your—"

Rand wrapped his arm around the back of her shoulders and pulled her to his side to will his strength into her. "Calm yourself, Rose. And tell me exactly what happened. Slowly."

The sensation in his chest squeezed tighter and tighter as she explained that she and Alison had searched all over the castle grounds and could not find Jason anywhere.

Rand chastised himself for not being more cautious in guarding the boy. He'd vowed he would protect Rose and her son, and he'd failed miserably.

Rose stared up at him, her eyes wide and trusting. "My lord, what are we going to do?"

Nay. He would not give in to his fear. Rose had come to him for help and he would not disappoint her.

"We are going to find your son, Rose. That is what we are going to do."

Rose was relieved when Rand quickly took charge. He rounded up every castle retainer who was in the outer bailey and organized a large search party. He broke them up into three groups, sending the third, the largest group to search the village. The other two parties began their search within the castle walls. Those folk who joined her and Rand began scouring the castle grounds to the rear of the Keep, while the others began working their way from the castle gate toward the Keep, where the two groups would meet.

"What is beyond the orchard, Rose?"

"The fish pond. It froze over two days ago and the—"

"Hush," Rand said as he raised a hand and halted. "Did you hear that?"

A gust of wind buffeted Rose. She pulled her fur collar around her neck and cocked her ear to listen. Boyish, enthusiastic shouts punctured the air. It sounded like it came from the pond. But the gusting wind could be carrying the sound from any direction.

Rose shot her gaze to Rand. "I think it is coming from the fish pond."

He nodded, his eyes bright. "Come. Let's go check. It sounds like some boys are playing. I imagine the ice on the pond was quite a temptation."

Clutching her arm, he led her through the rows of apple and quince trees. A denuded tree branch caught on her veil and yanked her head back.

"Ouch," she cried out.

Rand released her arm and stood face-to-face with her. "Are you all right?" His hands gently pried the branch loose and then dropped the end of her veil.

Rose rubbed her scalp where a pin was yanked from her head. "'Tis naught but a small scratch."

But Rand did not back away. He stood staring down at her. Their breaths intermingled. He rubbed his thumb over her cool cheek, the tender gesture suffusing her face with tingling warmth.

His hands dropped to her shoulders. "I promise you we are going to find Jason, Rose. He is probably just hiding from us. When I was his age, I was forever eluding my nurse so I could play with the peasant children. I know we will find him shortly. I shall not rest until we do."

She nodded, blinking back the sting of tears.

"Come," he said and grabbed her hand.

Warmth seeped into her palm. His strength flowed into her, giving her the courage and hope she needed to keep from wilting in despair.

Together, they turned and hurried to reach the pond. They emerged into the clearing where the pond, covered with a layer of ice, spread out before them along the southeast wall of the castle.

Golden shoots of dead grasses lined the far side of the pond. On the frozen white surface a group of castle pages were hitting a ball back and forth with sticks, purposely avoiding an area not far from the grasses where the ice was thinner.

Rose dug her fingernails into the back of Rand's hand.

"Aye, love, I see him, too."

Jason stood on the other side of the pond near the grasses silently observing the older boys who were yelling exuberantly in their play. A blond-haired older boy, roughly elbowing Geoffrey aside, shouted and smacked the ball with his stick. He hit the ball with such force it careened across the entire surface of the pond and disappeared into the grasses. The boys chased after it, then slid to a stop, realizing they'd have to walk on the thin ice.

The next events happened so fast Rose would swear they occurred in the blink of an eye.

Jason crashed into the grasses and hollered, "I've got it!"

Rose's heart crawled up into her throat. "Jason, stop! 'Tis too dangerous!"

Jason stopped. "Don't be afraid, Mama! The ball is right here! I can see it near my foot!"

He bent down and scrabbled in the grass. The movement propelled the ball out of the rushes and it rolled to a stop onto the thin ice. With nary a thought to his safety, Jason went after the ball. He leaned down, reaching for the leather toy. His fingers closed over it.

Beside her, Rand hollered, "Jason! You will obey your mother! Get off the ice, *now!*"

Startled at Rand's firm tone, Jason dropped the ball and it slid several feet away.

A loud crack shattered the hushed silence. A jagged line formed and spread out from beneath Jason's feet. The boy, his eyes wide, froze in fright.

Rose ran toward Jason, waving her hand for him to move. "Jason, get off the ice! 'Tis cracking!"

Another loud crack rent the air, and Rose watched in horror as Jason plummeted into the water.

A scream from a great distance echoed in her ears. Then Rose realized it was her own. Arms pumping, her booted feet crunched on the hard-packed snow on the ground. Rand shot past her, his longer strides chewing up the distance with amazing speed. But they'd never reach Jason in time. Jason's head bobbed above the water, his arms churning, but he did not know how to swim.

Jason slipped below the water. Moments passed, but he did not resurface.

Her heart slammed to her toes. "Naaay!" she screamed.

Then one of the boys, Geoffrey she thought, crawled out to

the edge of the ice, and dropping to his stomach, he reached his arm down into the pond.

Soon, Jason's wet, matted head cleared the surface. He clutched the edge of the ice with his free hand and sputtered, coughing and choking up water. Geoffrey held on to Jason but was too weak to pull him out.

Finally, Rand reached Geoffrey. "Are you holding on tight to Jason's hand, Geoffrey?"

Rose did not hear his reply, but Rand grabbed the castle page's ankles and pulled him backward.

Jason was freed quickly from the water's dangerous clutches. Had Rand moved to pull Jason from the water, his weight would have cracked the ice and put them all in danger.

Rand grabbed Jason and lifted him up into his arms. Rose slowed to a stop, but the leather soles of her boots slipped on the ice. She lurched, then clutched Rand's arm, preventing herself from falling.

She stared down at Jason. His breathing was quick and shallow.

"Jason, can you hear me?" She asked as she brushed back the wet curls from his face.

His beautiful blue-green eyes opened. He blinked, eyelids drooping from exhaustion and the cold water. "I am sorry, Mama. Can you forgive me . . . for disobeying you?"

Emotion clogged the back of her throat. Tears pricked her eyes. "Of course, darling. I forgive you."

He smiled such a beatific smile—the left side of his mouth quirked up, revealing his dimple, reminding her of his father's engaging grin—that Rose realized she'd done Jason a grave disservice denying him knowledge of his real father. His eyes fluttered closed and his head drooped to the side.

"We need to get him inside, warmed and dried. Quickly!"

The danger was not over yet. He could still succumb to the elements.

* * *

Rand cradled Jason in his arms with gentle care as he entered the bedchamber behind Rose. He kicked the door closed with the sole of his booted foot. Rose moved to her bed and pulled the bedclothes down.

Rand hurriedly laid Jason down on top of the bed and began stripping off the boy's cold, dripping garments. "Rose, I can undress Jason. Go ahead and get out of those clothes."

Turning back to Jason, he gently tugged the boy's arm free of the clinging wet garment. When Rand did not hear the rustling of Rose's clothes, he looked at her over his shoulder. She stared at him, paralyzed, her hand clutching her throat.

"Rose," he snapped. "What are you waiting for? Remove your clothes so you can warm up Jason as you did me last night."

She jumped and her blank stare disappeared. She dropped her hand to the brooch that attached her cloak and unpinned it. Jerkily, she removed the heavy wool and tossed it onto the floor.

Rand removed the remainder of the boy's clothes, lifted Jason into his arms, slid him onto the clean dry sheets, and pulled the fur coverlet over him. He heard the clunk of Rose's boots dropping onto the floorboards one by one.

Edith entered the chamber, wringing her hands. "My lady." Her anxious gaze settled on Jason in the bed. "I heard the little lord slipped through the ice on the pond and nearly drowned. Is there aught I can get you?"

"Bring some honeyed mead and warm blankets for Jason," Rose said.

"Right away, milady."

Rand added before she left, "When you've done that, send Will to me."

Nodding, she spun away and closed the door behind her.

Rand moved past Rose to the fire and crouched down. He tossed more logs onto the glowing embers then stoked the flames with the poker. The soft swish of Rose's garments—

heard over the crackling pop of the fire—taunted him. He shook his head at the wayward clamoring of his thoughts when all his energies should be directed toward the welfare of Rose's son. With that thought in mind, he got up to go to the chamber door.

Rose tugged her under tunic off over her head. Her surcoate, and wimple and veil headdress lay on top of her cloak. The tunic drifted to the floor. She stood wearing naught but a sheer chemise. Her long red-gold hair hung to her waist, shimmering in the soft glow of the fire. Blushing, Rose reached down and grabbed the hem of her chemise. Quickly, she pulled the undergarment up and flung it off over her head.

He caught an inadvertent peek of her naked, ivory skin, and flame-colored curls between her thighs, before she lurched to the bed and climbed in with Jason. He swallowed the lump in his throat and flung open the door. "Will! Blankets!" he shouted.

A few moments later, Will burst up the stairwell and loped toward him. "Coming, milord," he said, a harried flush on his face and brown hair flopping in his eyes. The blankets and furs tottered dangerously in his arms.

Rand grabbed the stack of blankets. His voice harsh with worry and fear, he barked, "Drink!"

"Aye, milord. Edith is not far behind me with drink."

Rand nodded, spun back inside the room, and slammed the door shut on Will's face.

Coming around the left side of the canopied bed, he shot his gaze to Rose. She lay buried beneath the bedclothes, cradling Jason tenderly in her arms.

Rand layered the rest of the blankets on top of Rose and Jason. "How does the boy fare?" He asked, keeping his voice calm for Rose's sake.

She looked up, biting her lip and shaking her head. "I don't know yet." Fear lurked within her eyes, turning them a murky shade of blue. "Jason has not responded to my overtures. But he's not getting any colder either."

She gazed back down at Jason and gently stroked his damp hair at the back of his forehead. "At least now, because of you, and Geoffrey, he has a fighting chance." Her voice trebled.

A giant hand seized his heart and squeezed. Jason was alive, but Rand certainly could not claim credit for rescuing the boy. He clenched his fists at his sides as helpless rage rose up to choke him. He felt useless, inept, reminding him of his dismal ineffectualness to save his mother and sister.

Blowing out a harsh breath, he seized his surcoate then tugged it off his head. He refused to continue standing there staring like a lifeless stone statue.

"Rand, what are you doing?" She asked, her voice croaking.

His sherte came off next. "I intend to help. With both of us sharing our body heat, I imagine Jason will warm up quicker. Won't he?"

Her eyes gazed off into the distance as though deep in thought, then snapped back to him. "Aye, my lord, I had not thought of that."

When he slipped his braies down past his hips, Rose stared at his groin, wide-eyed. Inexorably, his shaft swelled, pumping with blood. Rand swallowed, his tongue dry. Then suddenly, she darted her gaze away. A sigh of relief escaped Rand as he bent down and slid his undergarments off his feet.

He crawled quickly into bed next to Jason, facing Rose. He draped his arm over mother and son atop the blankets, and huddled up close to them. Long moments passed in tense silence.

At a scratch upon the door, he called out, "Enter."

Edith arrived carrying a tray with a flagon and three chalices on it. Lady Alison trailed behind her, her gaze dipped down in maidenly shyness.

Edith set the tray on the table beside the bed and poured mead.

"My lady," Alison said fervently, "by the grace of the Blessed Virgin Mary, I pray Jason will recover."

Rose squeezed Jason and stared down at him with love bright in her eyes. "With God's grace—"

Jason opened his eyes and mumbled, "Mama?"

Rand's breath hitched in relief as the boy looked up at them with his blue-green gaze.

"Aye, son," Rose said, her voice thickening with emotion.

"I'm thirsty. May I have a drink?"

"Of course, you may, darling," she said with a laughing sob of relief.

Rand propped Jason up while Rose pressed the chalice—which Edith had handed her—up to the boy's lips. He gulped greedily until his head slumped back on the pillow.

Rand noticed the boy's body no longer felt icy cold. He was warmer and his eyes clearer. Hope bloomed in Rand's chest, but he tempered it until he could be certain the boy was going to be all right.

"My lady, will the little lord be all right?" Alison ventured.

Rose smiled. "I believe the imminent danger has passed, but we shall have to watch him over the next few days to guard against infection." Her voice was cautiously hopeful.

Rand searched the boy's face. He *had* regained some color in his cheeks. The huge weight constricting Rand's chest lifted. He could not believe how quickly he'd become attached to Rose's son. Again, Rand marveled how his matted gold curls and dimpled cheeks were characteristics reminiscent of Juliana, his dead sister.

If Rose had not been pregnant when they'd made love all those years ago, he could almost believe Jason was his son. But the idea was preposterous. Unless . . .

Could Rose have lied to him? She'd claimed she was pregnant with Bertram's child; otherwise Rand would not have bedded her and risked getting her with child.

Rand frowned; Jason's natal day was October 12. The

timing of his birth made it entirely possible if . . . Rose had lied about being pregnant, and instead Jason had been conceived the night she and Rand made love.

The thought that Rose had lied to him would never have crossed his mind before. But he now knew she was keeping secrets. The night Bertram died she'd been planning to flee him. And there was more to what occurred the other night than she told Rand, evidenced by the dagger he'd found that morning.

Rose looked up at Rand. His brow was wrinkled and his eyes appeared distant as if he were trying to work out a puzzle. Her heart fluttered with panic as she wondered what he was thinking. Rose stared down at Jason. His smile, his dimples were an exact replica of Rand's more masculine visage. Surely Rand could not possibly suspect Jason was his son?

A pounding set up at her temples.

Rose pulled the furs up closer around Jason. "You may go now Edith, Alison. Jason needs his rest. I intend to stay with him abed for the night."

They left. It was just Rose and Rand now. Their eyes met, and held. Jason was asleep between them, his short even breaths testament to his strength and stamina. Her heart beat with an emotion she could not name. Rand smiled at her. Then leaned forward and pressed his lips against hers. It was a whisper, a breath of a kiss. Her lips tingled. Her pulse pounded.

The kiss lasted but a moment.

Rand slid out of the bed, the sheet wrapped around him. Taking his warmth and vitality with him.

"Are you leaving?" Surely that was not a plea in her voice.

"Nay," he said, a smile in his voice. Light from the sconce glowed in his eyes, sparking the amber bits in his green-gray gaze. "I'm just going to sit over here in the chair while you and Jason get some rest."

* * *

Later that evening, a knock sounded on the door. Rand climbed to his feet from the chair by the bed. When Lady Alison entered, he held his hand up for her to keep her voice low.

"My lord, may I speak with you outside for a moment?"

Rand frowned. What could the girl wish to speak to him about? "Whatever you wish to speak to me about, it can wait."

"Very well, my lord. But I thought you would wish to know immediately. I have discovered some information concerning who drugged Sir William."

"Go on, Rand," Rose said sleepily from the bed. "There is naught you can do for Jason. And if Lady Alison has any information about who gave Sir William a sleeping potion, 'tis best we learn the truth now." Her voice trembled as she added, "Geoffrey saved Jason's life. I am even surer of his innocence now."

Rand wavered with indecision. He absolutely needed to discover the villain who had dared to try and harm Rose.

"Speak to Alison, Rand. If there is a traitor at Ayleston, 'tis imperative we know who."

His gaze cleared. He nodded. "I will be back as soon as I am done."

Rose inwardly sighed with relief.

She wrapped her arms tightly around Jason's narrow rib cage. His breath wafted across her face, his heartbeat a cadence that stirred her emotions: fear, love, guilt. Now that she was alone, the rush of emotions surged up inside her and erupted in tears.

She'd come so close to losing Jason. And it was all her fault. Had she found him a moment sooner she could have prevented him from going out onto the pond and falling through the ice. But she'd lost precious time when, for her own selfish comfort, she'd reveled in Rand's tender ministrations after he had freed her veil from the tree branch.

"You are going to be fine, son. Mama's going to make you all better. I promise," she swore, voice ragged, a thicket of emotion clogging her throat.

Jason's eyes fluttered open. "Mama?"

"Aye, Jason. Mama is here." She smoothed his drying hair off his forehead with a shaking hand.

"Where's Papa? He did come back for us, didn't he?" His dark blond eyebrows drew down in a frown, while his chin quivered. "Or was I just dreaming?"

A dagger of guilt stabbed at her heart. Air whooshed from her lungs. Depriving her son of the knowledge of his father was unforgivable.

Her relief that Jason was alive and cognizant was so great she did not correct his use of the word "papa". "Nay, Jason. You were not dreaming. Sir Rand came back."

His eyes filled with tears, and he heaved a great sigh. "I am glad, Mama. I missed him."

The blade drove deeper; Rose paled. Jason loved Rand. And it seemed Rand cared greatly for Jason in return. She could not forget the tender care with which Rand had carried Jason in his arms, nor his deep concern for his son's health. The fact that Rand did not know Jason was his son made her love him even more.

She loved Rand? The stunning revelation reverberated inside her head like a drum beat.

She thought back over the last months since her marriage to Rand. She'd only agreed to the union so she would not be forced to marry Sir Golan, a man made from the same distorted mold as her first husband.

Once given power over her, though, Rand had never abused his dominion. In point, Rand was everything Bertram was not: a kind and considerate man who made her feel desired and worthy of love. He was not cruel or vicious, but understood the deep emotional scars she carried, for he too had suffered physical brutality at the hands of someone who was supposed to love and protect him.

Dazed with shock, Rose confessed in a breathy rasp, "I missed him, too, son."

An odd combination of wonder and trepidation rippled along her flesh. Without even realizing it, she had fallen in love with Rand. But how could Rand ever love her, a liar and an adulteress? A woman who was afraid of the passion he coaxed from her with one seductive look, or tender caress?

Chapter Twenty-Two

Using the last of the bed ties, Geoffrey kept his gaze fixed upon the knight lying asleep in the bed as he leaned over and bound the man's right arm to the bedpost. A single candle flame illuminated the knight's handsomely carved cheekbones, square jaw, and cleft chin.

Geoffrey inhaled a whiff of the strong scent of ale on Golan's exhalation. He'd easily slipped into Sir Golan's chamber at the inn near Chester Castle. Occasional bursts of laughter floated up the stairs from the common room below and penetrated the thin walls of the bedchamber. Geoffrey reached for his dagger in his boot and drew the blade from its leather sheath. The resulting hiss sounded ominous in the lull.

Golan snorted and tried to roll over, but the bed ties drew him up short. His eyes popped open at the same time he lurched up in bed. "What the . . ." he sputtered. Reaching the limits of his silken bonds, he flopped back down on the mattress.

He opened his mouth to shout for help.

Geoffrey thrust the dagger blade against his throat. "Go ahead and call for help, Sir Golan, and it shall be the last thing you ever do."

Golan gulped and nodded his compliance.

A sly, satisfied smile spread across Geoffrey's face. He held Sir Golan's gaze. "You have been very bad, Sir Golan. And I am just the person to punish you for your evil deeds."

Golan's eyes grew fever bright. He licked his lips. "Who are you and what do you intend to do with me?"

"Don't be coy. You know who I am and what I am going to do to you."

With a flourish, Geoffrey whipped the covers off. Golan jerked, the long, loose-flowing sherte he wore floated up with the gust of air and floated back down. His sherte covered him to his knees, with his arms and legs spread and trussed like a boar on a spit.

"Very good, Golan. I like obedience." He slid the sharp tip of the blade down Golan's neck to his shirt opening. The pulse at the base of his neck fluttered, but he lay absolutely motionless. Eyes narrowing, Geoffrey growled, "Nay, I demand it."

Switching the hold of the dagger to a downward grip, he grabbed the neck of the sherte in his free hand and slit the linen fabric from neck to groin.

Golan yelped, but the sound was quickly cut off. The knight's broad chest rose and fell rapidly. His upper lip beaded with sweat.

"Very good, Sir Golan. I shall have to reward you for your obedience."

Geoffrey parted each side of the slit sherte with a casual flip of his hand. Golan was now completely exposed and vulnerable, exactly how Geoffrey wanted him. Next, in a slow, steady caress, his eyes trailed down Golan's bared body. The cold kiss of his dagger blade followed in the wake of his perusal. Not a breath stirred as the blade descended down Golan's broad, muscular chest and taut, ribbed stomach, then circled around his manhood. Hard and thick, the vermilion appendage distended from a curly nest of dark hair.

Geoffrey smiled a small smile of triumph, his voice softly enticing. "The danger rouses you. Good. It shall make things so much more exciting."

He crawled atop the bed, straddling the bound knight's thighs, and knelt above him.

Golan's eyes narrowed and he tugged ineffectively at his binding. "You are playing a dangerous game. I do not like games."

Geoffrey chuckled light and seductive. "You do not like my game? Verily?" He clutched Golan's erection and squeezed. Golan groaned in ecstasy. "Oh, I believe you shall enjoy the pleasure I shall wring from your lips."

Geoffrey raised the dagger high and drove it down quickly, embedding the blade in the headboard above Golan.

The knight narrowed his eyes in warning, but Geoffrey ignored him. He knew he had Sir Golan exactly in his delectable power. There was not a man he could not seduce.

Then Geoffrey bent over Golan, wrapped his small lips around his erection, and sucked him deep inside his mouth. With his hands and legs tied, Golan lifted his hips off the bed violently to meet Geoffrey's up-and-down strokes.

Golan's panting groans filled the chamber, but Geoffrey released him before he achieved satisfaction.

A long groan of agony ripped from Golan's lips and his hips bucked up in violent appeal. "What are you doing? Finish what you started."

"Oh, I'll finish. But not before I get what I want." Removing all but his sherte, Geoffrey stood up on the mattress and, carefully balancing himself, straddled Golan's chest. Crossing his arms, he reached down and grabbed his knee-length, flowing sherte and tugged it off.

He was completely naked except for the thick woolen band of cloth wrapped tightly around his chest. Slowly, he unwrapped the cloth while holding Golan's desire-glazed eyes. A long sigh expelled from Geoffrey's, or more correctly, Lady

Lydia's lungs as her heavy breasts flopped free of the constricting linen. With a flick of her wrist, the fabric fluttered to the mattress.

In Rose's bedchamber, Rand leaned down and added another log to the fire. The flames flared up, licking hungrily over the timber. The scarred flesh of his back suddenly itched as memories of the fire that killed his mother inundated him. He closed his eyes tightly and spun around.

In an attempt to block out the visions, he stared at Rose and Jason sleeping in the bed as peaceful as angels. Not for the first time he wished Jason was his son. So much so that he was crafting wild scenarios in his head for how it could be possible. But he knew better than to wish for the impossible.

He arched his lower back to alleviate the twinge of pain. It was a permanent reminder of what would happen to anyone he loved. The moment he'd weakened and contemplated a life of love and companionship with Rose, Jason nearly drowned. It proved his fears were justified—his love was a curse to anyone unfortunate enough to trust him to protect him or her from the dangers and ills of this world. This time Jason survived, but Rand dared not risk falling deeper in love.

The quiet breathing of mother and son settled into a slow, steady rhythm, counterpoint to his shuddering heartbeat. With an ache in his heart, he gathered up his few belongings and moved to the chamber at the opposite end of the hall.

Lady Lydia de Joinville raised her hands and cupped her large breasts. Holding Golan's eyes spellbound, she squeezed and massaged the globes of flesh, arousing herself till her nipples grew turgid. Releasing her right breast, she sucked her middle finger into her mouth, pulled out the glistening digit, and skimmed her right hand down her stomach. When she reached her blond delta, she furrowed her finger through her moist cleft and slipped it inside her sheath.

"Take me inside you. Now!"

"Patience. This is my game." She pumped her finger in and out, enjoying tormenting him.

She loved having men in her power. They were so easy to manipulate and control. It had been almost too easy to escape the vile convent she'd been virtually imprisoned in by King Edward. The abbot had been long without the pleasures of the flesh. Lydia had employed her skills on the abbot with minimal effort, and in a short amount of time convinced him to let her escape.

She closed her eyes and licked her bottom lip in delicious memory of the enthusiastic . . . confessions she withdrew from the monk.

Another groan escaped Golan.

Lydia gazed down at him through her lashes, pouting. "You are a naughty boy, Golan. 'Tis time you atone for coveting your neighbor's wife."

"That bitch. Rosalyn was mine. She is going to pay for betraying me. I shall see to it."

Aye, Lady Rosalyn was going to pay for her transgressions. Lydia was convinced she had gotten away with murder. Lydia had been at Ayleston the night Bertram fell down the stairs in a drunken stupor. They had been lovers for years, and as much as she could love anyone, she had loved Bertram. Not only was he the most beautiful-looking man she had ever met, he truly knew who and what she was; he understood her and loved her for it.

That Lady Rosalyn was Alex de Beaumont's sister was an added benefit. No man had ever rejected Lydia until Alex had refused to break his betrothal and marry her. Alex had rejected her, just as Lydia's father had rejected her when he found her fornicating with a lowly peasant in the same bed her father had first claimed her body.

All she knew was betrayal from men. Now she used men for her own devices. She was the one in control, wielding her carnal favors in order to get men to do her bidding. Golan was no different from any other man.

Aye. He was just another pawn in her scheme to avenge herself on Rose for murdering Bertram. The woman was going to suffer the loss of someone she loved so she'd experience the pain and misery that Lydia carried around with her every day.

She shifted slightly, giving Golan a coyly seductive smile. "Aye. She'll get what she deserves. But for now, you are going to give me what I deserve. A reward, shall we say, for my help." Lydia nodded at the dagger above his head. "Proof of my effectiveness as a spy within Ayleston Castle."

"Where'd you get the dagger?"

"'Tis my dagger. I retrieved it from your squire's belongings. I left it as a warning to Rosalyn."

He chuckled with evil glee. "Sir Rand gave it to me before I left Ayleston. He thought 'twas mine. But you would not have gained access to Ayleston without me. I killed the merchant couple so you could be 'rescued' by Sir Rand's party."

"Aye, and you shall get your reward."

His arms twisted in the bindings. "Then release me. Now!"

"Soon, lover, very soon." She retrieved her glistening finger, and supporting herself on the headboard, she leaned over and swiped it across his lips. His tongue darted out and sucked her finger into his mouth.

She pulled it out, then crouched down over him. Her slick portal was inches from his lips. "Take me with your mouth."

His mouth closed over her nether lips and sucked the bud at her apex. Rewarding him, she reached around and pumped her hand up and down his cock as he licked her moist folds like a greedy child.

Having made him wait long enough, she moved back and slid down his manhood in one smooth stroke. She rose up slowly, then drove back down. She drew out the torture, increasing her strokes. Faster. Harder. Then changing the rhythm in slow, exquisite plunges up and down. Slow then fast, fast then slow, she rode him.

His groans mounting, Golan swore, "You are a witch, Lyla. Be done with it. Now!"

The fool did not even know who she was. She'd used a false name to protect her identity.

Smiling in satisfaction, Lydia raked her fingernails down his muscle-bound chest, creating red runnels. Golan, with a final thrust of his hips, roared his climax.

Excited by the power she wielded over him, rather than from any physical satisfaction, Lydia quickly followed, her inner walls quivering with her release.

Shuddering, panting, Golan licked his lips as he tried to regain his breath.

Lydia climbed off the bed, retrieved her dagger, and slashed the bed ties binding Golan's arms and legs.

Golan jumped off the bed, and in a sudden move, he jerked the dagger from her grip, shoved her onto the bed, and pressed the lethal blade to her neck. "What is to keep me from slitting your throat here and now?" His hot, fetid breath bathed her neck.

Pain shivered through her wrist. A clot of fear climbed up her throat, her heart and pulse pounding. Outwardly, Lydia gave him a seductive lift of her lips, all the while trailing her right hand down his arm and clutching his hand holding the dagger.

Lydia knew evil. She had seen and experienced it. But Sir Golan's smile encapsulated and surpassed even the worst depravity she'd seen and done in this cruel world.

"You won't kill me because the person you hate most in this world trusts me completely."

"How can you be sure Rosalyn trusts you?"

"Because I saved her son's life."

"You fool! Why would you save his life?" He pressed the blade closer, pricking her skin. A bead of blood dripped down her neck. It was a mistake he would live to regret. He continued, "I want the woman to suffer for humiliating me. Killing her son is only the first of the torments I mean to inflict on that bitch."

"By rescuing the boy from drowning, Lady Rosalyn now trusts me with the boy's life. With the plan I have devised, using the boy as a pawn, you shall have your revenge on Sir Rand and his wife in one neat, tidy package."

His eyes glittered with evil anticipation. "Tell me. What is this plan you have devised?"

"Give me the dagger," she purred. "You want what only I can give you. Don't you, Golan?" She eased the dagger from his loosened grip and ran the sharp blade down his chest.

The member between his legs hardened and surged against her stomach.

"Ummmm. That's it." She licked her lips as though in anticipation.

Lydia knew she had Golan exactly where she wanted him. And if her plan, God forfend, should fail, she could escape with none knowing of her involvement and leave Sir Golan to take the blame. And more importantly, suffer the consequences.

This time her machinations would prevail. Lady Rosalyn was going to regret murdering Bertram; and in particular, she was going to regret taking away the only person Lydia ever cared about and leaving her alone in the world.

As January advanced into February and then March, word trickled in to Ayleston that Edward's three-pronged attack in the southern, central, and northern portions of Wales was succeeding. The Welsh rebels, supporters of Llewelyn ap Gruffydd, were pushed deeper into the prince's northern mountainous holdings of Snowdonia. Tensions amplified as stories reached them of fierce deadly raids on nearby settlements.

Rand had increased the garrison, along with guard watches on the castle walls, in order to give advance warning should trouble arise. The ground was thawing and the first shoots of flowers and winter wheat were sprouting in the fields and meadows.

Training on the open ground in the outer bailey, Rand grunted as he fought fiercely with sword and shield against a nearly recovered Sir Justin. As he parried and thrust, he shouted instructions to the group of newly recruited men-at-arms who formed a circle around them. The sun shone down on him; sweat dripped itchingly down his back beneath his leather gambeson, a padded knee-length tunic, while the slight chill breeze cooled his exposed face and head.

At a sudden shout upon the castle walls, Rand whipped his head around. A guard on the battlements pointed to the north-west. Rand dashed to the stairs leading up to the castle wall walk and climbed up them two at a time. Once atop the parapet, he shielded his eyes against the late afternoon sun and saw about twenty men, women, and children running for the protection of the castle walls. A band of Welsh rebels on horseback was behind them in fast pursuit.

An agonized cry rent the air; a boy stumbled to his knees, an arrow piercing through his thigh. His mother, holding his hand as she ran, was yanked to a stop. She grabbed the boy around the waist to carry him along.

"Archers to arms!" Rand shouted.

Arrows continued to rain down on the peasants. The woman dragging her son jerked as an arrow pierced her torso. She fell dead, another arrow slicing through the boy's throat. They crumpled in a pile clutching each other.

When Rand saw a phalanx of crossbowmen emerge from

the gatehouse onto the parapet, he ran back down to the outer bailey and ordered his knights and men-at-arms to mount up.

As all hands readied their mounts to ride, Rose emerged from the stillroom brushing the back of her hand across her forehead. "Rand, what is happening?"

"Rose, I don't have time, rebels have—"

The whishing sound of longbow arrows hummed through the air. A shiver of fear raced down his back. "Get down, Rose!" he cried, then crouched down over her into a tight ball and braced his shield above their heads. An arrow *thunked* into the leather-covered wooden shield. Half a dozen arrows pierced the ground around them, fletching quivering. Beneath him he could feel Rose shuddering in fright.

Shouts and chaos reigned as servants rushed to seek cover.

Catching Justin's eye, Rand shouted, "Raise the portcullis and lower the drawbridge! Then prepare to ride out! I'll be back in a moment!"

He turned back to Rose. "Come, we head for the Keep."

Under cover of a return volley of bolts from Ayleston's crossbowmen, Rand pulled Rose up and propelled her backward using his shield for protection. "Where is Jason?"

Her eyes glazed with fright. "He's supposed to be in the chapel with Brother Michael. But you know how he . . . Oh, God—"

"Easy, Rose. Do not make trouble where there is none." He shifted and began heading in the direction of the chapel. "We'll go—" She yanked out of his arms before he could complete his thought and raced unprotected toward the chapel. "Rose! Damnation," he cursed in his fear and chased after her.

She pulled the arched chapel door open and scurried inside the hushed, darkened interior. Rand, on her heels, grabbed the open door and shut it behind him.

"Mama. Mama." Jason shimmied out from behind a table next to the wall and raced to her with his arms outstretched.

"I heard the fighting. Brother Michael would not let me go to you. He said it was too dangerous."

"Brother Michael was correct," she said, breathless, and knelt down wrapping her arms around Jason. "'Tis not safe for you to be outside right now."

"But who is going to protect you from the bad people if I don't?"

Rand clutched Jason's shoulder. "Never fear, Jason. I shall always protect you and your mother from danger. Now, I need you to do something very important. Until the fighting is over, I want you to stay here with your mother where 'tis safe. Can you do that, for me?"

"Aye, Sir Rand. I shan't fail you."

"Good, son. You are a very brave boy."

Rand turned and headed for the chapel exit.

"Rand, wait."

Rand spun around and Rose, unable to stop her forward momentum, collided with him. He clutched her shoulders and looked down into her eyes. Concern shadowed her eyes to a dark blue.

"What is it, Rose?"

Drawing a deep breath, Rose shot up onto her toes and, clutching his waist, pressed her slightly parted lips to his. Desire and tenderness swirled deep in his gut.

Rose drew her head back—briefly, her soft breaths mingled with his deeper ones—then she dropped back down and took two steps backward. "Be careful, Rand."

Rose left Jason's chamber, and for the third time that night, she marched to her bedchamber window, threw open the shutters, and stared out into the night seeking any sign that Rand had returned. Cool night air rushed across her skin raising goose bumps on her arms. She pressed her fist against her stomach to quell the worry roiling inside her. The quiet crackling of the fire could not soothe the tension that strung her as taut as a bowstring, even as her emotions threatened to burst free from her tightly constrained control.

Fear for Rand's safety paralyzed her. Somewhere out there he was pursuing the rebels who'd attacked Ayleston, exposing himself to the lethal accuracy of Welsh longbow arrows and ambush tactics.

"My lady?" said Edith, who emerged from Jason's chamber. "The little lord is abed, sleeping. You missed supper. I know you are worried. But you should eat something. Shall I go to the kitchen and get you a small repast before you retire?"

"Aye, go ahead. And bring a flagon of wine, too." Rose was not hungry, but she wished to be alone to sort out her thoughts.

Edith left, closing the chamber door.

After closing the shutters, Rose went into the other bedchamber and stared down at her sleeping son. He lay on his back, his right thumb in his mouth. Her heart turned over. Her precious son might never know his father should aught happen to Rand. A sob crawled up the back of her throat and escaped. Rose clutched her hand over her mouth to still her rising emotions. Nay. She would not come undone.

She bent down, smoothed Jason's curls off his forehead, and kissed his soft, sweet-smelling skin. Someone from her chamber called out, "Rose, my dear."

A chill raced down her spine. The voice sounded oddly like Bertram's. She entered her bedchamber and glanced around. The room was empty. At a scratching sound on the chamber door, Rose spun toward it.

The male voice called out again. "Rose, dear, come to me."

She rushed to the door and threw it open, then looked both ways down the hall. The voice came again from the spiral stairwell. "Rose, come to me."

"Whoever is playing this silly game, I do not appreciate it."

As her heart pounded wildly, she lied, "Nor am I afraid, if that is what you seek."

"Then come, my dear."

The torch at the stair landing had been snuffed out. Rose hastened to the end of the darkened corridor, refusing to show her fear. When she reached the top of the spiral stairs, she hesitated. An eerie masculine voice echoed up the stairwell. "Why, Rose? Why did you kill me?"

Rose cried out, "I did not kill you!" then rushed down the spiral stairs to catch the culprit who had played such a cruel trick on her.

As she approached the bottom stair, she spotted a pool of blood on the worn stone stair, "murderer" written in blood on the wall beside it. She jerked to a halt, a strangled moan bursting from her lips.

Heart palpitating like a trapped animal's, she spun around and ran up the stairs intending to lock herself in her chamber until Edith returned. But when she reached the landing, she noticed the door to the private chapel was ajar. Rose gaped, shocked. She was sure she'd locked the chamber the last time she was inside. No one else had the key.

Cautiously, a hand to her throat, Rose pushed open the door and took several steps inside. The chamber door thudded closed behind her. She whirled around, her heart racing triple time, and stared aghast. Piercing a piece of parchment was the extorter's dagger, which was embedded in the thick wooden door. But this time, Jason's stone necklace hung from the blade too.

Nay! The cry echoed inside her head. Rose snatched the dagger and retrieved the necklace and parchment. Hand shaking, she unfolded the message, angled it into the moonlight, and read the familiar slanted scrawl.

You murdered Bertram and so you must pay. If you ever wish to see your son again, deliver yourself to the lieutenant-justiciar of Chester and confess to Bertram's murder. Tell no one or Jason dies.

After a moment of stunned denial, her scream shattered the silence.

She ran out of the chamber. A sharp pain exploded inside her skull. White light flared briefly. Then darkness descended.

Chapter Twenty-Three

"Rose? Can you hear me? Rose!" Rand's voice penetrated the heavy blackness pressing down on Rose.

He softly patted her face and called her name again. She groaned, blinking, a nagging sense of alarm pricking her sluggish awareness. Pain reverberated inside her head, but she forced her eyes open. Gazing up, she saw her brocaded canopy. Beneath her, the soft mattress enveloped her body and her lavender-scented pillow supported her pounding head.

Rand sat beside her on the bed, his soft gray-green eyes shadowed with concern. "Praise the Lord. You are awake."

"Water," she managed to croak.

Rand fluffed the pillows behind her back and helped her to sit up. Someone handed him a chalice of water, and he supported her shoulders as he tipped the cup to her lips. She gulped several drinks, causing water to dribble down her chin. Rand gently wiped her chin with a linen cloth, which lay beside the basin on the table nearby.

"Thank you, Rand."

She strained to remember what had happened, and winced with pain. She reached up and felt the painful lump on the back of her skull. "What's wrong? What happened to me? Why am I in bed?"

Alarm glimmered in his green-gray gaze. "Do you not remember, Rose? Can you tell us what happened?" He nodded behind him. "Edith found you outside the private chapel. You were lying on the floor unconscious."

Edith, wringing her hands, moved next to Rand in the lamplight, where Rose could see her. "Aye, milady. Don't you remember? I went down to the kitchen to get you a late-night repast. When I left you, you were here in your bedchamber."

Rose frowned. "Of course. I remember now. You left and I went to check on Jason in his cham—"

A whimper escaped Rose as her memory rushed back with frightening accuracy. "Oh, God, Rand." She reached out and clutched his forearm. "Where is Jason? Have you checked on him? Is he all right?"

Rand's features were a stiff mask; beneath her hand his muscles tensed. "Rose, I am sorry," he said, his voice thick with guilt. He pulled something from his purse and pressed it into her hand. It was Jason's stone necklace.

Rose screamed, "Nay!"

She jumped from bed and slipped past Rand before he could stop her. She stumbled. Excruciating pain jabbed her skull, but she managed to tug the chamber curtain aside and lurch to Jason's bed. It was empty, the sheets cold. Her legs collapsed and she fell to her knees.

Rand hurried after Rose. She cried out in denial again and again. "Nay. He cannot be gone. He cannot. Not my precious baby." Sobs racked her body as she crawled onto Jason's bed and clutched his pillow to her face.

He sat down beside her and gathered her in his arms. A convulsive breath shuddered through her; she clutched him tightly and curled up in his lap. He rubbed up and down her back, trying to soothe her pain, but he knew nothing would allay her fears until he returned Jason safely into her arms. And he knew exactly where to start.

The burning anger in his chest expanded. *'Twas that bastard*

Golan. Rand had no doubt the man had abducted Jason. He just could not figure out how the wretch had accomplished it. But it no longer mattered. All Rand's energies were concentrated on finding Golan and forcing him to confess where he was holding the boy. He could not even contemplate that it might be too late; that Jason might already be dead. He had to believe Golan was simply using the boy as a pawn in order to draw Rand into a trap and kill him.

He had no intention of falling into a trap orchestrated by Golan. When they met, only one of them would come away from the confrontation alive. Should Rand not survive, he'd made a contingency plan to see Golan dead so he would never be able to harm Rose again.

Rose's sobs quieted and her breathing became deep and even. Rand kissed the top of her bare head. He inhaled deeply the lavender and rose scent of her silky copper hair. His body quickened at the soft feel of her breasts cushioned against his chest and her buttocks pillowing his burgeoning flesh. He shifted, embarrassed at his reaction.

To hide his response, he lifted Rose and took her into her bedchamber. He glanced around but Edith was gone. Rand laid her down on the bed, then sat beside her and brushed back the fiery locks of her hair. The gold highlights shimmered in the lamplight.

Slowly, she eased her white-knuckled grip open, revealing the stone necklace he had found by her body. "'Tis Jason's. I gave it to him. He always carries it with him." Her voice was raspy with misery.

Rand swallowed the clot of emotion in the back of his throat. "I promise, Rose," he said, his voice laced with steely resolve, "I shall get Jason back and see Golan dead for daring to lay a hand on your son. I have already made arrangements. I leave at first light."

Her eyes gazed up at him crystalline with her tears. He saw sadness, guilt, and love reflected back at him. His breath caught; his heart beat a rapid tattoo. Surely it was not love he saw reflected in her gaze, for at that moment, the blue depths of her eyes sparked with a ruthless light of determination. She reached over and placed the necklace on the table. Then turning back to him, she cupped both his cheeks in her palms and drew his face down to hers. He told himself to pull back, that Rose was vulnerable, was not in her right mind, and knew not what she was doing.

Just as she knew not what she asked of him all those years ago, when, in her grief for her brother, Alex, whom they all had believed was dead, she'd begged Rand to make love to her.

Now her desire-glazed eyes dropped to his mouth. Her pink tongue darted out and slowly licked her plump bottom lip to a glistening ruby red. As she swirled her tongue over her upper lip next, he imagined that tongue licking his erect flesh. Pleasure stabbed sharp and swift, and his phallus jerked.

Rand inhaled then exhaled to control his rampaging desire. But temptation was too great. A ragged groan escaped him and he pressed his lips to her softer, fuller, irresistible bowed lips. A soft moan skimmed his mouth when she deepened her kiss. With a patience he never knew he had, Rand allowed Rose to control the pace of the kiss, marveling at the wonder and joy thrumming through his heart at her bold yet shy explorations.

Rose reclined on the bed, pulling Rand down on top of her. His powerful chest muscles flexed against her breasts, radiating a tingling heat into the sensitive flesh of her nipples, making them harden into stiff points. The pressure and strength of him emboldened her. She reached down between their bodies and clasped her hand over the hard ridge of flesh pressing against her thigh.

Rand groaned long and low and surged up into her hand. He pulled his head back and stared questioningly into her eyes. "I have to know, Rose. Are you sure this is what you want? You're hurting and vulnerable right now. I don't want you to regret what we do, as you did last time we—"

She shook her head and pressed two fingers to his lips. A need unlike any she'd ever experienced demanded she explore it. "Nay, Rand. I have never been surer of anything in my life. I'm tired of being afraid. Golan has taken Jason from me." Her voice quivered with distress, but she bravely continued, "And you are going into danger to retrieve him. God forfend, should something happen to you or Jason, I do not want to look back and remember naught but my fear and terror. I want you to make love to me, nay, need you to. My only regret would be if you walk away from me now without showing me how much you truly want me. Unless . . . Do you still want me?"

"Oh, God. You cannot truly know how much."

"Then show me, won't you?" Her voice trembled, a small part of her still unsure whether he wanted her. As desperately, as recklessly, as passionately as she wanted him.

But Rand erased all her doubts when, his gaze searing hers, he crushed her to him and slanted his lips boldly over her mouth. His kiss was wild and passionate and hot. Then his tongue delved between her lips and seized her tongue in a velvety, seductive caress.

He groaned deeply. She moaned softly.

Rose had not lied about why she wanted Rand to make love to her. But she had not told him the whole truth either. Golan's note had demanded she tell no one of her sacrifice to rescue Jason. It was up to Rose to save her son. And she would gladly give up her life for Jason.

She loved her son so much she would die in order that he would live and be safely returned to his father. But until now, she'd never realized how strong she was. If she could face death, she knew her fears of intimacy were as inconsequential as fairy dust.

Indeed. Once she falsely confessed to murdering Bertram,

however many days she had remaining to her, she wanted to look back on her life without regrets. To remember that she had been loved and cherished by Rand, at least as much as he would ever allow himself to love a woman.

Rand quickly divested them of their clothing. Stripped down to her chemise, Rose tugged Rand's sherte over his head. Then he stood beside the bed, and, after untying the lace in the rolled band of his braies, he shoved them with his hose down to his ankles and stepped out of them.

She slowly perused his naked body, the glow from the hanging bedside lamp shimmering him with light and shadow. With his shoulders arched, Rand stood still, proudly displaying his form while she examined every exquisite muscle and tendon and sinew of his superb body, from his broad shoulders, to his narrow waist, to his thick, muscular thighs and sturdy calves.

But her eyes were drawn like a magnet to the thick shaft that sprang up from a nest of dark blond hair. Thick veins pulsing with blood twined around the tumescent, vermilion flesh. Ready to possess her. Ready to cherish her.

Rose shot her gaze up to Rand, her eyes wide and expectant. Rand removed her chemise, the last barrier, and crawled into bed with her. Then he shocked her when he turned onto his back, grabbed her waist, and rolled her on top of him. She sat on him, loins touching loins, her thighs splayed around his hips.

Her hair cascaded down around them. He grabbed a section, brought it to his nose and whiffed. A ragged moan emerged from his lips. She felt it rumble all the way down in his stomach and quiver in her feminine core with a tingling heat.

Then he cupped her cheek and stared into her eyes. His intense gaze deepened to the vivid green of a forest, which she nearly got lost in. "You are beautiful, Rose. Absolutely, breathtakingly beautiful." His voice was a raspy caress.

The air whooshed from her lungs. Her chest rose rapidly to catch her breath. Her heart filled with love and longing. And of regret—for what could have been, and for selfishly denying Rand his son.

He draped her hair back over her shoulders, exposing her breasts to his gaze. He stared as though spellbound, eyes glittering with desire, and then slowly lifted them to hers. Delving deeply into her eyes, he reached up and covered her breasts with his hands, massaging and kneading them. "Your breasts were made for me alone. See how perfectly they conform to my hands."

Her breasts swelled. She bit her lip as his palms abraded the aching peaks. His hand drifted down her stomach, in a slow, smooth caress. Her breath hitched when two fingers glided along her slick folds and plunged inside her sheath. Caressing her until she gasped in pleasure. Wet, she drenched his fingers.

She blushed, embarrassed. Bertram had upbraided her for the same reaction. "I am sorry. I did not mean to do that."

She rose partway to get off him, but Rand clutched her hips.

"Nay, don't move. You haven't done anything wrong. The moisture is your body's natural response, which allows me to enter you without you feeling pain. How can that be wrong?"

She chewed the corner of her lip and nodded. For too long she had allowed Bertram control over her thoughts and feelings, but she would no longer give him the power to reach from the grave to denigrate and demean her. She wiggled her hips. "What do you want me to do?"

"Take me inside you, Rose," he said, his voice hoarse. "Ride me. That way you control the pace. You direct me on the course we pursue."

Rose's eyes widened in surprise, but she did as he said, her eyes downcast with shyness. Rising onto her knees, she took him in her hand. His member, hard yet encased in velvety softness, seared her hand. She poised the bulbous head at her entry and slid down on him in one smooth, luxurious stroke.

Rand clutched her hips, groaning. His hands rotated her, grinding her against him. Her inner flesh rippled with contractions and she moaned.

"Jesu, you feel amazing, incredible. Why did we wait so long to do this?"

Rose smiled with a teasing grin. "Because you are amazingly stubborn and I am incredibly hardheaded?"

A deep chuckle rumbled through him, the vibrations quivering along his shaft and setting off a hot shivery caress between her thighs. She gasped, a breathy moan of surprise and pleasure.

With an instinct born of pent-up desire, she withdrew all the way to the tip of his shaft, then drove down again. Awkwardly at first, her movements slow and unsure, she thrust up and down his smooth shaft. His masculine scent of leather and pine mingled with the essence of their musky desire ensorcelled her. Soon she caught on to an exquisite rhythm that had him moaning in ecstasy, her back arched as she leaned back on one hand to give her leverage, hips pumping up and down in a wild gyration; the friction and heat of him inside sparked fire along her flesh.

Rose stared down at Rand; his tender gaze held hers, conveying his love and joy at the beauty of their joining. Then he lifted his hands off her hips, clutched her shoulders, and pulled her down to him. His lips seared into hers, her breasts cushioned against his hard strength. She gloried in this moment—their hearts beat as one. Gloried at her newfound courage to break free from the bonds of her abusive past.

Rose met the wild thrusts of Rand's flanks, the slap of the flesh of their bodies humming in her ears along with their panting breaths.

"Rose, oh, God, look at me, love." His desperate voice thrilled her. "I'm almost there. I need you with me."

Rose stared into Rand's eyes. With one heaving thrust, spasms of tingling heat exploded along her inner folds. Rose cried out. Her sheath contracted around his thick shaft. And ecstasy shivered through her.

Rand watched Rose shatter before him, her beautiful crystal eyes wide with wonder and revelation. Elated, his heart bursting with joy, he pumped his hips wildly as fiery pleasure shivered through his shaft. With one final thrust, his essence spurted inside her as he shouted out her name. Drained, he collapsed back upon the soft mattress.

He clutched Rose to him, her soft-scented breath panting heavily in his ear. She snuggled against his side, laying her head on his chest and her arm around his waist. A great shuddering sigh escaped his lips. Contentment unlike aught he'd ever felt before flowed through him. His eyelids grew heavy, but he reached for the coverlet and fur and draped them over him and Rose. Exhaustion overtook him and darkness descended.

Rand woke rolling over in bed, his first thought of Rose. Cold from the absence of her body heat, he reached out to pull her next to him. His hands came up empty and his eyes snapped open. He flipped the covers off and ran his hand over the indention in the mattress made by her body. The bedding was cool to the touch as if she'd risen from bed some time ago.

Likely she was anxious for the safe return of Jason, yet why had she not woken him? Rand jumped off the bed and reached for his clothes on the floor beside the bed. But they were no longer there. He moved to the chamber door to call for his squire and saw his garments folded neatly on the chest at the foot of the bed. He smiled at Rose's considerate gesture. It was so like her to think of others, even in the midst of her own unhappiness.

After he called Will, he began dressing. He'd pulled on

his braies and hose, but when he reached for his sherte a crinkling sound alerted him to the presence of a piece of parchment folded within the garment. Puzzled, he withdrew the parchment and held it up to the glimmer of sunlight now piercing through the double arched window.

"My lord, you called?"

Rand waved Will to hush and read the delicate slanted words addressed to him.

> *Forgive me, Rand. But I can't let you sacrifice your life for my mistakes. I know you do not understand, but soon all will be revealed. Until then, I beg you to stay at Ayleston, where, once I've done as Golan has demanded, word will arrive of Jason's whereabouts and you can get him back from his captor. I pray that you do not intervene on my behalf and that you leave me to my fate. Jason's life depends upon it.* Our son *shall need* his father *when I am gone.*

Disbelieving, Rand blinked and then reread the missive. When he reread the last line, a sick feeling rumbled in the pit of his stomach. Did Rose truly mean Jason was his son and not Bertram's? His body began to shake; legs wobbling, he stumbled backward and sat down on the chest heavily. He dropped his head in his hands as the world he knew suddenly spun around and flipped him on his head. He had a son. Jason was his son. His body began to shake harder as the implications of Rose's missive began to register.

Rand lunged up from the chest roaring with sick comprehension. Not only was Jason in Golan's brutal custody, but Rose was intent on sacrificing herself for Jason's return, although he had yet to understand in what manner.

"My lord. What is amiss?"

Rand reached for his sherte and tugged it over his head.

"Rose has gone to Golan in order to take Jason's place." He

waved the missive at Will. "She's explained it here in her letter. I need to catch her before she reaches Chester. Then I shall retrieve Jason even if it kills me."

"What can I do to help, milord?"

"Saddle the fastest horse we have in the stable. I ride for Chester anon. And send word to Amaury de Valence to meet me at my house at Chester without delay."

"I shall do so right away." Will rushed out of the chamber.

Rand sat back down on the chest and pulled on his calf-high boots. He ruthlessly ignored the fear that clawed inside him as though he'd swallowed a dragon. With raw determination he retrieved the sword belt and scabbard leaning against the washstand and belted it around his waist. Then he retrieved a voluminous, dark, hooded cloak.

He intended to forego his armor, shield, and spurs. Stealth and deception were required if he was to get Jason and Rose back unharmed. He refused to consider any other possible result. No matter Rose's betrayal, Rand did not want to live in a world without her.

Chapter Twenty-Four

On the road outside the gates of Chester Castle, Rose slid down off her palfrey's back. Trying to soothe her own nervousness, she stroked the mare's silky neck, her gaze straying to the large gray marble stone nearby. "I shall continue on from here by myself now, Geoffrey." She looked back up at the lad still mounted. "I don't know what kind of reception I'll receive. I would not forgive myself if aught should happen to you because you accompanied me."

"My lady. Are you sure this is what you wish to do?"

"Aye, Geoffrey. I have no other choice. Do not fear for me, though. I do not regret trading my life for my son's. Just as your parents willingly died protecting you, I am content that Jason will live on without me. Sir Rand will see that he is well cared for."

Geoffrey nodded, an odd gleam in his round blue eyes.

"Go on now, Geoffrey. Thank you for your assistance in sneaking the mare from the castle." She swatted her horse on the rump and it set off at a trot down Castle Lane, back toward Bridge Street and the road that led back to Ayleston.

Rose pulled her cloak tighter around her and entered through the castle gate behind a cart loaded with barrels of salted cod. Its wheels rumbled on the cobbles in the darkened tunnel, and a tremor of fear reverberated down her spine like a gloomy echo. The outer bailey was large, but wherever she looked it bustled with activity. Soldiers mustering for the summer offensive into Wales waited in a line near the northern castle wall where a castle official handed out supplies of blankets and bread to the new recruits. Supplies of wine, ale, fish, and grain were being brought in from the harbor and surrounding countryside and stored in the castle cellars.

Straight before her in the center of the bailey was the castle well. Rose veered to the left of it and headed toward the Great Hall, which lay along the southern defenses of the castle wall. Rose stepped between two carts and entered the arched door of the forebuilding attached to the Great Hall. Once inside, the castle porter, a tall middle-aged man with graying short brown hair, directed her to the lieutenant-justiciar's office.

When she neared the chamber, Rose threw back her shoulders, then walked proudly inside.

A young, pleasant-faced clerk sitting at a small desk rose and greeted her when she entered the antechamber.

She kept her hands folded demurely before her as she replied, "I am Lady Rosalyn. Sir Golan is expecting me."

He left and returned shortly. "The lieutenant-justiciar is tending to an important matter and shall speak with you when he's done."

The clerk sat down. The fear that had been Rose's constant companion since she left Ayleston before dawn suddenly altered to outright fury at the despicable man. Her worry for her son had twisted her stomach into knots, and Golan's obvious delay stoked her anxiety into a fine rage.

She marched into his chamber, her hands fisted at her sides and her face flushed. "Where is my son? What have you done with Jason?"

The clerk hustled into the room behind her. "My lord. Forgive me. I told Lady Rosalyn you were occupied."

Golan set down the missive he had been reading and

negligently waved his clerk away. "You may leave, Roger. I shall speak with Lady Rosalyn now."

"I have done as you have asked, Sir Golan. Now tell me where you are keeping Jason."

Golan stood up slowly behind his desk and leaned forward, resting his fisted knuckles on top of his desk. He smiled, satisfaction clear in his voice as he said, "Lady Rosalyn. Do you have something you wish to confess?"

A lump of emotion formed in her chest and constricted her breathing. "I will confess as soon as I know Jason is alive and unharmed."

Frowning, Golan straightened and came around his desk to stand before her. "You are in no position to bargain, my lady," he said with an insolent sneer. When he reached out and stroked her cheek with his knuckles, she flinched. It was not a caress, but a warning. "Confess."

She refused to move away and reveal her fear. She said softly, "If I confess, how do I know you will release Jason?"

"You do not. But if you do not confess, right now, this moment, I shall send word to my accomplice to slit the boy's throat."

She read the conviction in Golan's black hate-filled eyes. He would murder Jason. He had no qualms about killing an innocent boy.

"Very well. I wish to confess to murdering my husband. One night when he was drunk, I pushed him down the stairs. As you know, the fall broke his neck."

His satisfied smile broadened. He reached out and stroked down her arm. "Now was that so difficult?" She shuddered with revulsion.

Not expecting an answer, Golan shouted, "Roger!"

Roger hurried into the chamber, bowing. "My lord?"

"Call the guards. Lady Rosalyn has just confessed to murdering her first husband, Lord Ayleston."

When the clerk left, Rose jerked her arm free of Golan's

repulsive grip. "I have confessed as you demanded. When will you release Jason?"

"Not so fast. You will have to give your confession to the coroner, who will record it, and only then can it be used at your trial to convict you. He is due back on the morrow. That should give you plenty of time to consider your transgressions and repent your sins."

Two armed guards entered the chamber, their glowering presences dwarfing her.

"Take Lady Rosalyn to the tower prison," Golan ordered.

The guards seized her by her arms.

"Wait!" She twisted back to Golan. Tears flooded her eyes. His smirking face blurred. "Where is Jason? Tell me where he is!" She twisted and struggled in the guards' arms. Pain shot through her limbs as they shored up their fierce hold and dragged her inexorably forward. Desperate, she resorted to begging. "Prithee. Sir Golan, I beg you. Do not harm my son. He's just a boy."

Golan, crossing his arms over his chest, watched with ruthless satisfaction as the haughty Lady Rosalyn was reduced to a begging supplicant. 'Twas only the beginning of the degradations he had in store for her. She would regret spurning him and marrying Sir Rand instead. Passing through the outer portal, Rosalyn clutched the door frame with her hand. But the guards gave a sharp tug, and, with a final cry, her grip slipped and she disappeared from view.

Golan plucked off the desk the letter that he'd been writing when she had arrived. He reread it, a slow smile spreading across his face.

He folded the missive, retrieved the candle on the shelf below the single chamber window, poured wax onto the parchment, and then pressed his seal into the wax.

"Roger," he called.

His clerk returned and bowed. "My lord."

"See that this is delivered to the king in Northumberland

posthaste. The king must be informed that Lady Rosalyn confessed to murdering her first husband and her trial will be held at the next county court three days from tomorrow."

Roger reached out to take the message. Golan flicked it back out of the man's reach. He narrowed his eyes and glared. "Need I explain further the imperative nature of this message? Or why the king must receive it without delay?"

His clerk visibly gulped. "Aye, my lord. I understand. I shall not fail in my duty."

"Good," Golan said coldly and handed his servant the letter.

Rose turned and rubbed her arms as she gazed out the cross-shaped arrow-slit of her tower gaol cell. The sun was dipping down toward the western horizon, the last of its rosy rays shimmering on the water of the Dee River below. In the distance she could see the foothills of the Welsh mountains.

Behind her, the chamber door closed in back of the coroner, and then the key scraped, the guard locking her inside once more. Now there was nothing to stand between Sir Golan and his revenge. For with her confession recorded in the coroner's rolls, she'd sealed her fate. It would be a quick trial, her execution no doubt carried out with gleeful swiftness. Burning at the stake for murdering her lord. A whimper escaped her.

She rubbed her weary, burning eyes. Worry for her son had kept her awake all night. Her spirits were bleak, but since almost two days had passed and she had not seen Rand, she took hope that her husband had done as she had asked him. Rose rolled her shoulders, trying to ease the stiff tendons at the base of her neck. She reached up and rubbed the hard knot of tension. Her clothes were wrinkled and dirty, and her wimple and veil headdress were long discarded.

The sudden screech of the key in the lock raised the hairs on her arms. She jerked, startled, and spun to gaze wide-eyed as the door slowly creaked open. Her lips moved in silent prayer. "Let it not be Sir Golan, I pray you, Lord."

Rose breathed a sigh of relief when the female servant wearing a hooded cloak entered carrying a tray of food. Without speaking a word, the woman laid the tray down on the table near the door. Rose turned back to the miniscule view outside. Another reason why she had to be vigilant and not succumb to sleep was because Sir Golan would not be satisfied seeing her executed on the gallows. He wished to humiliate and debase her for repudiating him in favor of Rand.

Rose shuddered, trying not to think about what he intended to do to her. But unfortunately, she remembered all too vividly his vile attack in the chapel. Flashes of his assault pummeled her at her most vulnerable moments, when the ache at the separation from her son grew so intense that she just curled up in bed unable to eat, move, or think.

Tears welled in her eyes and she fiercely rubbed them away with her fists. She would be brave. She would not weaken now and give Golan the satisfaction of turning her into a weeping, cowering woman, as Bertram had. Jason was counting on her to be strong for him.

Don't worry, my beloved son. Somehow, someway, Mama's going to save you. I vow it.

"You should eat something to fortify you for your upcoming ordeal."

The soft, seductive voice of the speaker sent a curl of revulsion down Rose's spine. Surely her mind was playing tricks on her. Slowly, Rose turned around, her brow furrowed.

Not five feet from Rose, the cloaked woman reached up, pulled back the sides of her wool hood, and let it drape down her back.

Rose gasped. "Nay, it cannot be." She breathed a sigh of shock and disbelief.

Lady Lydia's full lips curled up in satisfaction. "Aye, 'tis indeed possible."

Short gold curls framed an exquisite heart-shaped face. Rose had never expected to see or hear from Lady Lydia again. The king had locked her away in a remote nunnery.

Sudden sick comprehension roiled inside Rose. Her chest rose rapidly with agitation. "You! You're the one responsible for my incarceration. I don't know how, but I know 'tis so."

Lydia threw back her head and laughed in wicked amusement. Then her laugh abruptly died. She began pacing around the room, taking in Rose's sparse cell.

Fury flushing her face, Rose demanded, "What have you done with my son, Lydia?"

Lydia ignored her. She flicked the soiled straw-stuffed mattress in the corner bed niche that was built into the wall, then strolled back past the cell door. She prowled like an animal trapped in a cage, stopping at the small table. Beside the tray of food and drink, a clay basin and water pitcher sat on the table. Lydia reached out a single finger and wiped it along the wooden surface.

She held up her forefinger covered with dust. "Tsk, tsk, tsk. Cleanliness is next to godliness. The sisters at St. Brigid's would be appalled if they were to inspect your cell. I should know." She held up both her hands, which were red and raw and chafed. "I spent hours on my hands and knees scrubbing the floors and walls until there was not a speck of dust covering them," she spat icily.

"Answer me! At least tell me Jason is still alive."

"Do not seek to dictate to me!" Lydia flung her arm out and swiped the tray of food off the table. Rose recoiled. The tray clattered against the stone wall. A brown, gooey muck of potage stuck to the wall and slowly dribbled down it.

The bright glitter in Lydia's blue eyes took Rose off guard. "Pray, have mercy, Lydia," she implored softly. "Jason is just a boy." Her voice cracked with emotion, deep despair breaking her heart. "Will you not at least tell me if he is safe and unharmed?"

Lydia delicately brushed her golden curls back off her temple. The glimmer of madness dimmed. "The boy is safe, for now. The sisters are taking good care of him. But that can quickly change. His safety depends on your docile co-operation." Her small upturned nose wrinkled in disgust. "It should not be so difficult for you. You always were a pathetic mouse."

But Rose barely listened to her scornful diatribe. Lydia had accidentally given her a clue to Jason's whereabouts. She'd said Jason was being well cared for by the sisters. That could only mean he was being held in a nunnery or hospital. But it was more likely he resided in a hospital where the nuns took care of not only the sick but orphans too. And he must still be in Chester or the surrounding area. She doubted they'd had time to secrete him in a more distant hospital. There were two hospitals near Chester. If only she could find a way to get word to Rand of what she'd learned.

But for now Rose had so many questions to ask of Lydia. Mayhap if she could get Lydia to open up, Bertram's mistress might give her a further hint as to Jason's location. She kept her voice calm, neutral. "I don't understand, Lydia. How is it you were released? And why were we not told?" Rose fisted her hands down at her sides, digging her nails into her palms.

Lady Lydia continued pacing. When she reached the corner opposite the straw mattress, she curled her nose up at the foul smell emanating from the bucket that served as Rose's chamber pot.

"The convent, Lydia? Why are you no longer within its walls? How did you come to be here?"

A soft trill escaped her lips. "How shall I say this?" Her hips swaying, she walked slowly toward Rose. "'Tis quite ingenious, I think you will agree. The abbot who presided over the abbess of St. Brigid's looked the other way when I bribed a fisherman to sail me across to the mainland. For a price, of course." Standing before Rose, she flicked her finger along the right side of her mouth and repeated the gesture on the other side as though wiping something from her lips. "Needless to say he was quite 'gratified' by the services I provided him, and was quite 'eager' to reward me with whatever I desired."

Rose blushed, knowing what the gesture implied. Bertram had forced Rose to watch as Lady Lydia had taken his aroused flesh inside her mouth and stimulated him until he spent his seed.

"Ahh, I see I have shocked the *innocent* Lady Rosalyn."

Rose stiffened at the contemptuous emphasis Lydia placed on the word "innocent," as though it were a curse.

Lydia laughed, the sound grating Rose's ears. "How I despised your innocence and verve for life from the moment I met you. Then when Bertram and I became lovers, I found the perfect opportunity to humiliate and demean you. I cleverly saw to it that he married you. That he stripped away your innocence just as my incestuous father stripped away mine," she spat out bitterly.

Rose gasped at the horrific revelation. Lady Lydia's father, her own flesh and blood, had ravished her body? How could a father do such a thing? It was evil and corrupt. No wonder Lydia was diabolically manipulative of every man she met. She must truly loathe all men.

As she despised them? Rose marveled in sudden insight. Nay, she thought, she did not despise the whole male race. But Bertram had severely damaged her trust in men. It took Rand's patience and kind understanding to teach her not to hate indiscriminately based on one bad experience. That there were good men and bad men, as well as there were good women and corrupt women.

With sudden understanding, pity welled inside Rose's chest for the innocent girl Lydia had once been.

"Don't you *dare* pity me, Rosalyn Montague." Lydia's delicate features twisted with hate. "You are the one to be pitied.

It shall not be long ere you are convicted and sentenced to death for killing Bertram. I shall revel as I watch the flames consume your body at the stake."

Rose blanched at the gruesome image, her pity forgotten. "Why, Lydia? You despised me for my innocence. But as you said, Bertram stripped me of my naïveté years ago. Why do you yet hate me? Contrary to what you believe, I did not kill Bertram. He tripped and fell down the stairs."

Lydia shoved her face in Rose's. "You may not have pushed him down the stairs, but he is dead because of you," she snarled. "If you had not been sneaking away from the castle that night, he would never have confronted you in the corridor to prevent you from leaving. And he would not have tripped and fallen when he moved to block your path at the top of the staircase."

Rose gasped. Her hand flew to her neck. "How could you know what happened? Unless . . ."

Lydia spun away, sat down on the bed niche, and crossed her legs. "Aye. I saw the whole confrontation. When I heard you arguing with Bertram outside the chamber I shared with him, I opened the door to see what the commotion was about. After he fell, you walked right past my cracked door in your haste to hide your involvement in the crime."

Rose did not refute Lydia's accusation. Lydia was determined to blame her for Bertram's death and would not be gainsaid. Rose rubbed the hollow at the base of her neck. "If you knew what happened, why did you not speak out before, or give the hue and cry when Bertram fell?"

"Because I did not wish to answer prying questions that might bring light to my affair with Bertram. I could not take the chance of my husband becoming suspicious and learning Bertram was my lover. But my caution was of no avail." A bitter light flamed in her cool blue eyes. She lurched up from her seat and paced to the cell door. "On Lord Joinville's deathbed, his heir apprised him of my infidelities and the miserable sod disinherited me. All he left me with were a few pitiful dower manors. And now even those are lost to me. And 'tis all your brother's fault."

Lydia spat out, "I curse the entire Beaumont lineage." Her contemptuous gaze flicked down Rose's body.

Rose held Lydia's sneering look, refusing to let Lydia intimidate her.

"Why has the king not yet learned you have fled the convent? Surely the abbess or one of the nuns must have discovered your disappearance and informed the king."

"The abbot told the abbess I was being moved to, and detained, in another convent. So no one but the abbot knew of my escape. I promised him I would never tell anyone he helped me. So everyone believes I am still withering away in that barren convent. Even Golan does not know my true identity."

"How is that possible? How is it Golan has not recognized you? And where have you been hiding all this time that no one else has recognized you?"

A look of unadulterated pleasure spread across Lydia's face. "You do not know? You have not guessed?" Lydia approached Rose and slowly walked around her. Rose remained completely still. Lydia's hand reached out and plucked a nonexistent piece of lint off of Rose's shoulder. Rose flinched but did not step away. "Why, I was in disguise, of course. My short hair and stature lent credence to my deception. But I had to conceal my distinctive light hair and skin." She stopped in front of Rose again. Pausing, she tapped her forefinger against her chin.

Rose stared at Lydia blankly.

Lydia tsked with contempt. "God, you are truly guileless."

After a dramatic pause, Lydia grabbed the sides of her bodice. She pulled the ruby silk taut against her body flattening her voluptuous breasts. Her sensual mouth curved in a slyly pleased moue. "Mayhap it will jog your memory if you picture me disguised as a boy, with my hair and skin darkened with dye?"

Rose's jaw dropped in horror.

Lydia threw back her head and laughed with maniacal glee. "Exactly. I have been right beneath your nose the whole time and you did not even realize it. You even required my help in delivering you to Sir Golan, the very man I've conspired with to destroy you."

A wave of disbelief washed over Rose. Her knees buckled. She staggered and reached out to catch herself on the bed niche. Her bottom smacked hard against the bench; the straw mattress crinkled loudly in the stunned silence.

Rose's skull exploded with pain. Her vision spun and she dropped her head between her legs to keep from fainting.

She barely noticed the biting cold seeping into her posterior. *Mother Mary, what have I done? Mother Mary, what have I done?* The blade of guilt stabbed deeper with each lament.

Geoffrey, the boy she had given hearth and board to was none other than Lady Lydia. She'd let a viper into their midst, endangering everyone she ever cared about. So many questions whirled in her head she did not know where to begin. But with a newfound reserve of strength she'd discovered deep inside, Rose raised her head.

"How long have you been conspiring with Sir Golan? Were you the one who drugged Sir William and delivered the extortion message? Why did you save Jason from drowning if you wished to punish me?" She gasped. "Who were those poor people who were murdered on the road that you claimed were your parents? Surely you did not—" Rose could not complete her question. The idea that the merchant couple was killed so Lydia could perpetrate her deception was too horrible to believe.

"The merchant couple was an unfortunate casualty."

"You had them killed?"

"'Twas Sir Golan's idea. We had to come up with a plan to get me inside Ayleston Castle. And it worked brilliantly. You never suspected Geoffrey's motives, or his loyalty to you. Sir Rand, on the other hand, was much more suspicious of me."

"So it was you who drugged Sir William after all, and not Sir Golan's squire?"

Lydia chuckled. Pride laced her words as she replied, "Aye. That was my idea. Sir Golan's man distracted the slut while I mixed henbane in William's drink. If anyone questioned the servants, Golan would take the blame. He was the obvious culprit, and he cared not what you thought of him."

"And the extortion note? That was you also, wasn't it? I saw you in the chapel that day. What was the purpose of your extortion plot?"

"After all these years you still do not understand. Bertram loved *me*." Her voice rose as she repeated, "He loved *me!*" and thumped her chest with her fist for emphasis. "He knew all about my sordid past. He knew what was inside my soul, yet he loved me anyway. Bertram was the only person who ever understood me and accepted me as I am. But you took him away from me. You killed Bertram. So, aye, I sent you the threatening note. I wanted to frighten you. To torment you and make you believe that at any moment you could lose everything."

"I don't understand why you did not try to harm me or those I cared for while you were at Ayleston. For months you had the opportunity to wreck vengeance upon me. It would have been easy to poison the food or wine. You even saved Jason from drowning. Why?"

"I do not want your death to be quick and painless; that would be too easy. By saving Jason's life, I gained your undying trust, giving me the time and opportunity to orchestrate Jason's abduction and your imprisonment. When I learned you had married Sir Rand, I began to hatch a plot to see you suffer for what you did. You do not deserve to be happy and in love. You are not worthy of Rand's love. Nor any man's love."

"Rand does not love me. He only married me because our families betrothed us." To her dying breath, she would never reveal the true deception of their marriage vows.

"Fool. Not only are you guileless, but you are blind too. The man has always loved you. He was too stubborn and afraid to realize it. But it's too late for you, Rose. Rand and Jason are lost to you. I have taken everyone you've ever loved, as you stole Bertram from me."

The key screeched in the lock, and Rose winced, the sound like the cry of a banshee in her ears. Lydia began to move to the door pulling her hood up over her distinctive blond hair. Nay. It was too soon. Rose still had not secured Jason's release.

"Lydia, prithee, I implore you. Do not harm Jason. Return him to Rand when I am gone."

The guard pushed the door open. His nose was smashed flat against his face and a permanent scowl etched on his face. "Your time is up, milady," he said, his voice deep and gravelly.

Lydia stepped out, her rich silk skirts swishing as she pulled them aside so the guard did not incidentally befoul them. Rose lurched toward the scarred oak door as it swung shut. She blared out in desperation, "What is to prevent me from exposing your identity?!" The door slammed in her face.

Silence reigned.

Rose dropped her head. Her shoulders slumped. Then the small door, which the guard used to peek into the chamber and check on her, snapped open. Lydia peered through the small opening covered with iron bars.

Rose straightened her shoulders and stared bravely at Lydia. "I have done as you asked. I confessed to Bertram's murder. My trial is the day after tomorrow and a conviction is a foregone conclusion. You have won. Will you do one last honorable thing and see that Jason is returned safely into Sir Rand's custody after I am passed?"

Lydia, her lips slightly pinched, nodded her agreement. An audible sigh whooshed from Rose's lungs. She was able to breathe easier, as if a heavy stone had been dislodged from her chest. Then Lydia crooked her finger for Rose to come closer. Rose dipped her head toward the woman.

Blue eyes flared with an unearthly light. "Betray me and Jason dies."

The words struck Rose in the heart like barbed arrows. She flinched, all the blood draining from her face.

Chapter Twenty-Five

Keys jingled. The guard fumbled around to find the correct key. Golan, his hand resting on his sword hilt, tapped the cool metal cross guard with his fingers, impatient for the bumbling fool to open the cell door. Finally, the garlic-reeking guard inserted the key in the lock and unlocked the door. Grunting, Golan elbowed him aside and shoved the door open.

He gazed around the dark and dank chamber. To his right inside the octagonal tower, Lady Rosalyn lurched up from a reclining position on the bed and stood up to move as far away from it as she could. Golan sneered. It would not stop him from bedding her. She should have been *his* wife. He deserved to get some sort of compensation for the prize being stolen from him.

Standing in the threshold, Golan turned back to the guard. He jerked his arm toward the door and pointed imperiously. "Leave us. Now! I want some privacy with the prisoner."

The guard smiled slyly, then turned and headed down the spiral stairs whistling. Golan closed the door and turned back to Rosalyn.

She'd folded her hands before her, and stood with her shoulders thrown back proudly. Conversely, her dark clothes were wrinkled and dirty, her hair was tangled and uncombed, and the chamber reeked.

"Lady Rosalyn," he said with derision.

Head angled as though she were a queen receiving one of her lowly subjects, she nodded. "Sir Golan."

Proud, cold bitch. Despite her reduced circumstances and approaching trial and execution, she still had the audacity to act as though she were better than him. He vowed he would wipe the look of disdain from her face.

"Remove your clothes." With slow, deliberate movements, Golan tugged the tie free at the neck of his cloak and tossed the outer garment on the table next to the water basin.

Her cheeks paled and a tremor shook her shoulders. He smirked, pleased. She was not so haughty now.

Golan grabbed the strap end of his leather sword belt, tugged it back freeing the pin from the hole, and slid it out of the buckle. He removed his belt and propped his scabbard and sword against the wall next to the cell door.

She had not moved from her position or done as he had ordered.

"I said take off your garments!" He strode the five feet between them, and she raised her arms to ward him off. But he grabbed the neck of her blue woolen bodice—and ripped. "Now! Or I shall remove them for you."

She clutched the ripped material closed, her chest heaving. "'Tis not . . . necessary," her voice faltered. "I will do it."

He watched, waiting until she did as he bid. She gathered the skirt of her surcoate and tugged it off over her head. A gray tunic and chemise remained.

Golan tossed his surcoate aside and reached next for the laces of his sherte.

Her fingers fumbled as she tried to untie the lace closing the neck of her undertunic. "Why are you doing this? Do you enjoy taking women who despise you? Who find you repugnant?"

Heat sizzled over his flesh. He swung his arm out and backhanded her. She cried out, stumbling, and fell to her knees against the bed niche. Satisfaction bloomed and spread, going straight to his cock. He hardened and grew as stiff as marble.

She reached up and propped her bent arm on the bed. Blood welled at the corner of her mouth. She wiped the back of her hand across her lips, smearing the blood across her cheek. Her blue eyes, smoldering with contempt, shot to his.

Slowly, she pushed to her feet. "Go ahead, take me against my will, but I shall not aid you, nor cower before you. You are a vile, cowardly man."

A bright light flared inside his head like a strike of lightning. Pain seared his skull. With a shout of rage he reached out and wrapped his fingers around her neck. "Goddamn deceiving bitch. Am I not handsome enough for you? Am I not aristocratic enough for you? Who are you to judge me? Just like my wife, you are naught but a cheating whore." Staring into her eyes, he watched them flare open wide in surprise. "Aye. Do not think I have not noticed the resemblance between Sir Rand and your son."

With one hand he squeezed her neck tighter, lifting her off her feet. She dangled before him, her legs swinging, toes twitching as she tried to touch the ground. Her face turned vermilion, while her delicate fingers clawed at his wrist and her eyes bulged.

Just as her eyelids began to flutter closed, he released her. She crumpled onto the bed, limbs akimbo, choking and wheezing as she gulped in air and rubbed her throat.

He jumped on her. Before she could move, he grabbed her thighs, spread them forcefully, and shoved up her skirts. She screamed, twisted beneath him. Her fingers reached out and her nails raked down his cheek. He roared in pain, clutched her hands and shoved them down beside her head.

He thrust his hips forward, rubbed his throbbing erection

against her vulnerable center. "I'm going to shove my cock so far up you I shall break you in twain, harlot."

Raising his sherte, he reached down and loosened the tie at the waist of his braies, then shoved them down till his shaft sprang free. She screeched, twisted and bucked beneath him. Her center was open and ready for his invasion. Golan panted, his skin feverish, sweat popping out on his forehead.

Rose bucked up against Golan. Her neck throbbed with pain and revulsion shuddered through her as his shaft pressed against her exposed flesh. She kicked out again. She gazed at him with blazing scorn. "You are pathetic, Golan. Just like my first husband, you cannot get aroused unless by perversion. You are not a real man. You are a weak, worthless, repulsive slug."

With a roar, Golan leaned up. A satanic light blackened his eyes.

Rose seized the opening and jammed her knee straight up into his loins. He howled in excruciating pain. Feral satisfaction soared inside her, lending her strength. She pressed her hands against his chest and shoved. Suddenly his head jerked, and groaning, he collapsed on top of her. Unmoving, his heavy weight crushed her, the stone bed jabbing into her back. Then his burden lifted from her and he was flung aside.

Her eyes grew wide as Rand's grim visage came into view. "Rand," she blurted out.

Rose's face blazed bright red. A rush of emotion—shock, disbelief, shame—knocked the breath from her. She darted her eyes away. Pushing up into a seated position, she shoved her tunic and chemise down to cover her nakedness.

I cannot bear to look at him. What must he think of me? she wondered.

Rand, his heart pounding in his throat, grabbed Rose's hand and pulled her into his embrace. "Oh, God, Rose, forgive me. I came as soon as I could. Tell me you are all right. Did the bastard rape you?"

"Nay. 'Twas close, but he did not—" She shuddered in his arms.

A red mist obstructed his vision as he remembered Golan, with his buttocks bared, poised over Rose. "Easy, love. I have you." Rand clutched Rose tightly, attempting to soothe her as much as himself. Every muscle in his body stiffened as he constrained the rage rippling through him. Any moment his body could snap. He tamped down the emotion. He needed to keep a cool head if they were to escape the castle without alerting the garrison.

Concentrating on Rose, he clutched her head to him, his hand caressing down her back over her loose coppery hair. Gradually the warmth of her body melted into his, easing his own jumping nerves.

"I fought Golan, Rand. I swear it."

"I know you fought him, Rose. I'm proud of you."

"You are? Why? Are you not sickened by what you saw?"

He leaned back and cupped her cheeks in his palms. "I'm sickened that that bastard touched you. But I would never blame you. Nor does it change how I feel about you. You have naught to be ashamed of. You are not at fault. Understand?"

As she shuddered once more, relief showed in her soft blue eyes. "I understand."

He kissed her, his lips clinging to the soft, sensual contours of her berry-sweet lips. She moaned, clutched his arms tightly and leaned into him. Her pert breasts burned into his muscled chest. Hard points stabbed him, the abrasion setting off a spark of heat. The sensation shot straight to his shaft.

Quivering, he pulled back with effort, breathing harshly. "Later, we shall finish this. But now we have to go. We don't have much time."

He released her and bent down to check on Golan. The man was unconscious, lying facedown, his undergarments bunched around his buttocks. Rand clenched his jaw, felt a muscle tic in his cheek. His fingers twitched with the urge to run the knave threw. But he needed the man alive for the nonce. Later, though . . . He would see to it Golan never had a chance to rape a woman again.

Rand glanced back at Rose. Her pale blue eyes glared daggers at Golan and then they grew shadowed with fear. "Rand. We have to go. They have Jason. Lydia and Golan, I mean. I think they're holding him at one of the hospitals. Lydia let it slip when she was gloating about her scheme for revenge. Lydia has been—"

As Rand listened to Rose's nonsensical babble, he wondered if her ordeal had stolen her wits. "Rose, what are you talking about? Lydia de Joinville is locked away in a nunnery in the north," he said as he moved to the bed and ripped the straw pallet apart. Straw fluttered into the air and stuck to every surface.

Rose reached out and grabbed his forearm. "Rand, listen to me." Her nails bit deeply into his skin. Shocked, his gaze jerked to hers. Her eyes bore into him. "Lydia escaped the nunnery. She is the one who concocted the whole extortion scheme. Yesterday, she came—"

"What extortion scheme are you talking about?"

"I don't have time to explain everything, but Lydia delivered a note to me at Ayleston the night of the raid. In the note, she promised to release Jason if I confessed to murdering Bertram."

"That explains a lot. I couldn't figure out why you would willingly leave Ayleston."

"'Tis the only thing that would have persuaded me to leave you. She lured me out of my chamber to the chapel, where I found her message, and then she knocked me out."

"I don't understand. How did Lydia get inside the castle to lure you away?" Now was not the time to ask her if Jason was his son. But soon Rand would need an explanation.

Her soft round eyes narrowed. "Because Lydia is Geoffrey."

"Jesu. How can that be?" Even as he asked he remembered

from their very first meeting thinking Geoffrey seemed familiar to him.

Rand ripped the thick woolen pallet cover into several long strips as Rose explained.

"She dyed her hair and skin dark. And bound her breasts. After escaping the nunnery, she joined forces with Golan and together they concocted a plan for revenge. She came to my cell yesterday and told me everything."

"The woman is a menace." Rand crouched down and tied Golan's hands behind his back. "'Tis getting late. We have to hurry. The guard can come back at any moment."

Rand lunged to his feet and grabbed the pitcher off the table.

"What are you doing, Rand?"

"I need to revive Golan so we can take him with us. If he wishes to live, he'll tell us where he is holding Jason. I have my ship downriver to take you away to safety. Once I see that done, I'll come back for Jason."

"You don't understand, Rand. Lydia swore she would kill Jason if I betrayed her. We have to get to Jason before she finds out I've escaped."

"First we have to escape without raising the alarm. Below the castle walls, outside the postern gate is a barge waiting to take you to my ship."

"I'm not going anywhere without Jason. Once Golan tells us where Jason is being held, I'm going with you to rescue him."

A whistle warbled from below through the tower arrow loop. Rand swore. "That's one of my men. The guard is returning. Hide behind the door." He set the pitcher down on the table.

Rose lunged behind the open door. He crossed to the opposite side, quietly drawing his sword. He pressed one finger against his lips and his back against the wall. She nodded, her face alight with courage and determination. Pride surged within him. Most women who had gone through what Rose had would have dissolved into a puddle of tears and been too distraught to think, or react, with resolve.

Footsteps pounded up the stairs. The guard paused outside. Steel scraped as the man drew his sword from his wooden scabbard and charged into the chamber.

Shouting, the guard spun about. His sword arched up to meet Rand's downward-slashing weapon. The edge of the guard's blade struck the flat of Rand's sword; sparks flew. Rand disengaged and attacked with several quick downward blows. The gaoler countered Rand's every move. Sweat dribbled down Rand's forehead as they fought, parrying, cutting, slashing, and dodging each other's attacks.

Aware of the passage of time, Rand struck out with a quick thrust of his steel, but lunging too quickly, he staggered. The guard warded off the blow with a diagonal slice of his blade, glancing Rand's sword away and slashing through Rand's unprotected thigh. Rose screamed. Rand did not pause but leapt away, avoiding a deadly cut. Pain seared his thigh. Blood poured forth.

With lightning speed, Rand recovered his blade and stepped in close to the guard, who was caught unprepared. Rand gave a hard glancing blow against the defender's mailed head. Stunned, the man fell to his knees. Rand stabbed the guard through the throat and withdrew his sword.

The gaoler grabbed his throat, choking as blood gushed through his fingers. Then he slumped over sideways and collapsed on the floorboards, dead.

Turning to Rose, Rand sheathed his sword. She was staring at the guard, her eyes glazed with shock and her hand clutching her throat.

Rand removed his cloak, and wrapping it around Rose's shoulders, he pulled the hood up so it completely covered her distinct red-gold hair. Rand clutched her cold hands and rubbed his thumbs over her palms, willing his strength into her.

She gazed up at him. Her vision cleared. "You're wounded." She raised his tunic and sherte and probed around the wound through the slash in his thin braies.

Rose bit her lip, frowning. "You are lucky. 'Tis a relatively shallow wound and the bleeding has stopped."

Her fingers glided delicately over his flesh, sensual caresses that stirred his loins. It was certainly not her intention, and his response was completely inappropriate considering the danger they were still in.

"Time is running out, Rose. We need to leave immediately."

"I agree. But first I need to bind the wound so it does not become infected." She bent down and ripped a long strip of linen from the hem of her chemise. She continued speaking as she tied the bandage tightly around his thigh. "Later it needs to be cleansed and treated with healing herbs—"

Footsteps thundered up the tower stairs. She spun toward the door.

Rand swore, drawing his sword. When Amaury stepped through the portal, Rand exhaled loudly and sheathed his sword.

Amaury glanced around the room, grimacing. "We need to hurry, Rand. Every moment we delay puts us more in danger."

Rand nodded. "Rose, listen to me. I need to rouse Golan and get him ready to go with us. Until we're safely away from the castle, all my attention must be on guarding Golan so he does not alert anyone of our escape. But I can't do that if I'm worrying about you," Rand said, holding his hands out to her. "Do you understand, Rose?"

She slipped her fingers trustingly into his hands. "Of course. What is it you would have me do?"

Warmth suffused his hands and spread up his arms and throughout his body. Gratitude and tenderness crowded his senses. Rose's confidence imbued him with a strength and determination unlike anything he had ever felt before.

"I need you to go with Amaury. He'll take you to the barge waiting to take us to my ship moored downriver. Do not worry. I shall be right behind you."

Do not worry, Rand had glibly decreed.

As Rose descended the steep steps cut into the sandstone slope, she glanced for the third time back up toward the postern gate. The high stone walls surrounding Chester loomed above her.

Rand may as well have said, *Do not breathe, I shall be right behind you.* Indeed, fear and worry coiled in her gut.

Distracted, she caught her toe on an uneven step and tripped. Heart pumping wildly, she flung forward.

Amaury caught her by her elbow, stopping her fall. "Careful, my lady. 'Twould not do for you to fall and break your neck."

A high-pitched giggle burst from her lips. How ironic it would be to die the same way her husband had died. And when she was escaping from the supposed crime of killing him. The bushy eyebrow Amaury quirked in wary concern provoked another inappropriate laugh. Rose slapped her hand over her mouth.

Amaury frowned, guiding her by the arm. She took mincing steps, more cautious now; she had too much to live for. Her son needed her. It broke her heart thinking of how frightened and confused he must be. Surely Jason did not think she had abandoned him? She fiercely prayed 'twas not so.

The ground beneath her feet leveled as they drew near the riverbank. Waiting for them in a flat-bottomed barge moored to the revetment were two men wearing wool fishermen's hats.

Rose shifted her gaze back to the castle.

Beside her, Amaury prodded, "My lady, 'tis best if you board the boat before Sir Rand arrives with the captive."

She nodded distractedly. In addition to her fear, she could not help feeling that she had abandoned Rand. At the time she'd believed it was the right decision, but now she wondered.

Assisted by Amaury, Rose stepped into the back of the vessel. It rocked slightly, but she steadied herself and then sat down on the planked seat.

While Amaury unwound the mooring cable, Rose looked up at the castle and stared fixedly on the postern gate.

Time seemed to draw out forever. Rose nearly lurched out of her skin when the gate finally swung open.

First Golan and then Rand stepped out. Rand slung his left arm over Golan's shoulder as though they were friendly acquaintances sharing a moment of camaraderie. But Rose noticed Rand walked behind Golan a little way, his right hand pressed up against Golan's side. Their bodies shifted, parting, and in that brief interval, light from the dying rays of the sun flashed off the steel blade jammed against Golan.

Soon they reached the bottom of the stairs. Golan glared at her, an unrelenting glint of evil menace in his dark eyes. She shivered but raised her chin and held his stare. Perhaps reading her smug satisfaction, he frowned and glanced away.

Rose shifted her gaze to Rand. He was watching her; his gray-green eyes lit with admiration and pride. She smiled slightly. He nodded, his lips curled in satisfaction.

Rand turned to Amaury. "Let's shove off. Though I didn't encounter any trouble leaving the castle, it shall not be long before they discover the dead guard and realize Rose has escaped."

Golan simmered with repressed rage. Thwarted lust and revenge clamored to spew out in violent cataclysm. He nearly shuddered with it. But he shoved it deep down where the darkest recesses of his soul resided. Corrupted after years of disappointment and frustration heaped upon him throughout his misbegotten life—by his whoring, seductive mother, his drunkard father, and his adulteress wife. The final insult came when Rose rejected his offer of marriage and scorned his physical advances.

Golan curled his lip and glared at the offending pair. "Do you truly believe you and your *whore* shall escape unscathed. The king knows Rose murdered Bertram. He shall arrive in Chester anon and will hunt you down like the dog you are."

"Shut your mouth"—Rand jabbed the sharp tip of his blade into Golan's flesh about an inch—"and get into the boat."

As Golan winced and groaned in pain, Rand shoved him. He stumbled into the boat. Rand squeezed his shoulder painfully, forcing him down onto the seat in the middle of the boat facing the rowers.

Golan opened his mouth to speak.

Rand sat beside him. "Say another word and I'll cut out your tongue."

Golan fumed as the boat glided away from the riverbank. He glanced back at the castle as they proceeded downriver. There was no sign of activity on the castle walls except the regular guard watch.

The cold wind whipped against his face like a bracing slap. His head throbbed painfully and his wrists, tied behind his back, were sore and raw. But his senses sharpened, every particle of his being focused on escape. Beneath the cover of his cloak, he twisted and pulled at his bonds. The wool fabric bit into his skin; a trickle of blood ran down his palm.

However, his persistence was rewarded when the bonds loosened enough for him to slip his hand out. Hiding a smug smile of satisfaction, he remained emotionless and quiet, unwilling to draw attention to himself. He would watch and wait, and when the perfect opportunity to escape came along, he would snatch it. He would finally kill Rand, show Lady Rosalyn the fate sluts deserved, and then kill her, too.

Beside him, Rand tensed. The barge rowed past the quayside, where guards patrolled and inspected ships' cargos before they were offloaded.

Golan hissed as the dagger pricked his side.

"I advise you not to do," Rand warned, "or say anything to draw attention to us. Understand?"

Golan nodded, lips turned down, disgruntled. But he was exactly where he wished to be. He had no intention of seeking rescue.

Trumpets blared loudly from the castle, sounding the alarm. Lady Rosalyn gasped behind him.

"Rand, we must hasten. Now the alarm has been raised, Lydia knows I have escaped. She's going to kill Jason if we do not get to him first."

Who was this Lydia she referred to? Golan wondered. It could only be Lyla, which meant the brazen slut lied to him about who she was. Naught about the woman would surprise him.

Once the barge slipped beyond Chester's walls, Rand barked, "Row faster."

The men at the oars pulled faster, emerging into the Dee estuary.

Golan could not prevent the gloating smile from spreading across his face. It seemed God had not forsaken him. With soldiers swarming over the countryside in pursuit, and Lyla—or whomever she was—determined to kill Rose and Rand's brat, the lovers were doomed.

Rand turned his head back to Rose. "We have only a couple of miles to travel until we reach my ship. We'll find Jason before Lydia can harm him. I promise."

Rand was deluded. The boy would not long be of this earth.

Golan twisted his hands once more. His mouth watered with anticipation as revenge crept ever closer. Soon. Very soo—

The dagger slithered between his thighs and pricked his ballocks. A streak of fire surged through his veins; he gasped.

"Is that not correct, Golan?" Rand smiled. Not the roguish quirk of lips Rand was famous for, but a snarl that said he'd enjoy severing Golan's cock from his body if he did not reveal the boy's location.

Chapter Twenty-Six

"Rand, I am going with you."

The woman is as tenacious as a bloodhound. Rand spun around and planted his hands on his hips. Rose halted in the tall, swaying grasses along the riverbank. He narrowed his eyes, glaring down at her. "Absolutely not. 'Tis too dangerous."

The shadows of dusk fell on the *Argo*, moored along the bank, while fog rolled in from the river and scurried lowly and thickly along the ground.

"'Tis dangerous for you, also. Jason is my son. How can you expect me—"

The anger he'd tamped down since learning Jason was his son flared hotly. Rand brought his arm up, swiftly cutting off her reply. "Jason is my son, too. Tell me, Rose, if Jason had not been abducted, would you ever have told me he was mine?" The pain of betrayal was still an open wound, which festered beneath his skin with feverish intensity.

She jerked her face away, flushing with guilt.

A cold prickling sensation skittered over the back of his neck. Rand glanced up onto the deck of his ship. Golan stared directly at him; a wave of hatred slammed into Rand. Then Master Harwood, standing next to Golan, opened the door to the sterncastle, shoved Golan inside, and locked the door behind him.

"Rand," Amaury called out, emerging from the thatched cottage, "my informant told me soldiers from the castle garrison have already searched this way. I purchased two horses for our use." He pointed to a track not far away. "He said that hay cart track is seldom used and should take us not far from the hospital."

Rand turned back to Rose, but she was already halfway across the small courtyard, making her way toward the stable. Rand hurried after her, Amaury on his heels. Rand strode into the small dark structure but did not see Rose. A horse nickered, hay rustled.

The interior of the barn had a hayloft opposite the entrance. Along the left wall hung horse tack and farm implements. To Rand's right were three stalls; two had occupants and a third was empty.

A brown Welsh cob with a black mane and tail, occupying the first stall, stuck its head over the stall door. Rand patted the horse's muzzle. A black plow horse stood with its head hanging down in the next stall over.

In the last stall, clothing stirred as though Rose was dressing, or undressing.

"Rose? What are you doing?"

"I have a plan. Just a mo . . . uumph." The rest of her words became muffled and indistinct.

Needing to be on his way, Rand grabbed the lead rope hanging on a peg outside the stall. He looped it over the cob's head, then opened the door and led the horse out of its stall.

Amaury moved to the horse in the second stall. At the sharp intake of the man's breath, Rand looked up from his task. Rose stood in front of the last stall, her stomach protruding as though big with child.

He blinked, twice, his gaze disbelieving.

Then as her intent registered, Rand clamped his jaw tightly.

"Nay, do not even think it. You are going to go on my ship, where you will be safe. As soon as I retrieve Jason, we will join you and we will all leave England together."

"Just hear me out." She walked toward him, hands raised pleadingly. "The religious at the Hospital of St. John without the North Gate will not wish to give shelter to two strange men in the dark hours. But if I come as your pregnant wife they would not be so heartless as to turn us away."

"Rand, she makes an excellent point."

Rand blew out a frustrated breath. "Amaury, leave us," he said, his eyes never wavering from Rose's.

With a dark chuckle, Amaury brushed past him, his heavy footsteps crunching on hay as he exited the barn.

Rose gazed up at him, her crystal blue eyes asking for his understanding. "I need to do this, Rand. Jason must be terrified. He needs me. Besides, we do not have time to argue any longer. You know this is the best chance we have of gaining entrance to the hospital."

Rand frowned. Though he hated to admit it, she was right. It mattered not to him that she had come up with the idea. What he hated was the thought of her getting hurt. It terrified him. Fear churned in his belly, yet, as always, he ruthlessly pushed it away and concentrated on what he had to do.

"Very well, Rose," he said grimly. "But you must do exactly as I tell you. You cannot second-guess me or question my actions. If we are going to do this together, you are going to have to trust that every action I take is to minimize the danger to you and Jason."

"I do trust you, Rand." The revelation jolted Rose.

Rand nodded stiffly.

As he began tacking their horses, her thoughts turned to her stunning realization. Bertram, a critical, tyrannical man who despised her for her passionate, trusting nature, had shattered her trust in men. So much so that she had annihilated all traces of her true self and become the docile, emotionless mouse Bertram required in his spouse.

Rand, on the other hand, had only ever tried to protect her. He had never disparaged her for her passion or for taking care of the inhabitants of Ayleston. Nor had he spurned her for the ardor he easily drew from her body. He did not try to change her or mold her into the image of a perfect woman. He accepted her as she was.

But could Rand ever love her?

Until now, she never understood how desperately she desired his love.

Rand, riding on the cob, peered up ahead, but the tracks disappeared about five feet before him in the eddying fog. The fog had become thicker and denser, slowing their progress. Rose wrapped her arms tighter around his waist. With her chest flattened against his back, he felt the tension in her body, her chest rising and falling with her rapid breathing.

Amaury rode ahead, reconnoitering, so they did not stumble upon a troop of soldiers out searching for them.

The night was eerily silent. The fabric he'd wrapped around the horses' hooves muffled the clip-clop of their steps. An owl screeched.

Rose shuddered. "'Tis an omen of death," her voice quivered, breath wafting across his ear.

The sudden clamor of pounding horses' hooves sent Rand's heart beating faster. Directly before them, Amaury materialized out of the fog like a specter.

Amaury's mouth pulled down in a grim frown, and the scar beside his lips whitened. He swung his arm back the way he came and pointed. "Soldiers," he said, his voice low and his breath short. "Perhaps a dozen. Coming this way."

"Rand, what are we going to do?" Her voice frantic, Rose dug her fingers into his waist.

* * *

Back at Rand's ship, Golan paced the small confines of the sterncastle. He had already freed the bonds from his hands. Now he waited for the man called Harwood to return. The ship had moved away from land and was anchored in the Dee estuary now. Looking through a small round window covered with iron bars, he could see the riverbank a short distance away.

At the sudden scrape of the key in the lock, Golan darted to the door. He leaned back against the wall and tensed.

The door swung open. A hand appeared holding a candle stand with a lit candle. As it cast a soft glow in the room, he struck out at Harwood's elbow. The candle fell and was snuffed out. Before the old man could react, Golan wrapped his arm around Harwood's neck and seized the man's dagger from the sheath at his waist.

Golan pressed the sharp blade against Harwood's throat.

Harwood tensed, panting heavily. "If you kill me, you shall never escape this ship alive. You cannot possibly fight every man on board."

A harsh laugh burst from his lips. "Why would I wish to kill you? As my hostage, no one on the ship shall gainsay me, guaranteeing my escape. Now move. And do not try any tricks."

"Amaury," Rand uttered, clutching the reins in his left hand. He covered Rose's hand with his free one in an attempt to soothe and reassure her. "Go back the way you came and head off the search party. Tell them you know where the escaped prisoners are hiding and you can lead them to their hiding spot. Just in case your ruse does not work, and they continue this way, Rose and I will veer off the track heading west. We'll circle round the armed party, then return to the road."

Amaury nodded his understanding, wheeling his horse around in the opposite direction. "I will lead them east to Boughton."

The ominous clatter of tack, heavy armor, and weaponry grew louder, the ground shaking beneath them. Rand kicked his horse into a walk, saying over his shoulder to Amaury, "We'll meet you back at the ship when we have Jason."

Soon the fog encapsulated them in a seemingly private world. He kneed his horse into a trot.

"Will Amaury be all right?" Rose's hot breath puffed against his ear, the pleasurable sensation making his stomach tighten. "What happens when they find out he's led them astray?"

Once they were about three hundred yards away from the track, Rand pulled the cob up to a walk again and answered, "You need not worry about Amaury. He is a very cunning and resourceful man. The king, on occasion, has even utilized Amaury's services to spy for him in Wales."

"King Edward!" Rose gasped, her hand inadvertently brushing the tip of his suddenly stiff shaft. Rand shuddered, clasping the reins tighter. "Do you not fear he shall betray you to the king?"

He swung the horse back in a southerly direction toward the hospital. "Amaury has a reputation for being discreet. He has to be in his occupation. But more importantly, the man is loyal to a fault. He shall not betray us."

"By helping us escape, is he not being disloyal to the king?"

"King Edward cares not what the man does. Now, if Amaury spied on the king for the Welsh that would be an entirely different matter. Besides, Amaury is in my debt for saving his life. He'd never betray me." He was reluctant to bring up the latter, but he wanted to put Rose's mind at ease.

"Do you hear that?" Rand queried, his voice low.

"What? I don't hear anything," Rose responded in kind.

"Exactly." Reining in his mount, Rand strained his ears to listen.

The rumble of troops in motion was now silenced. Then the contingent of men on horseback was on the move again. The sound of thundering hooves rapidly faded as they moved farther away.

Rose's head popped around his shoulder, her gaze bright with triumph. "Amaury has done it, Rand. The soldiers are heading in the other direction."

"Aye," Rand concurred heartily, "he most certainly has." Then he kissed her. Deeply. Hotly. Confidently.

Her breath hitched, her lips melded to his.

He pulled back. She was dazed, her lips berry red and moistened with desire. His mouth curled up in a huge grin.

"Hold on," Rand said before he turned forward again, kicked the cob into a gallop, and headed back east toward the track that led to the hospital. That led back to his son. The son he wanted to get to know much better. "Let's go get our son."

She clutched his chest, clinging to him with her small hands. "Aye, our son. He will be all right, won't he? Do you think Lydia could actually—" Her voice ended abruptly in a strangled moan.

"I don't know. But I believe he shall be safe until we can reach the hospital. Lydia, unwilling to draw attention to herself, will wait to commit her foul deed in the deepest hours of the night, when all but a few poor souls are asleep."

"I pray you are right."

"I am right; you shall see," Rand swore with conviction, bolstering Rose with a confidence he did not entirely feel.

So, in silence, Rand moved his lips in prayer, seeking forgiveness and intercession on behalf of Jason. Bargaining for his son's life. He had not prayed with such desperate fervency since he woke after the fire in excruciating pain and discovered he'd survived when his mother had not.

But now he had so much to live for. Rose. Jason. The family he'd always wanted but was too afraid to seek.

Yet doubt needled him each time he recalled the ease with which Golan had given up Jason's location.

Water lapped at the hull of the barge as Golan stepped out.

"Well, my friend. This is where we must part." Golan bent down and wiped off the bloody blade in a clump of tall grasses.

Slumped in the boat, Harwood remained mute and unresponsive. Blood gushed from his slit throat.

"No parting words?" Golan shrugged, then threw back his head and laughed.

He shoved the dagger inside his belt and headed across the moist ground toward the small hamlet in search of a horse. A huge grin of satisfaction spread across his face. God, he could not wait to see the surprise on the dastardly pair's faces when he confronted them. He would see the couple dead without a bit of remorse. Excitement quivered inside him, and pleasure coiled tight in his belly at the thought of it.

Chapter Twenty-Seven

Rose kept her gaze trained forward, seeking any signs of a settlement. Her lips moved in prayer, begging and beseeching the Lord to keep her son safe. But secretly she feared He would not hear her prayer for she had yet to confess her sin of adultery.

Yet she could not give up hope or give in to despair. She would not burden Rand's confidence with the doubts that beset her.

In the distance, a faint glow shone through the dissipating fog. "Is that a light?"

"Where?"

She pointed to the left. "Over there," she said excitedly. "Do you see it?"

"Aye. Now I do. It looks like . . . torches, two of them." Rand guided the cob toward the lights. It was not long before they came upon the eight-foot-high stone walls enclosing the Hospital of St. John without the North Gate, and its adjoining chapel and bell tower.

Directly across from the hospital soared the forty-foot-high wall protecting the northern approach to the town of Chester.

A gate about six feet wide appeared in the wall before the hospital, flanked by two torches. Rand threw his leg over the neck of his horse and jumped down. Then he reached up and grabbed her beneath the arms and lifted her down.

She stared up at him, eyes wide, breathless, heart pounding. Though it was dark, the glow from the torches cast a golden light upon his head like a halo. Her very own earthly guardian angel. "What now?"

Rand stared back at the closed gate, then back to her protruding belly. "When I ring the bell for admittance, if the gatekeeper shows any reluctance to admit us, faint as though you are too weak to walk." Rand reached over and pulled the bell string on the right side of the gate.

It rang loudly in the consuming silence.

Holding the cob's reins in his right hand, he embraced Rose's shoulders with his opposite arm. Bending to her ear, he continued, whispering, "If that does not work, I shall have to resort to more . . . drastic measures to gain entrance."

Rose, pressed against his left side, felt the hard imprint of his sword and scabbard.

A sharp scraping of iron reverberated in her ears. A wrinkled face peeked through a small square opening in the door, grumpily inquiring, "Who's there?"

Rand could just make out the black and white veil and wimple of a nun. "Good sister, may my wife and I seek hospitality for the night? I fear she is in a bad way. We have journeyed long and were unable to find lodging before nightfall."

When the woman hesitated, mumbling under her breath, Rose slumped gracefully in his arms. Rand caught her behind her knees and lifted her up cradling her like a baby.

The heavy wood bar screeched as it was shoved up. Soon a small door big enough for a person to pass through swung open. "Mercy," the nun said, scowling, "why did you not say your wife was in such dire need of care?"

Grateful the ruse worked, Rand did not point out that he had warned the nun of Rose's "condition." He shifted Rose higher in his arms and ducked as he passed through the low door. He followed the nun across the small courtyard and entered the porch. Rand had a brief view of the infirmary's vaulted chamber on his left before the nun picked up a branch of candles on a table by the door. Her strides swift, she turned right and headed down a long corridor. Their footsteps padded across the tile floor, while flames in lit torches flickered as they passed by, creating interesting shadows on the red sandstone walls.

Rose felt as light as a bolster and just as soft in his arms. Her fingers twined in the hair at his nape. She gazed up at him, her blue eyes fathomless; a deep sensation of connection and certainty to do whatever was necessary to save their son passed between them. No words were necessary.

The corridor ended abruptly at an arched doorway. The nun proceeded through it, taking them outside again. A pentice, or covered walkway that was open on one side, connected the hospital to a small thatched-roof cottage.

"You may stay in the guesthouse for the night." Using a key she retrieved from a leather belt beneath her scapular, a black sleeveless outer garment, the sister opened the chamber door and stepped back to allow Rand to carry Rose inside.

Rand glanced around the room quickly. It was small yet tidy and clean. He covered the ground to the canopy bed in two long strides and laid Rose down on top of the bedclothes.

"My name is Sister Hildegard." Rand stepped back to give her room to light a hanging lamp beside the curtained bed. With her hand she indicated the chest at the foot of the bed. "Extra blankets are inside, and you'll find firewood stacked next to the fireplace. One of the other sisters will return shortly with water for washing and a small repast."

"Bless you, sister. We thank you for your kindness," Rose addressed Sister Hildegard, her voice thready and her hands cradling her protruding stomach.

The older woman nodded to them both and left, closing the door quietly behind her.

Rand knelt before the fireplace in front of the bed, striking steel to flint. "I'll start a fire to give us more light."

Rose swung her legs over the side of the bed and got to her feet. She moved to the door and opening it peered outside. "What are we going to do now? Do you have a plan for how we are going to find Jason without raising anyone's suspicions?"

Once he placed the burning tinder under the kindling, Rand gazed over his shoulder at her. "I have an idea, but I doubt you are going to like it."

The fire blazed to life; Rand got to his feet, brushing off his hands.

Rose raised her chin determinedly. "I'm prepared to do whatever it takes to find Jason. We dare not wait any longer. But how do we even know if Jason is still here? Lydia could have taken him already. Or God forfend, she has already . . . harmed him." Her voice rose on a shrill note and her shoulders suddenly drooped.

Rand hurried to her and pulled her into his embrace. The cloth she'd stuffed beneath her tunic shifted easily. He kissed the top of her head, saying fervently, "Jason is here. I am sure of it. Lydia's days of terrorizing you will end this night. I shall personally see to it."

Her warmth seeped into him, her scent ensorcelling his senses. Overcome by tenderness, he pulled back and stared deeply into her wide blue eyes, desperate to convey the verity of his words, his conviction that they would prevail.

When her gaze dropped to his mouth, he groaned and pressed his mouth to her soft, intoxicating lips. Feverishly. Hungrily. His tongue stabbed inside her velvety dark cavern.

Fire shot straight to his gut, and lower still. Shaft marble hard, he pressed against her, rotating his hips and seeking her moist heat. With a breathy moan, Rose undulated her lower body against the hard ridge of his desire. Stroking,

teasing, penetrating, their tongues tangled with a burning,
desperate intensity.

He could not think for her passionate response. For her
brave action in trading her life for their son's. Aye. Their son.
Although it still hurt that she had not told him long ago that
he was Jason's father, Rand realized that she had wanted only
to protect Jason. But after Bertram's death, whom or what
had she been protecting Jason from? He could only surmise
it had been from him.

The reason she had kept it secret would have to wait. Jason
was somewhere in the hospital and in extreme danger. He
clutched her shoulders and pulled back. Breaths heavy, his
and hers, they stared at one another.

They had to find Jason. His son was alive. He could feel it.
But time was rapidly dwindling away.

"Rand—" Rose began.

At a strangled squeak, Rand started. He swirled to the
door. Rose jumped back, a hand to her throat. The pale-faced
nun in the open doorway stared aghast at them. The tray of
food she was holding slipped from her fingers and clattered
on the ground.

Slapping one hand over her mouth, the nun pointed at
Rose's stomach. "You are not . . . not with child."

Rand swung his gaze to Rose, who looked down. The
padding that was stuffed beneath her tunic had shifted and a
huge lump protruded from her side like a grotesque tumor.

"Oh no." Rose grabbed the stuffing and shifted it, but the
damage was done.

Just as the sister opened her mouth and screamed, Rand,
his heart crawling up his throat, lunged for her. He grabbed
the woman around the shoulders and clamped his hand over
her mouth, cutting off her cry of alarm.

Rose, meanwhile, moved to the door and closed it hastily.

"Have no fear, sister, I do not intend to harm you."

The nun stared up at him, her body shuddering. He kept his

hand over her mouth. "We only want to get our son. He would have been brought to the hospital about three days ago. He has blond curly hair, dimples, and is three and a half years old." As he gave Jason's description, the sister's watery brown eyes grew huge. His heart beat so hard he thought he might have an apoplexy. "Did a boy matching that description arrive here in the last few days? Nod up and down if the answer is aye. Nod side to side if the answer is nay."

Her head bobbed up and down rapidly. A great rush of air expelled from his lungs.

Rose moved around the nun to stand on the woman's other side.

"Does the boy still reside in the hospital?" she asked excitedly.

Her head nodding up and down once more, the answer was aye.

Rand's glance clashed with Rose's, a rush of emotions—wonder, relief, and worry—shimmering between them.

Then Rose jerked forward and clutched the nun's arm. "What about a woman, with short, blond curly hair, very beautiful, with a petite but shapely stature? Have you seen her? Is she a guest or mayhap an infirmary resident?"

The woman's head twisted side to side.

Rose, eyes bright, asked desperately, "Are you sure? She could be disguised, perhaps even as a nun. If so, she would have arrived in recent days."

Brown eyes slowly grew wide with shock. Then the nun nodded in the positive this time. Rand turned and stared at Rose. Her eyes became dark blue, shadowed with fear.

Rand narrowed his eyes on the nun, frown fierce. "Explain. I'm going to remove my hand. Do not scream or I'll snap your neck." God would forgive him for frightening a nun. "Do you understand?"

She nodded her head aye.

He uncovered her mouth slowly. "Tell us what you know of the woman."

She exhaled a soft, shuddery breath and explained in stops and starts. "S-Sister Mary. Trav . . . she is traveling from the north . . . on pilgrimage to Santiago de Compostela. She arrived just one day after two castle guards left the boy in our care."

His voice roughened with emotion, Rand asked, "Has she had any contact with the boy since her arrival?"

"Nay, I do not believe so. While Sister Mary is recuperating before continuing on her journey to Leon, she has been busy every day delivering alms to the poor of Chester."

Rose clutched a hand to her throat. Her pulse jumped at the base, fear and relief that Jason was yet all right clamoring in her blood. "How is the boy? My son. Is he all right?"

"He seems like a sad boy, but he is strong and in good health."

Rand asked, "Do you know where this Sister Mary is now?"

"She is attending the Compline services with the others before 'tis time to retire for the evening."

The nun raised big fearful eyes to Rand. "My lord, I pray you, let me go. I have told you everything I know." Then she took a short, mincing step backward, bumping against the door.

Rand closed the gap between them and clutched the slender nun's shoulders. "I am sorry. I cannot let you go yet." His voice was grim, determined.

The nun, clutching her hands before her, voice shaking, implored, "Prithee, do not hurt me."

Rose felt sympathy for the frightened nun, but her son was in danger and she could not falter now.

"I have no desire to hurt you, but . . ."

"Aye, but?"

"My wife has need of your habit. I shall have to ask you to remove it."

The demand surprised Rose. Suddenly, the nun's eyes widened in terror and rolled back in her head. She slumped in Rand's arms.

"Lord help us," he swore, exasperated.

Rose pulled the blankets down on the bed. "Lie her down over here, Rand."

Rand did so. "'Tis as well she fainted. It shall be easier to remove her garments." He motioned her to the other side of the bed as he began removing the nun's black sleeveless outer garment worn over her white habit. "The habit shall disguise you as we search the beds for Jason."

"'Tis a good plan." Rose did not hesitate at the notion of Rand doing such an intimate chore. Jason's life was worth any sacrifice. And the inappropriateness of Rand viewing a woman in her undress, and a nun at that, was inconsequential to Rose.

Not even death shall stop me from saving Jason. He is my life, and Rand, too. I love them both so much.

Rose and Rand stood behind a large stone column not far from the great arching entry of the infirmary. Behind her, Rand braced his hands upon her shoulders. The wide sleeves of a monk's robe he'd commandeered from the laundry brushed her arms. Rose stared straight forward, her eyes straining toward the infirmary, searching for any sign of movement. She could just make out the first two of several large columns that supported the vaulted ceiling. The darkness was vast, but tall, standing branched candles stood on each side of a column, creating subtle illumination.

"All right, Rose," Rand whispered in her ear, his heartbeat a comforting tattoo against her back. "You must not do anything to draw attention upon yourself. I see only one other nun in the infirmary, though there may be others. Casually stop by each bed as if you are seeking to give the inhabitants comfort."

Rose glanced over her shoulder at Rand. His face was barely visible within the voluminous cowl he'd pulled down over his brow. "Rand, I shall be fine. I believe I can reasonably portray myself as a nurse. I *am* accustomed to caring for others." She was covered from head to toe in the black and white of a nun's habit except for her face.

"'Tis Lydia I am concerned about. She shall be very dangerous. Do not confront her if you should come upon her. The moment you get into trouble—"

"Do you suspect there will be trouble?"

"Always. 'Tis better to expect the worst and be prepared than to expect the best and be unprepared." His gray-green eyes steadily held her stare. Calm, serene, confidence his gaze exuded. "But I don't want you to be distressed. I shall not let you out of my sight and will be there should anything untoward occur. Are you ready?"

Rose took a deep breath and nodded.

Rand smiled tenderly. "Good. Remember I am here for you—no matter what happens I shall be by your side in a thrice."

She smiled tremulously. With the bent knuckle of his forefinger, he tipped her chin up. Her lips tingled in readiness the moment before he dipped his head. Soft. Tender. His lips pressed against hers; a breath of a kiss that tantalized. Captivated. Enticed.

Then it was over.

Rose, her pulse racing, stepped out from behind the column and proceeded through a central area that separated the infirmary from the chapel. The chapel to her right was directly opposite the infirmary and designed so patients could view from their beds the daily offices the brethren sang for the comfort of their soul. A quick, surreptitious glance revealed the chapel was now empty. Only a single candle on the altar gave illumination.

Edging past the font, Rose turned left and entered the infirmary. Two rows of stone columns on either side of the vast chamber created a large, open central aisle down the middle. Behind the columns were two smaller side aisles where the beds ran in rows down each wall below stained glass windows. Each bed was enclosed by curtains, which hung on rods attached to long chains suspended from the high-beamed ceiling.

Suddenly, two nuns conversing quietly between each other emerged from behind one of the nearest columns. Rose, wearing the borrowed white wimple and black veil, tipped her head down and tugged the edges of the long veil beside her cheeks to conceal her face.

"Sister Agnes," the taller of the two called out. "Did you not hear the bells? 'Tis time to retire for the night."

She did not respond but continued walking over to the beds on the left wall. At the foot of each bed was a chest. Many of the beds had two patients in them, but a few had single occupants. Once out of the sisters' view, she sat on the side of a bed occupied by a woman with long, stringy gray hair who was snoring loudly. A lit sconce on the wall cast subtle shadows on the woman's craggy, age-worn face. Rose peeked around the curtain divider protecting the patient from drafts. The sisters were gone.

Checking to make sure no one else was in sight, she climbed to her feet. Hospitals such as this one that housed both male and female residents were segregated, which meant Jason was in one of the beds on the other side with the male patients. With a cautious eye on the entrance to the infirmary, Rose quickly crossed the center aisle to the other side. She began her perusal of the first bed, then the second. Neither of the dwellers were children. She hurried down the row, stopping at the foot of each bed, glancing to see that the patient wasn't Jason, and continuing to the next. Her heart plummeted each time she scrutinized a patient and realized it was not Jason.

Then a strange muffled sound emerged from one of the beds farther down. Rose cocked her head and listened.

The sudden cry of a child calling out, "Mama," caused Rose to start.

Caution flown, Rose screamed, "Jason!" She ran like a woman possessed shoving curtains aside as she sought to find where the voice came from. It was Jason. She knew it. A mother recognized the sound of her child's voice in the deep recesses of her soul.

She yanked the curtain aside at the last bed and gaped in horror. Jason's short legs kicked atop the bed as Lydia, garbed in a nun's habit, pressed a pillow over his face.

Agony wrenched Rose's chest. "Get away from my son!" she shrieked, lunging around the bed.

When she reached for Lydia, the woman drew a dagger from under her scapular and stabbed out at Rose. The blade slashed Rose's forearm, and blood spurted as fire sizzled along her flesh.

Lydia grabbed Jason's arm and yanked him from the bed. Jason whimpered in fear and pain. "Stay where you are, *my lady*," Lydia snarled. Her face contorted with hate, a stiff mask marring her refined features. Then she pressed the dagger to Jason's neck.

Rose froze where she stood, the blood draining from her face and gushing from her wound. She clasped her hand over the injury to staunch the bleeding.

"Lydia, prithee. Let my son go," she entreated, voice quavering.

"Nay, I think not."

"What do you want? Tell me. I'll do whatever you ask. Just do not hurt my son."

Jason squirmed in Lydia's arms. "Mama?"

Rose gazed at Jason, who stood barefoot in a big flowing sherte. His big blue-green eyes beseeched her. Her eyes blurred with tears. "Jason, darling, 'tis all right. I won't let her hurt you."

Lydia laughed, a short shrill sound quickly cut off. "You are in no position to dictate to me. You cannot help your precious son. You were supposed to die. Now your son shall pay with his life for your betrayal."

"You are right. I betrayed you. Let Jason go. I shall gladly take his place. 'Tis me you want to hurt. Not Jason."

"Certes. But now I have changed my mind. Indeed, I want you to suffer knowing 'twas your actions that brought about your son's death."

"Lydia, I beg you. Have you no heart? He is just an innocent boy."

"Nay, I have no heart. My father stole it, along with everything else I ever once valued."

Desperate, Rose glanced back toward the infirmary entrance. She could just make out the left side of the tall, wide arched portal. Where was Rand? He should have heard her cry out and come by now.

"He is not coming to your rescue." She cackled.

Rose jerked back to Lydia. "What are you talking about?"

"Rand. Your brave defender," she scoffed, a wave of scorn hitting Rose like flames spewed from a dragon's mouth. "He is not coming to your rescue. He has more . . . pressing matters with which to concern himself."

"Do not speak in riddles," Rose spat out, a spike of anger piercing her voice. She was tired of Lydia's tricks and constant manipulation. "What do you know?"

Lydia stiffened. "Brave demands, considering I have a dagger pointed at your son's throat." She pressed the dagger closer, puncturing his skin, causing a small bead of blood to trickle down.

Rose's heart jumped into her throat, thundered. Jason's

eyes, round with fear, gazed up at her. She cursed her
wayward tongue and remained silent, waiting. She must
not antagonize the woman. *Patience*, she told herself. *Until
I can get Jason safely away from Lydia, that is.*

"Golan," Lydia said, satisfaction dripping from her tongue
like honey.

"Golan?" She shook her head, straining to keep the satisfaction from entering her voice. "Golan can no longer help
you. He is secure in the hold of Rand's ship."

A deep masculine chuckle sent a shiver down Rose's spine.
She spun around and gaped, the pa-bum pa-bum of her heart
loud in her ears. Golan's wide sensual smile gleamed bright,
effusive, and terrifying.

"Golan? What . . . ? I . . . you . . ."

"Did you truly believe you and your pathetic lover could
keep me from exacting my revenge?"

Golan reached out with strong, blunt fingers and pulled her
into his arms. With her back to his chest, his left arm embraced her upper shoulders, while his other hand slithered
across her breasts in a parody of a loving caress, then down
her stomach and over her mound.

He clutched her between her legs and ground his erect
flesh between the cheeks of her derriere. "I'm going to enjoy
finishing what we started in the prison before that blackguard
knocked me out."

A quiver shuddered over her as though an army of black
beetles crawled over her flesh. Moaning, she begged, "Nay,
not in front of my son."

"Don't touch my mama," Jason piped up, tears trailing
down his face.

Golan's sickly hot breath puffed against her ear. "Ah, how
touching. Your and Rand's little bastard is a brave though
foolhardy boy. I shall give you that. But 'tis time he learn
what a whore his mother is."

"What's a bastard, Mama?"

Lydia, tugging Jason along, shuffled past Rose and toward the tall, lit iron candle stand near the column at the end of the bed. "Golan," she snapped, "we do not have time for your games now. Someone will be checking on the inmates soon. Have you taken care of Rand as we discussed?"

"Aye, Rand was so focused on this trollop, he did not even hear me approach him from behind." Smug satisfaction laced his words.

Rose gasped. "What did you do to him? If you hurt him—"

"He is not dead, if that is your concern. Yet."

A loud scraping sound on the stone floor drew Rose's glance back to Lydia. In stunned disbelief, Rose watched Lydia shove the candelabra over with the weight of her body. It crashed to the bed and, with amazing rapidity, the candle flames caught the coverlet on fire, spreading across the bed in a sizzling trail of destruction.

"What are you doing?" Rose asked in horror. "You'll catch the whole hospital on fire and burn it down."

A smile so evilly wicked spread across Lydia's face, Rose nearly doubled over as though from a punch to her stomach.

"Aye, when they find your charred bodies in the remains, you shall be unrecognizable. A fitting punishment for a woman who murdered her husband, do you not agree?" A menacing chuckle punctuated her rhetorical query.

Rose opened her mouth to shout fire, but Lydia narrowed her eyes and swore, "Shout a warning, and I'll slit Jason's throat right now."

Lydia's snide voice curled around Rose like a serpent and squeezed the breath from her. Rose clamped her mouth shut and glanced back down at Jason. Ghostly pale, he stood quietly, his countenance a mixture of fear and bravery. Pride surged in her chest. She held his gaze, her eyes conveying to him her love and strength.

Lydia, seeing Rose's compliance, marched away, hauling

Jason behind her. Rose breathed a sigh of relief when Golan
released her.

"Move it," Golan grumbled, then nudged her forward after
Lydia and out the infirmary's entrance.

But their ordeal had only begun. Smoke began to billow in
the chamber and taint the air with its acrid stench. On the
other hand, surely someone would detect the fire and extin-
guish it before it could flame out of control?

Chapter Twenty-Eight

When a sharp pain jabbed at his left temple, Rand groaned. He tried to open his eyes, but a dense blackness weighed him down and held him in the grip of a nightmare. He was in the stable fire, and the burning stench filled his nostrils and lungs. Only this time, the past merged with the present. It was Rose who was in danger, not his mother.

He thought he heard the drone of a man's and a woman's voices. It sounded like Golan's deep gruff tones, but Rand knew it could not possibly be him. It was just a dream.

A cool, comforting hand stroked his forehead, smoothing his hair back. He sighed, knowing it was Rose.

"Rand." Her soft voice, laced with fear, penetrated the thickness inside his skull. She spoke again, her voice louder, more insistent, "Rand, pray, answer me."

Rose needed him. And Jason. He could not let them down. Rand blinked once, twice, forcing his eyes open. It was dark, but he had no difficulty making out her features. She leaned over him, her normally smooth brow furrowed.

"Heaven's mercy."

He smiled at the relief evident in her voice. "Ro—" His voice cracked. He cleared his throat and tried again. "Are you all right? Do you have Jason?"

"Jason and I are fine, but—"

Rose jerked back suddenly.

"Very well, 'tis enough prattling."

Rand started at the male voice. Golan. How could it be him? He was locked in the hold of Rand's ship. Then Rand remembered hearing Rose scream a moment before he received a blow to his head. Heart racing erratically, he tried to get up from the hard stone floor, but his arms pulled tautly at the rope binding his wrists to a heavy altar column, and he was drawn back.

Rand strained against his shackles impotently. "Golan, you coward, show your face," he swore, searching the shadows.

Golan chuckled and stepped forward. He clutched Rose in his arms before him and groped her breasts, a grin of ecstasy on his face. Rose made not a sound, her face expressionless and eyes staring into the distance.

"Whoreson," Rand swore, his face flushing and fury pumping through his veins. "Get your hands off my wife."

He tried to lunge up again. Pain wrenched his shoulders. "Release me, Golan, and fight me like a man. Ahh, but we both know you are too inept to beat me in a fair battle. After all, you switched my lance during the joust to give you an unfair advantage."

Golan glared. "How did you find out?"

"The day of the joust something felt odd about my lance. When it shattered too easily, I suspected the fire was a diversion so someone could switch my lance for a defective one. You were the one person who stood to gain by my defeat. Until now, I only had suspicions." Rand smiled with smug satisfaction. "But you just confirmed them."

"Arrogant bastard. But I have the upper hand now." Golan pressed Rose's chin to the side with his left hand and kissed her. She jerked her head away and spat with contempt.

Rand gritted his teeth, loathing and frustration roiling in his gut like pitch. "Golan," he snapped, drawing his attention away from Rose. "Fight me, you coward. Or are you afraid you cannot beat me in a fair fight?"

Golan's lips rolled back in a snarl. "I am not afraid of you." He shoved Rose aside and swung his arm out.

Golan's white-knuckled fist slammed into Rand's jaw.

Rose screamed as his head whipped back and his teeth rattled in his skull. The metallic taste of blood filled his mouth. He spat out the blood onto the flagstone floor and glared icily at Golan.

"That's for the beating you gave me," Golan said. Surprising Rand, he knelt down and began untying the bonds at Rand's wrists. "After I kill you," he whispered in a sibilant voice, "I'm going to enjoy slaking my desire for Rose over your dead body."

A feminine voice slithered from the shadows. "Golan, what are you doing?" It was Lydia, Rand guessed. "You can't untie him. We have to go before the fire is discovered." Lydia grabbed Golan's arm and pulled him toward the door.

Fire? Rand jerked. It was then he realized the pungent odor of smoke had not been in his dream. His heart pummeled his chest and sweat popped out on his forehead as panic seized him.

"Don't order me about, wench," Golan said, shoving Lydia off him. "I'm not finished with this knave and his harlot yet."

Rand shifted his gaze to Rose, who clutched Jason to her. A small window high above on his right let in a shaft of moonlight. The beam slanted down across the chamber—which was about twelve feet square—and splashed onto the wall opposite, illuminating Rose above her chin. Their eyes met and held. He blinked. Hope, love, and determination shone bright in her gaze. Emotion clogged his throat. He wanted to reach out and hold her, tell her everything was going to be all right, that they would survive this latest challenge.

Golan reached for his waist. Rand jerked his head back toward Golan. The man withdrew a dagger from his belt. Rand recognized the blade. His heart plummeted.

"That's Harwood's dagger. How did you get it? What did you do to Harwood?"

Rand stared at the dagger as it drew closer.

Golan swiped the blade across his neck simulating the action of slitting a throat. "He's communing with the devils in Purgatory." A menacing chuckle scraped like a razor.

"You bastard. You didn't have to kill him. Your grudge is with me."

"You have no one to blame but yourself. When you involved Harwood in our feud, you sealed his death."

Rand blanched, guilt churning like acid in his gut. Golan reached down behind Rand again.

Lydia stepped around Golan and pressed her hands against his chest. "Golan, darling. You can't release him." Her voice coaxed with a seductive lilt. "We have schemed too long to give him an opportunity to escape. Come, let's not divert from our plan now. Leave them to their fiery death"—her hand reached down and pressed against Golan's loins, and her voice dropped to a throaty pitch—"while we attend to more pleasurable pursuits."

"Your wiles shall not work with me, you strumpet." His tone thick with disgust, Golan pushed her aside once more.

When she clung to him, he backhanded her across the face. Lydia cried out, stumbling toward Rose. As Golan bent down, Lydia sprang on his back and raised a dagger high in her hand. Rand's heart stopped a beat and his eyes widened in shock. With a guttural cry, Lydia plunged the blade into Golan's throat. He bellowed in excruciating pain. Lydia withdrew the dagger; blood sprayed into the air like a fountain.

A startled gasp came from Rose. "Close your eyes, sweetling," she told Jason, pressing his face into her hip.

Golan tried to stanch the blood, but it bubbled between his fingers. Face paling, he collapsed to the ground at Rand's feet. "The bitch killed me," he said in shocked disbelief. His eyes glazed over as his lifeblood drained from him. He stared blankly into space.

"Nay!" Rand shouted, jerking against the stout column. "I wanted to kill the conniving bastard."

"Don't move, Jason," Rose said, squeezing his shoulder. "Stay right here." Stepping forward, she dropped to her knees to check Golan's pulse. "He's dead," she said, her voice and face stripped of all emotion.

The door slammed shut. Rand glanced up. Lydia was nowhere in sight.

"The door!" Rand shouted.

At the same time, Rose screamed, jumping up. He heard the iron key scrape as it turned inside the wooden tumbler. Rose grabbed the door latch and yanked on it. But Rand knew it was too late. As he suspected, the door didn't budge.

His shoulders slumped.

"She's locked us in," Rose said, voice frantic, gazing at him over her shoulder. She spun back to the door. Banging on the wooden panel, Rose shouted, "Help! Someone, help us!"

"Untie me, Rose." The scent of smoke grew stronger. It billowed below the door and puffed up in thickening gray clouds. "Hurry. The fire is spreading quickly. We have to find a way out of here."

She rushed over next to him. Her foot slipped in a spreading pool of blood and she fell on her buttocks with a yelp of pain.

"What is it? Are you hurt?"

She crawled up onto her knees and reached up behind him. "Nay. I am fine. I just hurt my bottom." Rose jerked the altar cloth off and covered Golan.

Then stretching around Rand, she tipped her head down and quickly worked to untie the knots of his bonds. Jason moved closer to his mother, clearly scared and seeking her comforting presence.

Her fingers brushed Rand's wrists tantalizingly. Her

mussed hair fell over her shoulder and kissed his cheek silkily. He closed his eyes and inhaled. The subtle scents of rose and lavender lingered in the coppery strands.

"What are we going to do? How do we get out of here?"

At Rose's urgent prodding, he jerked his eyes open. He searched the four corners of the chamber looking for anything to help them escape. The chamber was the chapel vestry. A cupboard for storing the liturgical objects and vestments stood against the wall beneath the window. In addition, on either side of the cupboard were two freestanding posts that supported candles.

"I don't know, but I am not going to give up without a fight."

His hands finally slackened and he brought them around and rubbed the red welts ringing his wrists. He tucked his feet to his haunches and lunged to his feet. Having lain unmoving too long, a prickling sensation stabbed his lower limbs, and he stumbled.

Rose caught him. He clutched her shoulders and stared down at her. Soft blue eyes gazed at him; he fell into the shimmering pools, drawing ever deeper under her captivating spell. Jason nudged between them, tugging on Rand's surcoate. "Papa, the smoke is getting thicker."

Rand swallowed, clutched Jason's shoulder. "Don't worry, son," he said, then dashed to the door. "I'm going to get you and your mother out of here."

On the chance someone might hear them, he shouted at the top of his lungs and pounded heavily with his fists against the door. Rose joined him and added her voice to his, until it gave out and she began choking. Rand clutched her in his arms and rubbed her back while she coughed. When she finally subsided, he released a growl of frustration.

He spun around and looked around the room once more. His gaze shot back to the pair of wooden posts. They were about twelve inches thick and five feet tall. His heart soared.

He veered to the left of the altar, grabbed a post, and lifted it. It was heavy and made of sturdy oak. "'Tis perfect for what I have in mind."

"What are you going to do with it?" She stared, gaze puzzled.

He hefted it up in his arms and maneuvered it clumsily before the altar. "Come, grab the front end. We'll use it as a battering ram to break the lock bolt."

Her head snapped up, eyes brightening with excitement. "Brilliant. It may just work."

"Stand on the right side of the post so we can balance the weight of the beam."

She nodded, ducked beneath the beam, then gave him her back and couched the post like a lance under her left arm.

Rand said gently, "Jason, move back behind the altar."

He waited till the boy obeyed.

"All right, Rose. Together, we'll bring the post back then forward three times to gain momentum and speed. I'll count one, two, then three each time on the forward pass. Upon the final count of three, we'll ram the post against the door with all our weight behind it. And keep going till the lock or door shatters. Understand?"

"Aye. I'm ready."

"Good." He swung the post backward, and then on the forward swing he counted out, "One." Backward and forward, "Two." Backward and forward, "Three!"

The beam slammed into the door. Wood crunched loudly in the tense silence. They swung again and again. Each time the door shivered forcefully. The wood began to splinter and crack.

"'Tis working!" Rose cried excitedly.

"Indeed, 'tis," he concurred, a huge grin spreading across his face and his blood rushing in his veins.

On the eighth swing, the door smashed open with a shuddering crash. Smoke poured into the chamber and sinister shadows and light from the red glow of the fire coiled and writhed on the chamber walls. A flash of fear from his memory of the stable fire crept beneath his skin and set off prickling warnings. Cold sweat broke over his body.

Rose dropped her end of the post, whirled around, and flung her arms around him in a crushing hug. "Let's get out of here," she said in intense jubilation.

Embraced by her soft, supple arms, Rand determinedly tamped his fears into a coffer and slammed the lid shut. He lowered the post and hurried to Jason, who crouched behind the altar, with his hands covering his ears. Rand hoisted the boy into his arms. Jason trembled in fright, his chubby arms clinging like vines around Rand's neck. Rose glanced up at them, her eyes tearing with . . . joy, wonder, mayhap?

He swallowed a lump of emotion and wrapped his free arm around Rose's shoulder. As one, they surged through the chamber door and hastened down the chancel of the chapel adjoining the infirmary.

Rose clutched Rand's hand tightly as he pulled her along. The heat and smoke was cloyingly thick. Panting breathily, her nostrils flared. The fire's stench wafted into her nose and scratched the back of her throat. She coughed, expelling the thick fumes choking her.

As the smoke parted for a moment, Rose peeked through the infirmary's arched entry. The blaze consumed half the beds and spread like rippling waves along the wood-beamed roofline. Rand turned left and raced to the hospital entrance. Two nuns, supporting a limping, moaning woman between them, passed Rose and Rand going the opposite direction, back toward the church. A monk, running hurriedly up behind the women, waved his arms wildly at Rose and Rand.

"Stop!" The brother's cowl draped down the back of his

shoulders and the fringes of his gray tonsured head stuck out on end.

They pulled up as the monk approached.

Panting with exertion, he continued, "'Tis no exit this way. The doors are jammed and impassable."

"Where are the other exits? Have you tried them?"

"There is only one other exit; it leads to the cloister. But I've checked it too." He shook his head and continued, voice despairing, "A fallen burning beam blocks it. We are trapped. Unless someone comes to our rescue, all we can do is pray."

Rose shot her gaze to Rand's. A palpable wave of despair seemed to draw them together. The debilitating emotion hovered for several beats of her heart, until suddenly, a light of determination flamed in the gold flecks of Rand's colorful gaze. His confidence imbued her heart with courage. She rubbed Jason's back to ease his fear and in return to gain comfort and strength from him. His breath came in labored pants.

Rand turned back to the monk. "Pray, brother? I intend to do more than pray. I shall continue looking for a way to escape till my dying breath."

Rose blurted, "What of the windows? I noticed several windows in the infirmary." Her breath wheezed.

The monk shook his head. "The infirmary is almost completely ablaze. I'd not advise you to enter. 'Tis too dangerous." As if to emphasize the brother's words, a beam crashed to the ground in the direction of the infirmary, sounding like a crack of thunder. "You see, 'tis not safe. I beg you come with me. Those of us who were unable to escape are seeking refuge in the sanctuary to pray for our souls."

"Before long, nowhere shall be safe. I regret we must part here. But tell me, good brother, before you go, what of the windows in the infirmary? Are any reachable from the ground?"

"There are two windows in the west bay that are lower than the rest, but I am unsure how or if 'tis possible to access them."

"If there is a way, I'll find it."

Jason began coughing violently. Rand patted his back, worry marking his brow. Rose smoothed Jason's hair back from his forehead in a soothing gesture.

"Come, Rose. We must hurry."

The monk said, "May God and His angels be with you." He made the sign of the cross, blessing them, "In the name of the Father and of the Son and of the Holy Ghost. Amen," before he hurried away.

They followed on his heels, Rand leading the way again. As they approached the infirmary entrance, great billowing clouds of smoke discharged from the chamber, the flames flickering on the walls like ghastly images of what Rose imagined demons from Hell looked like.

Rand stopped suddenly. Caught unawares, Rose bumped into him. Above the din of the crackling fire, groaning timbers, and terrified moans of the remaining inhabitants, he shouted, "Take off your wimple and veil!"

Wondering what he intended, she nevertheless obeyed. As she removed the hairpins from her headdress, he set Jason down on the floor, pulled the cope he wore over his head, and shrugged out of it. When he stepped aside, she saw the stoup, a basin of holy water set upon a waist-high stone pedestal.

She handed him her wimple and veil and he dunked it, along with his cope, into the basin of holy water, ignoring the rose-shaped sprinkler attached to the basin by a chain.

"Put your arms up." When she did, he pulled the robe over her head and she shimmied to help ease the clingy wet material down her body. A quick, soft smile graced his face, and then he handed her the veil he'd wrung out. "Use this to cover your mouth and nose so you can breathe easier. The wimple is for Ja—" His words cut off abruptly as he looked down.

Rose glanced down too. Jason was nowhere in sight. They spoke in unison. "Oh, God, where's Jason?"

"Jesu. He's gone."

A pounding ache seized her chest. "We have to find him."

"We'll check the chapel first, then the infirmary."

She plucked his sleeve to stop him. "'Twill be quicker if we search separately."

He paused, frowning. "I don't like the idea of us parting, but . . . The fire has not spread toward the chapel yet. While you go check in that direction, I'll check the infirmary."

"Mama!" Jason's cry came from the direction of the infirmary.

They spun around as one and raced through the infirmary entrance. The monk was correct. Flames consumed the beds lined in rows down both side aisles. Several burning beams had fallen from the ceiling and were strewn about. The intense heat made it difficult to breathe.

Jason stood in the first bay and pointed at one of a handful of beds not on fire. "Mama. Look. Under the bed."

Rose knelt down beside him and hugged him tightly. "Darling, thank the Virgin Mary you are all right," she whispered fiercely. The tempo of her heart beat like a drum.

Rand squeezed her shoulder in sympathy. When Jason began to squirm, she pulled back and said sternly, "Don't leave my side again. 'Tis very dangerous. You can get badly hurt. Do you hear me?"

"Aye, Mama. I promise not to leave you. But I heard the woman moaning."

Rose turned and stared in shock. A woman huddled under the bed, raving as she yanked at her wiry gray hair. Her aged eyes stared unseeing through a milky film.

Rand coughed. Once he could speak, he said, "We'll leave the woman where she is, for now, till we can find a way out of the building. We don't need the distraction."

Rose nodded and covered Jason's mouth with the wet wimple. "Here, son. Hold the cloth to your mouth and breathe into it."

She duplicated the gesture with the veil to her mouth.

The cloying smoke lessened somewhat, and she could breathe easier.

As she stood up, Rand headed for the beds. Jason molded himself around the back of her hip, while his left hand tightly clutched her skirt behind her knees.

Near the second bed, a stained-glass window was situated about nine feet above the ground. It appeared to be about five feet high and four feet wide. Rose glanced at Rand, who yanked the bedclothes off the bed. She noticed he subtly angled his body away from the flames and averted his gaze.

"Do you think you can reach the window and climb out?" She heard the undercurrent of anxiety in her voice.

"I have an idea I think may work." He ripped two strips from the linen bed sheet and then tossed her the remaining material. As he wrapped the linen around his palms, he explained, "Tear the sheet in long strips and knot them end to end to make a rope. Time is of the essence. This ceiling can collapse at any moment."

Once she had about twelve strips, each one four inches wide by eight feet long, her fingers worked quickly knotting the ends together. "But how are you to get through the sealed window?" Nervously, she glanced at the approaching flames.

He raised his palms up, briefly. "I can tell you, but 'tis quicker if I show you," he said as he marched to the nearby tall branched iron candle stand in front of the stone column.

Grunting, he hefted the candle stand over his right shoulder and carried it to the bedside, where he set it back down. Then she watched as he jumped onto the bed, and once he balanced his right foot on the bed frame, and his left foot on the bed ropes, with both hands he gripped the rod holding the bed curtain and yanked it down with a strong tug, chain and all. He removed the other bed curtain the same way, clearing the bed of all impediments. Then he hoisted the candelabra again and smashed it through the window like a spear. Shattered glass sprayed down over the window ledge and clinked on the stone floor as it rained down.

A great whooshing sound like a gust of wind startled Rose. She looked up to see the fire was spreading rapidly over the ceiling beams toward them. "Oh, God, we have to hurry, Rand!" she shouted. "What can I do to help?!"

He jabbed the candle stand through the window several more times till there was naught but a few slivers of glass clinging to the rectangular window frame. He set the candle stand down on the floor, then sprang off the bed. He shoved the iron stand over so it propped against the wall under the window. The top of the three branches reached just four feet shy of the broad stone window ledge.

As he removed the linen strips round his hands, he spoke quickly of his plans. He tied and double knotted the two linen bands onto the candle stand, spacing them four feet apart in the center of the twelve-foot-long pole. The thickness of the knotted fabric served as foot and hand supports as he climbed up the candle stand to the branched top, where he jumped the few remaining feet onto the stone ledge jutting out in front of the window.

In a crouched position, he grasped the window embrasure. Their eyes met, a long, lingering gaze of shared elation, and dare she hope, love. It seemed to blaze in his eyes like a beacon, guiding her home, encircling her in safety and comfort, warmth and protection. She marveled, unable to believe her fortune. But they were not free yet.

A great thundering rumble erupted above them. Rand's eyes grew wide in horror. Rose gazed up at the ceiling, clutching Jason in a fierce grip, her fear so palpable she trembled. Then as if all the mythical Roman gods on Mount Olympus gave a shuddering roar, a section of the beamed ceiling broke apart and came tumbling down toward them.

Chapter Twenty-Nine

Rand, hearing the shrieking crack of the timbered ceiling, a distinctive sound he had been unable to forget, even after fifteen years, leapt down off the ledge, grabbed Rose and Jason in his arms, flung them against the wall, then crouched over them protectively.

A great whoosh of air buffeted him as the beams crashed behind him, and crackling heat pulsed at his back. He clutched Rose and Jason, both shaking with fright. Residual echoes of fear, shame, and guilt over the stable fire were subsumed in his desperation to get Rose and Jason safely out of the burning building. Then . . .

A keening wail rent the air, sending a chill down his body. He turned his head around and gaped in horror. Through a wall of fire shooting into the air, he watched the old woman jump up from under the bed, flames engulfing her. She ran around madly in circles screeching in agonizing pain.

Rand froze, paralyzed, gripped in a nightmare where truth and reality shattered in a prism of images. He could not move or think or feel. Just envision his mother consumed by flames till she was nothing but charred remains. His cognizance warped in a black void of pain and fear. The blaze of the fire coming ever near him, like a burning phantasm wailing in misery and despair.

A whirring, buzzing sound rushed in his ears. "Rand. Rand." A wraith reached out with long, bony fingers and sharp nails.

"Rand, prithee. I love you. I need you. Jason needs you. Come back to me." Rose's breath hitched with a ragged sob. "I love you so much."

Blackness shattered as Rose's words reached him and her tears bathed his cheeks.

He was crouched down on his haunches, his back to the infirmary wall. The fire was so close the heat blasted as strong and hot as a coal-fired forge. "Rose?"

Her eyes glimmered with hope and love. "Rand, we have to go. Now!"

Giving him the knotted rope she made, she lifted Jason in her arms. Rand jumped to his feet. His wits returned. Her confession that she loved him giving him strength, he took charge. "I'll tie Jason in your arms, then pull you both up once I've climbed into the window."

Jason clung to Rose face-first, with his legs around her waist and his arms around her neck. After tying them securely, Rand vaulted up the candle stand and into the window embrasure.

Rose twitched nervously back toward the chapel. "What about the brother and sisters?"

A sheen of sweat covering his face, he shook his head sadly. "The infirmary entrance is completely blocked with burning debris from the collapsed ceiling. 'Tis hopeless. Once free from here, we can try to get help for them. Toss me the end of the rope."

Snatching the rope out of the air, Rand coiled it around his forearm, then braced his body against one side of the window and pressed his foot against the other to gain leverage. "Use your feet to climb up the wall when I pull you up. Can you do that?"

She bit the corner of her plump lip and nodded determinedly.

"Very good," he said, smiling with encouragement. "I'll pull you up on the count of three. One, two, three."

Pressing his shoulder and foot against the embrasure, with a loud grunt, he tugged Rose and Jason up. Sweat broke over his back, while his leg and arm muscles flexed and strained. His jaw clenched tight, teeth aching. He pulled on the rope a foot at a time. Inexorably, Rose climbed up the wall step-by-step. When her foot hit the wide ledge, he gave one last great heave and pulled her into his arms. Jason was cradled between them.

His arms quivered, not with strain, but with the restraint not to squeeze her too hard, in an overwhelming urge to assure himself she and Jason were safe and unharmed. A huge pressure in the vicinity of his heart felt near to bursting with the need to confess all of his feelings—his fears, his hopes, his dreams. And more importantly, how much he loved them both.

But the groaning roof was on the point of collapse. Rand wanted to be as far away from the hospital as he could when it caved in. He removed Jason from his harness and carefully steadied him at Rose's feet. Rose was securely placed against the embrasure, crouched behind Jason and facing out toward the dark night.

Rand vaulted off the ledge, the cool breeze a relief after the blaring heat of the fire. He hit the ground with a jarring thump. Quickly climbing to his feet, he maneuvered himself directly below the window. In the shadow of the building, he gazed up at Rose, his arms stretched up to her. "Hand Jason to me and then I'll catch you when you jump down."

Clutching Jason's arms, Rose lowered him down. Rand

caught hold of his dangling legs. "I've got him. You can let go."

After setting Jason on his feet, he turned back to the window. Rose gazed nervously behind him at the city walls. "Hurry, Rose. Jump. I won't let you fall."

Rose held her arms out and jumped.

She slammed into him, causing him to stagger, but he held on to her tightly. Chest heaving, he flipped his hair out of his face. Her face was inches from his. He smiled. "We made it. Are you ready to go?"

She smiled back. "Aye, let's go."

Rand swung Jason into his arms, then grabbed Rose's hand. They ran and ran until Rose pulled up, clutching her side and breathing heavily.

Rand set Jason down and wrapped his arm around Rose. "Take a moment to catch your breath. But we need to find a place to hide. We're fortunate we have not run into any of the castle guard, who surely by now have come to investigate the fire."

Staring back at the hospital, Rand watched what was left of the roof collapse, causing a section of the wall to crumble. Debris floated above, illuminated by the red glow of the fire. He shuddered at how close they had come to being buried in the rubble. His eyes met Rose's, a shared gaze of gratitude and relief passing between them.

"Rand," Rose said, her head cocked, "do you hear that?"

"What?" Rand gazed toward the castle walls.

The sky was clear now and the full moon illuminated the outline of a small troop of soldiers rapidly advancing. They slashed their swords through the thick reeds lining the ditch they traversed as they approached the hospital.

He grabbed Jason. "We must hurry before they see us."

They ran headed west, away from the soldiers. Suddenly, Rose cried out.

Rand slid to a stop and spun around. He hurried back to where she was limping on one foot. "What is it? Are you hurt?"

"Mama," Jason piped up, fear in his voice.

She smoothed Jason's cheek. "I'm all right, darling," she said, a smile on her face, but Rand saw the pain glazing her eyes. Then she looked up at Rand. "I stepped on a rock and turned my ankle. I think it's sprained."

A shout came from the direction of the soldiers. A man in front pointed toward them.

"Jesu. We've been spotted. Can you run on it?"

She put her weight on her foot and tried to walk, but she pulled up short again. Tears sprang to her eyes. "I can't walk on it. It hurts too much. You must go without me. I'll only hold you back. Run. Take Jason with you and keep him safe."

"Absolutely not, Rose. I am staying with you. I shall not leave you alone to the mercy of the king's guard."

"Rand, I beg you." She clutched his hands as her soft blue gaze implored him. "Go. Before 'tis too late."

He shook his head, his voice tempered with steel. "I swore I'd never leave you. I have never broken a vow to you before and I shall not start now."

At that moment, half a dozen soldiers converged on them, their swords drawn. Rand wrapped his arm around Rose protectively.

He recognized their dark-haired lieutenant, who stepped several paces forward. "Sir Rand, you are under arrest by order of the king."

"On what charge, Sir Reginald?"

Sir Reginald shifted his head toward Rose, then back to Rand. "For abetting and harboring a confessed felon."

Rand jerked his gaze to Rose, curious why they were not arresting her. "What of Lady Rosalyn?"

"Sir Golan's clerk brought the king evidence of the lieu-tenant-justiciar's various corruption and extortion schemes, including Lady Rosalyn's coerced confession. Charges have been withdrawn. Lady Rosalyn is free to go."

Rose gasped.

"Will you give me a moment to bid Lady Rosalyn fare well?"

Sir Reginald nodded. "Make it brief."

Rand waited until the lieutenant rejoined his men. He gazed into his son's face, saw the familiar dimples, and jaw-line. The sweet smile so like his mother's. He felt his heart cracking. Jason patted his face. "Why are you so sad, Papa?"

Unable to speak for the emotion in his throat, he turned to Rose. Fear shimmered in her gaze. He leaned down and kissed her. Her lips, soft and supple, clung desperately to his. Holding her tightly, he poured all his love and devotion into his final, parting kiss.

"'Tis time, Sir Rand. Step away from Lady Rosalyn."

Rand handed Jason over to his mother.

She clung to Jason, her face twisted with pain and grief. "Rand, I need—"

"Do not grieve for me, Rose," he whispered softly in her ear. "Never doubt that you are worthy of love. One day you will find a man who will love you. I am sorry I cannot be that man." He embraced Rose and Jason one more time. "When he's old enough to understand, tell Jason I love him." Then he moved away from them, his hands out to his sides to show his cooperation.

Two soldiers rushed forward and restrained him, while a third clapped manacles on his wrists, pushed the cup in place, passed a chain through the cross-shaped slot, and securely locked it.

As Rand stood stoic while he was shackled, Rose memorized every detail of his precious face, from his green-gray eyes shrouded with thick dark eyelashes, to his sensual lips framed by endearing dimples, to his strong jaw clenched with courageous resolve.

As she watched him being dragged away, a terrible ache unlike any she ever felt tore her heart in twain.

"Nay. Don't want Papa to go." Jason reached out, struggling in Rose's arms. "Papa. Papa."

Legs trembling, she dropped to her knees. Rose tried to hold her emotions inside, but a deep, dark chasm, where she kept her feelings buried, burst free and would not be silenced. She sobbed, hugging her son, afraid she might shatter into a thousand pieces if she let him go.

Chapter Thirty

Upon receiving the latest refusal by King Edward for a private audience, Rose took long, swift strides in search of Edith and Jason. Rand's townhome in Chester had a small but magnificent walled garden. Meadowsweet, with its frothy white petals, betony, with its purple-hued flowers, honeysuckle, and roses of white and pale pink grew in profusion in raised planter beds, imbuing the courtyard with an intoxicating concoction of sweet fragrance. But Rose was oblivious to all but her mission.

As Rose passed under an arbor of honeysuckle, a warm summer breeze wafted through her long flowing hair, which was held back by a circlet. Jason's childish giggles drew a smile from Rose. In a back corner of the garden, Edith sat on a bench below a hawthorn tree, many of its green leaves tinged with a reddish hue. Jason, wearing just his braies, played in a pool of water in the middle of the courtyard, his feet kicking sprays of water into the air.

Flicking back a loose lock tickling her cheek, Rose raised the missive in her other hand and waved it at Edith. "The king has denied my request for an audience, again. If Edward thinks his refusal will deter me, well, I am afraid he shall be disappointed." Rose halted by the bench.

Edith gazed at her, raisin-brown eyes shadowed with concern. "Milady, what do you intend to do?"

"I intend to go to Chester Castle and stand day after day in the presence chamber like the rest of the supplicants petitioning the king." Rose tipped back on her heels and, staring down, smoothed her hands over the red silk stretched over her rounded stomach.

She calculated four and a half moon cycles had passed since she and Rand had made love and conceived this precious babe she carried. Her heart blossomed with profound love and tenderness. But she could not prevent a ripple of sadness from marring her happiness. Rand should be here with her. He missed his son's birth and early years; it was not fair he would never know this child either.

Rose continued, "My condition being glaringly evident, I am counting on the king showing mercy upon me. If not, perhaps the queen will take pity on me and use her influence with the king to get me an audience. I shall not rest till Edward frees Rand from prison." The conviction in her voice rang like steel.

"What do you hope to accomplish by speaking with the king?"

"I intend to persuade Edward that Rand did not truly betray him. The king knows Golan extorted my confession. Rand, therefore, should not be condemned for breaking me free from prison when I was not guilty of the crime Golan made me falsely confess to."

"Do you truly believe the king can be swayed with reason?"

"I pray Edward's love for his cousin shall outweigh his anger that Rand broke his oath of fealty, and the king will pardon him."

"You must not despair should you fail. You have Jason, and another child on the way to consider now."

Aye, Rose swore fiercely to herself, *I shall protect you, my sweet one.* Already she loved this baby more than her own life. She loved Jason just as much, but this baby was conceived in an amalgam of hope, love, and desolation; desolation because she'd thought she was going to die and never see Rand and Jason again.

Rose jumped, startled, when a small hare scampered into the garden. It froze not far from the pool. One beady dark eye stared at them. Jason scooped up water in his hands and, giggling, showered the hare with it. When the animal darted away, Jason leapt from the pool and gave chase. The hare, cornered, scrabbled beneath the hedge. Jason lunged for it with his hands outstretched. The hare made its escape. Catching naught but air, Jason fell onto his hands in the dirt.

Rose ran to his side, fearing he was hurt. But he just crawled to his feet, and laughing, he swiped his dirty hands onto his braies.

His eyes brightened upon seeing her. "Mama, did you see? I almost caught a hare."

"Aye, I saw all right. I also see what a dirty mess you are." She licked her thumb and wiped a bit of dirt off his forehead.

His feet and hands were muddy and his braies were covered with dirty smudges at the thighs and knees.

"I believe 'tis time for someone's bath."

"Ah, Mama, I want to play some more. Can I?"

Since Rand's imprisonment, it was rare to see Jason so happy. She did not have the heart to spoil his playtime.

"Very well, dar—" Feeling a sharp twinge in her abdomen, Rose gasped and clutched her stomach. "Oh my."

"Mama?"

"Milady, is it the baby? Are you all right?" Edith rushed over and wrapped her arms around Rose's shoulders. "I knew all your worrying was not good for the baby. I shall take you—"

"Nay, my dear friend, 'tis naught wrong with the babe. The opposite actually. The baby kicked me, I think." She marveled.

"Can I feel the baby?" Jason leaned toward her eagerly.

She beamed at his enthusiasm. "Aye, son, here." She grabbed his grimy hands and pressed them to the tiny bulge that protruded from her rounded stomach.

His eyes rounded, awe in his face. "I can feel him moving."

She laughed, ruffling his shoulder-length damp curls. "Aye, I can feel him, too. Though you know, son, it could very well be a girl and not a boy."

"Rose?"

Rose started at the soft, silken caress of the masculine voice. Slowly, disbelieving, she turned in the direction of the voice. Rand stood beneath the spreading canopy of the hawthorn tree, staring at her stomach. The leaves overhead fluttered in the breeze, dappling him with shimmering light. She skimmed her gaze over him from head to toe. His surcoate was ragged and dirty. His hair, long, lanky, and greasy, framed his dirt-begrimed, bearded face. Yet he never appeared more handsome to her.

His gaze shot up to hers.

She spoke in unison with Rand, shock palpable in both their voices.

"Rand, what . . . how came you to be here?"

"Rose, darling, verily? You are with child?"

A thrumming wonder and happiness began to beat in her breast.

She nodded, biting the corner of her plump lower lip, waiting for his response. She did not wait long. A huge grin spread across his bearded face; in a trice he loped toward her, then swung her up into his arms with one hand at her back and the other under her knees.

He spun her around, releasing a carefree laugh of exuberance she'd never heard from him before. She clutched his shoulders, laughing and crying with unbound joy. Then Rand set her down and clutched her face between his palms. His green eyes, lit with overwhelming pleasure, bore into hers.

"You are having a baby. I still cannot believe it. By the looks of it, Jason shall have a baby brother or sister in five months or so."

Jason nudged between them. "I am having a brother. Girls are no fun to play with."

Rand released her, and laughing, picked Jason up and hugged him. "Girls are fun too. One day I am sure you will agree."

Jason wiggled to be free. "I am too old to be picked up like a baby."

Rand stumbled, appearing as though Jason was too heavy a burden to carry. "Aye, you are so heavy, I cannot hold you any longer," he said, setting Jason down on his feet.

Jason giggled heartily. Rose smiled, so happy she felt like raising her voice to the sky.

"Milord, milady," Edith interjected, "you no doubt wish to have your privacy to discuss all that has occurred of late. I can tend Jason for the nonce, and he may sleep with me in the servants' quarters this eve."

Rose felt a flush on her cheeks, knowing Edith was giving them privacy for more than just talking.

Rand grinned, his eyes twinkling with laughter. But when he spoke his voice sounded calm and serious. "Aye, Edith, Rose and I do have much to . . . discuss. And I desperately need a bath to remove the filth of prison."

"Come, Rand. I shall order a bath for you and find you some clean clothes," Rose said.

But first, she turned and kissed Jason. "Good eve, son. Sleep well. Rand and I shall see you in the morn."

Rand knelt down, hugged and kissed Jason.

"Your beard tickles, Papa," Jason said, giggling.

Rand's throat visibly quivered. "Well, it appears I need to shave too. Good eve, son," he said, a crack in his voice.

He stood up and held his hand out for her. His eyes glowed like hot steel. Her heart missed a beat, then began racing wildly with anticipation. Without hesitation, she slipped her hand into his warm clasp interlacing her fingers through his.

Rose held Rand's hand tightly as they walked in silence, tension building between them like a sultry wave of heat.

She quickened her pace to keep up with his longer gait. Upon approaching the arbor, he released her, then swung his arm out with a flourish for her to go before him. She grinned, curtsied, and hurried beneath the arch. When he stepped through the arbor, he swept her off her feet again, clutching her to his chest. She squealed in delight. He laughed and hurriedly raced to the outer steps leading to their bed-chamber above the kitchen.

Rose had too many questions vying for an explanation. "How came you to be free?" she blurted out. "I wrote the king numerous times begging for your release. But every time he denied me."

"Edward was disappointed I broke my oath of fealty. But breaking an accused felon from gaol was a blatant defiance of his authority." She stiffened in his arms, about to refute the king's erroneous conjecture. "'Tis true you were not really culpable for Bertram's death, but appearances made you guilty all the same. So Edward wished to make an example of me. He may have planned to pardon me all along, but now that the main body of the army is to advance along the north coast of Wales into Llewelyn's territory of Gwynedd, the king pardoned me on condition I fight without remuneration in this or any other Welsh wars in the future."

"When must you leave?"

"We have three days together before Edward and the fighting force move out from Chester."

Her heart plummeted. "Three days! 'Tis not enough time. You have only just returned to us." She searched his pale, thin face. "And you are much too thin. I know what sort of swill they serve in prison. Surely you need time to recup—"

At the top of the stairs, he reached for the door latch and pushed the door open with his knee, spun around, and slammed it shut with his back. He let her legs down and still holding her placed his finger over her lips to still her words.

Her legs quivered at his touch, while her breath hitched.

Rand said, his own voice breathless, "You are right. We do not have much time. And I intend to make the most of every waking hour we have till I must part from you and Jason again. I am grateful for the time I do have, because I know once the war is over, I am coming back to you, to home, to family. No war, or enemy, or king shall keep me from you!"

Rose's eyes welled with tears. "Aye, Rand, we are a family. Can you forgive me for lying to you about Jason? For not telling you he was your son?"

Rand spun away, pacing to the large canopy bed draped in dark blue velvet curtains. "Why did you keep such a secret, Rose?" Despite how much he loved her, that still hurt terribly. He'd wondered every day in gaol if Rose just did not believe him capable of being a good father to Jason. He rubbed the pain in his chest. "Why did you lie to me? You had so many opportunities to tell me the truth. Good God, that day at the wharf—that is what your strange behavior was about. You could have told me then."

"I have no excuse, Rand. I was afraid—" She stopped abruptly, slow tears rolling down her cheeks.

"Afraid of what? Go ahead and say it. You are afraid that I shall make a terrible father, that I cannot even prevent my son from being abducted in my own dwelling."

"Nay, Rand," she cried out. "I have never believed such of you. How can you think that of me? Unless . . . surely you do not fear you cannot protect Jason? You saved Jason and me from the fire."

"What of my mother and sister? They are dead because of me."

"Nay, you were not responsible. Sometimes accidents happen. There is naught we can do about it."

Rand's vision blurred. He felt his sister's arms slip from his neck, saw her floating down into the depths of the river, her eyes staring at him with reproach.

"Rand." Rose's gentle touch upon his arm, her soft plea recalled him from his memories.

"I had Juliana in my arms, Rose, but I released her so I could live."

"You were just a boy, Rand. You tried to save her. If you had not let her go, you would have died too. I would never have met you, and Jason would never have been born. Nor would you ever have protected me from marriage to Golan.

"And as far as your mother, do not belittle her sacrifice."

"Her sacrifice?"

"Aye. Your mother *chose* to run into a burning building to save you. She risked her life because she loved you. Did you not do the same when we rescued Jason from Golan and Lydia and escaped from the hospital fire? Would you not do so again?" Her hands were alive as she talked, reminding him of the animated girl he knew before her first marriage. "Would you not risk any fear, any punishment, any torment to save Jason, or our baby who lies protected within my womb?"

Rand dropped his gaze to where her hands cradled their baby. Her red silk surcoate was smudged with Jason's muddy handprints. Without volition, he reached out and touched her rounded stomach, marveling that inside her belly was his child, a child they'd conceived as man and wife.

Rand raised his eyes back to her face. The last barrier around his heart shattered. Wonder filled him and his heart expanded. He'd discovered a renewed hope in the future and belief that their love for each other was strong enough to overcome their fears. Their love was forged in a cataclysm of fire, making them as strong and durable as steel. "You are right. Just moments before she died, Mother made me swear to never give up hope. She never gave up hope, and I am here, alive, about to be blessed with another child."

Rose's chest expanded and contracted. His gaze skimmed over her perfectly shaped breasts, which were plumper than he remembered, up her slender, graceful neck, where her pulse throbbed in the hollow of her collar, and stopped on her succulent reddened lips. Her hands came up between them and covered his chest muscles, squeezing and releasing in a massaging motion.

He dipped his head, blood raging through his veins. She lifted her lips toward his in anticipation. His breath grew ragged. The moment their mouths touched, it was as if a fire sparked an inexhaustible hunger. Their tongues melded, entwining in a sensual dance.

Rand groaned, marveling at the delectable, velvety softness of her lips, sweetness of her breath, and boldness of her caressing tongue. Lurching forward, he wrapped his arms around her and pressed his hips against her mons pubis. Wanting to get closer, to be absorbed by her, he trailed his hand down her back and then clutched her buttocks. He pulled her flush against his hardened flesh; his hips found a slow, stroking rhythm against her heated delta. She met him stroke for stroke, a mewling cry upon her lips.

Someone rapped on the door. Rose jumped and stepped away from him. She rubbed the jumping pulse in her throat. They stared at one another, breathing heavily. Rand swallowed, and then gathering his senses, he bid whoever was at the door to enter.

Several scullions brought in buckets of water and began pouring the contents into a tub in the corner of the chamber. Another carried soap and towels and laid them down on a stool nearby.

"I did not order a bath yet," she mused, her voice yet thick with desire.

He cleared his throat. "I ordered it when I arrived. I'd thought to bathe before I saw you, but Jason's laughter drew me to the garden."

When the last servant left, Rand began stripping off his stinky raiment. As he kicked off his boots, Rose boldly began unknotting the tie at the waist of his braies. Her silky fingers brushed his skin in teasing strokes. A rush of hot blood surged into his cock, making him throb with pleasure and pain. She shoved his braies and attached hose down to his ankles, and gazed up at him brazenly through her lashes, her mouth inches from his erection.

He hissed through his teeth. "You tease, are you trying to make me lose control?"

"Why, is it working?" Her heated breath puffed over his bulbous head.

He groaned in agonized pleasure, quivering with the need to delve deep into her slick sheath and glory in her loving embrace. Instead, he spun away and plunged into the hot water.

Rose smiled as Rand spun away from her in obvious arousal. His back to her, she gasped upon seeing the red-welted skin on his lower back and buttocks. It was an old healed scar from a burn. With his braies on, only a few inches of the rippled flesh would be visible. He must have received it in the stable fire when he was a youth.

Then why had she not seen his scar before? She thought back. The few times she'd seen Rand unclothed, either it had been dark or he'd always kept his back turned away from her. But surely she would have felt the scar while making love to him? Nay, then too. The first time he'd made love to her he'd worn a robe, and more recently, he'd lain on his back and pulled her atop him. She did remember feeling some rough skin on his back when she'd warmed him with her body the night of the blizzard. But, again, he'd rolled onto his back and distracted her with questions.

Now, Rose knelt behind him and ran her fingers delicately over the rough welts. He stiffened.

"Oh, my darling, how it must have pained you." Her voice was thick with tears.

Rand reached for a linen cloth on the stool. "'Twas long ago, my love. Do not distress yourself."

Rose plucked the towel from his hands and lathered it with soap and water. "Pray, take your ease. I shall bathe you." She skimmed the cloth over the back of his shoulders. "'Tis a wifely duty, is it not?"

A deep groan was her only answer.

She kissed his neck tenderly, her attempt to give him some small gesture to comfort him from awful, painful memories. The scar was a constant reminder of all he lost.

Next, she ran the linen down his back and buttocks. He released a sigh, then quivered when she ran the cloth between the crease of his bottom cheeks. She took pleasure in this domestic task. She moved around to the side of the tub and washed his muscular chest and ribbed stomach. Still on her knees, she bumped the back of her hand on the head of his upstanding phallus. She watched, transfixed, as the thick veined shaft bobbed in the water. With a guttural groan, Rand reached out, cupped her left breast, and massaged her with firm strokes.

She gasped as her nipple swelled with tingling heat against his palm. With his other hand, he cupped her head and pulled her so close their breaths mingled.

His voice rumbled like a caress. "If you must torment me, 'tis only fair I do the same to you."

His gaze dipped to her lips. The sensitive flesh tingled in readiness. His lips molded to hers like warm marble; his tongue stabbed between her lips. She moaned. Torment her, would he?

She pulled back. "Sounds like a challenge to me," she purred, then delved her hand into the water and took his shaft in a firm grasp. "A challenge I gladly take up." A long, shuddering groan escaped him. She chuckled seductively. "Hmm, I wonder who shall cry craven first?"

She punctuated her boast by stroking her hand up and down his splendid manhood, the water easing the slippery glide of her taunting grip. His eyes snared hers, glittering with a mixture of feral promise and need.

"Very well, but you are dressed and I am as bare as a babe in the womb. Hardly seems fair." He grinned teasingly, even as his eyes taunted her to strip off her garments.

She smiled, giving his manhood one last sensuous caress. If he expected her to be too shy and timid to disrobe before him in the light of day, he was going to be thoroughly shocked. She pushed up from the tub, leaning toward him, her lips inches from his, and kissed him. She slid her tongue between his lips, exploring, savoring, enticing him to lose all control. But soon she was ensnared in her own game. She pulled away breathless, heart drumming erratically and feminine muscles quivering with need.

But Rand was not unaffected either. His lids drooped languidly and desire blazed in his eyes, while his whitened knuckles clutched the tub edge.

She nodded to the no doubt cooling water. "Pray, do not let my undressing preclude you from finishing your bath while the water is hot. You'll find the soap for washing your hair on the stool."

"'Tis very generous of you," he said ironically.

When he dipped his head under water, she removed the broach that held the split bodice together, put it in her jewel coffer, and began brushing her hair in long, smooth strokes.

Moments of companionable silence passed, the carnal tension thickening as he stared transfixed upon her languorous movements.

"Your hair is so shiny, 'tis like gold leaf is sprinkled in your mane," Rand said, lathering his hair and scrubbing his scalp vigorously a second time.

" 'Tis a special oil I put in my soap to make it shine."

He dipped his head back and rinsed the lather from his hair.

He surged up, squeezing the excess water from his mane. Suddenly, a look of horror crossed his face. He picked up the soap from the stool and stared at it, his expression aghast. "Is this—"

Rose giggled. "Aye, 'tis the soap I use." She tugged the surcoat and undertunic she wore over her head, leaving her in a nearly transparent chemise.

"A man is not supposed to have shiny hair."

Rose arched one eyebrow. "Why not?"

He surged up out of the tub, his hands fisted on his hips. "Because, well, 'tis just not manly."

Rose gazed hungrily over him, appreciating the liquid sluicing down his muscled chest and stomach into his curly, light brown groin hair. His magnificent erection, long and thick and roped with purplish veins, stood straight up in the air.

"Well, do you have aught to say, woman?"

Having unlaced the ties at the neck of her chemise, she shimmied out of the garment and stood naked before him. Rand still had not said he loved her. She opened herself up to be vulnerable, believing in her heart he did. She prayed her newfound courage would show him that he had nothing to fear by confessing his love.

Rose dropped her gaze to his groin. She licked her suddenly parched lips. "You appear more than manly enough for me," she said pointedly. Then she shot her gaze up to his. "Of course, in order to be certain, I shall need some physical proof before I can render a final judgment as to your manliness or nay. Are you *up to* the test?"

Rand, gaze enthralled by the bold, brazen seductress

before him, felt a deep ripple in his gut that emerged from his mouth like the aroused roar of a lion as it seeks its mate.

He dipped his shoulder and lifted her up into his arms. Her breasts cushioned against his chest. "Are you casting aspersions upon my manhood? Because if you are, I shall have to vigorously prove my worth as a man."

She nodded as if extremely serious. "Aye, vigor is a very manly trait also. I await your proof of vigor with enthusiasm."

In three long, swift strides, he carried her to the bed and laid her gently on the mattress. Her arms eagerly clutched him to her, drawing his body over hers. She raised her thighs, cradling his hips. With a groan, he kissed her thoroughly, then licked a hot trail down her throat to one delicious peaked nipple. He drew the swollen nub between his lips and sucked. She moaned.

With a light, teasing caress, her hand skimmed down his stomach and took his cock in her hand. He groaned against her breast, the hard ridge of flesh throbbing with an overwhelming urge to plunder her honey-slickened sheath. But it was more than lust raging inside him. His heart contracted with an incredible feeling of love and tenderness for Rose that for so long he'd denied or suppressed.

Rand reached down and slid two fingers inside her sheath, caressing her, stroking her inner walls, while the rasp of his tongue lathed her nipple. When he tugged the hardened point deep into his mouth, her hips lurched up. He teased her with the graze of his teeth. The exquisite taste of her was like honeyed mead.

Panting, undulating, Rose clung to Rand. A sudden blaze of fire shot to her core. Prickling heat sparked a ripple of explosions and she released a breathy moan. Her inner muscles throbbed and pulsed. Her body shuddered, Rand's strong arms cradling her tenderly.

When her heart slowed, she opened her eyes. Rand hovered above her, his arms supporting him. She stared into his eyes, the most amazing expression of love she'd ever seen bright within his gaze.

"I love you, Rose." His voice was husky with emotion. "I think I fell a little in love with you that day you stumbled at my feet with pig dung covering your face, your impish grin shining full of life. After you married, my feelings only deepened, but I denied it to myself. You are so strong and compassionate and courageous, I could not help but fall in love with you. But I love you most of all for your consuming love and selfless defense of our son."

Tears filling the back of her throat, Rose croaked, "I love you, Rand. Your patience, and kindness, and generous heart humble me. I trust you with my life and Jason's life. Never doubt it. I shall love you forever."

His eyes shining with joy, he kissed her as he glided hotly, inexorably inside her. Impetuous, desperate, she clutched his taut muscular buttocks and thrust her hips up, driving him to the hilt. He groaned. Withdrawing to the tip of his shaft, he plunged back in. With a slow, exquisite rhythm, he drove inside her again and again. She met him with every deep lunge.

He quickened the pace, thrusting harder, deeper. Her heart pounded. The exquisite sensation of him inside her was unlike anything she'd ever felt. With every deep stroke of his shaft, the tingling heat between her thighs coiled tighter, higher.

She clung to him tightly, about to spin apart. Then Rand gave one last deep thrust. A sharp stab of pleasure throbbed deep inside her, and her inner muscles quivered.

"Rose!" he shouted, spasms shaking him.

As they soared together, an incredible feeling of being one body, one soul consumed her.

Rand, breathless, collapsed beside Rose and pulled her into his arms. Warm tears bathed his chest. His gut clenched. He leaned up on his elbow and searched her face. "Rose, why are you crying? Did I hurt you or the babe?"

She smiled. "Nay, these are tears of joy and relief. For so long I thought you were going to die. I'm just so happy."

"I never thought I could be this content either. I no longer fear what may come. I know our love is strong enough that together we can face any foe, or any trouble that besets us."

Rose's hand cupped his cheek. "I love you, Rand. And I know your mother and sister are at peace at last."

Rand sighed, not with misery or sadness or despair. For the first time in his life, he was at peace. Though he never realized it, all along he was blessed. Every day, from this day forward, he would thank God for bringing Rose and Jason back into his life.

Rand pulled the covers up over them. As if they had been sleeping together for years, they curled up on their sides, her back to his chest.

Propping his head with his right arm, Rand draped his left arm over her waist and caressed her extended belly. As he was about to drift asleep, he asked, "Have you thought about what we shall call the babe?"

"If a boy," she said, voice slurred with sleep, "I thought to call him Julian, if a girl, Juliana."

A tear dribbled down Rand's cheek. He was blessed indeed.

Romantic Suspense from
Lisa Jackson

See How She Dies	0-8217-7605-3	$6.99US/$9.99CAN
Final Scream	0-8217-7712-2	$7.99US/$10.99CAN
Wishes	0-8217-6309-1	$5.99US/$7.99CAN
Whispers	0-8217-7603-7	$6.99US/$9.99CAN
Twice Kissed	0-8217-6038-6	$5.99US/$7.99CAN
Unspoken	0-8217-6402-0	$6.50US/$8.50CAN
If She Only Knew	0-8217-6708-9	$6.50US/$8.50CAN
Hot Blooded	0-8217-6841-7	$6.99US/$9.99CAN
Cold Blooded	0-8217-6934-0	$6.99US/$9.99CAN
The Night Before	0-8217-6936-7	$6.99US/$9.99CAN
The Morning After	0-8217-7295-3	$6.99US/$9.99CAN
Deep Freeze	0-8217-7296-1	$7.99US/$10.99CAN
Fatal Burn	0-8217-7577-4	$7.99US/$10.99CAN
Shiver	0-8217-7578-2	$7.99US/$10.99CAN
Most Likely to Die	0-8217-7576-6	$7.99US/$10.99CAN
Absolute Fear	0-8217-7936-2	$7.99US/$9.49CAN
Almost Dead	0-8217-7579-0	$7.99US/$10.99CAN
Lost Souls	0-8217-7938-9	$7.99US/$10.99CAN
Left to Die	1-4201-0276-1	$7.99US/$10.99CAN
Wicked Game	1-4201-0338-5	$7.99US/$9.99CAN
Malice	0-8217-7940-0	$7.99US/$9.49CAN

Available Wherever Books Are Sold!
Visit our website at **www.kensingtonbooks.com**